MISSION
(un)Popular

MISSION
(un)Popular

by Anna Humphrey

Disney • Hyperion Books
New York

Copyright © 2011 by Anna Humphrey

All rights reserved. Published by Disney • Hyperion Books, an imprint of Disney Book Group. No part of this book may be reproduced or transmitted in any form or by any means, electronic or mechanical, including photocopying, recording, or by any information storage and retrieval system, without written permission from the publisher. For information address Disney • Hyperion Books, 114 Fifth Avenue, New York, New York 10011-5690.

First Disney • Hyperion paperback edition, 2013

1 3 5 7 9 10 8 6 4 2

V567-9638-5-11046

Printed in the United States of America

Library of Congress Control Number for Hardcover Edition: 2011041667

ISBN 978-1-4231-2321-7

Visit www.un-requiredreading.com

SUSTAINABLE FORESTRY INITIATIVE

Certified Chain of Custody
Promoting Sustainable Forestry

www.sfiprogram.org
SFI-01054
The SFI label applies to the text stock

For Jamila, who leveled with me:
Anna, I love you, but you know nothing *about frizzy hair,*
and then, like always, was with me every step of the way.

Hello, my name is Margot Button. I'm almost thirteen and I'm a total social dork. I look wrong, act wrong, and say all the wrong things at all the wrong times.

No, scratch that. Remember, "Positive thoughts lead to positive feelings."

Hello, my name is Margot Button. I'm almost thirteen and I'm a unique and talented individual with strong social skills, exceptionally good manners, and natural good looks.

I can't even *think* that with a straight face. How about this?

Hello, my name is Margot Button. I'm almost thirteen. I'm mostly a total social dork, but I aspire to greatness. And as for my looks, if I straighten my hair, don't stand too close to the mirror, and squint a little, I look almost like a younger, uglier version of Salma Hayek. Except she has an amazing figure (and I'm a twig). And she's Mexican American (and I'm part Indian). And her accent is so cool (and I sound like a regular Canadian). And guys go insane over her (and guys barely notice me). But you know, other than that, we're twins.

That's better. Or what about this:

Hello, my name is Margot Button. I'm almost thirteen. And as for the rest, can you come back to me?

1

I Resolve Not to Be Myself Anymore

DID YOU KNOW THAT there are literally hundreds of ways to start the new year off fresh?

When I was in second grade, my teacher gave us an assignment about it. Everyone had to pick a country and show how they celebrated. Since we were seven, this involved a lot of misspelled sentences under lopsided pencil-crayon drawings of people marching in parades, stuffing their faces with food, and lighting off fireworks.

Because my dad (who I've never met) is Indian, I chose India as my country. My drawing is still tucked inside my scrapbook. It shows a bunch of brown-skinned people with satellite-dish-sized heads. They're holding candles while standing beside a doggish-looking cow that, for some reason, is wearing a Christmas wreath on its neck. It was supposed to symbolize Diwali, the festival of lights. Underneath, I wrote: "In India there is Diwali where the lite ends the evil. They wear new cloths."

At the time I thought that sounded like the most disappointing party on earth—almost as bad as my grandma Betty's birthday, where we ate carrot cake and her main present was a cutlery organizer—but that just goes to show what I know. Now that I'm going into seventh grade, I would kill for a New Year celebration that involves a wardrobe makeover, not to mention the banishing of evil. You've got to admit, it makes more sense than wearing cardboard hats and watching a giant disco ball drop on TV.

Still, if you want my personal opinion, the *real* New Year's Eve—the one that crosses all races and cultures, uniting us equally in dread and anticipation—is in September. It smells like new sharpened pencils and sounds like the crunching of the first fall leaves. To keep from mixing it up with the hundreds of other New Year's Eve possibilities, from here on in, I will call it School Year's Eve (or SYE, because that makes it sound as important as it is).

On SYE, there aren't any fireworks, noisemakers, or wreath-wearing cows. And instead of going wild at some crazy midnight party, you stop celebrating altogether. You buy new gym shoes. You write your name very carefully on the front of fresh notebooks, swearing that this year, you'll keep your handwriting perfect all year long; and this year, you won't hit yourself in the face with a volleyball while trying to serve; and this year, you'll finally get higher than a C+ in math, and your crush will learn your name, and you'll dress so well that you'll be at the mall one day, minding your own business, when this lady wearing sunglasses will come up to you and say something like: "You! You are exactly what we've been looking for! Will you be our new teen model for Abercrombie & Fitch?" And then everyone will be so jealous they'll want to lick the ground you walk on.

In summary, you celebrate School Year's Eve by hoping desperately that this year, you'll find a way to be completely different from who you were last year. Or maybe that's just me.

Of course, this is my life we're talking about. I can hope and plan all I want, but it doesn't mean anything will go my way. Take the Friday before SYE, for example. The day it all began. It was supposed to be perfect. The last relaxing, lounge-around-with-your-best-friend time before a long school year. It could not have turned out worse.

Looking back, I should have known something was up the second I opened my eyes. The suspicious smell of pancakes was in the air, but I ignored it, heading straight to the bathroom, then back to my room, where I had important stuff to do.

My best friend, Erika-with-a-K, and I had big plans for the afternoon. We were going to watch *Charmed and Dazed*, our favorite soap opera, at 1:00 while eating lunch: salad (because we've both been trying to be more healthy) and nachos (because nachos are so good). After that we were going to go down the street to Java House and order mocha lattes. We hate coffee, but now that we're almost thirteen, we've decided to acquire a taste for it. Then we were planning to have a back-to-school outfit session, where first I'd try on all my outfits and she'd rate them on a scale of one to ten for:

1. Hotness and/or cuteness
2. Makes your butt look good-ness
3. Looks cool and unique, but casual enough that nobody would guess you'd spent two hours picking it out with your best friend.

Then I'd do the same for her outfits. But first I needed to prepare. Because of "our current financial situation" (more about that later), my mom had used some of the "future fund" money my dad sends to take me shopping for the bare essentials of back-to-school stuff—two pairs of jeans, socks, underwear, and some Walmart pens and binders. Technically, that money from my dad is for my university education. It comes a few times a year, tucked in a little card filled with barely legible writing about whatever place he's in at the moment. (Last time he was working on a radish farm in California; next time he could be scaling the Rockies in search of rare peregrine falcons. It's hard to say.) My mom puts the money in a special bank account and we never touch it, so that tells you how tight things had gotten. It meant I was mostly going to have to create my School Year's Day outfit by working with the clothes I already had—which wasn't going to be easy, trust me.

I sat back on my heels, pulling stuff out of my drawers and scattering it around until I was sitting elbow-deep in a nest of bad fashion decisions. There were last year's khaki cargo pants (What had I been thinking? That I was some kind of jungle explorer-slash-sixth grader?); a camisole with little flowers on it, which wasn't too bad except for this one subtle ketchup stain; a hooded sweatshirt with weirdly big pom-pom tassels; a Hello Kitty T-shirt (that would have been *really* cute . . . if I was still eight years old); and a hand-me-down argyle vest with the tags still on it from one of my mom's client's daughters (*she* obviously knew it wasn't cool enough to wear, so why was she inflicting it on me?).

I was just considering the pros and cons of a blue velour leopard-print hoodie from the same hand-me-down bag (Pro: velour was *sort of* in this season. Con: blue leopard print!! Really?), when there was a knock at my door. "Margot?" My mom peeked in, not bothering to wait for an invitation.

She opened the door wider then, but didn't flinch at the mess. If anything, the new layer of clean clothes made my room look better, since it hid the piles of stuff underneath. "Oh, that's funky." She nodded in approval, eyeing the blue leopard-print hoodie. I'm not trying to be mean, but this was coming from a woman who was wearing a purple peasant skirt and a belt covered in small silver bells. I dropped the sweatshirt into my "would not be caught dead in it" pile.

"Oh look, Margot." She picked up a rainbow-colored woven Peruvian headband. She'd bought it for me once at a hippie festival where she was reading tarot cards, which is what she does for a living. "I was wondering where this went." I used to wear that headband practically every day in fourth grade, until this girl Sarah said it smelled like hair grease and asked if I ever washed it. So, while it was pretty in its way, and might have been the kind of thing that a tarot card reader could get away with, I knew it wasn't going to cut it in seventh grade. I took it from my mom and threw it on top of the hoodie.

But before you go thinking I'm ashamed of my mom, or her clothes, or her job, let me say that I'm not really. Tarot Card Reader is *not* one of the more regular mom-type occupations—like accountant, lawyer, or kindergarten teacher—but the whole thing is very sacred and serious to her, and I think it's pretty cool. The only part I don't like about it is that she refuses to do readings for anyone under eighteen, no matter how much they beg and plead and give her a million reasons why they *must* know the future. Which is dumb, because I happen to be very mature for my age.

I wrinkled my nose as Mom picked up a red silk scarf from

the hand-me-down bag and tied it around her neck. Paired with the silver bells on her belt, it made her look like a psychic Christmas elf, but, using my advanced maturity, I managed to keep myself from pointing that out. My mom could be a little sensitive about my constructive criticisms of her fashion choices. And, really, as her hippie wear went, the clothes she had on weren't so bad.

Which should have been my second clue that something was terribly wrong. It was barely nine a.m. Shouldn't she still be wearing the baggy T-shirt and old maternity shorts she slept in?

"Ma-goooo!" Alice, one of my two-year-old triplet sisters came running down the hall, her arms flailing in random directions like small tree branches caught in the wind.

She barreled past my mom and launched herself into my lap. I hugged her, then hauled us both up from the depths of the clothes nest and swung her around until she squealed. "Fly me again!" she shouted the second I brought her down for a crash landing in the "possibly passable" pile.

"Did you make breakfast?" I asked Mom curiously, sniffing the pancakes in the air again as I picked the squealing Alice up off the floor by her wrists.

Especially since my triplet half sisters had been born, weekday breakfast had been a DIY meal at our house. It was made of three ingredients: cereal, milk, and a bowl. It wasn't like my mom had time to be whipping up low-fat smoothies seven days a week. Plus, it's never really been her style.

"I did. I thought it would be a nice change," my mom answered as my sister and I spun again. "And, it's a big day, Margot. I want you to get off to a really good start." Considering all the stuff she had on her plate, between her job and my sisters and our financial problems, I was more than a little surprised she'd remembered the important back-to-school outfit session, but I wasn't about to complain. "Come on, both of you. Pancakes are getting cold."

In the kitchen, my grandma Betty had already strapped my other two sisters, Aleene and Alex, into their high chairs and had just finished cutting their buckwheat pancakes into tiny, choke-proof bites. She looked up and smiled when she saw me.

"Good morning, sweetheart," she said, reaching into the drawer behind her and grabbing three toddler-sized forks without even looking. Technically, my grandma lives down the street in an apartment building, but she's always at our place taking a triplet to the potty or doing our dishes when she should probably be watching *Jeopardy* or playing bingo.

"Hi, Grandma." I sank down into a kitchen chair.

"What can I get you? Orange juice? Soy milk?" Grandma Betty lifted Alice into her high chair and turned to me.

I was just about to ask for orange juice when my mom, who had started scraping burned pancake batter off the bottom of the pan, cut me off. "You sit down, Mom," she said. "Margot can help herself."

Ever since my grandma Betty had gotten a little light-headed while mall walking a month ago, Mom and my stepfather, Bald Boring Bryan, had been on this campaign to get her to take it easy. Still, even though it was true that I didn't need her to serve me, I couldn't help feeling jealous. Sometimes I wished I could get a fraction of the attention the triplets did. They didn't even have to cut their own food, or wipe their own butts. Plus, since the second they were born they've been turning heads wherever we go, with their wispy blond hair and blueberry eyes. Even a trip to the grocery store is guaranteed to bring on a chorus of strangers going, "Oooooh, aren't they precious," or "Look at the way they're all waving"—like that's an especially brilliant skill. I mean, not to state the obvious but, hello, I can do it too.

It also doesn't help that they're the only identical triplets in our city. The day after they were born, there was even a story on the front page of the local paper. "Darling Family Gets Three Times the Joy." The picture shows my mom, my step-father, and the triplets crowded onto a hospital bed. But even though the reporter mentioned me in paragraph four, nobody thought to take my picture or interview me. It's too bad, really, because I think that even then I could have offered a unique perspective on the suckier side of being a sibling of multiple half sisters. For one thing, your entire life gets blown apart and put back together in a way you never asked for.

"Don't fuss over me, Catherine," Grandma Betty scolded my mom. "I like to take care of my Margot. Now, sweetheart, soy milk or orange juice?"

"Orange juice," I answered. "Please." My mom scrubbed at the frying pan a little harder in frustration, but if Grandma noticed, she just ignored it.

"Good choice. You need your vitamins. It sounds like you've got a busy day ahead." Mom had even told Grandma about my back-to-school outfit-picking session? Now that *definitely* shocked me.

"I guess," I answered. I walked my fingers across Alex's high chair toward her plate, where I snatched a pancake bite, popping it into my mouth and chewing noisily. "Um-nom-nom-nom-nom." All three of them laughed so hard you'd think I was a professional stand-up off the Comedy Network.

"Actually," Mom said, turning toward my grandma, with the spatula still in hand, "I haven't told Margot why this morning is so important. Margot, I have something planned for you."

I swallowed hard. If my best friend Erika-with-a-K's mother said she'd planned something for her, you'd know it was a manicure at the spa, or tickets to an expensive musical. But my mom's surprises were usually things like a new twelve-pack of one-hundred-percent cotton granny-style underpants, or a day of art appreciation at the gallery on a free Friday with the screaming triplets.

I waited for it, hoping against reason that maybe she'd planned something nice to thank me for babysitting all summer. Maybe we were going to a movie, just the two of us. Or shopping for some brand-name back-to-school clothes. Erika-with-a-K had just gotten a new pair of Parasuco jeans with tiny rhinestones on the pockets, and I would have sold my soul to get the same pair. I should have known better, though. My stepfather, Bald Boring Bryan, had been out of work for ages before finally landing a contract for a series of TV commercials the month before. We were still catching up on overdue bills, and Parasuco jeans probably weren't our first priority.

"I've signed you up for a session through Community Connections," my mom said. She saw the devastated look on my face and responded with a warning expression I knew well: *Margot, don't argue with me. This will be good for you.*

"What kind of session?" Knowing her, it was bound to be a workshop on finding your inner goddess or jazzing up second-hand clothing with beadwork.

"It's an all-girls workshop," she started carefully. "The write-up said it would be a safe space to talk about your sense of self. Bryan and I thought—"

I pushed my chair back from the table. My sense of self *so* did not need talking about, and since when did my stepfather get to help decide what would be good for me?

"Margot, don't get upset. You'll be done by noon, in plenty of time to meet up with Erika. And it's already paid for. This isn't up for discussion," she added, before I could even start to protest.

"Fine," I mumbled. I could tell from the serious look on my mother's face that I wasn't getting out of this class, but that didn't mean I had to sit there and listen to her go on about how great for me it was going to be. "But you know what? I'm not hungry. At all." Grandma shot my mother a worried look.

I went down the hall to the bathroom, shutting the door much harder than I needed to. Then I splashed water over my face and started my ten-step hair routine, which takes at least half an hour and is sacred. I'd only made it to the spray-on conditioner (step four) when my mom knocked on the door saying it was almost time to go.

All of which explains how, at 9:15 in the morning on the last real day of summer vacation, with my hair still an incredible frizz ball, I found myself buckled into the front seat of our rusty, million-year-old minivan, staring angrily out the window. As we backed out of the driveway, I bit my lip and tried not to cry.

"So, Margot," my mom said, once we'd rounded the corner, "just think. In a few days, you'll be starting seventh grade."

"Yeah," I answered. "Just think." I definitely didn't feel like talking to her, and of all the topics I didn't feel like talking to her about, school was number one.

"Are you excited?"

I shrugged. The truth was, it was complicated. The answer was "yes" and "definitely not." In just three days, Erika and I would be walking through the doors of Manning Middle School for the first time. (If you didn't count the orientation tour we took in June.) We would officially be leaving elementary school behind and starting fresh. Sort of. All the people from our old school—Colonel Darling Elementary—would be starting at Manning too. But still, in a new building, with new teachers, I had some reason to hope things might be better. At least, they could be if I managed to stick to my School Year's resolution for seventh grade:

Be More Normal.

My mother drummed her fingers nervously on the steering wheel, obviously trying to work up the courage to say something more. "You know," she went on finally, "I remember what seventh grade was like, Margot. I used to get teased. There were girls who gave me the cold shoulder because of the music I listened to."

"That sucks," I said. What I was really thinking was that my mom had officially checked out. She had no idea what kids today were capable of. The cold shoulder? Try watching your best friend cry her eyes out because someone wrote "NERD" on her chair in Wite-Out while she was in the bathroom, and she came back and sat in it. And, honestly, as bad as that was, even Erika agreed that I had it worse. And it had started *way* before seventh grade.

Try enduring weird looks and whispering when everyone

else makes a macaroni Father's Day card, and yours is for your grandpa. Get called poor because your mom was too busy changing diapers and forgot to read the notice, let alone help you make gourmet triple-chocolate-chunk cookies, and you showed up at the Book-a-thon Bake-off empty-handed. Then get used to being called ape girl because your leg hair is darker than the other girls'. Have the most popular girl in school casually suggest that you might want to "do something" about your clothes. Get picked last for every team in gym class, every time. Have a bunch of popular guys throw pencil shavings into your frizzy hair all through math class. Eat the vegan three-bean chili your mom packed for lunch and listen to those same guys make farting noises behind your back the rest of the day. Understand that you don't really fit in for about ten different reasons, and that the more you try, the worse it gets . . . and then tell me about the cold shoulder.

I shifted in my seat, annoyed that I was being forced to even think about school on this supposed-to-be-blissful last official day of summer vacation.

"What exactly do I have to do in this class, anyway?" I asked, changing the subject as we got out of the van. The parking lot of the community center was practically deserted.

"Well," Mom said, "you'll probably talk about your self-image. Maybe do some group exercises. It's really about putting yourself in the best possible frame of mind to start the new school year."

I sighed. A new frame of mind wasn't going to solve my problems. What I needed was a new life.

My mom glanced at her watch. "Oh, we're late," she said, holding the front door open for me. She hurried down the stairs so quickly I was out of breath by the time we got to the bottom. The sign on the door in front of us read: POWERFUL GIRLS! SELF-ESTEEM FOR PRETEENS. It had a bad clip-art drawing of a girl giving a thumbs-up.

My mother kissed me quickly on the cheek. "Margot, please give it a chance. This might be just what you need. You know, to help you deal with the pressures of being a girl in today's world. And to work through what happened *last June*." She whispered those words like *last June* was something too horrible to even mention, which it sort of was. "I'll pick you up at noon." She squeezed my arm, then started back up the stairs.

I was just considering making a run for it when the door opened and a woman dressed in a flowing turquoise top poked her head out. "You must be Margot," she said, in an extremely soft but high-pitched voice. Imagine if a baby goat in a petting zoo could talk. Her wavy gray hair was sort of goatlike too, and she had huge front teeth. "We're just about to start." She stepped back and motioned for me to come in.

Wonderful, I thought. I was about to spend the entire morning of my last real day of summer vacation learning about self-esteem from a goat. Would I be standing there if I was anywhere close to normal? I honestly doubted it.

2

I Suck at Having Self-Esteem

THE FIRST THING I NOTICED when I walked into Powerful Girls! Self-Esteem for Preteens was that the preschool room, where it was being held, seemed smaller than it had when I was a kid. Back then, I could ride a trike forever without hitting a wall, and the sand table had been filled with mountains and valleys and castles with moats. Not anymore.

The toys, which had seen better days, were pushed against the walls. The room was dark and dingy, and instead of happy, laughing kids, a group of eleven- and twelve-year-old girls was balanced awkwardly on kindergarten-sized plastic chairs.

I recognized one of them—this short, freckled fifth grader from Colonel Darling Elementary. Our moms used to be friends a long time ago. She came to my house to play Monopoly while they did this single women's group thing in the living room. I could tell she remembered me too, but she looked at the floor quickly while I glanced at a *Stay Alert, Stay Safe* poster on the wall. It was an unspoken pact. We would pretend not to know each other, then never mention this to anyone we knew.

As for the other girls, I'd never met them, but, at a glance, they seemed to belong there. One had braces and tons of acne. Another was so overweight her thighs spilled way over the edges of the chair. A third had greasy hair and was wearing a T-shirt with dolphins on it. Almost all of them had slumped shoulders. Really, I thought to myself, I'm the coolest person in the room. At least I'd taken five minutes to put on a new pair of jeans and the flowered ketchup-stain cami.

"Girls," said Goat Lady, "I'd like you all to welcome Margot to the group." Everyone mumbled "Hi" while staring at their feet, except for one girl who had red hair in two thick braids down her back. "Hi, Margot." She looked at the teacher to make sure she was watching. "On behalf of everyone, welcome to the group."

"Thanks," I said. There were only two itty-bitty chairs left—which were side by side. One was right beside braids girl, the other was next to the fifth grader I knew. I chose braids girl.

"My name is Mrs. Carlyle," said the teacher, "but since we're all friends here, I'd like you to call me Beth. Is that all right?" She glanced around nervously, like she was expecting one of us to jump up and bite her. "Welcome to Powerful Girls! Self-Esteem for Preteens. Today we're going to work with five basic principles as we journey toward self-acceptance." She walked over to a whiteboard and wrote with a squeaky marker. *Principle 1: Appreciate Yourself.*

I took a deep breath and tried to think of a daydream I could focus on to pass the time. This was something I always did in French class. Nine times out of ten the fantasies were about Gorgeous George, who had been my dream-boyfriend since third grade.

He was tall. He was cute. He was nice. He was good at sports. He was perfect. The only problem was that he was popular, and I, as you might have guessed, was not-so-much. I wasn't the nerdiest of the nerds or anything, but I wasn't part of The Group. They actually called themselves that too—The Group.

You probably know the type. They wear really expensive (really great) clothes and do cool things like pass notes all through class, have pool parties, and shoplift candy. They make fun of anyone who isn't like them, and the rest of us hate them but also secretly dream of being them.

I stared off into a corner over Mrs. Carlyle's head and let myself drift off. In my fantasy, Gorgeous George (whose real name is just plain George, obviously) was walking past my locker with Sarah J. (the most popular of the popular girls).

She was bragging about how awesome her summer vacation to Paris was when she spotted Simon, this kid in our grade who has to go to speech therapy twice a week for lisping. She smiled at George in this way that made it clear she was about to do something *hilarious* and that he should pay attention. "Hi, Th-h-himon," she said, but saying all those th's accidentally made her spit right in Gorgeous George's eye.

Needless to say, he was grossed out. (Sarah J. might be teen-model perfect, with long blond hair and aqua-blue eyes, but even *her* spit is disgusting.) He also wasn't impressed. Simon's a nice enough guy, after all. It's not like it's his fault the letter S is so hard to say.

But here's where it got good: just then, I stepped up and offered George a tissue from one of those cute and organized-looking ten-packs of Kleenex, which I happened to have in my bag. He took it from me gently, wiped the spit from his eye, and really noticed me for the first time.

"Thanks," he said, and then he took my hand (to further thank me), and he noticed, all of a sudden, that I have really nice brown eyes. And so he said, "Wow. I never noticed how pretty your eyes are, Margot." And I got kind of shy then, which he thought was cute.

This is just one of the parts where you could tell it was a fantasy. In real life, I would have been so nervous that I would have started babbling uncontrollably about how I got my brown eyes from my world-traveling radish-farming dad, and that, if I'd had the choice, I would have rather had blue eyes like his. And had he ever heard that brown eyes are dominant? So, if one parent has blue eyes and the other has brown, the children are, like, ninety-nine percent more likely to get brown eyes. So really it's amazing anyone in the world has deep blue eyes like his anymore. . . .

But no. In my fantasy I batted my lashes at him like some kind of delicate princess. And like in *The Little Mermaid* (which the triplets would watch endlessly if my mother let them), using just my pretty brown eyes, I spoke volumes to him about my undying love. He reached out and ran his fingers through my hair (which, in fantasies, is always magically straight and tangle-free). Then he cupped his hand gently around my cheek and leaned in to kiss me while Sarah J. stood watching, her mouth hanging open in outrage. . . .

"Margot." The sound of my name snatched me ever-so-cruelly out of my fantasy. The whole group was looking at me. "Won't you begin?" Oh great, I thought, but I didn't panic. My mind is always wandering, so this kind of thing happens to me a lot. I figured out a long time ago that, instead of guessing what's going on, you're better off acting like you know, then asking a question that makes it sound like you care. For example: "I'd love to, but first, can you give me a better idea of what you're looking for?"

"Certainly, Margot," the teacher said. "Let me clarify that." See? Works every time! "What I'd really like to know, when you introduce yourself to the group, is who do you think you *are*?"

Who do I think I am? Easy. "Okay," I said. "Hi. My name is Margot Button."

"And?" she said softly, waiting for more.

"And, I'm almost thirteen years old."

"And?" she said. "Start again, Margot."

"Hi," I tried. "My name is Margot Button, and I'm almost thirteen, and I live on Gormon Avenue. I'll be starting seventh grade next week?"

"Who are *you*, Margot?" She leaned forward in her chair.

This was obviously some kind of a trick question.

"I'm a person . . . named Margot Button. I hate goldfish and processed cheese," I continued, saying whatever popped into my head, even though I knew it probably wasn't what she was hoping for. "Processed cheese because it barely tastes like cheese." Nobody said anything, so I just kept talking. "And goldfish because of the way they grow to the size of whatever you put them in. Say, if you put them in a bowl, they stay tiny, and if you put them in a pond, they grow giant and, I'm sorry, that's not normal."

Mrs. Carlyle just smiled politely. "That's all interesting, Margot, but I wonder if you could tell us anything about who you are *inside*?"

Oh. My. God.

"Inside? Fine." I smiled back. "My name is Margot Button, and I'm almost thirteen—like I said. *Inside*, I am very *annoyed* to be here talking about *self-esteem* on my last day of summer vacation."

There was total silence in the room. Mrs. Carlyle bit her lip like she was trying not to cry. I instantly felt really, really bad—even though she'd kind of forced me to lose my patience. Still, I was seriously planning to work on that as part of my School Year's resolution to Be More Normal. Starting with the first day of seventh grade, I solemnly swore I would install some kind of filter between my brain and my mouth.

To her credit, Mrs. Carlyle recovered quickly. She gave an uncomfortable, neighing kind of laugh (do goats neigh?) and seemed to put it behind her.

"That's very honest, Margot. But I wonder if, instead of defining yourself with momentary characteristics or emotions, you could tell us what it is that makes you *you*?"

I took a deep breath. "I'd really like to think about it some more," I said. "Could you come back to me?"

She smiled and nodded like it was the best idea ever. "Maybe you could write up your answer," she suggested. "Share it with us after break." Then she moved on to the next girl, the Goody Two-shoes with red hair. "Gabriella, would you like to introduce yourself to the group?"

"Sure," Gabriella said, smiling this wholesome smile like a kid on a cereal box. "My name is Gabriella, and I'm a bright, assertive, and capable young woman."

Mrs. Carlyle practically nodded her head off. She would have probably given Gabriella some kind of self-esteem standing ovation, too, except that just then, we heard loud voices in the hallway.

"I'm not!" It was a girl who sounded about my age. If anyone answered her, I couldn't make out what they were saying. "I don't care! I'm not!" she shouted again.

"Excuse me a moment, girls." The teacher stood up, smoothing out her skirt.

"I don't have time for this," answered a woman in an annoyed voice. Then she changed her tone completely, obviously talking on her cell. "Dario? Debbie. I'm so sorry, don't hang up." Her tone switched again, and she hissed something I couldn't make out.

"You must be Emily," Mrs. Carlyle said, cautiously sticking her head out the door. "We've been waiting for you. Won't you come join the group?" I craned my neck, trying to get a look at what was going on, but Mrs. Carlyle was blocking my view.

There was a tense silence followed by the sound of high heels clicking up the stairs.

Mrs. Carlyle smiled as she opened the door wider and the girl came inside. She was wearing tight jeans with a long sweater. Her hair was short and bleached blond, but growing in with darker roots. She was definitely at least as old as me, maybe older. And she was at least as miserable to be there as I was, maybe miserabler. She didn't look anyone in the eye.

"I'd like you all to say hello to Emily," Goat Lady said as she motioned to the empty seat beside me. The girl dropped her canvas backpack on the floor with a thud and nudged it under her chair with one foot. "Emily, before you arrived, we were going around the circle introducing ourselves—sharing who we are. Would you like to go next?"

The girl tipped her head back for a few seconds and stared at the ceiling. "Fine. I guess," she said. "My name is Em."

"And? What can you tell us about yourself?"

Em lowered her gaze. "I'll be thirteen on November twenty-fourth." The teacher nodded for her to go on, but Em gave her a puzzled look. "Which makes me a Sagittarius."

I could tell Mrs. Carlyle was trying hard not to look heart-broken. I, on the other hand, was feeling much better. At least two of us were so bad at self-esteem that we couldn't even introduce ourselves right.

Mrs. Carlyle went around the rest of the circle, forcing the other girls to stumble through their introductions, mumbling embarrassing stuff they knew she wanted to hear—mostly about how bright and creative and special they thought they were. When she was done, she put on a brave face. "All right, girls, let's move on to some written work. I'd like you all to get out a piece of paper and list three qualities that describe you."

As everyone dug through their bags for pens and papers, I leaned over. "I'm a Sagittarius too," I whispered to Em, but she barely smiled.

Three qualities that describe me
(Margot Button, age almost-13):
  1. Not photogenic
  2. Not very popular
  3. Talkative/Sarcastic

The first one is especially true. I've never known anyone who looks worse in pictures than I do. The all-time most terrible one made it into the sixth grade yearbook. It's of me in family studies class, eating bad soup. Andrew put in two and a half cups instead of two and a half tablespoons of salt, so my lips are all puckered and my eyes are all squinty.

Which reminds me that I've forgotten to mention Andrew. He's my friend. He's a boy. But he isn't my boyfriend. He's just a boy friend. We've known each other since first grade, when Erika and I used to chase him around the school yard pretending we were going to give him cooties. And now he hangs out with us at lunch (if he's not playing basketball or Nintendo DS with his friends Mike and Amir). Sometimes all five of us go over to Andrew's house after school to watch movies in his huge rec room. But not often, because guys only ever want to watch movies about outer space, guns, or zombies, and it makes me and Erika practically fall asleep.

Which brings me to the second quality: not very popular. Andrew is my friend, and we hang out with his friends. And, of course, there's Erika-with-a-K, who I do everything with. So it's not like I'm so unpopular that nobody talks to me, but Erika and Andrew aren't exactly Mr. and Mrs. Popularity either. And at my school, you're either popular or you're not. It defines who you are, so that's why I put it on the list.

I think I've already explained the talkative/sarcastic part. Like I said, I'm working on it.

"Are we finished?" Mrs. Carlyle looked at us hopefully. I had folded my list into a little accordion and was squeezing it between my fingers for something to do. "I'd like you to swap papers with the person beside you and discuss how you feel about the qualities you've listed."

Em looked as thrilled about the exercise as I did, but I figured I'd a hundred times rather swap with her than with Little

Miss Knows-all-the-answers on my left. "Trade?" I asked. She handed me her list.

3 Qualities that describe me, Em Warner:
 1. Rebellious
 2. Spunky
 3. Smart

"Spunky?" I said.

"Yeah," she said, matter-of-factly.

"That's . . ." I was thinking *conceited*, but I caught myself in time. "Different," I said, and then, because it hadn't come out sounding very sincere, I added: "You have really nice handwriting." She raised her eyebrows and gave me a look like she couldn't care less.

Then, desperately trying to fill the silence, I said her jeans were cool and asked which she liked better: Lucky jeans, Mavi, or Parasuco. She told me that mostly she just wore vintage. So we talked about where the best stores in the city were. Or at least, I talked and she listened, because it turned out she'd just moved to Darling and she barely knew where the malls were.

Thankfully, Mrs. Carlyle only asked a few groups to present their answers, and she skipped over Em and me, since we were obviously total failures at self-esteem. After that, she made us chant mantras, repeating the words "I am powerful. I am unique," until our self-worth was affirmed. I glanced at Em out of the corner of my eye. She was sitting with her arms folded, not even pretending to mumble along.

Then we made magazine collages to show our "secret

selves." For some reason, Em cut out all these pictures of fruit, nail polish, and expensive cars. "What?" she said when she saw me looking at it. "I like fruit." She was obviously trying to mess with Mrs. Carlyle's mind. My collage had a lot of pictures of girls with perfect creamy skin and straight hair, along with one photo of a tombstone that Em passed me. I don't even know where she found it. "Put this in," she whispered. "She'll think you're deranged." Instead, though, the teacher held up my collage and said how powerful it was.

"Symbolically speaking, Margot feels like she's dying a little on the inside," she explained. She swept her hand around the circle of peach-skinned models, then tapped the tombstone. "She's struggling to define her beauty in a society that doesn't value differences." Em started laughing softly, and I could barely contain a snort. There was nothing symbolic about it. Other people just took all of the good pictures from the magazines in the pile. By the time I got there, there were mostly ads for skin cream left. And none of them had brown-skinned girls because, let's face it, magazines almost never do.

Gabriella, the star of self-esteem, had cut out photos of people doing wilderness activities and enjoying family time, and the overweight girl's entire page was covered with movie stars.

After we finished discussing our collages and did a closing activity, we finally got to go home. Em was the first to leave, getting into the backseat of a black car. She slammed the door. I waved, but through the tinted windows I couldn't tell if she saw me. A station wagon stopped off next for the red-haired Gabriella, and she climbed into the front seat, talking excitedly to her dad. Overweight Girl and Acne Girl, to my surprise, got into the backseat of the same car, but didn't say a word to each other. They must have been sisters.

Five minutes later, the van pulled in. My mom had the triplets with her. Aleene was crying hysterically, but I didn't even turn around to make funny faces to get her to stop.

"Was it a useful class, honey?" my mom yelled over Aleene's wailing.

"It was pointless!" I yelled back. "Can we just go home?"

She turned to hand a juice box to Aleene, who immediately shut up. "Margot," she said. "I'm sorry you're angry with me. I really hoped that class might be helpful. The counselor suggested that low self-esteem could be an issue."

I stared straight ahead. Obviously, my mom had magically forgotten what it's like to be almost thirteen. If she remembered, she'd know that sometimes kids my age just screw up (like I admit I did, in a huge way, *last June*), but even if I did have self-esteem issues, the *last* thing that was going to make me feel better about myself was a horrible, humiliating class. If she really wanted to make me feel more confident about the new school year, she could give me a fighting chance by taking me to a salon and paying for hair straightening, and maybe getting me some better clothes, or at least doing a tarot reading so I could prepare myself for whatever humiliations I was in for between now and next June.

But speaking of *next* June . . . I guess by now you're probably wondering what happened *last June*. It's kind of a painful story to retell, so promise not to laugh too much. Basically, I shoplifted a glazed ham so people would think I was cool. Because I know you're probably already laughing at me while shaking your head and marveling at what a loser I am, let me tell you why it isn't actually funny.

It's not funny because:

1. It didn't work. People didn't start thinking I was cool. Instead, they started to call me "Hamburglar," which is about as far from a cool nickname as you can get.
2. I got caught.
3. My mom and Bald Boring Bryan will probably never trust me again.
4. Did I mention I got caught?

I'll admit it was a stupid thing to do. What was I planning to do with a glazed ham? If I wanted to steal something, I could have at least gone for something useful, like an iPod.

So why did I do it? Since *last June*, I've been asking myself over and over, and the honest answer is still: I don't know. I guess I did it because Sarah J. and some of the other popular kids were standing around at lunch near the steps where Erika and I were sitting. One of them dared somebody to sneak out of the yard, go into the grocery store across the street, and steal something. Except that stealing something is no big deal for them. They steal things all the time just to prove that they can: candy bars, gum, lip gloss. Small stuff. That's why the dare was that the person had to steal something bigger than their head.

I overheard, and without thinking what I was saying (story of my life), I said I'd do it. It was the first time I'd stolen anything, and I swore it would be the last. My mom is always talking about karma: about how the good energy you put out comes back to you, and the same with the bad, and I'm usually thinking about this and holding doors open for ladies with strollers or offering my seat to cranky, funny-smelling old men on the bus.

But *last June*, in one of those moments where my brain had obviously left my body, I felt this surge of energy go through me, and I just knew I could do it. So I walked into the grocery store and picked up the ham. I didn't even try to hide it under my shirt or in my bag.

Instead, I held it in my arms, trying to make it look like it was the most normal thing in the world for a twelve-year-old girl to be walking out of the store with a huge chunk of one-hundred-percent grain-fed Canadian meat. I might have actually made it too, if one of the cashiers hadn't been coming in from her break and if I hadn't happened to walk right into her. "Sorry," I mumbled.

"Hey," she said, "did you pay for that?"

And I'm not sure why—I told her I didn't.

My mom doesn't believe in grounding—she says freedom is a basic human right—but she told me that if she did, I'd be grounded for life. She also said that she and Bryan were "very disappointed." I had to agree to see a counselor a few times. Plus, the next day I had to go back to school and face all of the popular kids, who seemed to think it was hilarious that I got arrested.

"You knew we were just kidding, right?" Sarah J. had said, giving me a condescending look. "When we made that bet, nobody was actually going to do it." Then this guy Ken stuffed three ham sandwiches into my backpack when I wasn't looking, and about ten different people oinked at me.

And not only did The Group disapprove, the other kids were just as unimpressed. This girl Michelle told me stories about how her cousin couldn't even get a job at McDonald's because he'd stolen a stereo when he was eighteen and got a permanent criminal record. Andrew's friend Amir brought me a lavender-scented note from his mom. She works with troubled youth groups at their mosque and offered to meet with me if I needed guidance. Even Andrew, who's always nice to me, gave me a worried look and asked why I did it.

Basically, everybody thought I was a moron, myself included. It had been the worst experience of my life. I'd been trying to block it out of my mind all summer, and so far I'd been doing pretty well.

Erika had been helping a lot. We met every weekday at 12:30 so we could make nachos before *Charmed and Dazed* came on. She shredded the cheese and I took care of the rest. Layering nachos is a fine art and—not to brag—I'm an expert. When we lived alone, my mom and I used to make them every Saturday night.

In the afternoons, if I didn't have to babysit, we'd either go swimming in Erika's giant pool, go to the mall and not buy anything, try to make the perfect playlist, practice juggling different kinds of fruit (oranges were easiest, peaches were a disaster), go to the coffee shop, or do whatever else we could think of.

Erika had even been trying to convince me that having been arrested would make me seem dangerous, and that when we got to high school, guys would think that was hot. I wasn't so sure. Maybe if I'd been caught recklessly driving a really cool motorcycle . . . But shoplifting meat just didn't have the same edge to it.

Still. I appreciated her trying to make me feel better. She was the best best friend on earth. I couldn't imagine my life without her.

3

I Am Devastated Beyond Belief, and Then Some

T HEN, THE WORST IMAGINABLE thing happened. I became a miserable, weeping disaster. A sad shadow of my former self. A pathetic, shriveled, liquefied pumpkin that had been rotting on a doorstep since last Halloween. And that doesn't even begin to describe how devastated I was.

After spending the morning confirming my lack of self-esteem, I had never been more ready to spend an afternoon with my best friend. I couldn't wait to tell her the entire shameful story, right down to the final activity where Mrs. Carlyle switched off the fluorescents and made us each hold a candle to symbolize shining our light.

And, of course, once that was out of the way, Erika and I already had our whole afternoon planned. After we were done picking my School Year's Day outfit, we were going to head to Erika's so she could try on her clothes, which is all Mexx and Lucky Brand stuff that her mom buys when it's not even on sale. Because all her mom does is shop. (How *perfect* is her mom?) And when that was over, we were going to take the bus to the mall so we could try on this magical Miss Sixty shirt that looks good on both of us. It's black and loose with a stretchy bottom, so it hides Erika's stomach (which isn't flabby at all, but she says it is) and disguises my twiggishness. Even if I couldn't afford to buy it, at least I could be in its presence.

But none of that ever happened, because Erika didn't show up.

For a while I figured her mom was probably just making her vacuum the stairs or something, but when *Charmed and Dazed* finished, and she was nowhere in sight, I started to worry.

I thought maybe there'd been a mix-up and she'd gone straight to Java House, so I put on my shoes and yelled to Grandma Betty that I was going to the coffee shop. But when I got there, the place was empty, except for the way-older semi-cute coffee guy who Erika had a mini crush on (the other reason we'd been learning to like coffee all summer). So then I walked to her place. But when I got there, her mom said, "Oh, Margot. I don't know where Erika is. She stormed out. She probably went to your house."

So I ran back to my house. By this time I was sweaty and sort of mad, but the minute I saw Erika, I forgot about that. She was slumped over, resting her arms on our kitchen table, crying so hard her shoulders were shaking.

My mom was making her a cup of tea with honey, which is her cure for everything. "This is organic alfalfa honey made by free-range bees, Erika," she was explaining, as if Erika, in the state she was in, should be worried about the welfare of bees—except that, knowing her, she probably was. "Oh, Margot," Mom said when she saw me, "I'm glad you're back. I'll leave you girls to talk." She put the tea on the table and left, closing the sliding door behind her.

All I could do was look at Erika and wait for her to say something. Anything. She kept trying to catch her breath long enough to get words out between sobs. Finally she managed: "It's . . . s-so crappy."

"What?" I reached out and put my hand on top of hers.

"I'm not g-going to Manning."

"What do you mean you're not going to Manning? School starts on Tuesday."

"I'm going to S-Sacred Heart," she answered, her voice cracking halfway through.

"The private school?" I said. "The religious one for girls? You can't! You aren't even religious." None of it was making sense. I started to get hysterical. "You HAVE to go to Manning. Sacred Heart? That's the stupidest thing I've ever heard." I was almost yelling at her.

"My mom is making me go," Erika sniffed. Her nose was running, so I grabbed a paper towel and shoved it across the table.

"I can't believe this. Why would she do that?"

Erika got really quiet. Tears were streaming down her cheeks, and she seemed almost afraid of me as she whispered the next part. "She thinks there won't be as many bad influences at Sacred Heart."

The words hit me like a soccer ball to the stomach. I knew instantly that it was my fault. Me and my stupid glazed ham.

"It isn't because of you," Erika tried to reassure me. "My mom says it's because of Sarah J. and the other kids who pressured you. She put me on the waiting list in June, and a space opened up today. She just told me. It's so dumb."

Now *I* was about to burst into tears. Of all the bad things that had happened because of (said in a whisper) *last June*, from the police showing up, to the look of disappointment on my grandma's face, to the mind-numbingly boring self-esteem workshop that morning . . . *this* was the worst punishment I could ever receive. I was going to lose my best friend. And not only was I going to lose her, she was being sentenced to private school, complete with ugly plaid uniforms, religion classes, and no boys, and it was my fault. I was officially the worst best friend on earth.

"Margot, I'm sorry." I could hardly believe she was trying to comfort me at a time like this. "Margot, don't cry."

How was I going to face a single day of seventh grade without Erika? Who was going to help me divide fractions and figure out what was going on in French class? Who was going to sit with me, secretly drawing pictures of Sarah J. as a vampire bat after she suggested I should "really comb my hair before leaving for school"? Or listen to my endless gushing about Gorgeous George? Who was I going to eat lunch with? Walk home with? I would be utterly best-friendless. An outcast. A miserable, hallway-roaming loser. This just wasn't okay.

"I know!" I said, suddenly coming up with a brilliant plan. "I'll go to Sacred Heart too. I just have to convince my mom that public school is an evil influence. That shouldn't be hard."

Erika blinked. "Really? You'd do that for me?"

"Of course!"

"But you'd have to wear a uniform."

"Uniforms can be hot."

"And you'd have to go to church."

"Notta problem!" I practically sang. "Bring on the church."

"And there aren't any guys."

I admit that last one made me hesitate, but only for a

second. "What does it matter?" I sighed. "Gorgeous George is the only guy for me and he barely knows I exist."

Plus, I thought, it could be a fresh start. None of the Catholic school girls would have seen the yearbook picture of me eating soup. They wouldn't remember the time when (while trying to answer a question about how insulation conserves heat energy) I accidentally called our science teacher fat. Best of all, I'd lose the nickname Hamburglar. Really, me and Erika going to Sacred Heart was the ideal solution.

Unfortunately, my mom didn't see it that way.

"Oh Margot. I know you want to be with Erika, but the answer is no," she said when I cornered her in the kitchen later that day. She was trying to clean crushed blackberries out of Alice's hair with a Kleenex.

"But Mom," I reasoned, "can't you see that public school is corrupting me? I need to be in an environment more conducive to learning and less conducive to criminal behavior."

She smiled, which I thought was insensitive. "Hold still, please, Alice," she said, then sighed and gave up. "I guess it's bath night anyway." She threw away the Kleenex before opening the freezer and taking out a package of tofu burgers.

"Why? Why won't you let me go? At least explain."

"It's just not practical, Margot. And it's not who we are." She tried to separate the frozen burgers with a knife, but they wouldn't come loose. "First of all, we aren't Catholic. But more important, public school is giving you opportunities to grow as an individual. It exposes you to people from different backgrounds *and* socioeconomic classes—unlike private school, where most students come from the upper class. Which brings me to my last point." She stuck the knife in farther and the burgers finally came apart, flying in opposite directions. One landed on the floor. She picked it up and washed it under the tap. "Do you have any idea how much tuition for private school is?" I didn't. "It can be upward of fifteen thousand dollars a year," she said, turning on the frying pan.

I wanted to scream, but I knew I couldn't argue with that last point. If we had to eat floor burgers, we definitely couldn't afford fifteen thousand dollars.

"What if I get a job?" I tried.

"Margot." She sounded sad. "I *really* am sorry. I know how hard this is on both of you. Personally, I think Erika's parents are being shortsighted, but the decision is theirs. You'll still see each other on weekends and after school. We need to be reasonable, here, okay?"

I didn't want to be reasonable. I wanted to throw tofu burgers at her head, and at Erika's mom's head while I was at it. . . . But since that wasn't really an option, I did the only thing I could: I stomped to my room and slammed the door. Then I pressed myself against the wall in the corner and slid down until I was crumpled into a ball. I cried forever, making a big wet spot on the pink carpet. I didn't care if I was being dramatic.

Eventually I dragged myself up, blew my nose, and turned on my computer so I could IM the bad news to Erika.

Margot12: She said no.
EriKa: That sucks. I h8 both our moms.

I stared at the screen. *I'm going to miss you so much that I don't even know how I'll survive,* I typed, but then I thought it sounded desperate and corny (even if it was true), so I erased it and wrote:

Margot12: We should run away and be circus freaks together and never come back. Then they'd be sorry for ruining our lives.
EriKa: We should. We already know how to juggle oranges. ;) You be the bearded lady. I'll be the midget.
Margot12: How come you get to be the midget?
EriKa: Because I'm shorter.
Margot12: Well, how come I have to be the bearded lady?
EriKa: Because you'd look better with a beard.
Margot12: What's that supposed to mean?

I was starting to get insulted about my best friend thinking I'd look good with a beard—I mean, it's bad enough that I kind of have a tiny bit of a mustache that I have to bleach with this disgusting-smelling Sally Hansen stuff every couple of weeks—but then I remembered that life as we knew it was over. It hardly mattered who got to be the midget and who had to be the bearded lady.

Margot12: This sucks. What are we going to do?
EriKa: We'll hang out every day after

```
school. Promise? Since I have to wear
a uniform, you can have my new jeans
for the 1st day of school.
Margot12: Promise to hang out. EVERY
DAY. Thks 4 jeans.
```

Honestly though, I didn't feel very excited about the jeans, and I didn't even ask which top she thought I should wear with them, because *that* was how depressed I was. I was going to have to face the first day of seventh grade, and every school day after that, best-friendless. Not even Parasuco jeans could make that not suck.

4

Bald Boring Bryan Has a Moral Objection

MY TRIPLET SISTERS are only two, so it's not surprising they've got a few things left to learn about the way the world works. For example, they still don't get how mostly unfair life can be.

That Friday night, Aleene screamed like a maniac when my mom washed Alex's hair first at tub time. "Nonefair!" she wailed. And she *hates* hair washes (they all do), but that wasn't her point. Her point was she didn't get to go first.

"Here, Aleene. You're next. Look at this," Mom said, distracting her with a rubber duck, which Aleene accepted, still whimpering.

It sucks, but soon she'll realize that being denied the first hair wash is nothing. The older you get, the more unfair life becomes, and the worst part is, no one even thinks about handing you a squeaky duck to console you anymore—even if your weekend, like mine, was nonefair in about ten different ways.

Every Labor Day weekend Erika's parents take her to Toronto to visit her rich aunt and uncle. And when I say rich, I mean mansions and sports cars rich. Even Erika thinks they're rich (and her pool is bigger than my house). Her aunt takes her to the mall and lets her pick out whatever back-to-school clothes she wants. And even though Erika was going to be wearing a uniform this year, they still went. I couldn't pretend I wasn't insanely jealous, but at least Erika made her parents stop on their way out of town to drop off the jeans.

"Hi," she said, holding out a Holt Renfrew bag.

"Hi." I took it. The jeans were folded perfectly inside. I think her mom had even ironed them.

We looked at each other miserably for a while, not knowing what to say, which—trust me—never happens.

"It's going to be all right," she said finally, but there were tears in her eyes.

"Yeah, sure," I said, but I was crying too.

We hugged and stood at my front door, sniffling into each other's shoulders until her mom started honking. Clearly, she was in a hurry to get to Toronto so she could browse for a new Gucci bag before drinking martinis at some fancy restaurant.

Erika gave me one last hug. Then she got in the car and pressed her palm against the glass. I stood on the lawn, watching them drive away until they disappeared around a bend. Then I moped back into the house to start my exciting long weekend at home with my mom, Bryan, and the triplets.

That afternoon I spent hours in the backyard drawing my sisters a city out of sidewalk chalk on the patio stones. It even had tiny roads for riding trikes down, an ice cream parlor, a railroad, and (by special request) a dog zoo. The next day I went shopping at the dollar store for a few last-minute school things—a new pencil sharpener and a few erasers shaped like Japanimation hamsters.

Finally, on Labor Day, I helped my mom bake zucchini

loaf and prune her hibiscus—then I plonked down on the sofa, ready to spend my last afternoon of freedom doing something *I* wanted to do—watching decorating show reruns. It wasn't easy, either, considering that I had to try to block out the deafening sounds of the triplets playing on their battery-powered TinyTikes electric guitars in the next room. Their grandma Dotty (Bald Boring Bryan's mother) bought them for their birthday, and I swear I'll never forgive her.

Still, even though I was getting a huge headache and was totally depressed, I had to admit it was inspiring what you could do with paint, some custom cabinetry, and a bit of crown molding. I'd just watched the decorating team turn a nasty green kitchen into a bright, cheery, retro space, and was about to tune in to the next half-hour episode—a bedroom—when Bald Boring Bryan sulked wussily into the living room and stood with his head tilted to one side, waiting for me to pay attention to him.

"Margot," he started finally, scratching at his temple. "It would be incredibly helpful to me if you could watch the girls for half an hour while I nip out to the convenience store and get gas for the van."

"Can't you take them with you?" I asked, not looking away from the TV. "I'm watching this." The *Decorating by Design* theme song played as they came back from commercial. I hummed along as the little cartoon theme-song lady walked into a falling-apart cartoon room, pasted up fresh wallpaper with the show's logo on it, then, *poof*, the room transformed into a tasteful space using a coordinating pallet of neutrals. Cartoon lady turned and winked at the camera. I winked back. There was something about her that always made me feel better. Like, no matter how bad things looked, with a little wallpaper and a snap of her fingers, she could make it beautiful. Now, if only she could come fix my life. . . .

Bryan stood, staring over my shoulder while they panned the camera around for the "before" shot of the bedroom. It had bright purple walls and curtains with geometric shapes on them. It looked like it had been decorated by a first grade math teacher.

I could hear him take a deep breath, trying to center himself. It's part of this new yogic-peacefulness thing he's doing. You're supposed to "rise above your challenges" and "ride a wave of calm." I know it's mean, but sometimes I like to see how far I can push him.

"Couldn't you turn it off?" he tried again. "I'd be back from the store in half the time. Also, you and your sisters could spend some quality time together. We would all benefit."

"That might be true, Bryan," I said, still not looking at him, "but I think I would benefit more from watching this show because I really want to redecorate my room."

I could hear him breathing even more deeply; so deeply I had this vision of him accidentally inhaling the magazines I had lying on the coffee table. And, I swear, the pages of the September *CosmoGirl* did flutter when he exhaled.

"I understand that you're enjoying your television program, Margot, but sometimes we need to make sacrifices in this family to help each other out." His voice was less yogicly peaceful now, but I honestly didn't care. I can't stand when he pulls that "in this family" stuff on me; like he suddenly gets to decide what "this family" does and doesn't do. He's *not* my father, and it's not like I asked for three sisters.

"I need some time alone right now, okay?" I said, looking

up from the couch. "I'm dealing with a lot. And
don't remember, I spent quality time with my s
much every day this summer. Can't you please tak
dren to the store so I can mourn the loss of my best friend in
private?"

Bryan took another deep breath, then turned and left the
room. Thank God, I thought, directing my full attention back
to the show.

But before you go thinking I'm a big unhelpful jerk, let
me explain. It's not that I don't love my sisters. I do. I've loved
them right from the start, but that doesn't mean I want to be
with them constantly, and it doesn't mean I feel the same way
about Bryan.

I was just about to start fourth grade the summer my
mom met him at a vegan potluck dinner. (They brought almost
exactly the same couscous salad with raisins, so it was like fate
or something.) If I'd only known how much damage he was
going to do to my life, I would have definitely tried harder to
scare him off. But Bryan looked so harmless with his flaxseed
cereal and drippy sentimental ways that he hardly seemed worth
the trouble. Plus, Mom had never gotten very serious about
the other guys she'd dated, and I figured it would be the same.
Huge mistake.

Eight months later he gave my mom a moon-and-star
engagement ring and proposed by candlelight on the winter
solstice—something she thought was totally romantic, but I
thought was kind of cheap. He could have at least sprung for a
diamond and some electricity. I mean, my mom's pretty amazing, as moms go. She's smart and resourceful, not to mention
beautiful—with light blue eyes and long blond hair that reaches

all the way down her back and is just starting to go gray.

Still, she said yes, and four months later I was the flower girl at their riverside wedding. All of Bryan's family came, including his horrible mother, Dotty.

"I think it will be nice for Margot," she'd said to her cousin Flo, as they heaped their plates full of salads and casseroles at the homemade buffet. "It's sad, you know, her father wanting nothing to do with her. But now she'll have Bryan." She didn't know I was crouched behind the nondenominational minister's podium with Erika, picking field mushrooms for something to do. "Now, what do you suppose this green stuff with the nuts is?" she whispered loudly, then snorted. "One thing's for sure. Bryan won't get fat eating the food she cooks." Flo guffawed and slapped Dotty's arm, and after that Erika and I spent the rest of the reception hatching a plan to sneak the field mushrooms into Dotty's next helping of vegetarian lasagna—Erika was pretty sure they were the poison kind—but we never worked up the nerve.

Next thing I knew, I found myself packing my stuff into cardboard boxes and walking through the strange emptiness of our little brick bungalow—noticing the dark spot on the wall where our embarrassing Goddess of Fertility painting used to hang; running my hand over the door frame my mom had been notching to measure me since I was old enough to stand.

When we got to Bryan's house, nothing fit. Our sofa looked too small. Our sari curtains looked too bright against the white walls. Still, my mom threw our Peruvian blanket over Bryan's ugliest chair, rearranged his furniture to make room for ours, and hung up the fertility goddess painting right in the front hall. I'll never know for sure if it's what gave him the idea,

42

but a few months later, Bryan decided he wanted to have a little bald baby. He and my mom found this top-notch doctor and went for all kinds of tests. By Christmas they were showing me a black-and-white photo from her ultrasound. "Surprise, surprise, surprise!" my mom said, pointing to each bean-shaped blur.

My mom was almost forty when my sisters were born, and she never stops saying what a miracle they are. She didn't think she'd be able to have another kid after me. I was ten at the time. I couldn't understand why she'd *want* another one. And I definitely couldn't (and still don't) understand why she married Bryan. I thought we were doing perfectly fine—and that we were happy. But I guess she wanted more from life, like a bigger house with more people in it, piles and piles of laundry, and someone to bore her to sleep at night . . . and, if that was the case, she'd definitely found the right guy.

Still, dull and wussy as he might be, I had to admit Bryan had a few surprises up his sleeve. The decorating team had just started to take down the hexagon-shaped light fixture when my mom came in, grabbed the remote from the coffee table, and switched off the TV in one motion.

"I'm doing a tarot reading in the front room, and I need you to watch the girls."

I was stunned. First of all, I couldn't believe that Bryan had had the nerve to interrupt my mom. There's a strict "don't even think about interrupting a client unless you want bad karma to rain down upon you" policy in our house. Mom put her hands on her hips. "Bryan has to get to the convenience store before it closes."

I stared up at her. Her jaw was all clenched, and her forehead was all wrinkled. She barely even looked like herself. "He's had a difficult enough week. I don't understand why you can't treat him with a little respect, Margot. Bryan is an important member of this family."

"If Bryan thinks he's had such a difficult week, he should try my life. In case you're forgetting, I just lost my best friend to another school. All I want to do is watch TV and try to forget about it, okay?" I made a grab for the remote, but my mom got in the way, which made me even more annoyed. "And why did he go crying to you? It's kind of pathetic, don't you think? Plus, why do I *always* have to babysit? They're not my kids. And Bryan's *not* my family."

There's an expression—about a straw and a camel's back. Maybe you know it. If you don't, what happened next is a good example of how it works. Basically, a camel can carry a lot of straws without even caring. But eventually, no matter how chilled out the camel is, or how light each straw is, there's a limit to how much any desert-dwelling animal in its right mind is going to put up with. My mom was the camel. That last thing I said was one straw too many.

"I'm floored," she began. She wasn't yelling, but her eyes were narrow. "Did you just say what I think you said?" It didn't seem like she actually wanted an answer. "I know you're upset because Erika won't be going to your school this year, but that's not an excuse for this behavior. Bryan is part of your family. I don't want to hear you say a thing like that again."

She turned to go. "He's not," I muttered under my breath. "You're the one who married him, okay?"

I obviously hadn't muttered quietly enough. "No. It's not okay, Margot," my mother snapped, turning back. "It's really not okay." She picked up *CosmoGirl* and threw it. The pages made a loud slapping sound as they hit the carpet.

I sat up straighter. My mother never yells. And she definitely never throws things.

"Okay. Fine. I'll watch them," I said quickly. Then I couldn't help adding: "But only for half an hour. And he has to stay until the next commercial break."

She shook her head like she was just too annoyed with me to discuss it anymore. "Thank you, Margot," she said, already on her way out. "I appreciate your help."

After Bryan got back from the convenience store, I went straight to my room—partly to avoid my mother, but also to try on the Parasuco jeans with this long brown waffle-material top I thought would look okay. There was no way around it: school would be starting the next day, and it would probably suck, but that didn't mean I shouldn't try to look decent. I packed my new binders into my same old green backpack, opened the package of hamster erasers, and tossed aside the waffle top, settling instead on a gray-and-black-striped Mexx shirt that Erika gave me because she never wore it anymore. It was a bit weird and bunchy at the bottom, but it was the best thing I had.

I was just sharpening a few pencils when there was a knock at my door.

"Can I come in?" my mom asked. Then, as usual, came in without waiting for an answer. She straightened out my butterfly quilt, sat on the edge of the bed, and traced a wing with her finger.

"Margot," she said finally. "I want to apologize. I overreacted this afternoon. I'm sorry I threw your magazine." I listened warily. I kind of deserved the apology, but it wasn't like her to admit her mistakes. "It wasn't all about the babysitting. You help out so much with the girls. Bryan and I appreciate it. I don't know what we'd do without you."

I picked some clothes up off my computer chair, dumped them on the floor, and sat down. This seemed like it might be a long talk.

"I *do* want you to treat Bryan with more respect," she said, "but the real reason I was frustrated had more to do with some news we got on Friday that I was still trying to process. Some bad news."

Mom looked really worried. I gulped, bracing myself for it. Had she predicted her own imminent death in a tarot reading? Was Grandma Betty sick?

"Bryan's contract for the travel insurance commercials got canceled."

"What?" I exclaimed. Just the month before, TC Travel Co. had told him he had the "trustworthy" look they'd been searching for. "I thought they loved him for that part!"

"They did," Mom said with a small sigh. "They still do. But Bryan had a moral objection to the latest script."

"A moral objection? To a travel insurance commercial?" I could feel my temper rising because I knew exactly where this was going. Bryan was unemployed again, and now we were all going to have to suffer because of it. Again. "You're kidding, right? Why couldn't he just say the lines and get paid, then object later?"

"Bryan is a man with strong principles, Margot. It's just one of the things I love about him." It took all of my willpower not to sigh loudly or roll my eyes. "I really think this could be an opportunity in disguise," she said. "I did a reading for him.

The Ace of Wands came up, suggesting he would chart a new course—and that's just what he's going to do."

"What do you mean?"

"He's decided to become a real estate agent. We called the college and there was an opening in a night school class. It's like everything is lining up to make this possible. He starts tomorrow."

My mom stood up and walked across my room, stopping at my bookshelf and looking at the stack of cards I kept there. They were all from my dad, postmarked from the different places he'd traveled through—England, Bangladesh, Peru. Each one had a few sentences scrawled inside. Mostly about the people he'd met or the work he was doing.

"Bryan's a good man," she said, idly picking up one of the few gifts my dad had sent me—one of those pocket-sized games where you tip a tiny metal ball through a maze. "He's giving up a big dream for us, Margot, so whether you consider him your family or not, I need you to be kinder to him right now."

I didn't know what to say. All Bryan ever talked about was acting (when he wasn't talking about yogic breathing, or quoting from his favorite self-help books). Rainbows of happiness practically sprouted from his ears whenever he told the story of the time he was Hamlet in Shakespeare in the Park and it never rained once during the whole three-month run. I couldn't picture him in a suit and tie, touring people around houses and pointing out the great light and new laminate flooring.

"Okay," I said. I guessed I could try.

"And I need to ask you another favor."

I swiveled back and forth in my chair, waiting for the next blow.

"Things are going to get easier for us soon. But while we're paying Bryan's tuition, money's going to be tighter than ever. Donatello has agreed to give me some morning shifts at All Organics, which means I'll get the cashier's discount on groceries." Soy cheese and organic beet casserole! I tried not to jump for joy. "And I'll have to do more tarot readings in the afternoons. Which is where you'll come in . . ." I already knew what she was going to ask. "I'll need you to babysit from 3:45 until dinnertime while I'm with clients." She didn't miss the look of disappointment that was clearly written across my face. "Just from now until Christmas, sweetie. And Erika can help you anytime she wants."

I sighed, thinking of all the reasons this was a bad idea. Like, first, even if Erika was allowed to come over, when were we supposed to actually talk, or have any fun, or go to the mall with three two-year-olds to watch? And second, there's supposed to be a lot of homework in seventh grade. When was I going to finish it all? And third, how exactly was this fair?

"This time next year," Mom went on, "things will be different. You'll see. But we need to come together to make that happen." I nodded miserably, and my mom stood up. "I'll let you keep getting ready," she said. "It's a big day tomorrow." She kissed me on the top of my head and left, shutting the door softly behind her.

After she went, I lay down on my bed and stared at my ceiling for a long time. It's one of those bumpy ceilings that looks like it's made of cottage cheese. I used to spend a lot of time worrying that one of the little cottage cheese bumps might fall off and hit me in the eye (I guess I still worry about that), but at that moment I had bigger things on my mind. Like the fact that we were broke, again. And the fact that, as much as I loved the triplets, I missed our old house and our old life, where my mom always made sure we had enough money for whatever we really needed, with a little left over for popcorn at the movies and brand-name shoes.

Also, I thought about how much I was going to miss Erika. The idea of facing Manning alone made me feel queasy, and the news that I'd have to babysit every afternoon made me furious. But mostly I thought about how I was sick of being almost thirteen and having absolutely no control over my life.

5

School Year's Day

MY GRANDPA BUTTON used to say this thing when he'd drive me to Brownies or swimming lessons, and I'd ask if he had candy in the glove box. I think it was part of a poem. "Hope springs eternal in the human breast." He'd laugh, ruffling my hair, and hand me a caramel wrapped in cellophane, or a Scotch Mint, or whatever else he had hiding behind the maps. "Now don't tell your grandma about our stash."

Back then I never gave his little saying much thought, but now I get what it means. It's about how, even when everything seems against you, it's human nature to dream of caramels—or better things. Which maybe explains why, when my alarm went off at 7:00 that Tuesday morning, I jumped out of bed, ready to get the day started.

It was still School Year's Day, after all—a new beginning, a reason for hope. Erika wouldn't be there, and just the thought made my throat close up, but another part of me couldn't help being curious to find out who would be in my class and who my teachers would be. Plus, I was excited to see Andrew, who'd been in Barbados all summer—not to mention Gorgeous George.

I managed to make it to the bathroom before anyone else woke up, getting off to a good start by giving myself a solid half hour for my ten-step hair routine.

1. Wash
2. Condition
3. Towel-dry
4. Spray on leave-in conditioner
5. Blow-dry
6. Put in smoothing gel
7. Flat iron
8. Apply mousse liberally
9. Flip head and shake vigorously to add oomph
10. Flat iron again

Then I put on the striped shirt and Parasuco jeans. All in all, I looked okay, at least until I started to walk to the kitchen. That was when I noticed that the jeans, which were a size seven to fit Erika, kept sliding down my hips, showing off my ladybug underwear. Definitely not great. I went back and rifled through my closet for a belt. The only one I could find was made of purple elastic and had a sparkly butterfly buckle, but as long as I pulled my shirt down, nobody would see.

By the time I got to the kitchen, the morning was already in full swing. My mom was dressed for her shift at All Organics, had the triplets set up with bowls of Oaty-O's, and was trying to wash some dishes. "Oh no!" she cried, dropping a fork into the sink. "Don't do that, honey." Aleene was taking big gulps from her sippy cup, then sticking out her tongue and making farting noises so that soy milk spurted out. "No, no,

Aleene!" Mom said again. But Aleene started laughing at her own hilariousness, and then the other two thought it looked like fun to be human soy milk fountains. "Alice, Alex, no. The milk stays in your mouth." It was too late. Fake milk was being spewed in all directions. Pretty much a typical morning.

I grabbed a slice of bread and buttered it with EarthBound Organic Spread. My stomach was way too queasy for a real breakfast. "I'm going now," I said, messing up the triplets' hair from behind, so I'd stay clear of the dairy supplement disaster.

"Oh, okay," my mom answered, taking away Aleene's sippy cup before wiping her chin. The protests started immediately.

"No no no no no NO, Mommy. My cup. My cup. MY cup."

"Have a great first day, Margot," Mom yelled.

"Thanks," I mumbled, even though I thought she should have said something more like "good luck," or even "be brave."

With all the general morning chaos and the sick feeling in my stomach, I was already past the park when I remembered that my mom had forgotten to take the back-to-school picture. Ever since kindergarten she'd taken a photo of me on the front steps. We even kept them in a special album. In the first picture I'm standing in front of our bungalow wearing a frog raincoat. I'm smiling crookedly with my gappy teeth showing. In second grade I have these dorky pigtails that I obviously did myself because one is way higher up on my head than the other. I'm holding the Powerpuff Girls backpack my grandma bought me, and I'm about to jump off the step like I can't wait to get to school. I'm actually kind of cute.

From there, though, things go downhill, with different variations of fashion mistakes and bad hair. By the time I get to the fifth grade photo, I can hardly stand to look at it. I've got on a pair of too-tight jeans with obvious fake fading on them, and I'm leaning over onto one hip, trying to seem cool.

Since fourth grade my mom has practically had to force me to stand still for the picture anyway. I wondered if she'd forgotten about it or just decided not to bother this year.

And not taking the picture wasn't the only thing about School Year's Day that felt weird. When I passed the corner where Erika and I always met up I had to take a deep breath and force myself to keep walking. I even tried repeating Mrs. Carlyle's lame mantra in my head. *I am powerful. I am unique. I am powerful. I am unique.* It *so* didn't help.

As I rounded the corner onto Wayne Drive I saw a group of four girls up ahead who I recognized from the enrichment program at Colonel Darling Elementary. They each had a brand-new backpack and a cute fall jacket and cardigan, even though it was still warm enough to be in a T-shirt.

"And he totally kissed her on the couch with, like, his dad in the next room," one of them was telling the others. They all mini-screamed. I tried to think of some way I could work my way into their conversation. *I knew someone who kissed someone on a couch once,* maybe—except that I didn't, plus, why would they care? Or, *That's so crazy!!* Or even, *Hey, do you guys know what time it is?* But they'd only think I was some kind of eavesdropping weirdo, so instead I hung back about six feet—just close enough that, to a casual onlooker, it might seem like I was with their group and had fallen a little behind . . . but far enough away that they wouldn't think I was trying to look like I was with them.

By the time we reached Manning Avenue the sidewalk was getting crowded with kids. I gave a small, subtle wave that none of the enrichment-program girls even noticed, and casually veered off onto the lawn, where I wandered aimlessly for a few seconds before I spotted Michelle, showing some photos to her friend Bethany. Michelle's this really tall, athletic girl who stood beside me in the chorus of the sixth grade musical. She was good at harmonies. Plus, she was captain of the volleyball team last year.

She looked different, but I couldn't quite pinpoint how. Had she dyed her hair, or at least lightened it? She'd definitely gotten even taller, which was saying something—she'd been the last person in the back row in every school picture since kindergarten.

I walked over. "Hey," I said. "How's it going? Is that a Ferris wheel?"

"Yeah," she said.

"Oh my God," I went on, seeing my opening. "I love rides. But not Ferris wheels. One time, my mom and I went on the one at Niagara Falls. And there was some kind of power outage. We got stuck right at the top for half an hour and I had to pee *so* badly. It *so* didn't help that I was staring right at the biggest waterfall in the world."

"Really?" she said. "That's funny." But she didn't sound like she thought it was funny at all. I could tell by the way she was looking down, a small smirk on her face, already flipping to the next photo.

"Oh." I pointed. "Wonderland, right?" Erika went every year. I recognized the big fake mountain in the background. As I was pointing, though, my shirt rode up a little. I tugged it down quickly, but not before Michelle had caught a glimpse of the sparkly butterfly belt.

"Wow," she remarked, raising her eyebrows. "I *love* your belt."

Now I could tell what it was that had changed: over the summer, Michelle had turned into a giant B-word.

"Yeah. Thanks. Anyway," I said, taking the not-so-subtle hint and giving them another of my lame little waves. "Better go see some of my friends." I shoved my hands into my pockets and walked away, hearing Michelle and her friend giggle softly behind me. Whatever, I thought. So she could sing harmonies and get a serve over the net. Big deal.

I kept walking, trying to act like I had someplace definite to go. Two boys I didn't recognize were having an arm wrestling match on the grass, so I stopped to watch next to these girls, Christine and Amanda.

"Hi," I said, turning to Amanda. We hadn't exactly been friends, but she and another girl named Kim had done a project about bugs with me and Erika in fifth grade. Basically all Amanda did was draw the bubble letters for the display, and she misspelled *antennae*, but we never complained to the teacher. She kind of owed me.

"Hi," I said.

She turned and squinted. I kept watching the arm wrestling match, which, by the way, was no contest. The smaller guy's face was already turning so red I thought his head might pop. "Margaret, right?" she asked.

"Margot."

"Oh my God. I can't believe I forgot your name. How many years were you in my class?"

"I don't know," I answered, even though I did know. "Three maybe."

"That's so weird," she said. I smiled, even though I didn't really think it was weird, just kind of insulting. She turned her attention back to the match. All of a sudden she looked at me. "You did the ham thing, right?" My face froze. "I thought it was either you or that other girl called Margaret. Your names are practically the same."

I nodded.

Just then, the bigger guy put the scrawny one out of his misery. "You suck, Tucker!" he shouted, jumping up and pumping his fist in victory. Christine and Amanda went over to talk to them, and I quietly stepped away.

All around the yard people were standing in groups. Girls were squealing and hugging, comparing tan lines and new haircuts. And the guys, who suddenly looked so much older and taller, were standing with arms crossed, leaning against the fence, or shoving each other around.

I spotted Andrew's friends, Mike and Amir, across the yard, playing one-on-one on the basketball court. Amir looked up and waved, and I waved back gratefully and started to walk over. "Hey, Margot," he said, passing the ball to Mike and coming to greet me.

Amir is one of the only other brown-skinned kids in our grade, so you'd think we'd have something in common, but besides the fact that we're both friends with Andrew, we really don't. Sometimes he talks about religious stuff—like fasting for Ramadan, and celebrating Eid, like he expects me to be all interested, or asks me questions about my dad, but I don't know the answers. Mike's nice too, but really quiet. His family moved here from Korea, and he only started at our school in fifth grade. When I first met him I wasn't even sure if he could speak English, because he barely said anything.

"Did you have a good summer?" Amir asked. He was dressed in his usual khaki pants along with a new collared polo shirt.

"Okay, I guess." I shrugged. "I babysat a lot. What about you?"

"Oh, you know," he answered, catching the ball Mike threw back to him. "Same as always."

I nodded. That was about the extent of our usual conversations when Andrew wasn't around.

"You want to play?" Amir asked, holding up the ball.

"No thanks," I said. Even though the idea of having nobody to talk to was terrifying, the thought of attempting to play basketball was much, much worse. I could just picture it now: me, walking into Manning on the very first day with a bloody nose. "I have to go look at something before the bell rings. See you."

"Later, Margot." He dribbled the ball and tossed it to Mike, who sunk a basket.

I wandered over to a lamppost near the sidewalk and pretended to be interested in one of the posters stapled to it: HEE-HAW HOEDOWN: A LINE DANCE FOR SENIORS!—only noticing too late that I'd placed myself dangerously close to Sarah J. and The Group girls. They'd already staked out a concrete ledge, a few feet from where I was standing. It ran all the way along the fence. Nobody who wasn't part of their group—not even the eighth graders—seemed to be brave enough to approach it. Sarah J. was sitting sideways on the ledge with her feet up, while her best friends, Maggie and Joyce, stood beside her. They all looked perfect in their fitted fall jackets with their long shiny hair.

"I'm so starving right now," I could hear Maggie complaining. "I ate like, half a piece of toast this morning so I could fit into these jeans."

"Well," Joyce soothed, "it was totally worth it. They look great."

"Thanks." Maggie's cell started buzzing, and she took it out of her pocket, walking away as she answered the call.

Sarah J. watched Maggie's back for a second too long, then turned and whispered something to Joyce. Joyce nodded and whispered something back. I could tell by the stupid fake-pity on their faces that they were probably saying mean things about Maggie's weight.

I stepped a little closer to the poster and leaned in like I was studying the fine print. I was just starting to wonder how long I'd be able to keep pretending I was interested in the biography of Rosie Bartlett, an experienced dance instructor who was "crazy for country," when I felt someone grab me around the waist from behind. I screeched and jumped twelve and a half feet in the air.

"So that's why you never wrote back to my last e-mail? You were too busy line dancing with seniors?"

"Andrew!" I practically sang his name. I was so thankful to see somebody who liked me. "How was Barbados?"

"About as much fun as hanging out with eighty-year-old people is." He shifted his backpack strap on his shoulder, revealing a sweat stain in the armpit of his shirt, which I pretended not to notice. Andrew spends every summer in the Caribbean, visiting his grandparents. He'd written me a few e-mails, but they were mostly just about how bored he was, and about how his grandma kept making him wear slippers when it was a million degrees out. And I mostly just wrote back about how sick I was of babysitting.

But then, about two weeks earlier he'd written one last e-mail where he'd said he missed me, and he'd signed his name with two X's and an O. That kind of freaked me out. I mean, how was I supposed to know what he meant? Were they regular X's or actual e-kisses? And what if I didn't XX him back? Would he get all offended? It seemed safest not to risk it.

"Yeah, well. Couldn't be worse than an entire summer of babysitting," I said.

"You sure?" He sucked in, shaking his head. "I went lawn bowling and ate cereal with fiber. But at least I got a sweet tan." He held out his arm so we could compare, but he was joking, obviously—making fun of the popular girls who have an unofficial tan competition every summer. Andrew is black—one of the only black kids in our old school, and definitely the darkest kid in our grade.

"I thought you looked different," I teased, squinting at him. But in actual fact, he kind of did. Like most of the other guys, he seemed to have grown a foot in two months, and his normally curly hair was cropped short, making him look older.

I was going to take a serious moment to make some excuse about not having time to answer his last e-mail, but before I could, the bell rang and distracted me. Andrew and I joined the pack of kids heading toward the door.

"I can't believe Erika is late on the first day," he said, whistling through his teeth as we started across the lawn. "She's gonna get it."

"She's not late. . . . She's not coming." And then I told him the whole sad story of what happened on Friday.

"Damn," he said when I'd finished. "That sucks."

"I know," I said. "I'm so depressed."

"Don't be," he answered. "You can still see her after school, right? Plus, it means you get to spend more time with your amazing friend Andrew."

I almost said, "Great!" but realized he might take it the wrong way. Instead I said, "You wish!" and punched him in the arm.

As we filed through the main doors, two teachers directed the seventh graders to the old gym and the eighth graders to the new gym. I shuffled along like a prisoner. I'd been inside five seconds, and the yellow cinder-block walls and smell of disinfectant had already confirmed the hopelessness of the situation.

Everyone found a spot on the floor, and the principal, Mrs. Vandanhoover, walked to the front of the room and tried to look imposing, which must have been hard for her. She was even shorter than some of the kids. She held up her hand for silence. "Good morning, ladies and gentlemen," she shouted. "And welcome to Manning Middle School. Most of you know each other from Colonel Darling Elementary," she went on, "but there are several students joining you from other schools—and even other cities. I urge you to look around for these students and make them feel at home. We're a big family here at Manning, after all." She paused as if she was giving us time to spot the new students, and a few people *did* look around. "We've got plenty of ground to cover, so I'm going to get straight into announcements, then I'll call out the seventh grade class lists."

That was what we were really waiting for, of course. Normally I would have been clutching Erika's hand, and we'd both be putting every fiber of our beings into willing our names to be on the same list, but things were so different now.

Mrs. Vandanhoover started a long speech about the school's anti-bullying policy and how there would be "zero tolerance" for violence and weapons. It was predictable stuff, so instead of listening, I started looking for Gorgeous George.

It only took me a few seconds to find him. He was sitting close to the back. I have his wardrobe memorized, so I could tell he was wearing a new shirt. His hair was shorter, but thankfully not too short. And he was leaning back, with both of his palms flat on the floor behind him. I could have stared at him all day, but I only let myself look for a second.

Vandanhoover was going on about the new healthier choices in the school vending machines, so I took the opportunity to drift off into a Gorgeous George fantasy. In this one, it turned out that finally, for the first time since fourth grade, we'd ended up in the same class. His name got called first, and mine got called right after, even though we're nowhere near each other in the alphabet (Button and Wainscott). This was partly how you could tell that us ending up in the same class was magical and meant to be.

When he heard my name, he looked at me and smiled slowly as I gracefully got up off the gym floor. I walked toward him, tossing my straight tangle-free hair. "Margot," he said, tipping his head to one side so his hair fell into his eyes. He pushed it back. "You look hot in those jeans."

And I was like, "Oh, these? Thanks." And then he motioned for me to come closer, so I did. He leaned in, cupping his hands around my ear, like little kids do when they're telling secrets. He smelled incredible. Like soap and ocean air.

"Know what I want?" he whispered. I smiled shyly and gave him this mysterious/confused/meaningful look. He cupped his hands around my ear again and whispered: "Be my girlfriend."

I looked deep into his eyes, but I couldn't tell you what I said back. The words "class lists" finally came out of Mrs. Vandanhoover's mouth, and I immediately snapped back to reality.

"We'll begin with Seven-A, first period teacher, Mrs. Collins." The teacher who stood up had shiny brown hair cut in a bowl shape with bangs straight across. Her lipstick was bright red, and she had excellent posture. She was wearing a sweater vest. In a way, she reminded me of one of those creepy puppets ventriloquists use.

"Amir Ahmed," Mrs. Vandanhoover called. "Tiffany Abraham. Bethany Bluffs. Charlie Baker. Margot Button. Michelle Cobbs."

"Bye," I mouthed to Andrew. Amir waved at me as I stood up to join the class. Tiffany, a quiet girl with braces, smiled. Michelle was too busy celebrating being with her friend Bethany to notice anyone else. Still, even though she clearly wasn't my biggest fan, she wasn't the meanest girl on earth, either.

"Hey, Margot!" Amir said, giving me a high five as I came to stand beside him. "Maybe Andrew will be with us too."

"Hopefully," I said, turning my attention back to Mrs. Vandanhoover. I couldn't afford to miss a single word that came out of her mouth.

One by one, people got up from the floor and joined the class. There was Erik Frallen, who can do crazy-hard math in his head; Laura Inglestone, who was also kind of quiet but seemed nice; and then—dammit—"Sarah Jamieson," Mrs. Vandanhoover called. Sarah J. got up, holding on to her friend Joyce's hand and pulling it away like they were star-crossed lovers about to be parted for life.

"Maggie Keller," Mrs. Vandanhoover called. Seriously?! Maggie was Sarah J.'s second-best friend. Not as bad as Joyce, but bad enough. "Joyce Nichols." Oh God, shoot me now. "Cameron Ruling, Simon Sable, Ken Shapiro." Ken is George's idiot best friend. He spends ninety-nine percent of his time making farting noises with his armpits. "Stuart Smythe."

But then Mrs. Vandanhoover recited the three sweetest syllables in the entire English language: "George Wainscott." Oh miraculous miracle! I could have practically kissed somebody (preferably Gorgeous George, but anybody would have done). I couldn't wait to tell Erika. It suddenly didn't seem to matter so much that everything else in my life sucked. I was going to get to see George five hours a day, five days a week, for the entire school year.

"Guys! Seven-A rocks!" I heard Sarah J. say as George and Ken joined her and The Group girls. I tried to shuffle a tiny bit backward so I'd be able to see over Erik Frallen's math-genius head to get a glimpse of George, but there were too many other people in the way. In fact, I realized with sinking hopes, Gorgeous George and I were standing about as far apart as we could get while still being in the same class. He, of course, was on the side of ultimate coolness. I was somewhere beyond Erik Frallen's giant head.

"And last but not least, Emily Warner," Mrs. Vandanhoover called. "Welcome, Emily," she said, and a girl sitting at the back of the gym stood up and unwisely (unknowingly) walked over to the cool side of the class. It took me about two seconds to realize she was the girl from the self-esteem workshop: the rebellious, spunky, smart Sagittarius with bleached-blond hair. I tried to catch her eye to see if she recognized me, but she was looking the other way.

Mrs. Collins called for everyone to please follow her, and I waved to Andrew. He ran a finger down his cheek like a pretend tear, but I just shrugged in response. We'd see each other at lunch anyway. He shrugged back, agreeing.

Or at least I thought that was what he was agreeing to. But as Mrs. Collins led the way out of the gym, and I turned to wave to Andrew one last time, Ken Shapiro, of the farting armpits, purposely kneed Simon Sable in the back of his legs for no good reason, causing him to lose his balance. He bumped into Laura, who tripped and stumbled into Cameron Ruling. He nearly groped Tiffany Abraham by mistake, making her jump back in surprise and crash into Erik. It went through the class like a chain reaction, ending with me and Amir both getting shoved hard in the back. Maybe, I realized, Andrew hadn't been *crying* about missing me at all. Maybe it was more of a symbolic show of sympathy. Maybe he knew as well as I did that Seven-A was going to be a very dangerous place, and that I was officially, unquestionably doomed.

6

I Am the World's Saddest Supermodel

B Y THE END OF FIRST period it was official: my new teacher hated my guts.

It turned out Mrs. Collins's room was in the basement, which had to be the most depressing place in all of Manning. It was dark and dreary with small windows way up high, just at ground level, so all you could see were people's shoes, and that was if you were lucky enough that someone was walking past.

To disguise how dismal it was, Mrs. Collins had plastered the walls with inspirational quotes and pictures of authors looking thoughtful. Cutout letters on the bulletin board spelled: LET'S MAKE LEARNING FUN FOR EVERYONE!

Even the I ♥ THE PUBLIC SCHOOL SYSTEM coffee mug on her desk seemed too cheerful to be real.

"You'll find a name tag on the desk that's been assigned to you," Mrs. Collins instructed as we funneled through the door. "Please stick it on your shirt and wear it for the rest of the day so all your new teachers can get to know you."

Most kids were still standing around in groups, talking to their friends, but since I didn't really have anyone to talk to besides Amir, I found my desk pretty quickly. I sighed a little when I saw that my name had been spelled "Margo."

"Mrs. Collins?" I raised my hand politely. "You spelled my name wrong. I'm Margot Button. Margot is supposed to have a T at the end."

She glanced down at some papers on her desk. "Oh. It wasn't spelled with a T on the class list," she said pleasantly, then went back to shuffling her papers.

"But it has a T in real life," I pointed out. "Like, on my birth certificate."

She looked up again, stretching her red lips into a grin. "Well, you're in seventh grade now. I'm sure you know how to write the letter T." She smiled even more tightly. "I'm sure you have a pen."

"I'm sure you have a pen." I mimicked her perky voice under my breath as I dug around in my backpack. "Great. An English teacher who can't even spell my name."

"Margot Button." I heard Mrs. Collins's voice, and by the time I looked up, she was standing in the aisle in front of me. "In this classroom we don't tolerate disrespect. Why don't you join me at lunch recess, hmmm?" I clenched my hands into fists underneath the desk, but managed to keep myself from saying anything else stupid. The second she started back up the aisle, I grabbed my name tag and furiously added a T to my name. I scratched so hard that the pen tore right through the label. Fantastic. Not only had I managed to get a lunchtime detention within the first two minutes of being in the classroom, I was also going to look like an idiot wearing a name tag with a hole in it all day.

But just then, like a single ray of sunshine bursting through the suckiness that was my morning, Gorgeous George walked up the aisle and sank down into the seat in front of me! Into the *permanent*, assigned seat in front of me. He was so close I could smell the laundry detergent his mom used. But before I could even fully appreciate the gorgeousness of his shiny brown hair, his friend Ken followed behind and threw a car magazine onto his desk.

"Button," Ken said, winking at me and my stupid name tag. "Don't feel bad. The letter T is a hard one. I didn't learn it until like, second grade." He flashed me a big fake smile.

"I remember you," I heard someone say. I looked to my left and saw that the girl from the self-esteem workshop had been assigned the seat beside me. She couldn't have sat down at a better time.

"Hi!" I said, way too enthusiastically. "Em, right?"

"And you're Margot," she said. For a second I was flattered that she still knew my name, then I remembered I was wearing the stupid name tag. "Are you still dying a little bit on the inside?" she asked, rolling her eyes.

"Depends. Are you still trying to live a healthy life in a world obsessed with consumerism?" I'd had to work so hard to hold in my laughter during Mrs. Carlyle's description of Em's fruit, nail polish, and sports car collage that I'd nearly started crying.

"That workshop was beyond lame," Em said.

I just smiled. Mrs. Collins had stepped into the hallway to talk to another teacher, and Sarah J. had taken the opportunity to get out her cell phone. She was standing one row over at Maggie's desk, reading a text off the display.

"Matt's coming to pick me up at lunch today," she

announced loudly. "He says he misses me too much to be apart for the whole day. Isn't that the sweetest?"

"That's *so* adorable," Maggie agreed.

"I know. Ninth grade guys are so much more mature and sensitive than guys our age."

Sarah had a boyfriend who was in high school? Wasn't that illegal or something?

"I went to that mall you were telling me about," Em said as she took a black binder and red canvas pencil case out of her bag. I was so absorbed in Sarah's conversation that it took me a second to remember what she was talking about. "At Southvale? Is that *really* the best one in this town? It was so empty."

All of a sudden, Sarah J.'s super-senses seemed to kick in. Maybe she'd sniffed out the fact that somebody in the room wasn't secretly paying attention to her, or maybe it was because she'd heard the word "mall." Whatever the reason, she suddenly flipped her phone shut and spun around.

"Oh, hi. You must be a new person," she said to Em. "I'm Sarah Jamieson." She smiled ever so sweetly.

"Hi," Em said. "Nice to meet you." Then she gave Sarah a strange look when she kept standing there looking at us. "So, about that mall?" Em prompted.

"You mean Southvale?" Sarah cut in. "It sucks. You want to go to Connor-Leaside. It's not as white trash . . . Hey." She squinted at Em like she was trying to measure her with her eyes to decide which level of loserdom she belonged in. "Do you girls already know each other from somewhere?" Sarah thinks everything is her business.

"Kind of. We met at this lame workshop—" Em started,

then thankfully stopped. I think because she noticed the look of terror on my face. If she expanded on that sentence, we might as well make big hats that said "superloser" and wear them all year long, because Sarah J. would never forget, and she'd tell everyone.

"A workshop?" said Sarah, sounding all interested.

"It wasn't a workshop." My mind was racing, trying to think of a way out.

"Yeah," Em said matter-of-factly. "It was more of a convention." She bent down and took another binder out of her bag, like there was nothing more to say.

"What kind of convention?" Sarah J. pressed.

I was on the verge of telling her to mind her own big, fat, hairy business when Em looked up and said with a completely straight face: "It was a junior modeling convention." She paused, giving Sarah a bored look. "In New York." You could practically see Sarah J.'s eyes pop out of her head with disbelief. "I won't get into the details," Em continued. "It was a really boring one, wasn't it?" She turned to me.

"Yeah. Well. Not the greatest," I answered awkwardly.

Sarah J. grinned wickedly. "Wait, Margot *models*?"

"What?" Em faked surprise. "Is that hard to believe?"

Apparently it was, because Sarah started laughing. Gorgeous George had turned around in his chair to look at me by now. Then things got worse. Ken, the biggest jerk on earth, who was still standing at George's desk, grabbed the car magazine they'd been flipping through. "Hey, Hamburglar. Is this you?" He held up a picture of a red car with a brown-skinned model draped across the hood. She had huge pouty lips and helium-balloonlike cleavage. Sarah laughed even harder, covering her mouth. I literally wanted to melt into a puddle and seep into the carpet. "I'm sorry," she said.

Em just shrugged. "Don't be. You've obviously never seen Margot's portfolio. She's totally photogenic, and all the casting agents say she has real potential. I mean, she's *so* thin." She had that part right. I'm a boobless twig. That hardly made the lie more believable, though.

Mrs. Collins came back into the room then, and called for everyone's attention.

"Here," Sarah said softly, slipping her cell phone into George's palm. "It's got the pictures from the pool party last week. There's one of that girl named Shawna my cousin invited, wearing a bikini. Now, *she* should be a model," Sarah said, giving me a look. "No offense, Margot. Don't get that confiscated," she said to George, then she walked back to her desk. While Mrs. Collins waited for the class to settle down and George scrolled through Sarah's pictures underneath his desk, I opened my planner and started counting the days until Christmas vacation.

"It's lovely to see you this morning," Mrs. Collins began. "I hope you all had a pleasant summer. Most of you know one another from Colonel Darling, but we have one international student joining us." Mrs. Collins paused. "I'd like you all to welcome Emily Warner." Everyone turned in their seats. "Emily just moved to Darling from *New York!*" Mrs. Collins said the New York part like it was some kind of unbelievable thing. Honestly, her tone of voice would have been the exact same if she'd said "Emily just moved to Darling from *the moon!*"

Everyone looked at her a second time. Even I did. I'd never met anyone from New York before. Come to think of it, it explained why she had such good hair and cool clothes. It's a commonly known fact that people from New York have better fashion sense than people from Canada. They're just born with it.

I glanced across the room at Sarah J., who was looking directly at Em, mouth open wide like she was trying to put the pieces together. If Em was from New York, maybe she *was* a model. I mean, she could be. And if she was, maybe—as unlikely as it seemed—Sarah J. might believe I was one too. It was a long shot, but it was my only hope.

Mrs. Collins spent the rest of the period doing a classroom orientation and going over how to make a book-cover protector using a brown paper bag. When she asked if anyone had questions, I raised my hand. "Why don't we just plasticize the book covers so kids don't need to do this every year?"

She didn't even take a second to seriously think about my very practical suggestion.

"Well, Margot," she said. "If you'd like to find a plasticizing machine and personally plasticize everyone's book cover, you're certainly welcome to do so."

"Awesome idea, Button," Ken snickered from the other side of the room. I glared back at him, but he didn't seem to notice. I left at the end of the period thinking three things:

1. Maybe I will find a plasticizing machine and plasticize every single book cover for every single person.
2. I hate Mrs. Collins.
3. Bad things always happen when I open my mouth. If I have any hope of being more normal, my first

step will have to be an oath of complete silence until the end of the year.

Next we had math class with Mr. Tannen, which included a second fascinating lecture about how to cover textbooks with paper bags. Then, as we were getting our stuff from our lockers before lunch, things took another turn for the worse. I heard The Group girls around the corner near the water fountain.

"She doesn't look like a model," I heard Sarah whisper.

"I know, right?" Maggie agreed. "She's not even very tall."

"Or very thin," Joyce added.

"She could be one of those fat models that are supposed to look like real people," Maggie suggested. "But I hate her hair," she added when that didn't seem to go over very well.

"Yeah . . . her roots are grown out, like, this much," agreed Joyce.

Em, who was putting her books away three lockers over, either had really bad hearing or really thick skin. She bent down and tied one of her shoelaces without even glancing in the direction their voices were coming from, then stood up and walked away.

Part of me wanted to run after her to tell her not to worry . . . that if she kept out of their way and didn't draw attention to herself, they'd probably get bored and start leaving her alone in a few days. But another, bigger, part of me was still mad at her for the weird modeling convention lie. Plus, I didn't have time. I had a 12:00 detention with my new favorite teacher, Mrs. Collins.

I stuffed my lunch into my bag. "Well, at least she looks more like a model than Hamburglar does," I heard Sarah J. say, and they all snickered. I couldn't help it. I stared hard at the floor as tears welled up in my eyes.

I had to give the new girl credit: sure, she might tell lies, and yeah, her roots *were* growing out . . . but I wished my hearing was half as bad as hers. I glanced at the hallway clock. Still three hours and twenty minutes to go. Besides finding a rock to hide under, the only thing on earth that would make me feel better would be hearing Erika's voice. Which was why, when the bell rang at 3:20, I was so relieved I didn't even care that I was about to face two and a half hours of babysitting. I practically ran the six blocks home. It wasn't easy, considering I was carrying four textbooks. (I had a long night of paper bag book-covering ahead of me.)

"Margot!" Grandma Betty exclaimed when I walked in the door. "How was your first day?"

I didn't have to say anything. She could tell by the look on my face. "Oh, I know, sweetheart." She gripped my shoulders. "You must have been missing Erika. I'm sorry. The world can be a difficult place sometimes." She flashed me a brave smile. "But we persevere." I nodded, feeling like a wimp.

When my grandpa died three years ago, Grandma Betty said the same thing to everyone as she accepted their hugs with a determined smile. "We persevere." I never even saw her cry. On the day of the funeral she had her hair pulled back into her usual neat French twist, then she put on her pearls and her bravest face. Meanwhile, I was sobbing my eyes out, and she was the one comforting me—and everyone else.

Grandma Betty took a step back so she could look at me properly. "I know." She clapped her hands together once. "Your mother's next client—the one with the lips—will be here in a few minutes." She was talking about Sheila Wheeler, this woman who wears black lipstick and needs an emergency reading every time she gets a new match on Lavalife. "The girls are watching *The Little Mermaid*." I could hear Sebastian the crab singing in the next room. "I'll make you all a snack. You go call Erika to see how her first day went."

"Thanks, Grandma," I said. "I'll only be ten minutes. I know you're supposed to leave at 3:45."

"Take your time," she said, opening the fridge door and giving me a conspiring look over her shoulder. "I think I'd better just stay until Bryan gets home so you can keep an eye on me. Maybe you'll get some of your homework done while you're at it."

The phone rang twice before Erika's mom picked up. "Hi, Mrs. Davies," I said, trying to sound extra polite so I'd seem like a good influence. "It's Margot. Is Erika there?" I already knew exactly how I was going to start the conversation . . . by saying how I almost died at school without her, but that at least I had a bit of good news . . . and that it just might be about Gorgeous George. . . .

"Oh, Margot." Mrs. Davies sounded distracted. "She's not home yet. She's out with a friend from school. I'll let her know you called."

"Oh," I said, at a loss for any other words. "Thanks." I set the phone back in the charger, feeling numb. All day long I'd been taking mental notes about everything I was going to tell Erika. All day I'd been wondering how her day was going. After so many years of telling each other about every crush, consulting with each other before every haircut, venting about every disappointment or parent-related frustration . . . one day at a new school and she had a new friend? I felt like I'd been punched in the stomach.

I dragged myself into the living room, where the triplets were watching the cartoon fish convincing the prince to "kiss the girl," and sank down onto the couch.

"Magoo?" Alice said softly, putting her little hand on my arm.

"What, Alice?"

"You smells like butter hearts," she whispered. I was pretty sure she meant the butter tarts Grandma made. The gooey ones with raisins. And it was the nicest thing anyone had said to me all day.

"You smell like butter tarts too, Alice," I said, wrapping my arms around her and rubbing my cheek against her soft hair.

In the end, Grandma Betty stayed until 5:30. I sat at the kitchen table wrapping my textbooks in brown paper bags while she fed the triplets ravioli. It took me an hour and a half to do four books. (It's no coincidence that every year, at least one teacher writes on my report card: "Margot has trouble focusing on the task at hand.") I was just finishing the last one when we heard the van pull into the driveway. Grandma kissed us each quickly, then grabbed her coat off a chair. "We won't tell your mother or Bryan I stayed so late, will we?" She grinned like a mischievous little kid before hurrying out the back door.

Bryan came in the front about thirty seconds later, lugging a ratty square briefcase with him. He was wearing his usual button-up shirt with a tiny poof of chest hair sticking out the top, but you could tell he'd made an effort to dress up to fit in with the real estate crowd, because he'd actually ironed it and he was wearing pants that weren't jeans.

"Daddy! Daddy! Daddy!" the triplets called. Judging by the joy in their voices, you'd think he'd just returned from a five-month trek across the Sahara.

"Hello, budgies," he said, putting his briefcase down and going to hug each of them. "Were you good girls?" They all grinned at him with tomato sauce mouths. "Look at this nice dinner Margot made you!" Bryan exclaimed. "What do we say, girls?" he asked. "Thank you, Margot?" None of them said thank you, but none of them said anything about how Grandma Betty actually made the dinner, so I was grateful enough just for that.

"Daddy. Look! I got a hurt," Alex whined. She held out one finger and showed him the cut she got while "helping" me cover *Destination Math, Level 7* an hour earlier.

"Oh," he said, looking at it with grave concern like it was a gaping wound instead of a microscopic paper cut. "That must have hurt. Poor budgie. I bet you were really brave." He kissed it better. I started to pack up my books.

"And how was your day at school, Margot?" he asked, still holding Alex's injured finger.

I knew he was only asking because he thought he had to pretend to treat us all equally. Even though, really, there was nothing equal about the way he felt. The triplets were his budgies . . . his sweeties . . . his funny-funny girls. I was just some kid he'd gotten stuck with.

"Fine." I zipped up my backpack.

"It's strange, isn't it?" He laughed. "Us both starting school on the same day."

"Yeah," I answered, already edging out of the room.

"You know," he said brightly, "I'd forgotten how tough it

can be, trying to take notes while the teacher's talking. How do you do it?"

I was trying to be nicer to him, like I'd promised my mom, but, honestly, I'd had such a long day. I was too tired to play along with the, "Gee, let's be buddies" routine. "Try point form," I said.

"Right, good idea," he answered cheerfully. Bryan really *was* a pretty good actor, but when I turned my back I could hear him inhaling deeply to a count of four. "Can I get you something for dinner?" he tried again.

"I already ate, thanks," I said, then felt the tiniest bit bad, so I turned around and added, "Oh, and Bryan?"

"Yes?" he answered eagerly.

"I *love* your briefcase. It's really . . . retro."

"Thank you, Margot," he said, smiling. Then I figured we'd both made enough effort for the night. I went into my bedroom and closed the door behind me.

7

My Hair, Like My Language, Is Shockingly Bad

ONE TIME, IN THIRD grade, Erika and I got an idea for improving her front yard. The whole thing was basically green grass and rose gardens. It was okay, in a boring kind of way, but what it really needed was a koi pond. We sat on her front steps imagining it for the longest time. It would go from the front path to the maple tree and would be surrounded by white stone. (We even knew where we could get some—from the neighbor's driveway across the street.) And it would have a waterfall, plus a small bridge with trailing vines where Erika could sit and feed the fish. Seriously, I wish you could have seen this thing in our minds. It was breathtaking.

But then Erika's mother—who came home from the grocery store to find a two-inch-deep mud hole in her new sod—would probably disagree. As it turns out, the vision you have and the reality you end up with can be entirely different. Another thing I learned, yet again, the hard way. . . .

After leaving Bryan in the kitchen I flopped down on my bed, feeling rejected. Erika still hadn't called. She hadn't e-mailed either. I knew because I'd run back to my room about ten times to check. Clearly, she was much too busy swapping Bible stories with her new Catholic friend to think about me. I stared at the ceiling for a while, checked my e-mail a few more times, then got up and went into the bathroom.

I spent a long time looking in the mirror, trying to come up with something new to do with my hair. I kept thinking of what Em had said: "You obviously haven't seen her portfolio. She has real potential." Even though I knew she was lying, I wanted to believe her. Maybe I *did* have potential. Maybe with some lipstick and some mascara . . . ? I pulled my hair back and made a pouty model face.

I didn't look awful—not really. It was just that, with my hair back like that, my bushy eyebrows took over my entire face. They were disgusting, like flattened caterpillars. I felt so relieved. Becoming the new, improved, more normal Margot Button was going to be easy. All I needed was twenty minutes, a pair of tweezers, and the "Beautiful Brows" article from the September issue of *CosmoGirl*.

The first step, according to the magazine, was to visualize a straight line from the base of my nose to the inner edge of my eye. That was where my eyebrow was supposed to begin. I wrinkled my nose at my reflection. The situation was obviously serious. Next, I was supposed to look straight ahead and notice the spot above my pupil. This was where the arch should go. It sounded easy.

And it honestly would have been, except for the fact that it hurt *so* much. I had tears rolling down my cheeks before I'd even yanked out five little hairs. It took twenty minutes just to finish one eyebrow. It looked good, though. Thank God. Otherwise I never would have been able to get through the pain of the second one. I turned on Mix 85.4 and sang along while I worked. Personally, I blame the really good Eternal Crush song for what happened next.

I started plucking to the beat, taking pain breaks to dance around the bathroom. I was so energized that I finished in about ten minutes this time. But when I took a step back and looked in the mirror, it was pretty obvious that the second arch didn't match the first.

I didn't panic. I just had to make the arch in the first eyebrow archier. It was going all right, too, until, through the blur of pain-induced tears, I accidentally got a bunch of extra hairs stuck in the tweezers and pulled them out all at once. I wiped at my eyes and stared at my reflection in horror. There was a huge gap in my left eyebrow right where the eye-enhancing arch was supposed to be. I tried to brush the other hairs over to see if that would hide it, but it only looked like some kind of pathetic eyebrow comb-over.

I dug around in the cabinet for makeup, but all I could find was a black eyeliner pencil. It was my mom's, left over from the pre-triplet days when I still slept over at my grandma and grandpa's sometimes, while she went out with friends for nice dinners. It was a little on the crusty side, but I grabbed it anyway and tried to draw fake hairs. But besides being crusty, it was the completely wrong color and just made the gap look worse.

More than anything in the world, I wanted to call Erika. She would know what to do. And, if she didn't know, her mom would. Mrs. Davies is the kind of person who gets her nails done professionally. She owns three different kinds of eyelash curlers. She *knows* girl stuff. But what would I say?

"Hi, Erika, I know you're busy socializing right now, but I'm having this problem with my eyebrows . . . Could I talk to your mom . . . ?"

So instead I did the only thing I could think of. I brushed my hair down in front of my face, folded it up a few times to test how it would look, measured just below my "ideal" eyebrows, grabbed the scissors from under the sink, and cut bangs.

I can't quite explain the few seconds that followed. It was like things were happening in slow motion, to somebody else. The radio must have still been playing, but everything seemed silent. The huge clump of frizzy hair I'd just cut landed softly in the sink. I stared at it for what felt like minutes before I set the scissors down and looked up.

I was a poodle with a human face. I wanted to die. The bangs didn't lie flat and hide my eyebrows. Not at all. Instead, they stuck straight out, making it look like I'd made a pom-pom out of my own hair and glued it to my forehead. I took some deep breaths and tried to think it through rationally.

Obviously, there had to be options. I could wear a hat at all times. Or I could get hair extensions. Only where do you get hair extensions at 7:00 on a Tuesday night, and how would I pay for them? I turned on the tap and stuck my head under it to see if I could wet the bangs and, somehow, force them to dry straight.

With the water running, I didn't hear the knock on the bathroom door, I guess, because suddenly it opened a crack and I heard my mom's voice. "Margot, is everything all right in there?"

"Fine," I shouted.

"In the middle of my shift this morning, I realized we

forgot to take the back-to-school picture," she said. "We could take it now, if you're still dressed. It won't be quite the same, but I think we could— What are you doing?" She opened the door wider.

There was no point hiding it. "Trying to make my bangs go straight," I said miserably, rubbing at my forehead with a towel.

"Oh, Margot." She stepped toward me to survey the damage. This made me feel ten times worse. I'd kind of been hoping she'd say something like, "Hey, bangs look great on you. Who'd have guessed?" But if my mom, of all people, was at a loss for something positive to say, then it definitely looked horrible. "Did you tweeze your eyebrows too?" She was obviously trying not to wince.

And here I'd just been starting to feel a bit better about the eyebrows. "Yes," I said, close to tears. My mom held up her hands.

"Wait here." In a few minutes she was back with a baggie of bobby pins and a bottle of green hairspray I recognized from when I used to do ballet recitals. "Close your eyes." She combed my hair down and sprayed. It reeked like chemical-coated apples. I almost gagged twice. "Okay." She stepped back. I looked in the mirror. The bangs were parted in the middle, hippie-style, and glued flat against my head. I looked a little like a greasy used-car salesman, but there was my mom, peering over my shoulder hopefully. "Thanks," I managed. "They're . . . flatter." She smiled, the little wrinkles around her eyes lifting.

"How about that picture, then?"

I ended up going out onto the front steps and letting her take it. "Actually," she said as she turned on the porch light and handed me my schoolbag to pose with, "I like your hair pinned back like that, Margot. Now people can see more of your pretty face." But it was way too little, and way too late, and way too untrue. I was hideous, and I knew it, and she knew that I knew it.

"Don't worry, honey," she went on, putting an arm around me. "It'll grow back. Someday you'll look at this photo and smile."

She showed it to me in the display. My head was tilted weirdly to one side, and I had red-eye. Right. *So* photogenic. *Real* potential. But I didn't ask her to take it again. Seriously, what difference would it have made?

When I woke up the next morning, I hadn't exactly forgotten that I'd uglified myself, but still, it was a shock to see how bad I looked. Overnight, the hairspray had dried my new bangs into two gross chunks on either side of my face, and the eyebrow gap seemed to have grown even huger, somehow.

After showering, I tried to fix my bangs with the blow-dryer and round brush, but it was useless. Then I soaked them in leave-in conditioner and gel and used my flat iron. My hair made a sizzling sound as I pulled it through the straightening plates, but as soon as I released it, it sproinged back, only now my bangs were frizzy *and* crunchy—like cotton candy gone partly stale.

"Margot, sweetie," my mom said, knocking on the door, "it's half past. You'd better get going." I sighed, shoved the horrible bobby pins back in, to at least hold down the frizz/poof, and went to get dressed. Maybe, I thought, if I just tried to be perfectly quiet all day:

1. I won't embarrass myself like I did the day before.
2. Nobody will even notice I'm there, let alone that I have a "new look."
3. If they _do_ notice me, they won't even recognize me. "Who _is_ that mysterious, perfectly quiet girl with the interesting bangs?" they will wonder. (Okay, so even _I_ knew that wasn't going to happen.)

Even though I was already running late, I checked my e-mail one last time. There was still no message from Little Miss Holy-Saint-of-Ditching-her-Best-Friend. So much for all of her IM promises. _I'll call you every day. We'll hang out all the time._ Lies, lies, and more big fat lies. In a fit of anger and frustration, fueled by bad hair and loneliness, I opened my e-mail and typed as fast as I could.

Dear Erika,
    I hope you had a great first day at Sacred Heart. I hope you had a wonderful time learning superior skills in a wholesome environment. I understand why you didn't have time to call me back. You've got a new friend, and you guys are probably really busy shopping for kneesocks and reading the Bible. She's probably really smart, too. And a good influence. I'm sure she would never steal a ham.

Whatever, Erika. I'm hurt, but life
goes on. I wish you and your new friend
all the best. Really, I do,
because despite what you might think,
I'm actually a good enough person that
I still care about you, even though
you have thrown me away like a moldy
tangerine.
    Sincerely,
    Margot

I hit SEND, then glanced at my clock. I had exactly fourteen minutes to get to school. I rummaged frantically through
my clothes piles for something to wear, finally deciding on a
slightly too baggy blue T-shirt from the Gap and the Parasuco
jeans again. (Just because Erika and I weren't friends anymore
didn't mean the jeans had to get caught in the middle, did it?)

I ran most of the way to school and made it through the
doors just as the second bell was ringing.

"Good morning, everyone," Mrs. Collins said as I slid into
my seat a moment later. "Margot." She paused. "I'm glad you
could join us." Everyone turned to look at me. So much for not
drawing attention to my "new look."

Thankfully, Mrs. Collins was feeling all eager-beaver and
didn't waste any more time embarrassing me. "Today is a special day," she said. "It marks the beginning of our poetry unit."
Groans of joy emanated from all over the room. Poetry is like
the square dance unit of English class. Only a few geeky people
actually get into it. Secretly, I happen to be one of them, but
I'd never admit it out loud.

"In the words of the great American poet Robert Frost"—Mrs. Collins pointed to the board, where she'd written a quote in perfectly rounded letters—"'Poetry makes you remember what you didn't know you knew.' If you're not sure what that means, that's okay. Just keep it mind as we move through the unit." She started handing photocopies down the rows. "I've divided you into groups of five. I want you to read the poem on the handout and look up the circled vocabulary word within it that corresponds to your group's number. Define the word, then take turns using it in a sentence. When we're done, you'll do a short presentation about its meaning in the poem." She read off her list. "Group one: Emily, Sarah, George, Simon, and Margot."

It figured. Of course, on the day when I looked like a human poodle *and* I was wearing the same pants for the second day in a row, I'd end up having to do group work *and* a presentation with Gorgeous George *and* Sarah J. Why didn't Mrs. Collins just rent a JumboTron TV, put it in the gym, project my picture onto it, and call a schoolwide assembly so everybody could see a giant close-up of my ugliness?

I took a deep breath and gathered my courage as we pushed our desks together.

"Hi, Em," I said.

She smiled at me. A good start.

"Hi, George. I like your shirt," I tried.

"Oh. Thanks," he said, then stared out the window, probably looking for interesting shoes.

"So, Simon," I said, "how was your summer?"

Simon, a skinny, mostly quiet kid, looked up from his binder in surprise.

"Oh my God, Margot," Sarah said pointedly as she pulled her chair out and sat down.

"What?"

"Everyone knows he has a lisp," she whispered loudly, "but that doesn't mean you have to throw it in his face." She shook her head sadly, like I was too hopeless for words. "There's a thing called manners. You might want to learn some."

Even George was giving me a disapproving look.

"I—" I started, confused, but a second later I figured it out. *So, Simon, how was your summer?* Could I have put any more S's in that sentence? "I didn't mean it like that! I was just asking if he had a good summer."

"Right," Sarah said. By now Simon's face had gone completely red.

"I'm so sorry, Simon." I clapped my hand over my mouth, realizing I'd done it again. Sarah J. sighed. "I honestly didn't mean it like that."

He nodded once and went back to looking down at his desk like he just wanted the whole thing to be over with.

Sarah took an aquamarine zipper-closure binder out of her bag, then squinted at me. "Don't take this the wrong way, but did something happen to your face?"

"No," I said, reading the poem Mrs. Collins had handed out so I wouldn't have to look at her. It was called "Away, Melancholy," and our vocabulary word was right at the top. MELANCHOLY.

"Did you burn your eyebrows off or something?"

I didn't answer.

"No offense, but whatever you did, it doesn't look that good." She wrinkled her nose and kept staring at me. "Are you sure you didn't burn them?" I felt my cheeks getting hot.

"Of course she didn't burn them," Em spoke up. "She tweezed them." I shot her a quick, pleading look. She was only going to make it worse. "Everyone does it. And actually," Em continued, "your brows are looking a bit bushy. You might want to think about getting them shaped."

The smile fell from Sarah J.'s lips. "Shut up," she retorted.

Em just shrugged. "Okay, be like that. I was just making an observation."

Sarah scowled. "Oh, and I guess you know everything about eyebrows, right? You probably learned all about it at *modeling school*."

Without blinking, Em said, "Yeah. But it's pretty simple. You always want to pluck from underneath and line the arch up with the pupil. Margot had the right idea." She looked at my eyebrows. "She just overplucked, which is better than not plucking at all, if you ask me." She shot Sarah an appraising look.

Oh, this was definitely not good. Did the new girl have a death wish? "We should get started," I said loudly, trying to change the topic to poetry before any blood could be shed. "I'll get a dictionary." I flew across the room, grabbed a *Canadian Oxford*, raced back, and threw it on the desk. "Why don't you look up the word, Em?" I suggested.

"Sure." She flipped through the pages. "'Melancholy,'" she read. "'Noun. A deep sadness or depression.' But you can also use it as an adjective." She slammed the dictionary shut loudly. "That's a cheerful word. How many sentences do we need again?"

"Five," I answered. "One each." We all stared blankly at our notebooks for a few seconds.

It was Gorgeous George who finally broke the silence—and

he broke it by speaking to me! "Does your look hair different?" he asked, but not in a mean way.

"Yeah," Sarah agreed. "No offense," which is what she always said right before saying something really mean, "but it looks kind of retarded at the front." And then she looked at Em. "But I guess that's a modeling thing too?"

"That," Em said, looking at me, "is just a bad hair day." Then she pointed her pen at Sarah. "Don't pretend you don't have them too."

"I use good products," Sarah J. said. "And at least I don't dye it some fake color and then let the roots grow out."

Normally, I would have been busy obsessing over the fact that Sarah J. was picking on me, yet again—and in front of George, no less—and wondering what it meant that he had noticed that my hair was different. *He'd noticed my hair on other days, when it wasn't different?* But right then I was too shocked by the way Em was standing up to Sarah J. on my behalf, and too worried about how she was going to pay for it. If only I'd warned her the day before when I'd had the chance.

"Let's just read this, okay?" Simon spoke up, not lisping once. I think we were all so surprised to hear his voice that we were shocked into silence. Everyone looked down at the poem for a few seconds.

"Hey, where's Nerdette, anyway?" Sarah said, her attention span for English literature coming to an end as quickly as it had begun. She was talking about Erika-with-a-K, who always got straight A's in everything but gym.

"None of your business," I mumbled. The last thing I needed was for Sarah to find out that my ham stealing had gotten her sent to Sacred Heart, or that we weren't even friends anymore, which meant I officially had no friends at all except Andrew. "Can we please do the sentences?"

"Fine," Sarah snapped. "It makes me feel *melancholy* when people whose names start with M are so rude." She shot me a look. "And it also makes me feel *melancholy* when new people show up and think they're all that just because they're from New York, because honestly, they're not, and that's the most *melancholy* part—because they don't even realize it."

Em considered this for a few seconds, tapping her pencil calmly against her notebook. "It's a run-on sentence," she said, "but it'll do. Extra points for using the word *melancholy* three times. You're really smart. Okay," she went on, not pausing long enough for Sarah to make a comeback, "here's mine: 'A feeling of melancholy was in the air as the girl mourned the loss of her father.' What's yours, Margot?"

"How about . . . 'The love song on the radio made the girl feel melancholy because she wasn't with her true love'?" I looked at Gorgeous George as I said it, but he didn't react.

"Sure," Em answered, moving things along. "And you?" She looked at George.

"He has a name," Sarah J. snapped, but Em ignored her.

"'The man was melancholy'"—he stared out the window again—"'because he lost his shoes.'"

"Good," Em said. She looked to Simon.

"'The boy that thhhat alone felt melancholy,'" Simon supplied.

"Cool. We're done," Em said. "Anybody want to play hangman?" She reached into her backpack and took out a lined notepad.

Sarah J. glanced at George and raised one eyebrow like,

hangman? I had to admit, I hadn't played hangman since fourth grade. I would have thought that, being from New York, Em might have known a cooler, more current game. Hangman was older than my mom.

"Dirty hangman," she added.

Gorgeous George grinned. "I'm in," he said.

"Me too," I added quickly, eager for any chance to redeem myself in his eyes after the whole accidentally insulting Simon thing.

"Have fun with your game." Sarah waved one hand at us in this floppy-wristed way, like she was dismissing us from her royal throne room. "I'm going to write a note to Matt."

"Simon?" Em said, ignoring Sarah completely, but he just shook his head. "Okay, then. Go."

"E," I tried.

Em flashed me a Vanna White smile as she filled the letters in. We went back and forth picking letters until we had this.

m _ _ _ E _   _ u C _ E _

"All right, groups. You should be almost ready to present by now," Mrs. Collins called, holding up her hand for silence. Suddenly, in a flash, I could see it.

"Oh!" I slapped the desk. At that exact moment, two things happened: the room went completely quiet and I shouted the word—the bad word—the *very* bad word—the one that rhymes with BROTHER TRUCKER.

In the hush that followed, the sound of my swear word echoed off the walls.

"Margot Button," Mrs. Collins said in a soft, scary voice. "To the office."

8

Em Warner Is an Ultra-Mysterious Hair Genius

I KNOW I SOMETIMES SAY THE wrong thing at the wrong time, and that I don't always "focus on the task at hand," but the truth was, besides the glazed ham, I'd never really been in serious trouble. So as I sat in the principal's office, staring at my warped reflection in the supermodern stainless steel counter the secretary sat behind, many questions were racing through my mind. Questions like:

1. Do normal people shout swear words at the top of their lungs in English class? And do guys like George think it's hot? (Somehow, I doubt it.)
2. Can you get expelled for something like that?
3. Do I really look as bad as I do in my reflection?

Needless to say, when the secretary finally told me to go in, I was freaked out. I ended up getting lucky, though. Mrs. Vandanhoover was on her way out to some kind of principal's jamboree with the school board, and didn't have much time to talk to me. She also completely bought it when, in a stroke of genius, I told her the bad word slipped out when I stubbed my toe on my desk.

"Oh. Well. That can happen. But you know, Margot, it's important to watch your language—especially at school." She was packing things into her sleek black laptop case. I nodded like I shared her concern.

"Do you know what I say when I'm frustrated, or when I've hurt myself?"

I knew I wasn't supposed to answer, so I waited, looking interested.

"Fish sticks."

"Oh." I nodded as if this were an extra-wise and original piece of advice.

"I just scrunch up my fists and I say . . . FISH STICKS!" she shouted, and banged her open palm on the metal desk, which made this awful, hollow, clanging noise. She smiled calmly. "And then I feel so much better. I'd like you to try that, Margot."

"Okay," I said. "I will."

"Right here, with me."

"Okay . . ." I answered. "Fish sticks?"

"A little louder."

"Fish sticks."

"As though you've just stubbed your toe."

"FISH STICKS!" I yelled. I hoped to God that nobody could hear me in the hallway.

"That's it!" Mrs. Vandanhoover shouted, as though I'd accomplished something big. "Off you go."

Armed with my new inoffensive swear word, I was in my next class before Mr. Tannen even had time to start our introduction to fractions. Of course, it was the last place on earth I actually wanted to be. Everyone seemed to be staring and whispering.

While Mr. Tannen was busy helping Cameron Ruling with a problem, Ken walked past my desk to sharpen his pencil. "What did you say, Button?" he asked. I hadn't said anything. He cupped one hand around his ear and pretended to listen. "Button! I'm outraged at your inappropriateness. My virgin ears will never be the same!"

Charlie Baker, Maggie, Joyce, and the volleyball girls snickered.

"What?" He leaned in again. I still hadn't said anything. "Margot, honestly. You're offending us all with your potty mouth." The same people laughed.

I was just about to tell him to shut up when Amir, who sat in front of me, suddenly pushed his math book off his desk. It landed on the floor with a huge thud, and he turned to stare hard at Ken before bending down to pick it up. "What are you looking at, Amir-a-med?" Ken asked, pronouncing his name like it was all one word. But thankfully the noise of the book hitting the floor had caused Mr. Tannen to look up.

"Everything all right over there, Amir?" he asked.

"Yes, Mr. Tannen," Amir answered. And Ken walked back to his desk.

At lunch, I wandered dejectedly into the yard. Andrew, Mike, and Amir were at basketball tryouts, which meant I had nobody to sit with, and I wasn't about to face the cafeteria alone. At least it was still warm enough to be outside, where people were less likely to see me. I picked a tree, slid *CosmoGirl* out of my backpack, and sat down.

I'd been reading for about half an hour and was just

flipping through the "Must-Have Fall Accessories" article when I heard a voice. "Is that *CosmoGirl?*" A second later, Em slid down beside me, stretching out her legs. I noticed she was wearing Diesel shoes. I wasn't surprised. Besides having good fashion sense, people from New York also have a lot of money. I crossed my legs and tucked my feet underneath my thighs to hide my Payless Converse knockoffs, then quickly readjusted my T-shirt to make sure it was hiding the butterfly belt.

"Yeah," I said. She just kind of nodded, leaving me wondering if she thought *CosmoGirl* was kind of cool, or really lame.

"That was *so* funny in English class," she said. Well, at least that made it official. Everyone was enjoying my misery. "Did you get in trouble?"

"No," I said. "She basically told me to say *fish sticks* next time."

"And you didn't tell her it was my idea to play dirty hangman, right?"

"No," I said. I might have been weird and loserish and have had bad hair but I wasn't a tattletale.

"Good. So then?" Em slapped my arm. "What are you so mopey about?"

"I'm not mopey."

"You *look* mopey."

"Okay then. First of all, everyone is making fun of me. And second, would you look happy if this was your head?" I pointed to my poodle face.

"I see your point," she said. "Want me to fix it?"

"It's un-fixable." I pulled at my bangs.

"I've seen worse."

"Where? At modeling school?" It came out sarcastic, and I felt bad the instant it left my mouth. "Sorry," I mumbled. "I didn't mean that. So, it's true? I mean, you actually model?"

"Yes!" she said, clearly offended. "Not in this kind of magazine," she said, fluttering the pages of my *CosmoGirl.* "My agent mostly gets me cast for commercial modeling jobs, like clothing stores, toothpaste. Stuff like that. I once did this billboard shoot for Chuck E. Cheese's when I was little. I had to hug a guy in a stinky mouse costume for, like, two hours."

"That's really cool," I said. "Not the stinky costume but, you know, modeling."

"Yeah." She shrugged like it was no big deal. "So?" She paused. "Do you want me to do your hair or not?"

"I guess," I said. What did I have to lose? She pulled a brush out of her backpack, motioned for me to turn around, and took out my bobby pins.

There was something I'd been dying to ask ever since the first time I'd seen her, but I glanced around first to make sure nobody was close enough to overhear. "Quit moving your head," Em said.

"Sorry," I answered. "Hey, you know that thing? That stupid thing we were at? When we met?"

"Yeah?" she said.

"Did somebody make you go?" I remembered how she'd shouted at the woman in the hall. How the goat lady had opened the door and peered out cautiously. "Or did you want to be there?" I added, so it wouldn't sound like I already knew the answer.

"Why would anybody want to be there?"

"What were you doing there, then?" I asked.

"What were *you* doing there?" she answered. I hesitated. Em was new. She didn't know anybody. More important, she didn't know me, and she didn't know the glazed ham story. And, sure, she'd probably find out one of these days, but that didn't mean it had to be today. She yanked the brush through my hair, hard. I yelped.

"Sorry," she said, but she didn't sound very apologetic.

"I was there because my mom made me go."

"Me too," she said.

And then, since neither of us wanted to talk about it, I changed the subject.

"So, what part of New York did you live in?" I asked, trying not to wince as she brushed, no more gently than before. "The east part, or the west part, or the middle? Which would be Central Park, of course," I added.

"Brooklyn," she said, brushing my bangs straight back and holding them down with one hand.

"Oh. That's a nice place," I said, in a tone that made it sound like Brooklyn and I went way back. The second I'd said it, though, I started to have doubts. Was Brooklyn the part of New York where everyone got mugged? You know, the *projects*? Or was that Harlem? I'd never been very good at geography. "I mean, I've heard it's nice," I confessed. "I've never been there personally. Did you like it?"

"It was pretty great," she said.

"Then why did you move?"

She didn't answer for a few seconds. "We just needed a change. Our lifestyle was really hectic there." Her parents were probably high-powered stockbrokers, I figured. Pretty much everyone in New York was.

"So, where's your new house?" I asked.

"Lakeshore." Just like I'd thought, she was rich. The front lawns there are so huge you practically need one of those ride-on mowers just to cut the grass. "It's near the water. The one with the turrets."

"I love that house!" I almost screamed. You've got to understand, though, I *love* that house. Ever since I was little, I've wanted to live there. Obviously, I needed to know. "Is your bedroom in one of the turrets?"

"Yeah," she said, like it was nothing.

And then I went off on this big embarrassing thing about how it must be really challenging to decorate a round room when practically all furniture is designed for square or rectangular spaces. "I don't think you should get discouraged, though," I finished breathlessly. "A combination of custom pieces, window seating, and a round area rug would work. . . ." I finally trailed off, realizing I'd talked for almost five minutes straight without asking her any questions or bothering to check if she was actually listening.

"You know a lot," she said, but I couldn't tell if she meant it in a good way. "You're done." She handed me a compact out of her bag.

"Put some of the dark brown shadow on your bad eyebrow. It'll look better. You can keep that." The bell rang, and she stood up to go. She was already halfway across the yard before I'd managed to put my stuff away and push myself to my feet to follow. I flipped open the compact and looked at my reflection.

I actually smiled.

Using only a brush, her fingers, and a silk scarf that had

been tied around her wrist, Emily Warner from New York had performed the greatest hair miracle of the twenty-first century. She'd done better than make me look human again. I pretty much knew right then that I'd do whatever it took—I needed to be her friend.

9

Old Friends Are the Best Friends

I MANAGED TO GET THROUGH the rest of the afternoon without embarrassing myself. Unless you counted gym class, where we started our basketball unit and I accidentally threw the ball to someone on the other team. (The girl was on the yellow team, but she was wearing red shorts so it was very confusing.) Or French class, where Mr. Patachou asked me if I was a good student, and I said something like, *"Oui, je suis enceinte,"* which I thought meant, "Yes, I'm a saint," but actually meant "Yes, I'm pregnant." But compared to the events of the morning, that was nothing.

I was halfway down Manning Avenue, psyching myself up for babysitting duty, when I felt something hit my heel. I looked down and saw a pop can skidding away. "Hey!" Andrew was running toward me. He picked up the can and slam-dunked it into a recycling bin. "I've been calling your name since you left school. You didn't hear me, so I had to resort to kicking stuff at you."

"Thanks!" I said sarcastically. "I needed that."

"I know." There was real sympathy in his voice. "Bad day, right? Amir told me you got sent to Vandanhoover's office this morning. What happened?"

"I just said something I shouldn't have," I answered.

"You? Say something you shouldn't have?" He faked surprise. I hit him hard, and he started laughing. "Remember that time you told my mom her cornmeal muffins tasted like sawdust?"

"I only said they had a *texture* like sawdust," I corrected him.

"Or the time you told Erika not to worry because having such big feet made her ankles look smaller."

"Okay, you're twisting my words." I tried to defend myself again. "I was making her feel better after she said her feet were like boats. And they *are* like boats . . . but I didn't tell her that, did I?"

"But you just told *me* that," he said, grinning.

"Yeah, but your feet are like bigger boats." I motioned to his Nikes, which were at least size ten. "So you understand."

"What?! My feet are big?" He pretended to start crying, and I whacked him again. We walked in silence for a while, except for the quiet sound of him still laughing at me.

"This time was different," I explained. "It was worse. I was playing dirty hangman and I yelled a swear word. Really loud. Mrs. Collins hates my guts, plus everyone else thinks I'm an idiot."

"No they don't," Andrew tried to reassure me. "At least the people who matter don't. They probably just think you have a really colorful vocabulary."

He wasn't making me feel much better.

"How's Erika, anyway?" he asked, changing the subject.

"Busy," I muttered. "Making lots of new friends."

"Tell her hi for me next time you talk to her, okay?"

"*If* I talk to her," I replied. He let that one go. He's known Erika and me long enough to know it's best not to get involved in our fights. They usually don't last long anyway. But now something had changed. She was at a new school, with new friends, and she hadn't even returned my phone call.

"What's with the new look?" Andrew asked, changing the subject yet again and pointing to the scarf in my hair.

"Just something I'm trying."

"I like it," he said, then he touched my arm and left his hand there for a second. I stared at it like it was a strange butterfly that had landed on my jacket, and he moved it away. We both glanced down at the sidewalk for a second while we waited for the weirdness to pass. The whole rest of the way down Manning, all I could think about was that e-mail signed XXO, and I couldn't come up with a single normal thing to say to him.

Because here's the thing: you know how I said that Andrew's not my boyfriend, he's just my boy friend? Well, it's true. But it's also maybe not. It depends how you look at it. Just before school ended last year, and Andrew left for Barbados, we were watching movies at his house with Erika, Mike, and Amir. It was dark in the room, and while he was reaching for his pop on the shelf behind the couch, his arm ended up resting on my shoulder, just for a second. I guess I liked it. Or maybe I was just curious. Because after he moved it away, I kind of started moving closer to him on the couch, very slowly, until our shoulders were touching, just to see what would happen. And this is what happened: inch by inch, he kind of moved his hand over until it was partly touching my leg, and then I moved my hand over, to meet his . . . and we sat there like that, with our hands touching, for the whole movie. But that's all that happened. And we never talked about it or did it again. Even Erika doesn't know. If she did, she'd freak out.

I mean, Andrew's great. He's one of my best friends. But he's not the kind of guy you're supposed to have a *crush* on. And anyway, what if I *did* like him? Wouldn't it just mess up our friendship? And what about Gorgeous George? Hadn't anybody thought of him in all this? I hadn't wasted the past three years obsessing over his shiny hair just to give up on him that quickly, had I? Especially when I was finally in his class again?

"You around for lunch tomorrow?" Andrew asked when we reached the corner. There was a hint of nervousness in his voice.

"I dunno," I said cautiously. "Maybe." It wasn't that I didn't want to eat with him, but what *exactly* did he mean. . . .

"Well, if you are, meet us beside the basketball court, okay? Amir's bringing his Nintendo DS. He just got War of the Druids, Strike Three." I breathed a small sigh of relief. Druids at war with Amir and Mike. I couldn't think of a single thing less romantic.

"Sure," I said. "I'll try to come, unless I end up with another detention."

"Yeah, well. I won't count on it, then." He grabbed my waist to tickle me, jumped back before I could retaliate, then started running, turning and waving when he was safely out of reach.

I smiled as I watched him go. The weird arm touch had been nothing. Everything was normal with Andrew. Plus, I thought to myself as I walked along, Em seemed like she might turn out to be a friend. Of course I missed Erika so much I could hardly stand it, but I would get through it, wouldn't I? It was like Grandma Betty said: we persevere. Because what other choice was there? Nachos would never taste as good, *Charmed and Dazed* would never be as dramatic, drinking coffee with nobody to make faces with would be totally pointless . . . but I had to carry on.

I dug my hands deep into the pockets of the Parasuco jeans, bent my head against the wind, and shuffled through some fallen leaves. And that was when I felt the paper. At first I hoped it might be money, but when I pulled it out, I saw it was a piece of loose leaf folded into a little square. I knew it wasn't mine, but I unfolded it anyway. I'm nosy like that. It was dated September 1, Labor Day.

> Dear Margot,
> I know you're reading this note you found in my pocket, because you're nosy like that!
> My mother is heartless and as cold-blooded as a tarantula, lizard, or other ectothermic tetrapod. I hate her for making me go to Sacred Heart. I am going to miss you every second. And for the record, I don't agree with her that you're a bad influence. You're one of the best people I know. No matter what, we'll always be best friends. Promise?
> Meet me at the gates of the cemetery right after school. We can go to your house, and you can tell me everything about Manning. I'll call my mom and say I'm doing a project for school. She's organizing our closets anyway (she put it on her schedule!!), so she'll be too busy to care.
> Your Best Friend,
> Erika

I read the note twice as I walked, my steps getting faster and faster. I could just picture Erika standing alone at the cemetery gates, pulling her sleeves over her hands and glancing back nervously in case any dead people suddenly popped out of their graves. Since first grade she'd been my best friend, and then on the worst day of her life I'd accidentally ditched her . . . at a cemetery . . . and then written her the meanest e-mail on earth.

But maybe it wasn't too late. Maybe I *didn't* have to picture my life without Erika. I broke into a run.

"Grandma," I said, bursting into the kitchen. "It's a friendship emergency. Can you stay ten more minutes? I *have* to talk to Erika."

She looked up from the counter where she was chopping apple slices and smiled. "Of course. Take all the time you need, sweetheart."

I ran to my room, shut the door, turned on the computer, then wrote Erika a long e-mail, explaining the whole thing about how I didn't find the note until just then, and how I called her house and her mom said she was out with a new friend, and I got jealous because I'm a moron that way, and that I wished I'd never written the e-mail I'd sent that morning, and I didn't mean the thing about the moldy tangerine, and what was an ectothermic tetrapod? Then I begged and pleaded for her forgiveness by saying that I was so so so so so so so so so so sorry. And then I hit SEND and checked my instant messenger. She was online, of course.

Margot12: So? Do you still hate me?
EriKa: My mom was mad at me for not coming home to help organize the

```
closets. She never even told me you
called!!! I cried all night, and I was
miserable all day.
Margot12: You think I wasn't??! I
thought you didn't want to be my
friend anymore!!
EriKa: I thought that too.
```

There was a long pause while we both tried to think what to say.

```
Margot12: We're both kind of stupid, eh?
EriKa: We're totally dumb. Still
friends?
Margot12: Are you kidding!??
```

A few seconds later, the phone rang. Or at least it half rang, because that's how quickly I picked it up. "So?" Erika said. I gave her almost the full list of everyone in my class, saving Gorgeous George until very last. She screamed. "You haven't been in his class since fourth grade! That's the greatest news! What was he wearing?"

"Which day?" I asked.

"Both."

I felt so relieved. I literally couldn't imagine my life without Erika.

Eventually, after we'd analyzed George's wardrobe, we moved on to discussing my hair-and-eyebrow disaster and the Sarah J. encounter.

"I can't believe she actually asked if you burned them off!" Erika said.

"How's it going at Sacred Heart?" I asked.

"Okay, I guess." She sounded sad. "Everyone's been there since kindergarten, so they've already got their groups of friends. But this one girl let me borrow her hole-punch."

"Oh," I said, feeling horrible for her.

"Yeah, I know," she added miserably.

Then I heard her mother in the background saying something about homework. I hadn't even had a chance to tell her about Em, but I decided it could wait until next time. It might just make her feel worse about not having met anyone.

"Gotta go," she said. "Say hi to Andrew for me, okay? I have an orthodontist appointment tomorrow, and then we're leaving right after school on Friday to go to Toronto again. The fall stuff's on sale. But meet me at the cemetery gates at 3:30 on Monday, okay? I can help you babysit. And *actually* show up this time!"

I swore on the Parasuco jeans that I would.

10

I Stare at the Wrong Person's Butt . . .

WHEN YOU'RE almost thirteen, there's nothing more important than your friends. Not TV, not money, not clothes, not your family, not food, not water, not air . . . Okay, maybe air, but friends are a really close second.

So, with Erika back in my life, lunch plans with Andrew, and Em as a possible new friend, I woke up the next morning feeling great.

It took me an extra twenty minutes to re-create Em's scarf/hair-band styling technique and to fill in my brow gap with eyeshadow, but I still made it to Mrs. Collins's class with a millionth of a second to spare. "Pleased to see you, Margot," she said, giving me a big red phony smile as I slid into my seat. "I trust you'll be treating us to some more appropriate vocabulary words today." I hated her more every instant.

"Overall," she said, "your presentations yesterday were very well done. And now that we've explored a poem in detail, it's time we experienced one. Collect your books, go to your lockers, and come back with your jackets on." Mrs. Collins looked so excited I thought she might explode. "Come on," she said, "hop to it."

At my locker, I put my books on the top shelf, checked my hair in my magnetic mirror, and glanced at the only locker decoration I had up so far: a photo of Erika and me dressed as pears for Halloween last year. Her dad had thought up the idea. "A pair of pears!" We thought it was so hilarious.

"Sweet fruit costumes," Em said sarcastically. I jumped. I hadn't even heard her coming up behind me. "Who's your friend?" I caught a glimpse of myself grinning stupidly in my locker mirror and quickly tried to settle my face into a cooler, calmer expression. I was just so glad that Em had come over to talk to me.

"Oh, that's Erika." I grabbed my coat and closed my locker before Em could get a closer look at the picture. Erika and I had made the pear costumes ourselves by putting inflatable pool rings around our waists and stretching size XXL green sweaters over them. Then her mom sewed stems on to the tops of green toques. Girls in New York probably wore hot costumes, like French maids or sexy kittens. A pair of pears? It was still funny, but maybe more dorky-funny than hilarious-funny, now that I thought of it.

By the time we got back to the classroom, Mrs. Collins had put a clipboard on everyone's desk with a piece of paper attached. She held up her hand for silence. "What do you think of when I say the words *poetry in motion*?" Everyone stared at her blankly. "What about the idea that poetry should be experienced? You should smell poetry. Touch it. Taste it. Walk through poetry and come out the other side changed by it." She was pacing back and forth in front of the blackboard. "Today we'll be going out to Manning Avenue and walking up and down—carefully, quietly, and respectfully—looking for poetry. When you spot something that could become a poem, you'll write down some notes about it on your clipboard. Your assignment tonight will be to write the poem you've experienced."

I rolled my eyes with everyone else, even though it sounded kind of cool. I'd been thinking about the quote that Mrs. Collins had put on the board the day before: about how poetry makes you remember what you didn't know you knew. I think the guy who said that was right, because my grandpa Button used to read me this poem called "The Cremation of Sam McGee." He'd pull up a chair and lean forward, talking with his hands, while I sat, spellbound, on the carpet. I've never been to the Yukon like the characters in the poem, but I swear, by the time he was finished, I was always chilled right through.

Dressed in our coats and fully prepared to experience poetry (or at least to make fun of it and waste time), we shuffled up the stairs, blinking in the light. People broke off into their regular groups. Sarah J. led the way with her followers/worshippers, Maggie and Joyce, who were both wearing exactly identical pairs of black Pumas. George and Ken walked behind Laura and Tiffany, the two quietest girls in the class, pretending to pinch their butts. Amir had made friends with Erik Frallen the math genius and Simon, and Cameron Ruling and Stuart Smythe— these two really smart guys who codesigned and programmed the entire Web site for our old school, including this crazy animation of the school mascot that cheered when you clicked on its face. They were laughing over some un-understandable gigabytes joke. As for me, I was behaving like a more-or-less normal person on the outside, but inside I was doing the happy dance of joy about the fact that Em had decided to walk beside me.

We went slowly down Manning Avenue, kicking leaves. When I closed my eyes for just a second, I could swear they made the same sound a campfire does when it crackles, hisses, and pops. I started writing a poem in my head:

> The fiery leaves glow warm in the sun.
> Walk softly, they smolder,
> To hear them burn, run.

"Found any poetry yet?" Em asked sarcastically. She was holding her clipboard under her arm and picking at her nail polish in a bored way. I didn't think she'd care about the sound of autumn leaves.

"Nope," I answered.

We'd already reached the end of the street, so we turned and walked back. In the parking lot, Gorgeous George was pretending to club Ken over the head with his clipboard. His shiny brown hair reflected the sunlight as he tossed his head. Bethany and Michelle, the girls from the volleyball team, were walking alongside Sarah J. and her friends, laughing just a little too loudly at their jokes. And while Mrs. Collins was busy talking to Tiffany and Laura—the only two people in the class who actually seemed to be doing the assignment—Amir and his friends had ducked behind a hedge on someone's front lawn to chuck acorns at each other.

"Okay. Dude. I just experienced a poem," Ken said as Em and I passed the parking lot. "Wait for it." He paused dramatically.

> "My buddy, George,
> He beat up my head.
> My buddy, George,
> He made me brain-dead."

Sarah J. came up behind them and said something that made them laugh even more. Her outfit, as usual, was perfect—a cute, tailored plaid jacket with a wide belt, paired with super-tight dark-wash jeans. The back pockets had this cool swirl stitching done in light blue thread, plus just a sprinkling of tiny rhinestones, like the Parasuco jeans, only better because they fit her so perfectly you'd think the denim was painted on and the rhinestones had been individually bedazzled to her butt cheeks. Unluckily for me, she turned her head at just the wrong second and noticed me noticing.

"Take a picture, Hamburglar," she said as they passed us. "It'll last longer"—like that wasn't the most unoriginal insult ever. I guess she realized how dumb it was too, because she turned and added: "Oh my God, Margot. Were you just checking out George's butt?" He looked around at the sound of his name. "Or were you checking out mine?" She threw me a disgusted look. "No offense, but even if I was a lesbian, which is gross to even think about, you wouldn't stand a chance."

"Excuse me?" Em said, her mouth dropping open in disbelief. "Was that a homophobic comment you just made?"

"Oh please," Sarah countered lamely.

"Because if it was"—she glared at Sarah—"that's harassment." I pretended to be brushing away some imaginary fluff that had landed on my clipboard.

"Okay." Sarah got right in her face. "It's not my fault if

Margot was looking at my butt." She turned to walk away like she considered the conversation over.

"Don't flatter yourself." Em raised her eyebrows. "Margot wasn't looking at your butt. She happens to be straight. But the point is, you can't go around saying lesbians are gross. It's discrimination."

Even though it was *not* smart of her to be talking to Sarah like that, I had to admit, Em definitely had a good point.

"I get it," Sarah said, fixing Em with a stare. "You're a lesbian too. Is that why you're so offended? I don't know what they do in New York"—she made the name sound all lah-di-dah—"but here, we think it's pretty perverted to stare at people's butts, okay?"

Gorgeous George and Ken were both laughing uncomfortably. And things would have probably gotten way uglier if Mrs. Collins hadn't called us all to come inside just then. Em shot Sarah a look of death, but didn't say anything else.

"Do people actually like that girl?" Em asked as we walked toward the doors.

"She's been the most popular girl in school since third grade." I didn't want to scare Em, so I didn't mention that now that she'd seriously crossed Sarah, she was going to pay for it. The stuff she did to me was nothing compared to what she'd put some kids through. In fourth grade, April Morgan had called Sarah a name behind her back. The next thing April knew, everyone was talking about how her family ate bone marrow and blew their noses into their hands. Since Sarah was the one who'd started the rumor, nobody was brave enough to be April's friend after that, and a bunch of kids even refused to hold her hand during the pass-the-peanut game on Fun Run

Day. Eventually she just changed schools.

When we got inside, Em dragged me along with her to the bathroom. "Why does she call you Hamburglar?" she asked from inside her stall.

I should have known the question would come sooner or later, but still, it caught me unprepared. All the same, based on the way she'd just taken on Sarah J. for me, I figured I could trust Em. I told her a short version of the glazed ham story. "I don't even know why I did it," I finished, as she fixed her hair in the mirror beside me. "It was just one of those dumb things." Em made an understanding noise. We headed for the door.

"I ate dog food once," she said, out of nowhere. I looked at her to see if she was serious.

"Wet or dry?" I asked.

"Dry," she said.

"Why?" It was the obvious question.

"Just one of those dumb things," she answered. "I guess I wanted to see what it tasted like."

"And?"

"Don't try it."

As we walked down the hall to our lockers, I couldn't help but smile. After all, you didn't admit to *just anyone* that you'd eaten dog food. It was really happening. I had a new friend. And not just any new friend. A cool friend from New York who knew how to make my hair look awesome and who stood up for me . . . as unwise as that might be.

I met Em at her locker after math that day, hoping, now that we were officially friends, she'd sit with Andrew, Mike, Amir, and me at lunch, but she glanced at her watch.

"I'll catch up with you later, okay?" she said. "I have to take care of something."

"What is it?" I asked. "I can help."

"Thanks, but no," she said. "It's a personal thing."

"Sure." I nodded, not wanting to seem desperate or clingy, or to let on, just yet, how nosy I could be.

I watched her walk down the hall, then went out to the yard to find the guys. They were near the fence, crowded around the tiny Nintendo DS screen, watching Andrew's druid beat up a bunch of evil mythical woodland animals.

"You've got the magic dart," Mike said, "*and* the force field. Plus the golden arrow."

"So?" Andrew asked, his shoulder swaying as he dodged gnomes.

"So! Use one of them! Now!" Amir shouted, but it was too late. Amir and Mike threw up their hands. "Oh, man. He smashed your brains out."

"Shoulda used your weapons," Mike put in.

"I was saving them."

"For what? A gift for your granny?"

Andrew shoved Amir's shoulder, then smiled at me. "Hey, Margot."

"Hey." I sank down on the bench beside him, hugging my knees to my chest. Andrew handed the Nintendo off to Mike, then sat down beside me and pulled some ketchup chips from his backpack, breathing in deeply as he broke the airtight seal. "Oh, yeah. That's the stuff," he said, savoring the stench. "Want one?" He held out the bag.

"It's tempting." I leaned away from the smell.

Amir sat down on the other side of me and reached across my lap into the bag, grabbing a handful. He put one in his mouth and crunched. "You have English this afternoon?" he asked Andrew, when he'd finished chewing.

"Yeah. Fourth period."

"If she makes you do the poetry walk, there's tons of acorns at the big brick house with the huge tree. Me, Erik, Simon, and Stuart played torpedoes with them." He reached across for another handful of chips, leaving a trail of fine red dust on my white coat sleeve. I brushed it off. "Sorry, Margot," he said. "Here, want to switch?" We traded seats, and I think Andrew shot Amir the smallest annoyed look—like, *Hey man, I wanted her to sit there.* But maybe it was just my imagination. All the same, to make him feel better, I reached across Amir and grabbed a ketchup chip from the open bag. "Not bad, actually," I said, crunching it. Andrew grinned.

"Do you like her?" Amir asked. For a split second I thought he was asking Andrew about me, and I nearly choked.

"No way," Andrew answered. "She's evil. She's going to assign homework every day this week."

"Plus, she looks like this—" Mike, who was sitting on the other side of Andrew, suddenly sat up perfectly straight, made his lips into a pinched line, and turned his head stiffly from side to side, like a constipated owl. Everyone burst out laughing. Mike didn't talk that often, but when he did, he usually said something unexpected, funny, or just worth listening to.

"Collins totally has it in for Margot, too," Amir added. "Since the first second of the first day."

I sighed heavily. Weirdly, though, the fact that Amir had noticed made me feel a lot better about how much my English teacher hated my guts. At least I wasn't imagining it.

"Want me to kick her butt?" Andrew offered.

"I could actually kick it for you too, if you want," Amir put in.

"We'll triple kick it, evil-wood-nymph style," Mike pledged seriously, without looking up from the DS.

I reached for another chip, smiling. Obviously, nobody was going to be kicking any English teacher butt. But somehow, hearing them say it made me feel like I had the magic dart *and* the golden arrow *and* the force field of friendship on my side. I had Em and her quick comebacks *and* Erika-with-a-K's total devotion *and* Andrew, Amir, and Mike's goofy, boy-style loyalty—which meant that Sarah J., her friends, and even Mrs. Collins could try what they wanted. None of it would kill me.

11

I Make an Extremely Unwise Bet

XCEPT, YOU KNOW THAT whole thing about anything that doesn't kill you making you stronger? Turns out it's a complete lie. It's just a thing people say to keep you from giving up on life completely, barricading yourself in your room, and refusing to come out except to use the bathroom. The warm fuzzy feeling I had on Thursday didn't last long, and the next day, instead of making me stronger, the things that didn't kill me definitely made me wish I were dead.

That morning, energized by the respectable outfit I'd picked out (a new pair of Levi's skinny jeans my mom had bought me from Walmart, and a stretchy plaid shirt I'd rediscovered under a pile of books), and excited about the good friends who were waiting for me, I actually got to school early. I walked with a pep in my step past the old gym, where the girls' volleyball team was gathered, reading some kind of pink sign. "Hey, Michelle. Hi, Bethany, Brayden, and Claire," I called out.

"Um. Hi," Michelle answered, eyeing me strangely. I figured she was just taken aback by the unusual amount of morning energy I had.

"Simon! How are you?" I asked, careful not to use a single S in my sentence, except for the one in his name, which couldn't really be avoided. He turned, seeming surprised that I'd spoken to him, and shoved a pink piece of paper into his locker. What were these posters? Maybe there was a dance? Or some kind of student body election I hadn't heard about yet?

I spotted Em down the hall at her locker. "Hey, Em." I smiled widely as I approached. She turned, a cold look on her face. "What's wrong?" I asked, but she didn't answer. Instead she just ripped a pink poster off her locker and shoved it at me. Sarah J. (or one of her evil followers) had obviously gotten creative overnight. NEW YORK LESBO, read the sign, in big block letters.

Em walked over to my locker and ripped down a second. NEW YORK LESBO'S INDIAN LOVER. I gulped. Obviously, *Hamburglar* wasn't the worst nickname ever, after all.

"This is *not* cool," Em said, clenching her fists. "*So* not cool." She walked a few steps, turned on her heels, and walked back like a tiger pacing.

From where I was standing, I could see pink signs all the way down the hall. I grabbed one. EM + MARGOT = LESBIAN LOVE. Another, with little hearts all over it, said MARGOT & EM, TOGETHER 4EVER. A third one read: MARGOT & EM FOR PROM DRAG QUEENS.

"Come on," I said, starting down the hall, ripping off posters as I went. "Help me with this, okay?" All I wanted was to get rid of them before anyone else (especially Gorgeous George) saw them. "Then we'll go straight to Vandanhoover's office and tell her."

"Right," Em said. "Because that's going to do us any good."

"Well, what else are we supposed to do?" I asked.

She didn't answer, but went to the opposite side of the hallway and started ripping down the pink sheets too.

As it turned out, Em was right about Vandanhoover being useless. At 10:30 she called us down to the office and asked about the posters. And when we told her who we thought had done it, she just nodded. "I'll speak to Sarah and see if we can't work together to get to the bottom of things," she promised in that important-sounding but vague way adults have. But obviously, Sarah J. wasn't stupid. She was just going to deny it. There wasn't going to be any "getting to the bottom of it," and we all knew it. Seriously, between this and the fish sticks thing, I was starting to wonder what kind of skills they even taught at principal school.

By the time Mrs. Vandanhoover sent us back to class, things felt ten times more hopeless. "I'll see you in math," I said to Em. I had to pee, plus I needed a minute to myself.

As I was washing my hands, the door opened and Tiffany Abraham—one of the quiet girls—walked in. I breathed a sigh of relief that it was just her, and started to fix my hair. But a few minutes later, when she came to wash her hands at the sink beside me, she kind of cleared her throat. She seemed to be taking forever, rinsing the soap off each finger individually. Eventually I glanced over.

"Hi," she said softly. I smiled a little, then flipped my hair upside down to tousle it. When I flipped it up again, I could feel her watching me in the mirror.

"Listen," she said finally, reaching for a paper towel and not looking me in the eyes, "I think it sucks, those posters and everything." Her cheeks were going a bit pink. I could tell it was taking a lot out of her to say this.

"Thanks," I said, and I meant it.

Tiffany seemed to gain courage from my response. The words were coming easier now. "Like, really. I don't think it's anybody's business that you're a lesbian." My mouth must have fallen open a little. "Not that it's my personal style," she explained quickly. "But—my older brother is gay. So I'm really cool with it. I don't think you should be ashamed of who you are." Then she turned and left.

As soon as the door swished shut behind her, I banged my open palms down onto the countertop, then took a deep breath before looking up and staring at myself miserably in the mirror. The great outfit I'd picked out that morning suddenly looked all wrong. Em's head scarf, combined with the plaid shirt and my general scrawniness, made me look like a skinny, ten-year-old farm boy. It was no wonder people thought I was a lesbian. I ripped the hair scarf out furiously and splashed water on my bangs to wet them down, but it didn't help, so I put it back on. Then I went into a bathroom stall, where I pressed my back against the pink partition and stayed for a long, long time.

"How's it going?" Andrew said when I went out to meet him at lunch that afternoon. Em, who'd had another "personal thing" to take care of, had left me at our lockers again. I'd watched her walk off down the hall, but hadn't had the energy to follow.

"Fine," I answered. Then I threw my backpack on the ground like everything was normal, but I saw them all exchange a quick look.

"Do you want to play War of the Druids?" Andrew held out the DS. I have the world's suckiest hand-eye coordination. Erika and I played Mario Kart in Andrew's rec room once, and I kept accidentally driving backward, or veering off the track and crashing into shrubs. But after all that had happened that morning—call me crazy—I had a serious urge to stab someone through the heart with a poison dart. I reached for the DS.

"Okay," Andrew said, leaning in so close that I could smell his BO. "You're the Druid King—a master warrior. And this is your horse. To make it rear up and kick, you hold down A and press X. Try it." I did, and the horse kicked an evil wood nymph in the face, sending him flying off a cliff. It was pretty satisfying.

"Nice," Amir congratulated me, leaning in on my other side. I turned my horse and headed for the magical forest, where Andrew told me the enchanted sword of Elron was hidden.

I made it through most of level one, with Andrew beside me coaching, and was just about to face off with the first forest dragon, when I heard Em's voice.

"Hey," she said. "What are you doing?"

"She's slaying the Dragon of Elron Woods," Andrew said, his voice full of pride. "You should see this. Have you seriously never played War of the Druids before?"

"Seriously," I said.

I squeezed over on the bench to make room for her.

"War of the Druids?" Em said. "Sounds awesome." But it was clear from her tone that she didn't really think so. At all.

"I've got Mario Kart too," Andrew offered, leaning down and reaching into his bag.

And that was when I saw it: the corner of a familiar piece

of hot pink paper. . . . Andrew shoved it down when he saw me noticing it, but it was too late. Em had seen it too.

"What's that?" she asked sharply.

"It's not what it looks like, Margot," Andrew said quickly, giving me a pleading look.

"It's not?" Em said. "Because I'm pretty sure it is."

She reached past Andrew and pulled a sheet out of his backpack.

"We were taking them down," Andrew explained. "But we didn't want to put them in the recycle bin in case someone saw them and put them back up or something."

We? I nudged Amir's backpack with my foot. It made a crunching noise. Mike looked on sheepishly. I didn't know what to say.

"Where were you taking them down from?" Em asked.

"Downstairs hallway, near the gym. We saw them before basketball practice this morning," Andrew said. "I think we got them before anyone else saw."

"But there were more upstairs before lunch," Amir added. "They must have put them up after the bell went, I think. Plus, there were a bunch near the guys' bathroom."

"Idiots," Em said.

I handed the DS back to Andrew, tears welling up in my eyes.

"That's it." Em stood up like the matter was decided. "Sarah J. and her friends have gone too far." She kicked a glass bottle, sending it skidding across the yard. I saw Amir and Andrew exchange a look. "Margot, stop," she said. "Don't cry."

"Maybe we should report it to the office," Andrew suggested. Em just rolled her eyes.

She grabbed my hand and pulled me off the bench. "I need to talk to you alone."

Andrew shot me a worried look, but I just shrugged. Em had been right, after all. Vandanhoover hadn't been able to do anything.

"Look," she said, once she'd dragged me to the maple tree. "Your friends took down a few posters and that's great, but honestly, there's nothing else anybody can do for us. We have to look out for ourselves. Stop crying. Right now. Are you listening to me?"

I nodded, but tears were still running down my cheeks.

"I'll make you a bet. I'm going to make *her* cry."

I just kept crying. In fact, I wasn't planning to stop. Ever.

"Are you listening to me?" Em asked again. I nodded, but I didn't believe her. Make Sarah J. cry? It was impossible. "Give me a few weeks," she added.

As much as I wanted to see Sarah pay, I also happened to like Em—and need her. "Don't," I said, sniffling. "She'll make your life hell."

"Like I care," Em said. Then she added with a glint in her eye, "But there are always two parts to a bet. If I make that girl cry—and I mean bawling her eyes out in a bathroom stall—you have to kiss floppy hair guy."

"What?" I said.

"You heard me." She adjusted her backpack on her shoulder. "Floppy hair guy. I think his name is George. You like him. You're always staring at him. It's *so* obvious."

Was it? Now I really wanted to die.

"So?" she pressed, holding out her hand. "It's a bet?"

I dried some tears off my cheek with the back of my hand.

"Sure." I shook on it. "Because I guarantee you it won't work!"

"It'll work," she said. "You just met me. Trust me. You have no idea what I'm capable of yet."

Em Warner: rebellious, spunky, smart. I wondered, was it possible? If anyone could pull this off, maybe it was her.

"I don't even know how you're going to find his lips, though," she said in an offhand way as we started to walk back toward Andrew, Mike, and Amir. "With his hair flopping all over like that." Despite my misery, I half smiled.

One thing was certain: whatever happened, at least it wasn't going to be a boring year.

12

I Buy Toilet Paper in Bulk

ET OR NO BET, IT WAS, however, a boring weekend. Well, boring in some ways. Humiliating in others, and disgusting, to top it all off.

On Friday night, Mom came home from covering a late shift at All Organics and called Bryan, the triplets, and me into the kitchen to make this announcement:

"We've been selected for an exciting promotional opportunity," she said, shrugging off her coat. "We're going to be a VTV Dinners test family!"

"VTV?" I asked.

"Vegan TV dinners," she said, grinning. "It's a new line of one-hundred-percent-organic vegan convenience foods. When Donatello was placing the store's order, the subject of our family came up. And the moment VTV heard about the triplets and our busy lifestyle, they just knew we'd be a great fit."

Bryan hugged my mom tightly, practically weeping, like we'd won the lottery. "This is fantastic," he said. "Our luck is really changing." But it *so* wasn't.

The first shipment of food arrived by special delivery on Saturday. For dinner that night we had microwaved veggie loaf with a spinach confit. Mom wolfed it down. The triplets mushed it between their fingers (which is what they do with everything). I stared at it. Even Bryan didn't seem so sure about its edibleness. "I've never seen spinach in liquid form before," he said, taking a tentative mouthful. "It's an interesting consistency."

The next morning, Mom tried to convince me to start my day with some delicious scrambled tofu a-la-microwave. I declined. After eating my normal bowl of cereal, it was time for some shopping—but not the good kind. While Erika was once again in Toronto, browsing for designer jeans at chic boutiques, I ended up on the hellish flip side of shopping—at Costco, cruising the aisles for toilet paper. I was hoping that if I tagged along, I might be able to get some new hair products. But if I'd known how traumatizing buying in bulk could be, I would have definitely stayed home.

When we got to the store, everyone had a job. I pushed a cart the size of a small house while my mom handled the triple-seater stroller and Bryan navigated using the Costco map. "It says diapers are in aisle G, but here it jumps from D to H." He scratched at his bald patch like he was trying to unearth the answer from inside his skull.

While I waited for him to figure it out, I steered the cart over to a display of mineral blush. I'd read about it in *Cosmo-Girl*. It was supposed to be good for your pores. "Mom?" I said, showing her.

"No, Margot," she answered, barely looking at the makeup. She was busy straightening the stroller's wheels and squeezing it over to one side so a family could get past.

"Oh my God," a woman cooed, stopping in her tracks and abandoning her cart in the middle of the aisle. "What sweethearts! Are they triplets?" she asked my mom, leaning in to get a better look.

"They are."

"Hello!" Alex said, on cue. "I'm two." They started waving—always a crowd-pleaser—and the woman laughed.

"I gotsa guitar for my birthday," Aleene informed the woman, like that was somehow relevant to anything.

"Did you really?" the woman asked with wide eyes. "You lucky girl." Then, to my mom: "You must have your hands full." People *always* say that.

"It's a challenge." My mom *always* answers that.

"Mom?" I held up a 600-pack of makeup sponges. They were only $12.50, and they'd last forever.

"No, Margot."

"Are they identical?" the woman asked, predictably.

"They are," Mom answered. Then there was a bunch more gushing about how cute and how verbal they were before someone asked the woman to please move her cart, and she disappeared down the home entertainment aisle.

"Come on, Margot," Mom said. Bryan had finally found aisle G on the map. I put the sponges down and followed. If my pores looked bad, it would be all their fault.

Half an hour later, with a truckload of mega-value diapers, twenty lightbulbs, one hundred rolls of toilet paper, and six jugs of laundry detergent, we finally approached the checkout. And we would have actually made it all the way there, too, if some cruel person hadn't decided to put a display of Dora the Explorer canned pasta right at toddler eye level.

"Dora!!!" all three triplets shouted joyfully, reaching for the cans.

"Oh no, girls, that's garbage food," my mom explained, wheeling the stroller a little to the left so they couldn't reach. Meanwhile, I went to get in line with our stuff. I could see where this was headed, and I didn't want any part of it.

Aleene started whining, and when that didn't work, she tried climbing over the stroller's snack tray to get out. Mom asked her to sit her bum down and told her we could have VTV whole-wheat pasta at home. But Aleene isn't dumb. She knew a lame substitute when she heard one. All hell broke loose.

If you've ever seen a two-year-old throw a tantrum, you'll know what this looked like. It basically involves a lot of screaming, whining, and hysterical flailing of limbs—not to mention a flood of tears and snot. It always reminds me of this one time when Mom and I were pet-sitting for her friend, and Erika and I decided to give the cat a bath. The whole thing is messy, moist, loud, and totally out of control. Plus, when it happens in public, people stare at you like you're totally dysfunctional, which maybe we were.

I grabbed a magazine off the rack near the checkout and started to read an article about Oprah's dogs.

"Really," the woman in line in front of me said, looking at my sisters, then turning to her husband. "I don't know why people bring small children to places like this. It's obviously too much for them to handle."

I looked up over the magazine at her. She was wearing expensive workout wear with full makeup, and the only items in her cart were two huge decorative urns overflowing with fake fall foliage. It was pretty obvious she didn't have kids. The lady saw me looking at her and smiled, like she thought I was sympathizing with her about the squalling going on by the pasta display. I just smiled back, thankful that the toilet paper was covering up the mega-pack of diapers in the cart, and for once, grateful that I didn't look anything like my family.

I'd just turned the page in my magazine when . . . "Margot." I pretended not to hear. "Margot!" My mom's tone was more urgent now. "Can we please get your help over here?" I glanced back. Both Alex and Aleene had managed to climb out of the stroller by now and were kicking and screaming on the floor. Meanwhile, Alice had quietly wiggled most of her body under her snack tray, but couldn't get her shoulders or head through. She was stuck, and whimpering softly.

Bryan and my mom were both crouched down on the floor, talking soothingly and trying different useless techniques like counting to five and threatening to put the girls' giant Legos away for the rest of the day. I could feel the woman's eyes watching me, watching them, and suddenly I couldn't stand it a second longer. I put the magazine back in the rack.

"Sorry if my sisters ruined your bulk-buying experience," I said, giving her a nasty stare.

Then I abandoned our cart and walked over to hoist Alice back into sitting position in the stroller. I marched past my mom and Bryan, picked up three cans of Dora pastas, and handed one to each triplet.

"Margot!" Mom said sharply, looking up from the floor.

"Just let them have it," I said, my voice shaking. "It costs fifty-nine cents. Just make them shut up. Please." I glanced at the line, but the woman had turned her back. "Let's just go home," I said. "Okay?"

So we did, the triplets holding tight to their Dora pastas the whole way, and my mom staring, exhausted, out the window.

13

I Wear the Jacket of Extreme Coolness, and Sarah J. Wears Onions

HAVE YOU EVER HAD ONE of those moments when your karma just changes? One second you're wandering around like a total disaster, getting stared at by strangers in Costco, blurting out swear words and accidentally insulting people who lisp, and the next thing you know, you're actually a little bit cool? No? Well, me neither. Except for this one time . . .

Determined to get things off to a better, more normal start, and not to give my English teacher the satisfaction of pinching up her lips and going, "Oh, Margot, soooo nice of you to join us," I actually left for school on time the next Monday morning.

And when I walked into English class I practically let out a yodel of joy. Because unless Mrs. Collins had had a sex change operation, gone bald, and gained one hundred pounds . . . we had a substitute. "Mr. Learner" was written across the board in big sloppy letters, and a short hairy man was reading a paperback novel at Mrs. Collins's desk.

Amir, who was talking to Erik at the back of the room, gave me a thumbs-up. I smiled and slid into my chair. Gorgeous

George, looking totally hot in a new black-and-red-striped shirt with the sleeves rolled up, was there already too. He was across the room, talking to Sarah J., but I swear he looked up at me when I walked in.

"Matt was, like, no way. She's with me. And then they totally had to let me in," Sarah was saying in a loud voice. George just nodded. "And, honestly, high school parties are so much cooler. There were eleventh graders there, even, who were totally nice."

Em sighed. "Does she ever shut up about her boyfriend?"

"No," I answered. "He's in *high school*, by the way."

"Yeah. I heard. About a hundred times." Suddenly her face lit up. "I know. Let's talk about the cool things *we* did this weekend." She flipped her hair, Sarah-style. "Oh my God, Margot," she said loudly, drowning out Sarah J.'s voice. "That go-see in Toronto on Saturday was the coolest. I can't believe how much the casting agent loved your book. You're definitely getting that catalog shoot. I'm really jealous." I stared at her, my eyes going wide. Toronto? Saturday? Me? A book? What was a go-see? The coolest thing I'd done on Saturday was play solitaire online.

Sarah J. had fallen silent. She was staring at us, which, I realized, was exactly what Em had been aiming for.

"I hope so," I answered awkwardly. "I mean. You know me. I love modeling. All the free clothes and stuff."

Just then, the bell rang and a hush fell over the room as we waited for Mr. Learner to stand up or say something. He held up his index finger and, without even looking up from his book, said, "Give me a minute, guys. I'm almost at the end of this chapter."

Everyone hesitated, then slowly started talking again. After making sure that Sarah J. had gone back to ignoring us, Em shot me a look like, *Really? "All the free clothes and stuff." That's the best you could do?* I shrugged in response.

Finally, Mr. Learner put his book down.

"Done now," he announced, laying his hands flat against the desk and leaning forward. "Quiet, please." Nobody paid much attention. "I said DONE NOW," he yelled in a huge, booming voice. "QUIET, please." That worked.

"I'm sure you've noticed," he continued, stepping out from behind the desk, "that Mrs. Collins isn't here today." His pants were all wrinkled and part of his shirt was hanging out. He obviously wasn't married. "She's dealing with a family emergency. She'll be away for the rest of this week, at least, so we'll be getting to know each other."

I felt like jumping up and cheering. A family emergency! Despite how mean she'd been to me, I still hoped nothing *really* bad had happened to her family . . . but, still, an entire week Collins-free sounded kind of like heaven.

"Since I assume you can all read, you know that my name is Mr. Learner." He didn't smile. "And let me say up front that I can read your predictable preteen minds. In fact, I can hear the wheels in your brains turning as you imagine how you're going to get away with murder this week, so here's fair warning: I know every trick in the book. And I'm watching you." I could see a few people exchanging glances. "And now"—he walked over to a trolley full of books and grabbed one off the top—"we'll be leaving the poetry unit behind until Mrs. Collins returns." There were a few cheers. "I'd like to introduce you to William Golding's modern classic, *Lord of the Flies*." There were a few groans. "It's a story about the downfall of a society run entirely by children," he said. The cover had a picture of a bleeding pig's head covered in flies. Lovely. A story about rotting meat.

"As you read chapter one to yourselves, I want you to think about how you would organize a society if you found yourselves in the same situation as the characters. That's right. Picture an entire island of hormonal preteens with no parental supervision. A terrifying thought, I know."

I had to admit, even though the book looked horrible, I liked the question. We all started to read. It was a bit confusing in parts, but not as bad as I was expecting.

Almost the whole hour went by before Mr. Learner stopped us. "Books down," he instructed. "Thoughts, anyone?"

Nobody raised their hand, but Sarah J. made the mistake of leaning across the aisle at that moment to pass a note to Joyce. "Note passer," Mr. Learner said, "in the blue shirt."

Sarah looked up. "What was the question again?" she asked.

"If you found yourself stranded on an island, what's the first step you'd take in organizing your society?"

"Nothing," she answered. "Everyone could do whatever. It'd be like a big bush party."

"Ingenious," Mr. Learner said. Sarah shrugged like it was nothing. "A bush party. And what would you eat?"

"Just, like, whatever food was on the island, I guess."

"And what food is on the island?"

"Ummm . . ." She stalled. "Pig," she said finally, sounding all pleased with herself. She pointed to the book cover. It was pretty obvious that she'd barely gotten past page one. "It'd be like a pork party," she added with a giggle.

"I see." Mr. Learner stroked his chin. "And who would like to come to"—he paused—"your name, please."

"Sarah."

"And who would like to come to Sarah's pork party?" Almost everyone except me, Em, Amir, and Erik Frallen raised their hands.

"What if there was a typhoon?" he asked. "What if you were stranded on the island for more than a year, and there was only enough pork for a week? What if there was no fresh water to drink? Would you still want to come to Sarah's pork party?"

Most people put their hands down. As cool as being at one of The Group's parties might have been, the starving-to-death part probably put them off.

"For next Monday, you'll each write five hundred words about the steps you'd take to organize your society. Then we'll talk about which of you would survive the year. Obviously, the people at the pork party need to do some rethinking." He gave Sarah a condescending look.

"Any questions?" he asked. There weren't any. "Good." Then he said, almost cheerfully, "Now get lost. I'm already sick of looking at you."

You know what I hate? People who make out in public places.

It's disgusting. And not only is it disgusting, it's rude (especially to those of us who've never had anyone to make out with). And not only is it rude, it's unsanitary, considering all the spit involved. And not only that, but it's also disgusting, which I know I've already mentioned, but I think it's probably worth saying again because it explains why, thanks to Sarah J.'s noon make-out session, I literally lost my lunch.

Em had another mysterious "personal thing" to take care of when the bell rang, but she came to get me right after, from the side of the basketball court, where Amir, Mike, and Andrew were shooting hoops, while I almost passed level two of War of the Druids.

"Come on," she said, taking the DS from me and shoving it into Andrew's bag. "Let's go over there."

"Why don't we just stay here?" I suggested, motioning toward the court. "They're almost done, I think."

"Yeah, but they'll be all sweaty. Anyway, we have girl stuff to discuss. Let's go where it's quieter."

I stood up, looking toward Andrew. "Okay, well, just let me say bye, then."

"Why? We're just going over there." She pointed to the red maple. "They'll be able to see us." She was right. And anyway, the guys were busy, so I nodded and followed her.

But unfortunately, even though it *was* quieter, our new lunch spot put us directly in view of Sarah J., who was French-kissing Matt, her high school boyfriend, on the sidewalk.

From all her talk, I'd been expecting some kind of ultra-cool surfer dude with a six-pack. He didn't look anything like that. For one thing, Matt was kind of skinny. He was also shorter than Sarah, but to make up for it, he had very tall hair that rose from his forehead in a stiff wave. Still, he was well dressed in a gray Abercrombie sweatshirt and worn-in jeans, which Sarah must have liked, and he seemed to know what he was doing when it came to kissing.

"That's just nasty," Em said, taking a bite of her sandwich and looking toward Sarah J.'s display of lip slurping.

"Tell me about it. I'm glad I'm not eating right now."

"Forgot your lunch?" she asked with her mouth full.

"Yeah," I said. "It's okay. I'm not really hungry." The truth was, my mom had sent me to school with a VTV Power Pack lunch of organic vegetable stew, and I was not about to risk ridicule by heating it up in the cafeteria's kitchenette microwave.

"I'm not hungry either," she said, and passed me half of her sandwich. "Eat this for me?"

I was starving, actually, so I took it. It looked like something you'd buy at an open-air deli in Venice. It was on a big fresh bun, with baby spinach, cold cuts, red onions sliced thin, tomatoes, and mozzarella cheese. Seriously gourmet. At first I figured her mom must be a great cook, or something, but then I glanced at the wrapper in her hand. It had a Whole Foods sticker on it.

"What does your mom do?" I asked.

"Gets her nails done and shops and stares at herself in the mirror," Em said. "She's an actor."

"Really?" I couldn't keep the tone of amazement out of my voice. "So's my stepdad. Well, he used to be, anyway. He did Shakespeare in the Park, and a bunch of commercial work. What has your mom acted in?"

"Soap operas mostly."

I bit my lip to keep from gasping. I knew watching soap operas wasn't a cool thing to do, but if she was on *Charmed and Dazed*, I wouldn't be able to help myself. I'd definitely scream.

"Which ones?"

"*Destiny's World* for a while. Oh, and she played Chloe on *Chicago Dreams* for like, years."

I'd never watched either of those. Still, it must have been

pretty cool to have a soap opera actress for a mom. Way cooler than having a Shakespearian actor, or that bald-guy-in-the-travel-insurance-commercial for a stepdad. Now that I knew her mom was kind of famous, more and more things about Em were starting to make sense, too—like the black car with the tinted windows that had picked her up from the self-esteem workshop, how she was so good at hair and makeup, and probably even how she'd gotten into doing modeling work.

"Oh," said Em, reaching for her bag, "I almost forgot. The girl stuff we have to take care of. I brought you something."

"What?"

"Just something. Take off your coat."

"Why?" I complained. It was kind of cold out.

"Because I said so."

"No," I said.

She fixed me with a serious stare. "Okay, Margot. I really like you . . . and that's why I have to be honest with you. Your coat is ugly."

I took in both those bits of information at once. First, she *really* liked me? I tried not to let my face break into a smile, which was made easier by the fact that she'd just insulted my coat. "It's not that bad," I said lamely. It was a white Gore-Tex jacket with blue stitching. My mom bought it for me last Christmas. I knew it must have practically killed her to pay almost a hundred dollars for it when there were perfectly good, affordable coats at Walmart. But everyone had a Gore-Tex jacket, and I'd begged. Of course, that was last year. I looked around the yard. Nobody was wearing their Gore-Tex jackets anymore.

"Margot," Em said, halfway between kidding and serious, "this is an intervention. I'm rescuing you from your ugly jacket.

Give it to me." I handed it over. "And now for the ceremonious banishing of the ugly coat." She walked to the trash can on the other side of the yard and dropped it in, brushing her hands off as she came back.

"Close your eyes," she said. All I could think about was how my mom was going to kill me when she found out I threw away my jacket. I could hear Em opening the zipper of her bag, then felt her put something around my shoulders. "Open!" she said.

I was wearing the coolest green army jacket ever made. It had a million zippered pockets in it. I put my arms into the sleeves. They were the perfect length for scrunching my fingers up inside. "Is this yours?" I asked.

"Yours now," she said.

"For real?" I hugged the jacket around me. "Thanks!" I could hardly wait to show it to Erika.

"Don't mention it," Em said. "Friends don't let friends wear bad clothes."

While Em took another bite of the sandwich, I pretended like I was concentrating really hard on my fingernails so she wouldn't notice the big dorky smile on my face.

"Okay, enough. Gross," Em said. Sarah J. was running her hands through Matt's hair now—at the back—not in the wave part, where they'd probably get stuck.

Suddenly Em stood up and cupped her hands around her mouth. "Hey! Get a room!" she shouted. Without coming up for air, Sarah J. took one hand off Matt's head and gave us the finger. Em turned to me in exaggerated shock.

"Did you see that?" She put her hands on her hips. "That's it. This has to be stopped or else I'm seriously going to barf."

She seemed to think for a second, then stood up and walked over to the fence. "Excuse me," she said. "People are trying to eat here." I couldn't believe what she was doing, and apparently, neither could anyone else. Practically the whole school yard was staring, waiting to see how Sarah J. was going to react.

She pulled away from Matt and turned to glare at Em. "Do you want to stop staring at us, lesbian pervert? You too, Hamburglar." She laughed at her own offensive joke, then turned away, putting a hand on Matt's cheek and looking into his eyes.

"Come on, baby," he said, trying to lead her away to someplace more private.

"No way." She stood her ground. "We have a right to be here. They're the ones being perverted by watching." She started kissing him again.

Em just sighed, turned to me, then hopped up on the concrete ledge so she was leaning over the top of the fence barely three feet above Sarah and Matt. "This is your last warning," she said. When they still didn't come up for air, Em shrugged.

"I know you really like pork and everything, Sarah," she said. "So have some. It's capicola with veggies." She lobbed her half of the part-eaten deli sandwich right at Sarah. The bread split open when it hit her perfect blond head, then tumbled down to the ground, leaving a trail of mustard and mayo on her plaid jacket. Sarah gasped and looked up in shock, a purple onion clinging to her hair.

"You *didn't* just do that," she said.

"You little—" Matt started, heading toward the gate.

"Quick, Margot. Your sandwich," Em said.

If I'd taken a second then to pause and weigh the questions of right versus wrong, revenge versus forgiveness, and whether or not possibly getting beat up by a ninth grader was worth the five seconds of satisfaction I was about to feel, I might have made a different decision. But, as it was, I was mad. *Really* mad. I was sick of being Hamburglar and getting called a lesbian when I wasn't one. I was tired of watching the unpopular kids get pushed around while the evildoers got to call the shots and French-kiss their boyfriends wherever they wanted. And I was grateful to Em. First of all, for giving me the coolest jacket ever made . . . but also for having the guts to do things I never did. And that's why, without thinking, I jumped up onto the ledge beside her, and I threw my half of the sandwich. And, thanks to War of the Druids, which had totally improved my hand-eye coordination, I hit Sarah J. right in the shoulder. . . . I would have gotten her face too, I swear, if she hadn't blocked it with her arm at the last second.

"Oh, that's it," Matt said, breaking into a run. Moving fast in the opposite direction seemed like our best—maybe only—plan, but Em held me back.

"Wait," she whispered furiously. "I'll deal with this."

I stood there frozen, wondering why she was setting us up to get murdered in broad daylight. I caught Andrew's eye across the yard. He, Amir, and Mike had stopped their game, and Andrew especially was watching with big worried eyes.

"You're dead," Matt said, coming through the gate.

His feet had barely hit the school yard pavement when Em took a huge breath and shouted so loudly and so suddenly it almost made me lose my balance: "Help!! There's an intruder on school property! Somebody help us! I think he has a weapon!" Matt froze, staring at her in bewilderment. Within seconds, a teacher was there, then two teachers, then three.

As Mr. Munka, the boys' phys ed teacher, grabbed Matt by the arm, and general panic broke out in the school yard, Em hopped off the concrete ledge, smiling calmly at Sarah J.

If it were possible to murder someone through a chain-link fence using only the fury in your eyes, I'm pretty sure Em would be seriously dead right now. But as it was, all Sarah could do was pick the onion out of her hair and mumble a vague threat.

"You're in so much trouble now, New York, you know that? You and your little friend Hamburglar, too."

14

I Don't Buy Any Girl Scout Cookies

DOES ENDING UP IN THE office three times in the first two weeks of school officially make you a badass? I don't know. Personally, I think "badass" is a state of mind. It's *not* about getting in trouble. It's about *not caring* that you're getting in trouble, and I definitely didn't feel relaxed as Sarah, Matt, Em, and I sat in Mrs. Vandanhoover's office explaining ourselves.

"I hope you realize, Matthew, that you're no longer a student here. Manning could choose to press charges against you for trespassing, as well as for threatening two students and bringing a weapon onto the premises. I shouldn't need to tell you how serious this is." Vandanhoover's face was stony. It was just lucky for Em and me that Matt *had* been carrying a weapon. It was only a Swiss Army knife, but it still counted.

"I wasn't threatening them—" Matt started, but Em interrupted, clearing her throat.

"He said, and I quote: 'That's it. You're dead.' If that's not a threat, I don't know what is. You can ask anyone standing in the yard. They all heard him."

Mrs. Vandanhoover looked at Matt.

"It's just an expression," he said. "All I meant was that I was going to kick their butts."

Mrs. Vandanhoover frowned, not seeming any happier with that.

"Anyway, they were throwing stuff at us," Sarah said. "Look at this stain on my jacket."

"Okay, that," Em explained. "Margot and I were sitting there eating. And we were just trying to ask them, politely, to stop engaging in disturbing sexual behavior so close to school property. We were forced to throw the sandwiches in self-defense after Sarah made a rude gesture and yet another homophobic comment." Em gave Vandanhoover a meaningful look to remind her about the posters.

I couldn't tell if she was buying Em's self-defense plea, but it didn't matter. Vandanhoover seemed way more concerned about Matt and his pocket knife than a couple of Dijon mustard stains anyway.

"Matthew, I'm going to let you off with a stern warning this time. You are not to come within fifty feet of the Manning school property. If a similar violation takes place, we won't hesitate to press charges."

"But—" Sarah started, obviously planning to complain about her lunchtime make-out privileges being taken away. Vandanhoover cut her off.

"I'd suggest you return to Sterling High now." Matt stood up and left. "Emily, I'd like a word with you. Sarah and Margot, you can return to class." Sarah J. got up to follow Matt. "*Straight* to class," Vandanhoover added in a no-nonsense tone.

I glanced at Em, wondering if I should ask to stay. After all, I'd thrown half the sandwich, so this was half my fault—but she was playing with a ring on her pinkie finger like she wasn't worried at all. I stood up and left, pulling the door almost all the way closed behind me.

Despite Vandanhoover's warning, Sarah had run after Matt (I could see them talking in the hallway outside), and the secretary must have been in the bathroom, because the front office was empty. Maybe it was because I felt partly responsible for Em getting in trouble, or maybe it was just because I'm nosy like that, I took two small steps toward the doors, then stopped and stood as silently as possible, listening.

"You realize, Emily, that I'll have to call your social worker and your mother to report your involvement in this incident."

"But I wasn't even—I was minding my own business, and Sarah was *way* out of line."

"I'd like to believe you, Emily. I really would. Because I want to see you get off to a fresh start here in Darling. A better start. So does Mrs. Hoolihan at Social Services and Mrs. Martine in Student Support. It may seem harsh to you, but the reason we're keeping such a close eye on you is to help you find your way."

If Em gave any answer, I couldn't make out what it was.

"You're obviously a bright, creative girl, Emily. If you apply that energy to your studies, you'll be amazed at what you can achieve here. Now, tell me," Vandanhoover said, taking a softer tone, "how was your first week? Have you made any friends?"

"It was fine, I guess," Em mumbled. "I met Margot. She's all right." All right? I leaned in slightly, more than a little bit offended, waiting to see if she'd say anything more about me, but she didn't.

"That's wonderful," Mrs. Vandanhoover said. "A good

peer group is key to a student's success." She pushed her chair back from her desk, so as much as I wanted to hang around, I didn't wait to hear anything more.

I didn't really get a chance to talk to Em again until after school, but I did spend a lot of time watching her out of the corner of my eye, trying to guess what Vandanhoover could have been talking about. Em had a social worker? She needed a "fresh start"? Clearly, she had a sucky glazed-hamlike episode of her own.

"Everyone's talking about what happened," Em said, coming up behind me after the bell rang. I saw her reflection in my locker mirror. "That was *such* sweet revenge. She's never going to get that mustard stain out."

"I know," I said. "It *was* pretty good, wasn't it?"

"It didn't make her cry." Em sounded a bit disappointed. "But don't worry. I'm just getting started."

I gulped. If that was "just getting started," I couldn't even imagine what else she had in mind. "What did Vandanhoover say to you?" I asked casually.

"Not much," she answered. "She just wanted to hear my side of the story again. You know, to write it down in case they want to press charges next time." I closed my locker door. "What's wrong?" she asked.

"Nothing." I pretended to look for something in my bag. I obviously couldn't tell her I'd been eavesdropping, that I knew she was lying to my face, and that I'd overheard her say she thought I was just "all right." "I guess I'm worried about what's going to happen now." That much was true. Not only had we crossed Sarah, we'd also crossed Matt—her ninth-grade,

146

Swiss-Army-knife-carrying boyfriend. And maybe he wasn't allowed within fifty feet of the school, but who said that was going to stop him from finding us?

"What do you mean?" she said.

"Like, what if he's waiting for us outside?"

"He won't be," she said. "Anyway, did you see how small he is? We could take him if we had to." But there was the tiniest bit of uncertainty in her voice. "Look, he has better things to do than wait around for us." I wasn't reassured. "Okay. If you're all uptight about it, I'll walk you home. Where do you live?"

"It's fine," I said, too quickly. "You're probably right. He's got better things to do. It's out of your way anyway." Gormon Avenue was about ten blocks from Lakeshore. But that wasn't the only reason I didn't want her to walk me home. First, I was a bit mad about her lying to me, but also, I didn't want her coming to my house, meeting my psychic mother, and seeing how dirty and disorganized everything was. I could feel my cheeks start to burn as I thought about my babyish butterfly quilt and our mismatched furniture.

"Whatever," she said. "Shut up. I'm walking you home."

"But—"

"No buts," Em said. "I don't really feel like going home anyway." She bit her bottom lip, possibly thinking of the phone call her mom and social worker would be getting from Vandanhoover that afternoon. "Seriously. I'll be your bodyguard. Let's go."

I glanced nervously around every corner and behind every bush, but we didn't end up seeing Matt—or Sarah. "She probably ran straight to the dry cleaners," Em said. "I heard her telling Maggie how much that coat cost." When we got to my place, I was desperately hoping Em might just turn around and go home, but instead she asked to come in to use our phone. "My cell battery's almost dead," she explained.

"You have a cell phone?" I couldn't hide the look of envy on my face.

"What? You don't?"

"I'm getting one," I lied. "Probably for my birthday." I opened the front door. "Hi," I called. I was expecting to see Grandma Betty. Instead, I heard my mom's voice.

"Oh, Margot. I'm so glad you're home." She came out of the living room wearing her I'M 100% ORGANIC T-shirt. I glanced at Em, who was busy kicking her Diesel shoes off into our giant avalanche of a front-door shoe pile. "Donatello has strep throat," Mom went on, doing up her watchband. "He needs me to cover for him at the store. I canceled all my tarot clients. Grandma was going to come help babysit, but she's been held up at the doctor's office waiting for her flu shot, and then she's got a visitation that she really can't— Oh. Who's this?" she asked, noticing Em, who was still dealing with the shoe-pile situation.

"This is my friend from school—Em. She just has to use the phone."

"Oh. Hello, Em."

Em just smiled slightly and kind of nodded.

"It's fine," I told my mom. "Go do your shift. I can babysit on my own until Bryan gets home."

"Well, that's the other problem," Mom went on. "He has his first test tomorrow, so he has a study group until eight."

"I can put them to bed," I said. "I've done it before."

"Oh, Margot. You're a lifesaver. There are VTV dinners in the freezer. Call me at the store if you need anything. Do you like eggplant bharta, Em? You're welcome to stay and keep Margot company."

Em pulled her eyes away from our goddess of fertility painting to look at my mom. "Um, sure," she said.

"That's Venus of Lespugue," Mom said, smiling at the painting. "Just one interpretation of the divine feminine."

I winced. The goddess of fertility was fat, naked, and had droopy boobs.

"Mom," I said urgently, helping her into her coat. "Aren't you going to be late?"

"Right." She flashed me a quick apologetic smile. "Nice to meet you, Em," she called as she dashed out the door. I breathed a sigh of relief. But the feeling didn't last long.

"Magoo, look. I did a craft." Aleene had walked into the front hall and latched herself onto my pant leg. She held up her hand to show me a Popsicle stick she'd painted red. It had two googly eyes glued to it.

"That's nice, Aleene." Then I noticed that the paint was still wet. And not only was it still wet, it was all over my pants. "Oh, God, Aleene!" I shouted, grabbing the Popsicle stick from her, taking it to the kitchen and throwing it in the sink. I got why my mom was all for encouraging the triplets to express themselves creatively, but couldn't she let them do it with crayons or building blocks? Something that wouldn't get stains all over my stuff?

Aleene immediately went into hyperventilation mode. "Okay, fine," I said. "Here." I took off the green jacket Em had given me, then fished the Popsicle stick out of the sink and handed it back to her. I honestly didn't care if she got red paint all over everything in the house (except that jacket), as long as it kept her quiet.

"Magoo?" Alice came into the kitchen then, holding two Popsicle sticks of her own. "Juice?"

"Oh my God!" Em said, "How many of them are there?" Alex came in behind her, without any Popsicle sticks, but with her hands covered, back and front, in red paint.

"Too many," I answered, grabbing a dishcloth and going to work on Alex's hands. I glanced at Em to see if she was noticing how messy our kitchen was, but she was busy looking at the clock.

"What time do they go to bed?" she asked.

"About seven thirty," I answered.

She looked deep in thought for a second. "Do they know how to tell time?"

"They're only two."

"Wait here." She waved good-bye to the girls, who looked at her with big curious eyes, then she went into the living room, closing the sliding door behind her.

"Juice," Alice reminded me.

"Right." I opened the fridge. Apparently, with the exception of a freezer full of VTV frozen entrées, we had approximately nothing to eat. Thankfully, I found one can of concentrated orange juice in the freezer door. By the time I'd finished blorping it into the jug, Em was back.

"Is that orange juice?" she asked. "Oh, goody!" She could have been Cinderella herself the way the triplets were mesmerized by her every move. "I think we should drink our juice in the living room, don't you, Margot?"

"Okay," I said, still not quite sure what she had in mind. Em closed the kitchen door behind us as we stepped into the nearly pitch-black room. She had already closed all the blinds, and then she started propping throw cushions against the gap under the door. We sat down on the floor and played a half-hearted game with giant Legos for a few minutes, then Em started to yawn.

"It's already dark out. Aren't you sleepy, Margot?" she asked.

That was about the time I caught on. I faked an exaggerated yawn. "Yeah," I said. "It's late."

Em leaned toward me. "What are their names?" she asked. I told her. "Forget it," she said immediately. "I'll never remember." She patted Alex's head. "I know three little girls who should be in bed soon," she said, tickling Aleene's tummy. Alice moved closer to her and sat down on her lap. "Ooooh, goodness!" Em said, yawing again. "I am *so* sleepy." She batted her eyelids.

"I'm sleepy," Alex mimicked. Aleene yawned. I couldn't believe it was actually working. Half an hour later, at 4:30 in the afternoon, we'd brushed their teeth, read two stories (short ones, plus Em skipped pages), tucked them into bed with their unopened cans of Dora pasta (they'd been toting them around like teddy bears ever since we got back from Costco the day before), and turned out the lights.

"What?" Em said, after we closed the door softly and I glanced at my watch, amazed. "You didn't think we could outsmart a bunch of babies?"

"They're going to wake up at, like, two in the morning."

"Do you have to get up with them?" she asked.

"No," I answered.

"So?" she countered. And then she seemed to forget all about the girls. "I'm starving. What do you have to eat?"

This might sound weird, but I loved the fact that Em didn't seem to love, or actually even like, my sisters. Every time Erika-with-a-K came over, she wanted to play dollhouse or cuddle with them, and she always repeated whatever latest cute thing one of them had said. It had started to get a little annoying a few weeks ago, when she wouldn't stop calling french fries "bench guys" because Aleene was saying it that way. It was refreshing to have some mature conversation.

I went into the kitchen and opened the fridge, even though I knew the situation was beyond dismal. "We've got mustard and chutney," I said. "And this box of baking soda. Sorry. We're doing this frozen meals thing, but they're really gross."

"God. I know all about it. My mom's on this macrobiotic brown rice and seaweed diet. Wait!" Em shouted suddenly. "I know a game." She grabbed two dish towels and tied them together. "Put this on like a blindfold," she said. "Sit." She pulled out a chair.

I could hear her opening and closing drawers as I adjusted the tea towels over my eyes. "You're not going to throw knives at me, right?" I asked, only half joking.

She laughed. "Margot, when are you going to learn to trust me? Are you ready?"

"That depends. Ready for what?"

"Mystery on a spoon!" she announced. "The greatest game ever invented. I mix together mysterious things on a spoon, feed them to you, and you try to guess what they are."

"Couldn't you just throw knives at me instead?" I said, shuddering. I knew what was in our kitchen.

"Don't worry," she said. "There are rules. Rule number one is that you can mix no more than three things, so that limits how disgusting it can get." I heard her close the fridge. "Rule number two: only edible things can go on the spoon. Rule number three: you have to swallow it, no matter how gross it is. But don't worry. I have to go next, so if I feed you something really bad, you can make me pay."

I heard a few cupboard doors open and shut. "God, you weren't kidding," Em remarked. "You have no food." I heard a shaking noise like a box of cereal, except I knew I'd eaten the last of it that morning. "Oh, disgusting," Em said. A drawer opened and closed. "Okay. Open wide."

I took a deep breath and was just about to open my mouth when the doorbell rang. "Gotta get that." I jumped up, reaching for my blindfold.

"No!" yelled Em, grabbing my hand away. "You'll see what's on the spoon. Just answer it like that." Em put two hands on my back and pushed me so hard in the direction of the front hall that I practically had to run to avoid tipping forward. I reached up with one hand and pulled off the blindfold before opening the door.

It was Erika.

I suddenly remembered. It was Monday. "Oh my God," I said. "I forgot."

"I waited at the cemetery for an hour," she said. "Again." I racked my brain trying to think of some believable excuse or, at the very least, something to say. She beat me to it, though. "I thought maybe you were sick, or got abducted by a stranger, or that something was really wrong, like maybe one of your family members was in a car accident."

"No," I said, stuffing a corner of the tea-towel blindfold into my back pocket. "I'm so sorry. My mom had to cover a shift for her boss at All Organics, and I'm babysitting alone because my grandma's getting the flu shot. I just . . . forgot." I'll admit I didn't say it in a very apologetic way. It came out sounding more amazed than anything because, honestly, I was so surprised myself.

Tears started to spill silently out of Erika's eyes. I stepped toward her, putting a hand on her shoulder. "I just *completely* forgot," I said in a pleading tone. "Look, I'm doing something right now." I glanced back toward the kitchen nervously. "But what if we meet up tomorrow? Three thirty, by the cemetery gates. I *swear*, honestly, I'll remember this time. . . ."

"Who's there?" Em yelled from the kitchen. Erika's eyes widened.

"That's just," I explained, "this girl from school. We're . . . doing a food sampling project together. For health class."

Em came into the hallway. "Are you coming?" she asked. "It doesn't matter how long you avoid it, that spoon isn't getting any less nasty." When she saw Erika, she sighed heavily, pushed past me, then smiled sweetly. "Thanks," she said to my best friend, who was tugging at the sleeves of her white school-uniform shirt, "but we don't want any Girl Scout cookies." Then she slammed the door shut in her face.

"Em!" I shouted, the second the latch clicked.

"Oh, wait! Do you know her?" Em asked.

"Yeah," I said, grabbing frantically at the doorknob.

I stepped onto the front walk, but it was too late. Erika

was running toward the street, and I knew that even if I called after her, she'd keep going.

"Oh, sorry," Em said in an offhanded way. "I didn't know she was your friend. Anyway, come on. You can call her later or something. Blindfold back on."

I stood there another second, watching Erika go, her backpack bouncing up and down heavily, the edges of her kilt flapping. I felt numb, and sick, and empty—like everything my best friend and I had had for so many years had suddenly fallen into a bottomless pit and there was no way to get it back.

"Come on," Em urged again. I blinked back tears and shut the door, then tied the tea towels over my eyes. There was nothing else I could do at that moment. Erika was furious with me. I'd just have to let her cool down, then apologize later, and somehow make it right. She *had* to forgive me. . . . She was the person who could still remember the names of every doll I'd ever had, every favorite song I'd ever danced to; the one who was there when my grandpa died, when my mom got married, when my sisters were born. . . .

"Okay, brace yourself," Em said, sitting me back in the chair. "This is going to be pretty bad." I felt the tip of the spoon against my lips. "Smell it first," she suggested, but I didn't want to. I opened my mouth and swallowed as quickly as I could.

In case you're wondering what was on the mystery spoon, it was peanut butter, honey, and pepper—which was disgusting, but not nearly as gross as the mayonnaise, vinegar, and Tabasco sauce I got her back with—or the counterattack of vegetable oil, horseradish, and hot mustard. By round four, Em and I were both laughing our heads off. She even called me "the Master of Mystery on a Spoon." But the whole time I was secretly watching the clock, thinking about Erika crying her eyes out in her bedroom, and waiting for Em to leave so I could write her a long e-mail, explaining and apologizing.

Unfortunately, though, Em didn't seem in any hurry to get home.

"Show me your room," she said, when neither of us could handle one more spoonful of disgustingness.

I hesitated. I *really* needed to write that e-mail. Plus, there was so much babyish stuff in there. "It's pretty messy," I said, hoping she'd take the hint. She didn't.

"Here it is." She showed herself down the hall and pushed my door open. It wasn't hard to find. I have this embarrassing Winnie-the-Pooh nameplate my grandma bought for me at the dollar store off one of those racks of personalized key chains and things. It was the only time I'd ever seen one that actually had my name on it—spelled right, too.

Em stepped into the room, kicking aside some piles of junk to make a path to the bed. She flopped down on my butterfly quilt and looked up. "You're kidding, right?" she said. "Eternal Crush? In New York, fourth graders listen to that." On the wall over my bed was a magazine photo of Ian Donahue, the lead singer of our favorite band, Eternal Crush. Erika and I had plasticized his lips with Scotch tape so we wouldn't wear them out from kissing him. *Our* favorite band. It made me nervous just thinking that. What if I was too late? And Erika didn't forgive me? What if there wasn't any *us* anymore?

But before I could dwell on it, I was distracted by Em, who rolled over and looked up at me disapprovingly. "Oh, that. I barely listen to Eternal Crush anymore," I said. "Only when

I'm in the mood for something corny." I silently prayed Em wouldn't notice the huge pile of Eternal Crush CDs on my dresser, or the full-sized CRUSHING ON YOU tour poster that was, thankfully, hanging on the back of the open door, facing the wall.

"Who do you listen to?" I asked.

"Ummm," she said, letting her head hang over the edge of the mattress while she pretended to think. "Punk, hip-hop, like SubSonic. . . . Not Eternal Crush."

"Oh," I said, sitting down on the bed beside her. "I like that stuff too. Especially SubSonic." The truth was I'd never heard of them before.

Em sat up and glanced around at the rest of my room. "You don't look like your family." Her eyes had landed on this framed photo on the dresser. It was of me, my mom, Bryan, and the triplets. We got it taken last year for Christmas cards. The photo-studio lady nearly had a nervous breakdown trying to get all three triplets to sit still. "Are you adopted or something?" she asked.

It wasn't the first time in my life I'd been asked that question, but it still caught me off guard. "No." I stood up and looked in my full-length mirror while I tucked some stray hairs back under the hair band/scarf. "My dad's Indian. But he's in California right now, working." I don't know why I said that, but I liked the way it sounded. Like he was some kind of important businessman who had a perfectly good reason for not being around—instead of the not-at-all-reliable, more-than-a-little-selfish person my mom says he actually is.

In case you're curious, the way the story goes is that my mom met my dad at this interfaith retreat center in Massachusetts when she was thirty-one. She was there to meditate. He was there to find God and kick his habit of smoking marijuana. None of that quite worked out for him, but he met my mom in the communal kitchen one night while they were washing dishes, and one thing led to another, I guess.

When my mom found out she was pregnant, she says she was scared but really happy. She settled down in Darling to be close to Grandma and Grandpa Button. She also contacted my dad to let him know. He said that new life was beautiful, and that he'd send money for me whenever he could—but that was about it.

My mom says he's just that kind of person. He lives life in the moment without thinking too much about other people. She says she feels sad for him that he hasn't bothered to get to know me, and that it's his loss because I'm beautiful and interesting and very, very special, etc. Twice he's written to say he was passing through our part of Ontario and would definitely visit, but he never showed up. It made my mom furious, but it wasn't the end of the world. To tell you the truth, I'm so scared of meeting him that I've never even tried writing back to the addresses on the envelopes of his cards. What if the shape of my nose reminds him of some relative he hates? What if we just have nothing to say? What if, after he *does* get to know me, he decides I'm still not worth sticking around for?

All the same, sometimes at night, if I'm feeling depressed, I'll get the ball-and-maze game he sent me down from the shelf, and do it over and over, wondering if he tried playing it before putting it in the envelope, and if he made it to the end. If he ever does end up coming, I'll show him. I've practiced so many times I can do it with my eyes closed.

"Is this your stepfather?" By now, Em had walked across the room and picked up the photo. Her hand was dangerously close to the stack of Eternal Crush CDs, but she still hadn't noticed them.

"Unfortunately," I said, tucking the last strand of hair back under my headband. "What about you? Do you have brothers or sisters? Or stepparents?"

"No," she answered simply, and set down the photo.

"Why did your parents pick Darling when you decided to move?"

She sproinged the bobble-head turtle on top of my computer screen while she answered. "My mom picked it off the map. She liked it because it was in the middle of nowhere and she figured nothing would happen here. The total opposite of New York." I tried not to take offense at her description of my hometown. It was kind of true, after all. "Like I said, we wanted a break. I was worn out from modeling. And my mom was burned out from so much acting." That made sense, even if it didn't explain the social worker. I knew Bryan was always exhausted after a day on set, and that was just for a thirty-second commercial. Since Em's mom was on soap operas, she probably used to film every single day.

"But we'll only be here a year, I think," she went on. "Then we'll go back to New York."

I gulped. Of course she wasn't staying. She was nice to me, and cool. Plus, she was a model with a famous mother. It was all too good to be true. I shouldn't have been so surprised there was a huge catch. Em noticed the look on my face.

"I said I'm going to be here a whole year," she said. "Stop looking so depressed. We have tons of time to have fun."

She went up to my mirror and started smudging her eyeliner a little with her pinkie finger, then she looked up, noticing a necklace that was hanging over the corner. It was one of those heart pendants broken in two that says "Best Friend" on it. Only, the words are stacked one on top of the other, so instead of one half saying "best" and the other saying "friend" it has half of both words. . . . Mine says $\frac{BE}{FRI}$ and Erika's says $\frac{ST}{END}$. Her mom bought it for us two Christmases ago, but we'd both decided it was too dorky to wear in seventh grade.

"I used to have one of these," Em said, fingering it idly.

I was about to ask her who had the other half when I glanced at the clock. It was 6:30—almost two full hours since Erika had run off. If I wanted to have any hope of holding on to my $\frac{ST}{END}$ I *needed* to write that e-mail, $\frac{ST}{AT}$.

"Oh my God. You never called home!" I said suddenly.

"Oh my God, relax!" Em imitated me. "Don't worry. My mom won't care. She probably hasn't even noticed I'm not home yet."

I glanced at the clock again. 6:31. "Yeah, but . . . it's getting kind of late. I should probably do some homework or something, so—"

"You're kicking me out?"

"No," I said quickly. She'd been so nice to me, giving me the green jacket and walking me home. And now, especially with Erika at Sacred Heart, seriously mad at me and potentially never planning to forgive me, I couldn't afford to lose her as a friend, too. "You can stay!" My voice sounded too eager. "My stepdad won't be home until eight. We can do our homework together." She raised her eyebrows, giving me this look that made it clear she wasn't interested in being study buddies. I took a deep breath, determined to act normal. "I mean, if you want."

"It's fine. I have stuff to do. I probably should have left ages ago, actually. Where's the phone?"

About ten minutes later, the same black car with tinted windows came to pick Em up, and she waved from the sidewalk, seeming to have forgiven me.

"See you tomorrow," she called. "And don't forget to wear lip gloss. You never know if it might be your big day for kissing floppy hair guy." I forced a smile.

The second the car drove away, I ran back to my room to see if Erika was on IM. I knew she would be. She always was that time of night, but her status must have been set to invisible. So I sat down and wrote her the long e-mail, telling her how sorry I was. Then I sent it, and waited ten minutes. When there was no response, I called her house.

"I'm sorry, Margot," her dad said. His voice sounded tired. "Erika's indisposed at the moment."

"Well, could you ask her to call me back?" I said. "Please?"

"I'll ask," he promised.

After hanging up, I wandered miserably to the kitchen. I cleaned up the stuff from the spoon game, drank a huge glass of water to get the lingering tastes out of my mouth, and went back to my room to recheck my e-mail. Nothing. But as I turned off the monitor and looked around, I couldn't help noticing that the room was full of Erika. Her Parasuco jeans were still on the floor, but that was only the beginning.

On the dresser was a stuffed platypus she bought me for my birthday in third grade. The sticker books we were obsessed with in fourth grade were shoved sideways on a shelf, right beside this chapter book series about magical horses she'd lent me, which I'd never really gotten into. The note she'd put in my pocket for School Year's Day was still sitting unfolded on the dresser. I knelt on the bed and kissed the Ian Donahue lips picture. I didn't care what kids in New York listened to. He'd always be my eternal crush.

After turning on the computer one more time, checking my e-mail and sighing, I went to microwave some eggplant bharta. It was mushy and brown, but it tasted okay. I ate it in the quiet kitchen and was just throwing the carton into the recycling bin when I saw the bag of onions sitting on the counter. I don't know what made me do it, but I grabbed three and glanced at the second hand on the clock. I threw them into the air and got a good rhythm going. I didn't look up until the first one hit the floor.

And it was while I was bent down, crawling under the kitchen table to pick it up, that I finally lost it. I'd just hit twenty seconds, blasting the all-time summer orange juggling record out of the water. Plus, I had exciting new information— Spanish onions are even easier to work with. But Erika didn't want to talk to me, and there was nobody else in the world who would even care.

15

I Share a Personal Connection with the Lead Singer of the World's Coolest Band

WHEN I WOKE UP on Tuesday morning, I found my mom in the living room. She was lying on the couch watching a yoga video while the triplets ate VTV organic oatmeal on the carpet. The oatmeal looked awful—like beige snot. My mother looked worse.

"They've been up since four thirty," she said, blinking heavy eyelids. "I don't understand. They've been sleeping so well lately."

"That's weird," I said, feeling slightly terrible. "I hope it wasn't my fault," I added. "I put them to bed a little early." Somehow this made me feel better, even though it was still a lie.

"Did your new friend end up staying to help you babysit?" my mom asked, switching off the TV and sitting up. I nodded. "That was nice of her," she said. "Speaking of friends, I haven't seen Erika since school started. How's she doing at Sacred Heart?"

"Good," I lied. "She's been busy. Tons of homework."

I turned my back and walked to the window to open the blinds so my mom wouldn't notice the sad look on my face.

The last thing I needed was for her to get all concerned and bug me about "working things out" with Erika—like I wasn't already trying. I'd checked right before going to bed, and again first thing that morning, and she still hadn't answered my e-mail, which made it clear: she was pretending I didn't exist anymore.

My mom stretched out her back before bending to pick up the oatmeal bowls. "I found a green jacket on one of the kitchen chairs this morning. Does it belong to your friend, Em?"

"Oh. That's mine. She gave it to me."

"Are you sure she cleared that with her mother first? It looks like an expensive jacket."

"It's fine," I said. "It's like nothing to her family. They're really rich. Her mom's a soap opera actress and her dad's like, a stockbroker or something." I didn't technically know if that last part was true. Actually, now that I thought about it, Em hadn't said anything about her dad at all . . . but he probably did something like that.

My mom looked surprised—and doubtful, I think. I could tell by the way she paused and looked up at me for a second before picking up the last oatmeal bowl. I couldn't exactly blame her. It wasn't like soap stars and stockbrokers were flocking to Darling, Ontario, by the dozen. "Anyway," I added, tickling Aleene, then scooping her up off the floor and flipping her upside down so she squealed like a piglet, "I have to get ready for school."

I ended up doing a near-perfect job on my hair. And I chose a plain white T-shirt, which looked good with the army jacket. The only problem was my pants. All my jeans were in the wash, so I chose a pair of black cords. They would have been normal looking, too, if they hadn't been so short. I put on a pair of black socks with them (hoping nobody would notice that they ended practically an inch above my ankles), dodged a bowl of VTV oatmeal snot my mom held out to me, and ran out the door.

I rounded the corner and was partway down Delaware when I spotted the enrichment-program girls from Colonel Darling who I'd walked behind on the first day of school. You could tell they were good friends. Just the way they were talking to each other made me miss Erika.

"Did you honestly forget?" one of them was asking.

"No, I just didn't remember," another one laughed.

"Don't worry. You can copy mine," a third said. "I owe you anyway. You've saved my butt a squillion times."

"Thanks," the girl answered, pulling her red hair back into a ponytail and fastening it with an elastic band from her wrist. They walked in silence a few steps. "Hey, did you hear about that thing yesterday, with Sarah J. and the sandwich?" My ears perked up.

"I had band at lunch, but Caroline saw the whole thing," the first one answered. "She said there was mustard all over Sarah's clothes *and* her face."

"Oh God. That could *not* have been pretty."

"Well, personally, I'm glad. I hate that girl," said the one with the red hair. "I used to be friends with Maggie Keller until Sarah brainwashed her against me last year and turned her into a clone. Now she won't even talk to me."

"Yeah," one of her friends consoled her. "But you're better off now, right?"

The girl nodded, and I felt a small burst of pride. I mean,

it was only a mustard stain, but still, I felt like I'd made some small contribution toward righting the wrongs of popularity for the little people.

"Margot!" I heard somebody call. I turned to look over my shoulder. It was Andrew, running to catch up with me. I stopped, letting the enrichment-program girls walk ahead. "Hey. What's up?"

"Not much." I spun a little in a pile of leaves.

"Not much?" he said. "I saw what happened yesterday. Everyone's talking about it."

"They are?" I answered, curious to find out what else people were saying about how Em and I had heroically and permanently rid the school yard of Sarah J. and Matt's lip slurping.

"Yeah. Amir said Sarah was glaring at you all through French class. And Mike heard that her boyfriend tried to beat you up after school."

"What? Sarah J. *always* glares at me. But nobody tried to beat me up." I raised my fists and smiled, hoping to erase the worried look from Andrew's face. I threw an incredibly wussy fake punch into his shoulder. "Anyway, did you see Sarah's boyfriend? He's four feet tall. Okay, four and a half if you count his hair. He wouldn't stand a chance." Andrew smiled weakly. The truth was, Matt could pulverize me, and we both knew it.

"Yeah, well," Andrew went on, fake punching me back. "Just be careful, okay? Amir's sister knows that guy Matt. She says he's a jerk. If you want me to walk you home after school or anything . . ." He let his words trail off. I didn't miss noticing that he couldn't seem to look me in the eyes.

"Thanks," I answered. "That's really nice of you. . . ." I ran my fingers along the fence as we came up to the school yard, then grabbed a leaf that was sticking through the chain link and studied its thread-thin veins. "But you have basketball after school most days, right? I don't want to make you miss it."

"Right." He shrugged and smiled at the same time. "But you know, still . . . if he ever bugs you."

"I'm pretty sure Em and I can handle it." I smiled a little because I liked the way that sounded: *Em and I.* What I didn't know, of course, was that my *very new* friendship was about to get *very* complicated.

"What's with your pants?" Em said first thing when I walked into class. So much for nobody noticing how short they were. But I was glad I could count on my new friend to be honest with me—at least when it came to fashion.

"They shrunk in the wash," I lied.

"Come here." She lifted my shirt up a little. "The waist is big. Just pull them down."

I grabbed the waistband and settled them as far down on my hips as they would go. They still didn't touch the tops of my shoes.

"You want to talk about who should get a room?" I heard Sarah J.'s voice before I saw her. "New York just told Hamburglar to pull her pants down," she announced. Maggie and Joyce started laughing like it was the funniest thing they'd ever heard.

"It's like a lesbian love affair over there," Maggie added, backing Sarah up. Had she really been friends with the nice red-haired enrichment-program girl last year? Now that I thought about it, Maggie *did* used to do stuff like collect the money on pizza day. She also brought doughnut holes for everyone at lunch once. It seemed crazy that someone could turn so evil so fast.

"Seriously, you want to talk about disturbing displays of sexual behavior," Sarah said, making a gagging noise.

Then again, with Sarah J. as an influence, maybe it wasn't that hard to imagine.

My cheeks were burning, but I started to take my books out of my backpack, fully prepared to ignore them, when Em spoke up. "Oh my God, Margot." She tilted her head to one side like Sarah had just done the cutest thing. "Sarah is pretty much repeating everything I said yesterday word-for-word. I think she wants to be like me."

Just then, Mr. Learner walked in and set his briefcase on the desk. "Good morning, eager young minds," he said sarcastically, clapping his hands together.

Sarah was glaring hard at Em, but Em just smiled back, giving her the finger underneath her desk. Then she turned to face the front. As for me, I gave Maggie a tight, satisfied smile before flipping open my copy of *Lord of the Flies*.

For the rest of the morning I heard people talking about the sandwich incident wherever I went. But unlike the enrichment-program girls, most people seemed to be siding with Sarah J. "I think it's so immature to throw food, not to mention wasteful. I mean, hello. People are starving in foreign countries," I heard Michelle Cobbs tell her best friend Bethany as they walked around the bend and past Sarah's locker on their way to volleyball practice.

"That new girl is wack," Ken said to Gorgeous George, motioning toward Em as she took a drink from the water fountain after math. "I heard she's like, mentally deranged."

As usual, Em had "a personal thing to take care of" when the bell rang for lunch. She left me at our lockers and disappeared down the hall, turning right before the bathrooms. I couldn't help myself. I mean, if getting called lesbian lovers, then hitting the most popular girl in school in the head with a sandwich and living to tell about it wasn't a bonding experience, I didn't know what was. . . . We were friends. There wasn't any reason for secrets between us. I followed, hiding behind a group of eighth graders when Em stopped to check her reflection in the trophy case. Then I watched as she slipped into a room and closed the door behind her. As soon as the coast was clear, I wandered over casually, stopping to tie my shoelace. The nameplate on the door read: MRS. MARTINE, STUDENT SUPPORT OFFICE. So this was Em's "personal thing." What were they talking about in there? Was she honestly mentally deranged? I decided enough was enough. She owed me an answer. And I didn't waste any time. The second she came out to the yard, I paused War of the Druids level three, looked over to make sure Andrew, Mike, and Amir were still busy doing free throws, then turned to face her.

"What do you do in the Student Support Office at lunch every day?" I asked. She stopped midway through taking her Whole Foods sandwich out of her bag. "Are you seeing the guidance counselor or something?"

"No!" She began to unwrap the cellophane angrily, and I glanced down, worried that I might end up being the one covered in mustard today if I didn't say this just right.

"I just saw you go in," I said as gently as I could. "Are you in trouble for something? You can tell me if you are. I told you about the ham."

"I'm not in trouble for anything," Em said, bunching the plastic wrap into a ball and throwing it hard at the garbage can, where it bounced off the rim. "Why would you even say that?"

"It's the reason most people see a guidance counselor, or a social worker." I added that last part, waiting to see how she'd react.

"What do you mean social worker?"

"I heard you talking to Mrs. Vandanhoover in her office," I admitted.

She took a bite of the sandwich, staring off into the distance for a while before sighing. "Okay. Fine. I did something bad at my last school. I cut class a lot. That's all. To spend time with my dad."

"Why?" I knew people cut class to go to movie theaters or malls—but not to hang out with their dads. Actually, most people our age went out of their way to avoid their parents. "I mean, don't you see him enough at home?"

"No. He's a really busy person."

"Is he a stockbroker?" I asked.

"No," she said simply.

"Oh. Well, why's he so busy?"

She sighed like I was asking too many questions. "He's an agent for musicians. So he's like, at shows all the time. And he travels a lot. He didn't even move here with us. He stayed behind in New York to work. So, not that it's any of your business," she went on, "but I go to the Student Support Office to talk to him on the phone. Mrs. Martine lets me use her desk so I can have some privacy. Okay? Are you happy now?"

I didn't get why she was so pissed off, or why she'd been trying so hard to keep it a secret. I only *wished* my dad cared

170

enough to want to talk to me on the phone every day—or even once in a while. She was lucky!

"Are you mad at me for snooping?" I asked.

"I'm not mad." She kicked at a pile of leaves. "I just don't want anyone to make a big deal about my dad." She turned to look at me.

"Why would anyone make a big deal?" Just then I noticed Andrew waving me over. Mike and Amir were crouched down in one corner of the basketball court, looking at something on the ground. It was probably an old robin's eggshell or something. There was a nest on the school roof, and sometimes they fell.

"My dad represents some big names, okay?" she said suddenly, just as I was about to stand up and go see what Andrew wanted. "Like huge. Like, SubSonic, just to name one." Okay, so I still hadn't actually listened to their music, but I had Googled them after Em mentioned liking the band the night before, and this was amazing news. All of their albums had gone platinum and their videos were topping the charts. "One sec," I mouthed to Andrew, then turned to face Em.

"I don't want *anyone* to know," Em went on seriously. "I told you we moved to Darling to get a break from the entertainment industry, right?"

I nodded. "Okay."

"So swear you won't tell anyone." She fixed me with a steady stare.

"Okay," I said again. "I swear."

And I really, really meant it. It was just that my big mouth sort of got the better of me. It happened on Wednesday morning in the yard.

I showed up a full fifteen minutes early (a new record for me), wearing the Parasuco jeans again, but this time with the ketchup-stain cami. Still, underneath Em's green jacket, you couldn't even see the stain. I looked good, which was a lucky thing since, little did I know, I was about to have my first actual conversation with the guy I'd been in love with since third grade.

"Hey," Em said, catching up to me in the yard just as I was about to walk over to see Andrew, Mike, and Amir. "You're early. Come on."

"Come where?"

"Over there." She pointed to the far end of the yard, where Ken and Gorgeous George were standing near the bike racks. Ken was balancing on some kid's banana seat while George leaned against the fence.

"No way," I said. They were popular. It wasn't like we could just walk up to them anytime we wanted to.

"How are you going to kiss him if you can't even talk to him? Seriously, come on." I didn't budge, even when she grabbed the sleeve of the green jacket and pulled. Or at least I didn't until she started shouting, "Hey, guys!" and they both turned to look at us.

"I'm going to kill you," I said under my breath, but I followed her over.

"Can we ask you something?" she said as we approached.

Ken narrowed his eyes at us, and George looked surprised, but he nodded once.

"I've seen you reading those magazines about cars," Em went on. "Margot and I have this question. We were hoping you could help us. What handles better? A Porsche Nine-eleven or a Camaro?" Ken gave us a strange look. You could tell he didn't believe we really cared, which was funny because he was right. I barely knew what a Porsche or a Camaro looked like, and the subject of cars hadn't come up once in the time Em and I had known each other. "My mom's getting her driver's license this year," Em explained, "and she's looking to buy something. She said we could help choose."

"Your mom doesn't have a driver's license?" Ken asked.

"We're from New York," Em explained. "Nobody drives there." I was learning more facts about New York by the minute.

"She probably wants to start with a Ford Pinto or a second-hand station wagon, then," Ken suggested, and they both laughed, although I had no idea why that was funny.

"Oh. Ha-ha," Em mocked them. "You haven't met my mother. She wouldn't be caught dead in a crappy car—even in this town. Anyway"—she grabbed my coat sleeve again—"let's go, Margot. These guys don't know enough to help us." That seemed to do the trick.

"Hey, hey. Hold up." Ken raised his hands. "Is that a challenge?"

Em turned. "You want to make it one?"

"The Porsche Nine-eleven comes with a six-speed manual transmission. If she's never driven before, she'll probably want an automatic. The Camaro SS looks like a sweet ride. I'd go with that."

"Regular V-six powered or SS?" Em asked.

"SS," Ken replied. "More horsepower."

"You agree?" she asked, turning toward George.

"Totally," he said. "My dad test-drove one once. He said it was nice."

"All right, then." She nodded. "Thanks." It looked like we were about to turn and go, which made me panic. This was my big chance to make an impression and I hadn't said a single word to George yet. Because what could I say? I didn't know anything about cars . . . unless you counted knowing how to jiggle the stuck seat belt buckle in our minivan to get it undone. I was an expert at that.

"Hey," I said instead, changing the subject as I motioned to the earphones hanging around George's neck. "What are you listening to?" I don't know why I said it. I didn't know the first thing about music, either . . . unless you counted Eternal Crush, which Em clearly didn't.

"SubSonic," he said.

Then the words leaped out of my mouth. "Oh my God. I *love* them. Especially their last album, *The S.U.B.*" From my Google search two nights before, I'd learned that the band was made up of two big black guys who wore sunglasses and suit jackets, and a blond girl in a push-up bra who wore a lot of eyeliner and looked mad all the time. They also had a serious thing for too much punctuation. One of the guy's names was K.wack'ed and the girl's was something like Des.ti.nee. Their old English teachers must have wanted to write directly on the screen with a red pen every time they saw them interviewed on TV.

"Yeah. They're awesome, eh?" George said . . . to me!!

Which is maybe why, in a fit of stupidity fueled by true love, I said this: "Em's dad actually knows them."

The second the sentence left my mouth, I wanted to pull it back in. Em turned to glare at me. George's mouth fell open in disbelief. Ken smirked. "Yeah, right," he said.

"Margot!" Em said in a sharp, exasperated tone. "I told you not to tell anyone that."

"Sorry!" I squeaked. But the truth was, I didn't get why it had to be such a big secret. So what if a few people knew that her dad was their agent? She could still lead a quiet life in Darling. Plus, wasn't the greater good of my love life and our reputation worth something to Em?

"What?" George said, looking between us. "Is it actually true?"

I'd already pretty much spilled it. It didn't seem like it could do any more harm. "Yeah. Em's dad is their—"

She cut me off. "Friend. My dad knows them. My whole family does. We're family friends with K.wack'ed. But we call him Shane." Family friends? Em had definitely said her dad was their agent, but there must be a reason why she was covering that up, and I knew better than to open my big blabbery mouth again.

"Shane Marlowe," George said, obviously recognizing the singer's real name. "So you actually know him?"

"Yes," Em answered.

"You're not for real," Ken said, like he still wasn't sure he believed it.

"Yeah," Em said, glaring at me again. "I *am* for real. But I don't like to tell people because they go all insane and bug me for autographs and stuff. Shane hates that. Anyway," she said, tugging at my jacket again, much harder this time, "if you guys don't mind, don't spread it around. Like I said, people go nuts." The bell rang, and she dragged me away.

I waved.

"What part of 'don't tell anybody' did you not understand,

Margot?" she hissed as soon as we were out of earshot.

"Sorry! I was just . . . trying to think of something to say to him."

"Yeah. Well. Next time, say something else." She squinted like her head was about to explode.

"Em. Honestly. I didn't think it was such a big secret. So what if your dad's their agent . . . ?"

"Shhh," she said, glaring at me. "Family friend. From now on, it's family friend."

I looked at her in confusion.

"It's bad enough that people are going to find out I know K.wack'ed. If they know my dad's their agent, do you know how many people are going to bug me for free SubSonic stuff?"

"Okay," I promised. "Family friend. But anyway, you told Ken and George not to tell . . . so I'm sure they won't."

"Right. Just like you didn't tell."

I winced. She had a point.

"Sorry," I said again. "Em, I'm so so sorry."

"Margot, be quiet," she said, rubbing at her temples. "Just please stop talking, for once, and let me think of a way to fix this."

16

I Make a New Resolution

OVER THE YEARS, my habit of saying the wrong thing at the wrong time has had different kinds of consequences . . . from not-so-serious ones (like when I was in first grade and my grandpa Button laughed the whole way home after I asked this scruffy man wearing a bandana outside the liquor store if he was a pirate) to more serious ones (like being arrested after opening my big stupid mouth and volunteering to shoplift a glazed ham), but it had never before helped to make me more cool.

"Big news," Em said, coming to join me at lunch the next day. "Can you give us a minute?" She turned to Andrew. He'd been leaning over my shoulder, coaching as I used my teleporter star to zap myself to the enchanted forest of Orr to do combat with a troll. I handed him the Nintendo.

"Sure," he said, shrugging. "I'll keep it paused, Margot." Then he went over to join Amir and Mike, who were playing one-on-one. I'll admit, I breathed a small sigh of relief as Em threw her bag down and sat beside me. She'd barely said a word to me all morning, and after my giant screwup the day before, I'd been expecting the worst.

"What's up?"

"We're having a party," she said.

"What?"

"A party. My mom's going to visit a friend out of town next Saturday morning. She won't be back until Sunday—and besides having her new friend Conrad check in on me once in the day, she's letting me stay on my own. Next Saturday night my house will be completely empty. We're having a party."

I could picture it now: us, sitting all alone at Em's house, drinking pop with the music turned up loud while we waited for nobody to show up. "No offense," I answered. "I think it sounds fun, but who would come? Besides you and me? And them?" I motioned toward Andrew and Amir, who were doing some sort of chicken dance to psych Mike out and make him miss his shot.

"Lots of people. Anyone we want. We have a rec room with built-in speakers and a pool table. And anyway, this isn't going to be just any party. It's going to be *the* party. Things are going to change around here. We're about to get noticed, Margot. In a big way."

She was obviously in denial about how popular we *weren't*. I didn't say anything, though. I was happy enough that Em was talking to me again, and I didn't want to make her mad.

"My dad's going to help us out," she went on, taking her lunch out of her bag.

"What do you mean?"

"I was just talking to him, in the Student Support Office," she said. "Now that it's out, we can't do anything to stop people from talking about how I know SubSonic, but at least we can use it to our advantage. My dad's going to send some stuff for our party."

"Like decorations?"

"No," she said, as if it should be obvious, and I shifted a little on the bench. I wasn't about to admit it, but I didn't have any experience with parties . . . other than the pin-the-tail-on-the-donkey or pizza-party-sleepover kinds. What kinds of stuff would we need? "Just stuff. I'll tell you when it's all confirmed. Don't take this personally, but I don't need you starting any more rumors." I bit my bottom lip and looked down at the pavement.

As she'd predicted, Ken and George hadn't kept their mouths shut either. By lunchtime the day before, everyone seemed to know that Em was claiming to know SubSonic, and nobody seemed to believe it.

"Right," I'd overheard Michelle Cobbs say to her friend Bethany, while I was getting my books from my locker. "My aunt lives in New York, so I'm close personal friends with K.wack'ed, too." In the reflection of my locker mirror I could see Bethany roll her eyes in agreement. "I don't know if that girl is a lesbian or not, and I don't really care," Michelle went on, "but one thing is for sure. She's a fake. You can just tell."

Unfortunately, Em's outfit choice for the day wasn't doing anything to divert attention. She was wearing baggy jeans, a tight vintage T-shirt with a picture of Bambi on it, a huge gold belt, and spike-heeled boots. It looked good, don't get me wrong—like something straight out of *CosmoGirl*—but she definitely stood out in the hallway full of hoodie sweatshirts and Converse sneakers.

"Make sure to ask your mom tonight if you can sleep over, okay?" She took a bite of her trademark Whole Foods sandwich.

"I'll see if I can find you something to wear." She glanced at my clothes—a pair of jeans, my Converse knockoffs, and a blue V-neck sweater. I knew I didn't exactly look runway-ready, but honestly, it had seemed good enough when I'd picked it out that morning. My pants were even long enough. "Also, you're probably right," she said, looking out across the yard. "We need to work on making more friends between now and then. What about those volleyball wannabes to start?"

Michelle Cobbs, Bethany, and their two friends Brayden and Cynthia were coming across the yard. "Hi, Michelle," Em called out as they got closer—as if they were already friends, which couldn't have been further from the truth. If Em hadn't been ignoring me that morning, I could have told her what Michelle had said about her being a fake, but it was too late now.

"Hi," Michelle said coolly, glancing at Em's boots.

"Oh. Do you like?" With her legs still crossed, Em swung one leg up in the air to show off the spiked heel.

"Um," Michelle answered, "they're definitely tall." Her friends snickered.

"Yeah, well, we're not all lucky enough to have your height," Em said, in an actually sweet way. "Some of us have to fake it." You could tell Michelle was taken off guard by the way she stopped chewing her gum for a second.

"Hey. What size are you?" Em asked. "Want to try them on?" She was already undoing one zipper.

"Thanks, but I don't think so," Michelle answered.

"You look like a seven. Try!" Em said, holding them up. "They're Manolo Blahniks."

Michelle didn't really react, but that definitely caught the attention of an eighth grade girl with dark curly hair who was walking past with her group of friends. "Did you just say you had Manolo Blahniks—like from *Sex and the City?*"

Em nodded.

That made Michelle pause. After all, anybody who knew anything about shoes—and even most people who didn't—knew that those were crazy expensive. "They're not that hard to walk in. I'll teach you." Em held them out to Michelle again.

"Can I try them on after you?" the eighth grade girl asked.

Em got up in her sock feet and handed the boots to Michelle.

"I can't believe I'm doing this," Michelle said, but she sat down on the bench and checked the label before pulling them on.

"Where did you get those?" the eighth grader asked.

"They're my mom's," Em said. "She's a soap opera actress, so she goes to these fancy parties all the time. Plus, she only wears heels. Even to the grocery store."

Michelle finished doing up the zippers and stood, teetering a little.

"What do you think, Margot?" Em asked.

The truth was, Michelle was usually so sporty that she looked kind of weird in such girly boots—like she was dressing up as a sexy vampire for Halloween but had forgotten the top two-thirds of her costume. Also, she was already so tall that the four-inch heels made her tower above the rest of us—but since Em seemed serious about inviting them to this party, I could tell that wasn't what I was supposed to say.

"They look hot," I said instead. "Except"—I crouched down and unzipped one boot—"you should tuck your jeans into them." I'd seen that in *CosmoGirl.* To my amazement, Michelle bent over, unzipped the second boot, and tried it. And to my even bigger amazement, it looked way better. Even Em seemed impressed.

"Try walking," Em said, holding out one arm to steady Michelle, while I took the other side.

"Oh my God, how do you do this?" Michelle asked, laughing a little as she toppled into Em.

"Heel first, then toe," Em instructed. "Small steps. It's practically the first thing you learn in modeling school. And let your hips sway when you walk. That's the whole point." Michelle tried it and got a high-pitched whistle and catcall from Ken, who was watching with George from across the yard. She ignored it, but Em didn't.

"Sorry, guys, but she's way out of your league," she shouted back.

Michelle grinned as she sat down on the bench to pull the boots off. "I think I could get used to high heels," she said, handing them back to Em. "I mean, not every day, but they're kind of cool." I couldn't tell if she felt bad for what she'd said about Em in the hallway, but at the very least, she was pretending it had never happened, which counted for something.

As the week went on, some of the other people who weren't so sure about Em also seemed to be coming around.

"Okay," George said, turning in his seat when Em and I sat down on Friday morning in English class, "if you can answer these three questions, I'll believe you: where did Shane Marlowe grow up? What was the name of his first band? And what was the first city on their second North American tour?"

Em tapped one foot in the air. She had on a pair of tan

knee-high boots that had square heels. . . . Still high, but not as treacherous as the stilettos she'd worn the day before.

"George?" She hesitated. "Your name *is* George, right?" He nodded. "Look, I have nothing to prove to you. Anyway, anybody could look up that stuff online. Either believe me or don't. I don't care."

George seemed to think about that for a second, but didn't give up. "Like, how well would you say you know them?" he pressed.

"Put it this way: they came to our house for Thanksgiving last year. Jump.U.P. ate like, all the cranberries. K.wack'ed used to come to my jazz recitals when I was little. Of course, that was before he was famous. He's got this ring with twelve yellow diamonds in the shape of a pineapple." George nodded. He obviously knew the one. "Once when he was over, it fell off and we found it between the couch cushions. My dad had to send it back to him in an armored vehicle. To thank us, the next day he sent a plasma TV." George stared at her in wonder. "Margot met him too," she said. I looked up. "At a pool party for our modeling class this summer. He stopped by. He's so nice, right?" She turned to me.

I nodded. "Yeah," I added lamely, wondering why she couldn't at least warn me in advance when she was going to drag me into these things. "And he had a really nice bathing suit."

"Now, please," Em said to George, "I didn't finish reading the homework chapter yet." George turned to face the front, and I looked over at her, a little bit baffled, but mostly impressed. I wished someone would give my family a plasma TV.

Em still hadn't told me exactly what her dad was planning

to send us for the party, but if it had anything to do with SubSonic, and if things kept going the way they had been . . . maybe it was possible. . . . Next Saturday. *Our* party. I took out my agenda, flipped ahead a week, and wrote it in. Then, while the class settled into their desks and Mr. Learner arranged his things at the front, I came up with a new School Year's resolution. After all, why would anyone settle for being normal when they could *Get noticed. In a big way?* Things were definitely starting to change.

17

I Learn How to (sort of) Legally Acquire a Swamp Water Slurpee

UNFORTUNATELY, MY newfound kind-of popularity at school didn't do a thing to change my bizarre home life.

"Hi, Margot!" Kathy Malloy—one of my mom's clients—was stepping out of the tarot reading room when I got home. "I haven't seen you in a while. How's school going?"

"Great." I smiled. For once it was true. "How was your reading?"

"The Ace of Wands came up today," she said. "It's a good sign. Your mom thinks I'm on the right track with my idea to start a feng shui landscaping and shrubbery business." She swept her hand in front of her so I could picture the words. "I'm thinking of calling it Yin Yang Yard."

I had no idea who in Darling, Ontario, was going to buy feng shui shrubs, but still, I was honestly very happy for her . . . at least until I showed her out, and my mom opened the reading room door and totally ruined my good mood.

"Oh, Margot," she said, "while you're babysitting, could you help the girls pack some toys to bring in the van for the trip to the Finklemans'?"

"We're going to the Finklemans'?"

"Yes," she said, like she was surprised I didn't know. "For the reunion tomorrow."

"That's not tomorrow!" I couldn't even hide the horror in my voice.

"It's always two weekends after Labor Day," she answered. "I reminded you yesterday."

"You didn't remind me!" I whined. "You *so* did not."

"Well," she answered apologetically, "I meant to, then. I'm reminding you now."

"What if I have plans?" I didn't, actually, unless you counted window shopping online for new pants and high-heeled boots. But I still didn't want to go.

Every year Bald Boring Bryan's family has this big reunion picnic in Blumeford. They roast an entire pig with the head still on. It makes me feel sick just thinking about it. Also, Bryan's mom, Dotty, has T-shirts or ball caps specially made for everyone, and we *have* to wear them so we don't hurt her feelings. Last year's T-shirt said "It's Fantastic Being a Finkleman." I almost died. Plus, everyone just spends the whole time going ga-ga over the triplets . . . marveling at the way they know how to clap their hands or roll a ball, like they're the first babies on earth to attempt such feats of amazingness. And nobody ever knows what to say to me besides, "How's school, Margot?"

"Plus, I have *so* much homework. I have a five-hundred-word essay due on Monday. And anyway, remember how much fun we had last year?"

Dotty had basically forced us to eat pieces of pig by saying it was a delicacy and that she'd bought it fresh from a hog farmer she went to high school with. . . . And, since we hardly ever eat meat, and also because it was disgusting, it was enough to make my mom and me both throw up in the Porta Potties.

Mom's forehead wrinkled. I held my breath, waiting for it. This would, of course, be the part where she'd tell me we had to try our best to be good sports about it, because it meant a lot to Bryan. For some reason, though, she didn't bother.

"Okay, Margot," she said. "If you really feel you'd rather stay home and do your homework, I understand. You don't have to come with us." The doorbell rang just then—my mom's next tarot client.

"Really?" I said, but I didn't actually want her to answer that, so I quickly added, "Thanks," then backed out of the room quietly. I even waited until I was safely out of her sight before doing a little victory dance.

The next morning, as Mom and Bryan got the triplets ready, I lounged around in my pajamas, window shopping online and enjoying the morning. An hour later, I heard the van pull out of the driveway. According to the clock on my computer it was only 10:15. I couldn't believe they were going already. But what I couldn't believe even more was that they hadn't said good-bye.

I muttered under my breath as I stomped to the front window to watch them pull out. Nobody even looked up or noticed me standing there. They braked just before the street while Bryan adjusted the rearview mirror, and my mom turned to say something to the triplets. She laughed, pushed a button on the radio, and they drove off.

This just went to prove my point: I wasn't part of Bryan's family. Not at all. And since the day Bryan showed up, I was barely part of my own family. No wonder Mom had been so quick to let me stay home. She didn't want me there anyway.

I sulked into the living room, where I watched an infomercial for a miraculous food dehydrator that could dehydrate anything: meat, fruit, vegetables. They even showed how you could make your own raisins out of grapes. How convenient is that? When it ended I wandered into the kitchen, ate some Organic Oaty-O's, and put the bowl in the sink. I went to the window. I looked out. I watched a bird landing on different branches. I half squashed an ant that was crawling along the windowsill, then felt terrible and tried to nurse it back to health by giving it drops of water to drink. I accidentally drowned it, then gave it a decent burial in a potted plant. I took a shower and did my ten-step hair routine. Then I bleached my mustache, holding my breath practically the entire time for the smell. When I was done, I sat on my bed, picking at one of the butterflies on my quilt and looking at the clock, waiting for the numbers to change. When I'd watched four full minutes go by, I decided this was dumb and grabbed my house keys. If there was nothing to do at home, I could at least leave, even if I wasn't exactly sure where I was going.

It was a nice day, so I walked to the park at the end of my street, thinking I'd swing on the swings. But when I got there, there were all kinds of little kids, and I would have felt too stupid, so I just kept going.

Then I thought I could go to the coffee shop. But I realized I'd only end up thinking about Erika and feeling depressed, so I kept walking. As I approached downtown Darling, the bungalows and tacky split-levels gradually gave way to nicer brick houses, until I was solidly in rich people territory. Eventually

I realized I was going in the direction of Lakeshore, where I'd probably meant to go all along. Soon I was strolling past towering stone mansions with perfect lawns and three-car garages.

The turret house was the biggest of the big—right on the corner of Lakeshore and Miles Crescent. My heart started beating a little faster as I walked up to the giant wooden door and reached for the bell. I waited for it to finish singing its elaborate doorbell song, half expecting a butler in a suit to answer, but instead it was this lady who looked about ten years younger than my mom, wearing a regular-looking white bathrobe—Em's mom, obviously. I wasn't sure what I'd been expecting—big hair, tons of makeup, and a huge tumbler full of gin, maybe?—but if I hadn't already known, I never would have guessed she was a soap star.

"Yes?" she said, as if my existence was inconveniencing her.

"Um. Hi," I answered. "I'm Em's friend. Is she here?"

"Oh." Her face got friendlier. "I thought you were a disadvantaged child selling chocolate. Come in." She stepped aside. The hallway had marble floors, stained glass lamps, and two giant arrangements of real flowers. If I had been selling chocolate (I glanced down at my dirty discount-store shoes and frayed jeans. Did I honestly look that disadvantaged?), this would have been a good place to come. They obviously had cash.

"Emily," she called up the massive, curved staircase. "You've got a friend waiting." She ran one hand lightly over her hair, then looked me up and down.

"So, you go to Emily's school?" she said. "Is she fitting in there?"

It was such a strange and direct thing to ask that I wasn't sure how to answer at first. Did she want Em to fit in, considering

I was the kind of kid who went there? "She's making friends," I said. "She's definitely got a way with people."

"Well, that's one way to put it." Em's mom smiled coolly. "Emily!" she called again.

Em came down the stairs a few seconds later. Her hair was sticking out in about twenty different directions, and she was wearing sweatpants. She looked surprised to see me. "You just dropped by?"

"Yeah," I said. "Sorry."

"No. That's cool." She shrugged. "That's so *small town*."

I shrugged back. "You never gave me your phone number."

"Oh," she said. "Right. Well." She hiked up her sweatpants, which were falling off her hips.

"Emily, those look awful. I thought I told you to throw them out," her mom said.

"They're comfortable," Em shot back, returning her mom's stern look with identical green eyes.

"Give me a sec, okay?" she said to me. Her mom turned and walked into the next room without saying good-bye, and Em ran back up the stairs, leaving me in the huge hallway alone. A minute later I heard the sound of Em's feet on the stairs. The baggy sweatpants had been replaced with dark-wash jeans and a tight black sweater. Her hair was completely styled in its usual perfectly messy way. "Let's go," she said.

"Go where?" I asked.

"Wherever that's not here."

I glanced into the other room. "Should we tell your mom we're going out?"

Em shrugged. "She'll figure it out when we're not here." She noticed the look of surprise on my face. "Oh, fine." She yelled very loudly in no particular direction: "Debbie. We're going out."

"Have fun," her mom shouted back.

Em locked the door behind her, then looked at me. "Pick a direction."

"Okay. North," I answered.

"Great," she said. "Which way is north?"

"No idea," I admitted.

"How about this way, then?" Em turned right, and we started walking.

"So," I said when we'd walked for a while, "your mom kind of looks like you."

"Ew," Em retorted.

"I mean, except that she's old."

"She's not *that* old. And she still looks good. I mean, she has no trouble getting parts. But she barely even looks like herself anymore. Half of her is made of silicone."

"Why do you call her Debbie?" I asked.

She shrugged. "She hates the word *mom*. It makes her feel frumpy."

We walked a few steps in silence.

"You have a really nice house," I said, for something to say. "I can't believe you just moved there in August and you already have it decorated. When we moved we had boxes everywhere for like, a year."

"We hired people," Em said.

"I wish we had a bigger house," I said miserably. "I wish we hired people. You should try getting a turn in the bathroom at my house. Or finding a sandwich container with a lid that fits."

"I like your house," Em said. "It's cozy and interesting."

I shrugged. That was easy for her to say. I was sure Em would change her mind about how cozy and interesting my house was if she spent even a single day living there, tripping over sticky toys and searching for two shoes that matched in the shoe pile.

We walked along in silence again. "I forgot to have breakfast," she said suddenly. "I'd kill for a swamp water Slurpee, wouldn't you?"

"I don't know," I answered. "What is it?" It didn't exactly sound like a breakfast food. But then again—I glanced at my watch—it was already 11:40, so it wasn't exactly breakfast.

"Take me to the 7-Eleven," she commanded, and so we stopped walking in whatever direction we'd been walking and went in a different direction (possibly north, but really, who knows?) toward the 7-Eleven near the high school.

When we got there, Em picked out the biggest possible Slurpee cup, which I swear was the size of the garbage can in my bedroom.

"It's important to layer." She walked back and forth past all the Slurpee spouts, stopping at each one. The cup was see-through, and at first it looked like a messy rainbow, but then the colors started to melt together, and it looked, well, brown and disgusting . . . like snow and mud and purple food coloring mixed together.

I picked up a cup and followed along behind. "This looks so gross," I said. "Are we actually going to drink it?"

"Oh, you're going to drink it," Em said. "And you're going to love it."

I made a mini gagging noise, and the 7-Eleven guy shot us a suspicious look.

"Somebody needs to chill out." Em glanced at him. She stuck her hand in her coat pocket. "Crap," she said. "Forgot my wallet. Can you pay?"

"Sure," I said, but a split second later I realized I hadn't brought any money either. Em must have seen the look of panic cross my face. I'd heard stories about people who went to restaurants and couldn't pay. They ended up washing dishes for a week. What if 7-Eleven guy made us scrape gum off the sidewalk or pick up garbage with pointy sticks in the parking lot, where everybody would see us?

"Don't worry," she said. "Wait here. I'm going to go make friends."

I watched as Em approached the cashier and did what she did so well. "Hi," she said, plunking the giant Slurpee on the counter with complete confidence. "How's it going?"

"You want me to ring that in for you?" he asked.

"Ummm . . . not yet." She cocked her head to one side and studied the candy display. "I'm looking for a really good chocolate bar. Something sweet, but not too sweet. You know. Crunchy, but with a soft center."

"There's Mr. Goodbar."

"Oh yeah?" she said, tucking a piece of hair behind her ear. "You like that one?"

"It's pretty good. Lots of peanuts. Or an Oh Henry! bar. It's really fudgy. Or Mars."

"Huh. That's a lot to think about. Come here, Margot. This guy is good. He's like a chocolate-bar genius." She said it so sincerely that if you didn't know her you could have easily missed the fact that she was making fun of him. "Plus," she whispered loudly, "he's kind of cute." I had to concentrate to keep my mouth from dropping open. 7-Eleven guy was at least fifteen. Maybe sixteen. But more important, he wasn't cute. He was oily-looking and nervous, like a gerbil with acne.

She tilted her head to read his name tag. "Hi, Jason," she said. "It's nice to meet you. And thanks a ton for the chocolate-bar advice. I'm Em. This is Margot."

I waved weakly.

And then she just started talking to him about things. Like, asking him if he was on the football team (he wasn't), and if he had a girlfriend (he didn't), and saying she bet a lot of girls came in just to talk to him. He didn't say much. Just kind of nodded.

"Anyway," she finished, "I'll give you my number." She looked down at her shoes, then glanced up quickly, like she was shy. "We're having this party next Saturday. Maybe you want to come? Bring some of your friends? It's going to be really awesome."

He pulled a cell out of his back pocket and handed it to her. She added her name and number to his contacts list. "I might be around," he said. "I'll text you if I'm free."

"Great." Em smiled, then she snatched up her Slurpee and started to pull me toward the door. She kept hold of my arm and said in a hushed, measured voice. "Look back and wave, okay?"

When we'd gotten far enough away, I almost screamed. "Okay. What was that? He's in high school! If he texts you, are you actually going to text him back?"

"Of course I'm not going to text him back," she answered, making a face. "I was getting us free Slurpees, stupid." She pulled her hand out of her pocket. "And an Oh Henry!

bar. They're really fudgy, you know."

I looked down at the cup in my hand and felt a chill go through me. "I can't believe you made me shoplift!" Visions of glazed hams were dancing in my head.

"That wasn't shoplifting." She sucked on her straw thoughtfully. "He wanted to give them to us."

"He did not." I started walking really quickly. Em didn't try to keep pace. "And anyway," I said over my shoulder, "what if his boss finds out and makes him pay for the stuff we took? He probably only makes minimum wage." I plopped onto a park bench with my illegally acquired beverage.

"Relax. Slurpees only cost a dollar thirty-three. If we'd asked, he probably would have bought them for us." Em sat down on the next bench. "Plus, it's not like we didn't pay *any-thing* for them. Jason's going to spend the rest of the month walking around thinking he's some kind of superstar because two girls wanted his number."

"But you're not actually going to text him, right?"

"I already said I'm not," she answered. "So?" She motioned toward my Slurpee.

"It's really good," I admitted. We sat in silence, slurping for a while. "I can't believe it's already Saturday afternoon," I said finally.

"Are you kidding?" Em answered. "I can't wait for Monday." She smiled, showing all her teeth. They were covered in brown sludge.

I shivered again. The sun had disappeared behind dark clouds, and I stared down Park Street in the direction of Erika's house, wondering if she was home. Not that I could stop by to hang out even if it did start pouring rain. I was the last person she'd want to see. "Anyway, we should probably go home before we get soaked." I glanced up at the darkening sky. "Plus, my mom will get all paranoid if I'm not back soon." Untrue. At that very second she was probably making a toast to the joys of family around the disgusting roast pig and wasn't giving me the slightest thought.

"All right," Em said. "Get lots of rest. And keep practicing your kissing on that poster boy. I have a feeling it's going to be a big week."

I smiled as if to say that I doubted it, then waved as we walked off in separate directions. Even though I wasn't halfway finished, I put my shoplifted Slurpee into the first garbage can I passed, pushing it underneath an old newspaper, just to be safe.

It was 10:32 p.m. when I finally heard the garage door open. I sat up in bed and switched on the light, waiting for my mom to come check on me . . . or to show me her new Finkleman T-shirt and, you know, maybe say good night, but she didn't.

Nobody did.

I could hear Bryan and my mom tiptoeing around and talking in low voices. Then, a few minutes later, their bedroom door closed.

Nice, I thought. For all my mother knew, I could have been out drinking wine with a bunch of railway hoboes; sitting on a street corner sniffing heroin; or balancing along a guard-rail, recklessly juggling knives.

She used to read my horoscope to me every morning, and tuck me in with a kiss every night before the triplets and Bald Boring Bryan took over her life. She volunteered in my

Brownie unit even though she couldn't use a glue gun to save her life, and she worried obsessively that I didn't eat enough veggies. And now she didn't even have time to say a simple good night.

The next morning, my mom acted like nothing was wrong. "Morning, Margot," she said cheerfully as I dragged myself into the kitchen for some Organic Oaty-O's.

"Cheerio," Bryan added, holding up a spoonful of Oaty-O's and winking, so I'd know he was making the lamest joke on earth. I ignored him. He was only being nice to me to impress my mom anyway. I started rummaging in the sink to find a spoon to wash. "Did you have a good day to yourself yesterday?"

"It was fine," I muttered, and turned to take my cereal back to my room.

"I'm making buckwheat pancakes for a special weekend treat," my mom said to my back. "You want some, sweetie?"

"No," I answered. Because, first of all, "sweetie"? And also, leave it to my mom to put buckwheat in pancakes and then call them a treat.

"Girls, look!" she shouted suddenly, pointing out the window with her spatula. "The bus!" The triplets broke into squeals of toddler ecstasy as Mrs. Troubleman, a Colonel Darling Elementary bus driver, pulled her school bus up in front of our kitchen window and parked it there.

"Da bus! Da bus! Da bus!" the triplets chanted, running circles around the kitchen. I don't know if you've ever seen a two-year-old near a school bus, but it's like an addiction. They can't get enough. Sometimes I think I should warn my sisters that one day that yellow bus—and everything it stands for—will be the cause of all their misery, but I know they wouldn't get it.

"Hurray. The bus!" Bryan rejoiced, picking the girls up one at a time and swinging them around. That made it official. I lived in a house full of crazy people.

"Oh, Margot," sighed my mom. "You have to stay and join us for breakfast now. How often is the school bus parked right outside our window?" She had a point. Mrs. Troubleman usually parked her bus one block over. How could I think of missing this golden opportunity? Aleene was tugging excitedly at my hand, though, so I gave in, sinking down into a kitchen chair and taking a pancake off the stack.

Big mistake. Once they had me captive, my mom and Bryan spent the whole breakfast telling me about the mini quiche they ate at the Finkleman reunion, going on and on about how flaky the crust was. "And Uncle Eddy did the most amazing magic trick with a quarter and a box, Margot," Mom added. "I wish you'd seen it." Honestly, could they have rubbed it in any more?

As soon as she'd finished eating, my mom jumped up and started washing dishes, not even bothering to ask for details about what I'd done or to bug me about finishing my homework. Instead, she and Bryan talked loudly over the triplets' chatter: could they really afford winter tires *and* dental cleanings for themselves this year? Did Aleene's latest bowel movement seem soft? Were the girls getting enough social interaction with peers, and what about the woman down the street with a two-year-old? A possible playdate? Should they confront Grandma Betty about how she secretly fed the girls Fudgee-O's? I picked at my pancake and tried to tune them out.

I was almost relieved when breakfast was over, and my mom, Bryan, and the triplets all went outside to drool over the bus. It meant the house was quiet and I could go back to my room and work on my essay for Mr. Learner.

How I Would Organize a Society Without Adults
An Essay by Margot Button

To start, let me say that I don't think living on a preteen-filled desert island would be much fun (or one big pork party). Without adults, we wouldn't have the rules and regulations we're used to—not that adults, in my experience, are always so on top of things.

If I was in charge, the first thing we'd do would be to take care of the basics, like finding fresh water and nutritious food, as well as firewood for heat. We'd also want to set up some shelters. There could be dangerous animals or disgusting insects that could come out at night, and we would want protection from those.

Next, I would get everyone together to start a system of government for making decisions. But the leaders wouldn't be picked because they're prettiest, or most athletic, or because they know how to make especially realistic farting noises with their armpits. I think, more than anything, a leader should be a nice person, and a fair person, and should be able to see past how others look. And also, they should be able to recognize what people are good at and concentrate on that instead of trying to make everyone the same.

For example, my former best friend, Erika, knows everything about wildlife and science, so she could be the island's animal expert. My friend Em is a fast thinker, which would make her good at setting traps or leading hunting expeditions. And I like decorating shows and poetry, so I could be the island's interior decorator/poet. (Okay, maybe not the most useful talents in a desert island situation, but it's something, right? And everyone's contribution should count.)

After that, the main thing we should do is try to get rescued. We could either build a boat out of fallen logs or make a signal fire and hope that somebody in a passing ship sees us. But really, what are the odds of that? More realistically, we could hope somebody has a cell phone with them and that the island is in satellite range.

In conclusion, if we made sure to take care of basic needs like food, water, and shelter; if we worked together instead of against each other; and if we used each other's strengths, we would have an excellent chance of making it through the year alive (despite how bad my hair would look without access to an outlet for a blow-dryer, but that is probably not relevant to this essay).

Not that it was going to win any Nobel prizes, but I was pretty proud of my paper. It at least beat the pork party for an intelligent way to organize a society.

And that was when I had a brilliant idea.

18

The Art of Accessorizing

I RAN MY IDEA BY EM THE next morning in English class. "Okay, so what if we call it the Anti-Pork Party?"

She smiled. "I like it." I basked in the glow of her approval. "Okay. So we've got the name. And I was thinking, my rec room can probably fit about fifty people, but it would be crowded. So let's make it *really* exclusive."

"Exactly," I agreed. "Only the people we really like." We both looked across the room at Sarah J. and shook our heads. She was too busy examining her reflection in her compact mirror to notice anyway.

"Matt's taking me to see *In the Name of Love* on Saturday," she was saying to Maggie and Joyce while she smoothed expensive-looking face cream onto her cheeks and forehead.

"Awwwwww," Maggie and Joyce cooed on cue.

"That movie looks barfarific," Ken put in, as he came down the aisle and threw his bag on his desk.

"Sorry, Ken, but you don't know the first thing about romance," Maggie answered, rolling her eyes.

"True," he answered, popping a gummi candy into his mouth and chewing thoughtfully. "But being a dude, I *do* know how dudes think. If he's taking you to that movie, Sarah, he's got motives, if you know what I mean. . . ." He raised his eyebrows in this dirty way. Maggie just smacked him.

"He's right," Em spoke up. The Group girls turned to stare at her as if they were scandalized by her nerve. She just stared back. "If you don't want people joining your conversations, don't talk so loud." She paused. "I mean, come on. Did you see the preview? No guy in his right mind would waste his time otherwise. Jake Cassidy usually has great taste in roles. But his wife left him for the guy who played Butch in that biker movie and took all his money. He must *really* need the cash." She leaned forward on her desk and squinted her eyes with the intensity of it all. "'If I could be anywhere, baby . . .'" she quoted the scene in the preview where the girl and the guy meet on a bridge in the rain.

I couldn't let her do it alone. "'. . . I'd be right here in your arms,'" I finished, making the same pained, swooning expression as the actor.

Ken started laughing. "What?" he said, turning to Sarah as she shot him a withering look. "They kind of nailed it."

Amir and Simon walked in then, looking at some kind of weird electronic radio antennae thing. "Okay. Let's ask for a second opinion from a real man," Ken suggested. "Hey, Amir! Would you go see *In the Name of Love* for the fun of it?"

Amir handed the antennae thing off to Simon, who shoved it into his bag. "No," he said, shooting me a quick nervous look as he passed by my desk. "I'm not interested in that movie."

"Okay, what if Margot wanted to go and you knew you'd get some action? You two are into each other, right?"

Amir pulled out his chair, ignoring the question. I stared straight ahead. "Yo, Amir, man. I'm talking to you," Ken pressed. "You and Margot. Dark theater. Would you do it?"

"Shut up, Ken," I said, turning to face him. "Amir's not a sleaze like you. And for your information, we're not into each other." It wasn't the first time someone had made a joke about it, though . . . just because we ate lunch together . . . just because we both had the same skin color.

"Ooooh," Ken said, like I'd just burned him, which I guess I sort of had. "What's the matter, Margot? I guess you're a model now, right? Amir-a-med's not man enough for you anymore?" He walked over and picked up Amir's arm where his bicep would be if he had one, squeezing it. I wanted to kill him. I really did.

Amir just shook him off and started to take out his notebooks. "Do you want to take your seat, please?" he said firmly.

"Take my seat, please? Wow, them's fighting words. . . ."

Throughout all of this, Em had been watching silently. Then she just turned to face the front. I didn't get it. She always had the perfect comeback. And now, when we needed one more than ever, she had nothing to say? After all, if we owed anybody, it was Amir. He was the only person in our class who'd been on my side since school started . . . the only one who interfered when Ken teased me. He, Andrew, and Mike were the only ones who'd helped to take down the lesbian posters. I looked across the aisle at Em urgently, but she pretended to be watching the door like she was waiting for someone. Thankfully, George walked in, distracting Ken by holding up the latest issue of *SportsCar Weekly*, and Mr. Learner followed close behind, putting his paperback down on his desk and clearing his throat for our attention. Before I turned to face the front, I glanced back, hoping to catch Amir's eye, but he was looking down, studying his notebook like his life depended on it.

"Okay," Em said, as we headed in the direction of her house that day after school. "I've been thinking about this . . ." I had a rare afternoon off from babysitting because my mom and Bryan had decided the triplets needed to socialize outside the family setting—even if it meant my mom did fewer tarot readings. They were at a playdate down the street with a little boy named Dante, who was always chucking Matchbox cars, screaming, and biting people. Meanwhile, Em and I were using the time to put together the guest list for the Anti-Pork Party. ". . . and I've decided," she went on as she balanced along the curb, "Ken's a definite yes."

"What?" I dropped back and balanced along behind her. I was still seething about the whole thing with Amir that morning, even though when I'd seen him at lunch, he'd acted like it was no big deal. "Haven't you noticed he's the biggest jerk alive?"

"Oh, I noticed," she answered. "But he happens to be a big *popular* jerk. And anyway, he's kind of funny." I hoped she wasn't talking about what he'd done to Amir, because, personally, I couldn't think of anything *less* funny. "You know, like the way he made all those stupid pig jokes when Mr. Learner was talking about *Lord of the Flies*."

Okay, so I wasn't a fan of pig jokes in general (having had enough of them directed at me *last June* to last a lifetime), but it *had* been pretty hilarious when Mr. Learner asked why the characters called Ralph and Piggy joined Jack's feast, and Ken had answered, "to pig out," and then later he'd made this other comment about Jack being "pigheaded," and then he'd raised his hand and pretended to have forgotten he was in English class and started his question with the word "*pork-quoi*," and basically just kept mentioning pigs so much that, eventually, Mr. Learner banned him from participating.

"I don't know . . ." I said.

"So, Ken. And your floppy hair guy, obviously," Em went on, ignoring my hesitation. "Michelle, Bethany, and the rest of the volleyball team. That girl in eighth grade who tried on my shoes after Michelle, plus her friends. And Charlie Baker's okay. Also his girlfriend. She seems cool."

"Andrew, Mike, and Amir," I added. Em stopped abruptly, and I walked right into her, knocking us both off the curb. She got back on.

"Sorry." For a second I thought she was apologizing for making us fall, but then she went on. "Don't take this the wrong way, Margot, but I don't think that's such a good idea."

"Why not?"

"How can I put this nicely?" she said, starting to balance again. She turned, looking back over her shoulder. "They're kind of like that belt."

"Huh?"

"That butterfly belt you're always wearing." I looked down. The two bottom wings of the clasp were sticking out slightly, and I tugged my shirt down over them. "It's like: even if you do everything else right . . . right jeans, right attitude, good posture, decent hair . . . but you add just one wrong accessory—or, say, one wrong friend—everyone can tell you're not the real thing."

She must have noticed the sadness in my silence. "They're nice guys, Margot. I'm not saying they aren't. You can be friends with them if you want. . . . It's not like I'd stop you. But they're just not the people *I* want to hang out with. And they don't belong at this kind of party. They'd be out of place. That's all I'm saying."

I stepped off the curb and dug my hands into my pockets as Em walked on a few steps ahead. She didn't stumble when the sidewalk curved, even though she was wearing heels again. I hated to admit it, but maybe she was right. Andrew, Mike, and Amir didn't like hanging out with tons of people or listening to loud music. They didn't dance at all—unless you counted their funky chicken routine on the basketball court. They'd probably just feel completely awkward at a party like the one Em and I were planning. Maybe it was for the best. I mean, I'd still hang out with them, obviously, just not on that one night.

"Oh, and speaking of belts," Em said, as we neared her house, "I have some clothes for you if you want. Mostly some old clothes of mine in size four. They're kind of last season in New York—but still better than what you've got here. I think they'll fit." She unlocked the door and called into the big echoey hallway. "Hi, Debbie. I'm home. I brought Margot. Remember? You met her before."

"Just a second," Debbie's voice came back. Em showed me where to hang my coat and leave my shoes, and a minute later her mom's bare feet appeared on the thickly carpeted stairs. She was dressed head to toe in some kind of gold-and-green-spandex yoga wear, her long blond hair tied up in a bouncy ponytail. A few seconds later, a blond man followed behind her, also in bare feet and spandex. He towered over Em's mom, with shoulders at least three times as wide. My mouth dropped open. It was like a Viking had entered the room. A yoga Viking. "Emily, you remember Conrad, my personal trainer. We're just doing some Pilates in the back room." The man touched her gently on the small of her back and she looked up at him and smiled. "Margaret, hello." I didn't bother correcting her, and neither did Em. "I guess you have homework to do," she said, seeming in a hurry to get rid of us. "Conrad and I will leave you to it." Em pushed past them on the stairs, and I didn't know what else to do, so I followed.

I'd always wondered what the upstairs of the turret house was like, and I was more than a little excited to get the chance to see. Em's room was at the end of the hall, and it wasn't anything like I'd expected. I guess I'd always thought a girl's bedroom in a turret would have a canopy bed and matching pink curtains—like Erika's room did. The curtains were nice, but just plain white. The walls were mossy green. There wasn't a single babyish thing in the room.

"Here," Em said. She started pulling things out of the closet and throwing them on the bed. My heart leaped up as I saw the labels fly past. Calvin Klein, TNA, Mexx. A lot of them had the sales tags still on. "This will probably fit." She picked up a shimmery gray top. "Take whatever you want." I picked up the gray top and walked to the mirror, holding it against my chest. It matched the gray in the hair scarf Em had given me exactly. "Oh, and you need some more of these." Em pulled a few extra scarves out of the closet and handed them to me. "It's going to take a few more months for your bangs to grow out, and you can't wear the same one every day. This might be good for you, too." She grabbed a bottle off the dresser and threw it onto the bed. The label on the front said Flounce Frizz Control Serum. I picked it up and turned it over in my hand, already dreaming of the magical powers it might hold. "And this." She took a wide brown braided leather belt out of the closet and passed it to me, then held out her hand like she was waiting for a tip. "The butterfly," she prompted. I undid the clasp, pulled it out of the belt loops, and handed it over. She dropped it into her trash can.

"Thanks," I said, gulping a little. Then I sat on the white down comforter to look around the room. "Did you and your mom do this yourselves?" I asked.

"Paint the walls and stuff?" Em asked. "Are you serious? Debbie doesn't do home renovations. She's too busy with other things, like her personal trainer."

"Is he . . . ?" I paused, not sure how to say it. "I mean . . . are they? Doesn't your dad mind?"

"What?" Em turned, looking confused. I'd obviously done it again. Me and my giant mouth. "Oh, you mean . . ." she said, getting it. She put on a shocked and serious expression. "No. Conrad is just her personal trainer. Are you kidding?"

I nodded, even though I was thinking of the way the yoga Viking had touched her back. It was the same way Bryan touched my mom's back absentmindedly while standing behind her, waiting to get a fork from the cutlery drawer, or while she stood in line to step onto the escalator at Walmart.

"Anyway," Em said, bouncing onto the bed beside me, "are you ready?"

"Ready for what?"

"Ready to find out why our party is going to be the party of the century. It's all confirmed." I pushed myself closer to the edge of the bed, waiting for it. I don't know what I was expecting—a live DJ her dad had paid for, maybe, or some posters autographed by SubSonic. What she came out with was way, way cooler.

"Our party is going to be the world premier of the newest SubSonic single—'Velocity.' My dad's getting us an exclusive advance copy." I must have seemed stunned. "You know. 'Velocity.' Off the new album—*SubZero*. You know about it, right?"

"Oh, totally," I said. She could tell I was lying.

"Seriously, Margot." She stood up and went to her desk, where she flipped open her laptop and pulled up a band blog. "'The December release of SubSonic's new album, *SubZero*, is being hailed as the music event of the season. Preorders for the CD are already starting to pour in, and DC Records, the band's label, expects unprecedented digital sales,'" she read, then added, "It's a big, big deal that my dad is letting us hear it first."

It was. And for some reason, it made me sad. I was envious—I guess. What must it be like to have a dad who loved you that much? Not to mention a parent who actually understood how much your social life mattered and who was willing to do something so big to help you improve it? Based on what Em had just told me, our party was about to make Sarah J.'s legendary poolside bashes seem totally lame. "A really big deal," I agreed.

"Exactly. Now"—Em grabbed a notebook and flipped it open—"let's keep working on that guest list."

After we finalized who we'd invite, we spent the next hour planning the food (chips, salsa, jelly beans, full-size chocolate bars), the playlist that would lead up to the single (starting out kind of mellow and building in intensity), and the decorations (none, because decorations are lame, but the lights would be low). It wasn't until Em's mom knocked on the door that I even noticed how late it had gotten.

"Hello." She stuck her head into the room and looked around in this calm way that was entirely different from Bald Boring Bryan's post-yogic peacefulness—less zen, more zoned out. "I brought you a snack." She pushed the door open and held out two plastic takeout cups. "Conrad went out to the juice place for smoothies." Em stood up and grabbed them, handing one to me. She took a long sip. "Thanks," she said, when her mom kept standing there watching us. I tried some too. It tasted amazing—like it was squeezed from mountain-fresh elderberries, or something.

"Mmm," I said, taking an even bigger sip. Then, worried that my frantic drinking was making me look like a starving, disadvantaged kid, I slowed down. "Thanks," I added, taking the straw out of my mouth. "This is good."

"Hear that?" Em's mother said. "Somebody likes my cooking." She laughed a little too loudly at her own joke. Em stared off at the corner like she couldn't bear to make eye contact with her embarrassing mother. I couldn't say I felt sorry for her. Debbie was stylish and sophisticated. After finishing my homework the night before, I'd watched an old clip of *Chicago Dreams* online. In the episode, Debbie's character had just been in a car accident, and even when she was in a coma, she looked put together. Plus, she actually made the time to check in on Em, which was more than I could say for my own mother lately.

"Are you staying for dinner, Margaret?" Debbie asked me. "I'm ordering Thai for Emily."

That was when I glanced at the clock. It was already 6:45. "Oh, no, thanks," I said, already making a grab for my backpack and shoving the clothes, belt, and frizz control serum into it. "I forgot. I'm supposed to be home." Even if I ran the whole way, it would be past 7:00 by the time I got there. My mother was definitely going to kill me.

When I speed-walked into the kitchen, practically panting, my mom, Bryan, and the triplets were already sitting around the table over steaming cardboard containers of VTV Thai tofu with some sort of floppy green vegetable.

"Where have you been?" Mom twirled a noodle tightly around her fork. Somehow, I was willing to bet that whatever food Em's mom was ordering—probably crispy spring rolls and mango salad from Bangkok Gardens—would be more appetizing.

Bryan tilted his head like he had a right to be mad too, but I just gave him a look. He turned back to his dinner, trying to pick up a green thing that flopped off his fork back into the container.

"You told me you'd be home in time for dinner."

"And I am," I answered, hanging my backpack over my chair and sitting down.

"Margot, if you're going to be late, you call. You know that."

"I know," I muttered. Obviously, I knew. "I just lost track of time. I thought you were going to be at a playdate anyway."

"I was. But when we got home, and you were nowhere in sight, I started to worry." She wound up another noodle. Meanwhile, Aleene started squishing soft tofu chunks in her palm, watching as they came through the cracks between her fingers like worms.

"Sorry," I said again, poking my fork into the cardboard box.

"Well, just try to keep better track of time from now on, okay, Margot?"

"Food snakes," Aleene squealed. "Look!!" Everybody, unwisely, ignored her. "Look, look," she cried, and when we still didn't pay attention, she lobbed the tofu mush directly at my mother's chest.

"Aleene," Mom exclaimed, standing up, "in our family we don't throw things." She went to the sink, where she started blotting at her shirt with a dishcloth.

While my mom's back was turned, Bryan speared the green thing again, sniffed it, then put it back down. He caught me watching and gave a little shrug of defeat. I had to agree with him on that one point. VTV had definitely outdone themselves tonight in the disgusting and unidentifiable categories. I watched as he reached for the special notebook we were supposed to use to record our observations about the food. *Vegetables overcooked*, he scribbled underneath the heading *Thai Tofu*. He slid it across to me. *Slimy*, I added. *Mysterious*. He read my entry and nodded gravely.

"Didn't I tell you?" my mom said to Bryan. She was still standing at the sink, working on the stain. "Dante was throwing toys the whole time we were over. His mother doesn't step in. And here you see the influence he's had."

"Mom?" I interrupted. I knew it was a bad time, but then, it was always a bad time in our house. "Can I sleep over at Em's house next Saturday?"

She blotted at the stain again. "I don't know, Margot, give me a second here."

"They have this really great rec room," I said. "Perfect for sleepover parties." It was true. Em had taken me down there to see it. They had the hugest plasma TV I'd ever seen—probably the one K'wack.ed had given them.

"Well." Mom dropped the dishcloth back in the sink and sighed. "I suppose you can. I don't see why not."

I bit into a chunk of tofu, washed it down with a huge gulp of soy milk, dumped the rest of my dinner into the garbage while my mom was busy washing Aleene's hands, then went to my room.

When I got there, I checked my e-mail—like I'd been doing night after night—hoping against hope that there might be an answer from Erika. And when there wasn't, I knew it was time to face the facts. Em was right. Things were changing for us at school, and maybe that meant it was time to let go of the past. After all, I couldn't force Erika to forgive me. . . . So, taking a deep breath, I looked around the room, then grabbed a big Walmart bag off my dresser and started to gather things up. First the fun-fur headbands she'd bought me in fifth grade, then some magazines she gave me in the summer, and a bracelet from this time we were obsessed with making bracelets with embroidery string. I even took down the Eternal Crush poster from the back of the door, and the babyish Winnie-the-Pooh nameplate while I was at it. I added in the bobble-head turtle, the magical horse books, kissed Ian Donahue's lips good-bye, and finally, choking back tears, dropped the $_{FRI}^{BE}$ necklace into the bag. When I was done, I tied up the top, shoved some junk aside in the closet to make space, and buried it under some old sweaters.

I sat down on my bed and looked around. With Erika's stuff gone, the room looked different. Emptier—even though it was still messy. And plainer—like the person who lived here had no story. But more grown-up, too. I knew it would never compare to Em's room, with her mossy green walls and gleaming hardwood floors, but that didn't mean I couldn't try. "Mom!" I yelled into the living room. "Do we have any empty moving boxes left?"

"In the garage," she shouted back. "Near the outdoor stuff and the bikes."

I went to the garage and pulled the stuff aside, took three flattened boxes, and got to work.

19

Fuchsia Is the New Black

CLEANED AND SORTED AND rearranged until after eleven o'clock that night. When I was done, the result wasn't exactly minimalist, but it wasn't a pigsty either. And for a budget of zero dollars, I hadn't done that badly.

The Ian Donahue lips poster over my bed had been replaced by this cool gold-and-black Japanese wrapping paper I'd found in the closet, and the butterfly quilt had been turned upside down to the plain white side—only slightly stained. I'd swapped my heavy blue curtains for some gauzy black fabric I'd used once for a cape at Halloween, tying it in the middle with a gold ribbon I'd found attached to a crumpled gift bag. My fake wood dresser looked almost respectable with its top draped in a black-and-white polka-dot scarf; plus, I'd expanded the space visually by pushing my computer desk against the far wall and shoving a bunch of floor junk under the bed. The *Decorating by Design* theme-song lady would have been proud.

And it turned out my room wasn't the only thing that got a makeover. When I arrived at school the next morning, it seemed my social life was getting an overhaul too. Everyone was talking about the slips of hot pink paper that had appeared taped to the lockers of a select few.

"It's supposed to be some kind of world premiere for Sub-Sonic," Tamara Smith, a chunky girl with glasses was telling her friend Meredith as I passed. "But only like, twenty people are invited." Neither of the girls was holding a fuchsia paper, but even if they were envious, they didn't seem especially disappointed about it—probably because they wouldn't have expected, in a million years, to be invited. It was exactly the position I would have been in only a few weeks before.

"Hey," I said, approaching Em. She handed me an invitation with a flourish. "Thanks." I took it. The background had this black-and-white faded-out photo of the band, with the lead singer wearing her trademark push-up bra and scowl.

The Anti-Pork Party
Hosted by Em Warner & Margot Button
Your chance to dance to the sounds of
SubSonic's unreleased single, "Velocity."
Extra exclusive. By invite only!
Saturday, 7 p.m. till dawn
554 Lakeshore Drive

"So?" Em said.

"It looks good," I answered.

"Do you want to do the honors?" She motioned with her head toward Ken and Gorgeous George, who were sitting on the steps, each drinking a Big Gulp–sized Coke. I looked at her uncertainly. Even dressed in the clothes Em had given me—a pair of skinny jeans with the brown belt and the silky gray top—I didn't feel that confident. Plus, I still hated Ken's guts. "Here." She put two invitations in my hand and shoved me toward the guys. "Go talk to Floppy Hair. It's no big deal. He's just a normal guy. You'll thank me for this later."

I took small slow steps, as if I were approaching two unpredictable and possibly dangerous wild apes instead of two guys my own age, which maybe wasn't a bad description for one of them, considering the way Ken was burping the alphabet directly into George's face.

"Dude, you're *so* nasty!" George was saying as he leaned away. My thoughts exactly.

"Hey," I said, hooking one thumb into my pocket. Neither of them noticed me standing there. "Hi," I said again. "Hello?"

Ken got to Z and looked up. "Button," he said. "Would you care for a serenade?"

"It's tempting," I said, my voice full of sarcasm. George kind of laughed, which gave me the courage to go on. "Anyway." I held out both invitations. "We're having a party. You might have heard."

"'Velocity'?" George said after reading the invite. "Is this for real?" His deep blue eyes were looking directly into mine, and if only my hair had suddenly gone straight and tangle-free, it would have been exactly like my fantasies. Except, of course, for the fact that Ken was staring at me too.

"Yeah, don't mess with George here when it comes to SubSonic," he warned. "You'll break his heart. Just like you've already broken mine." Ken put one hand on his chest and flopped back against the step. He was making fun of me, and I felt my cheeks go hot with rage and embarrassment.

"It's for real," I said. I could never break Gorgeous George's heart. "So, I'll see you there." I didn't say it like a question, and I didn't wait for an answer. Instead, Em-style, I spun around on one foot and walked away, leaving (I hoped) an invisible trail of intrigue behind me. Or at least I would have if I hadn't accidentally tripped over a crack in the pavement. I heard Ken snort softly, but more important, I heard this: "Hey, shut up, man." And when I looked back over my shoulder, I saw that George was still reading the invite.

Over the course of the day, the difference between the people who *did* get an invitation and those who *didn't* became kind of obvious. Everyone who *did* get one was talking about it, and everyone who *didn't* was talking about it too—it was just that they were saying totally different things. For example:

"Why would I want to listen to a CD in someone's basement when I could be out with Matt?" I overheard Sarah say to Maggie and Joyce as we did basketball practice drills in gym. "It's stupid. Plus, it's probably not even the real single."

"Exactly," Maggie agreed, dribbling the ball lazily over to Joyce and placing it in her hands instead of throwing it. Mrs. Rivera, our joke of a gym teacher, was in her office with her favorite soft rock radio station turned up loud, ignoring us. Nobody was putting much effort into the drill, except for Michelle and the volleyball girls, who were always trying to stay in shape. Even Em and I were just walking pointless circles around the gym, occasionally tossing a ball back and forth.

"I don't get why everyone's making such a big deal about this party," Maggie finished, redoing her ponytail. As she lifted her arms, her gym shirt rode up a little, revealing a roll of stomach fat. I saw Sarah J. raise her eyebrows, but I didn't think anything of it until later, in the locker room. Maggie was in the bathroom when Sarah J. whispered to Joyce: "I've said it before, but now it's serious. Maggie *really* needs to cut out the macchiatos with whipped cream."

Which, again, I didn't really think anything of until we were in French class that day. As Mr. Patachou was busy explaining the wonders of the *passé composé*, Em slid a note onto my desk.

"Pass this behind you when nobody's looking," she whispered. The note had Maggie's name on it. But as you know by now, I'm nosy. I unfolded it a little. *Sarah thinks you're fat*, it read in big loopy letters. There was no signature. Em looked over at me, grinning. I didn't exactly grin back. I mean, Maggie wasn't my number-one-all-time-favorite person, but still, the note was mean. And I'd had enough anonymous notes passed to me in my day to know how much it sucked. At the same time, I couldn't *not* pass it. Em would know.

I refolded the note along the creases, passed it back, then watched anxiously out of the corner of my eye as it made its way up the aisle beside me and over to Maggie. She opened it, frowned before glancing around the room, then quickly tucked it into her pocket.

A minute later, she raised her hand.

"Mr. Patachou? *Puis-je aller aux toilettes?*" He handed her a hall pass. She left the room and was gone a full ten minutes. But after the bell rang, I saw her hanging out at her locker with Sarah J. and Joyce, making fun of Em's eyeliner, so I guessed she'd probably survive.

* * *

As I bounded across the yard after school, I couldn't help noticing how something in the air had changed. Obviously, it was getting colder—that brisk, stick-your-nose-in-the-freezer feeling of October approaching, but that's not really what I mean.

Charlie Baker smiled as I passed him; Michelle waved. Even people like Simon Sable and Laura Inglestone, who weren't invited to the party, seemed to look at me in a new way. "Smell ya later, Button," Ken shouted from his perch on the bike rack. Well, even that wasn't so bad, compared to the things he normally said to me.

"Hey, Margot." I turned at the sound of one more voice. It was Amir, walking fast to catch up to me, his thumbs hooked under the straps of his heavy backpack. "You going home?"

"Yeah," I said, pausing.

"I'm meeting my family at the community center for Maida's ballet recital." He didn't wait for an invitation. "I'll walk with you." I glanced back into the yard to see if Ken was watching, but he and George were busy looking down at his iPod. Still, I started up the sidewalk quickly. Neither Amir or I needed more rumors going around about how we were into each other.

For a while we just walked in silence. I started counting red cars. I got up to four before he spoke. "So, you're hosting a party or something, right?" he asked suddenly. I took a deep breath. I'd kind of been dreading this moment.

"Yeah," I said. "It's just going to be a few people at Em's house, though."

"Oh. Cool, I guess." We walked in silence a little longer, then he looked straight at me. "Do you really like that girl?" he asked.

"Em? Of course I do."

"Why?"

It was such a weird question. Amir liked Andrew and Mike because they shared a passion for ketchup-flavored snacks, zombie movies, and video games. When you're a guy, it's as simple as that. But when you're a girl, it's more complicated. First, there are friends like Erika-with-a-K, who you like because you have a history that spans a million sleepover parties, and includes a thousand inside jokes, plus fourteen tons of nacho cheese eaten over the years. . . . But there are also friends like Em, who are new, exciting, and spontaneous. They take you places you never thought you'd see, like the inside of a really cool party, just as one example . . . and they can make you into something you never thought you'd be. But I knew that was all stuff a guy like Amir probably wouldn't get.

"She's nice," I said instead, pulling the sleeves of my green army jacket down over my hands.

"I don't think she's nice."

I turned to him. "You don't even know Em. How would you know if she's nice or not?"

"I just noticed. She kind of tries to keep you away from Andrew. Me and Mike, too." He picked a big stick up from under a tree and started dragging it along the ground. "Shireen had a friend like that last year. This girl Monique turned her against all her old friends, then she ended up dumping her the second she found someone else to hang out with. Girls are evil like that. They make the dragons of Elron Woods look like bunny rabbits."

Shireen was Amir's older sister. She was in tenth grade at Sterling High. I didn't know much about her except that she got a poem published in a magazine once—something that had always made me look up to her and assume she was super smart. But then again, if she'd really fallen for a friend like that, maybe she wasn't as brilliant as I'd imagined.

"Not all girls are like that," I said defensively. "And Em's *definitely* not." I probably should have stopped right there, but I didn't want him thinking such bad things about Em after she'd done so much for me. "She might even invite you to her party," I went on, unwisely. "I mean, the guest list is really full, but if she can fit three more."

"Really?" Amir looked surprised.

"Really."

He shrugged. "I don't even know who that band is anyway. SubTerrain."

"SubSonic."

"SubSomething." He ran the stick along someone's picket fence. "But that's nice of her, I guess."

"Yeah," I said. "It is."

"Andrew will be excited."

I hesitated. "He will?" I couldn't picture Andrew liking a band like SubSonic either . . . so, obviously, if he would be excited about getting invited to Em's party, there had to be another reason. "Why?" I asked.

"Just because."

We were approaching the community center now, and I could see Amir's family waiting out front. Little girls in tutus, fall jackets, and running shoes were all over the sidewalk, giggling and spinning while they waited for the doors to open. I spotted Amir's little sister, Maida, right away. She was easy to find since she was the only mini-ballerina wearing a head scarf.

All the women in Amir's family wore them. I spotted his mom and older sister, Shireen, in the crowd as well.

"Just because *why*?" I pressed. I wish now that I hadn't pushed Amir, but I guess I wanted to know how Andrew felt for sure.

"Why do you think?" He put the question back to me with a meaningful look. I didn't say anything. Thankfully, Maida ran up to us just then, coming to a jumping stop that made her tutu spring up like the petals of a rose.

"You were almost late!" she said, grabbing Amir's hand excitedly. "It's time to go in! Right now!" A few people were starting to file into the community center, but Amir's mom, older sister, brother, and father, all came over, not seeming in any rush.

"Hello, Margot," his mom said, giving me a wide smile.

"Hi." I tried to act natural, but Amir's family made me nervous, even though they were always totally nice to me. I think it was because I couldn't stop staring at their clothes— his mom's and sisters' bright head scarves, especially. It's not that I thought they were weird or anything, but I couldn't help wondering: what would it be like to have something so obvious like that, that made you so different from everyone else, but so the same as your family? Probably nice, in a way. Nobody would ever ask if you were adopted . . . not to mention the side benefit that you'd never have to worry about how bad your hair looked. . . .

"How's school going this year, huh?" Amir's mom asked me. I knew she was politely referring to the glazed ham, and hinting that I could always come talk to her if I needed to. I still had the embarrassing lavender-scented note she'd sent to school with Amir, tucked into my top drawer. Not that I ever really planned to call her.

"Good, thanks," I said quickly. "I'm sorry. I have to go." I looked off down the sidewalk. "I babysit my sisters after school."

His mother nodded, then put her hands on Maida's bouncing shoulders. "Okay then, Miss Ballerina. Let's go." Maida grinned, jumped a few more times, then started for the stairs. "Bye, Margot," Amir's mom said. "Take care. I hope we'll see you again soon." The rest of the family waved and started to follow—everyone except Amir, who was looking at me with worry.

"You're not going to tell Andrew I said any of that stuff, though, right?" he asked. "About him, you know"—he seemed too mortified to get the words out—"liking you," he finally managed.

And if I thought I'd been embarrassed talking to his mom, now my cheeks felt *really* flushed. "No," I said, looking down at the ground. Obviously, I wouldn't.

"Okay, then. I'll see you tomorrow," Amir said, turning.

"Yeah, see you," I answered.

Then he jogged up the community center steps behind his family, leaving me feeling weirdly scared and alone as I started to wind my way down the sidewalk, dodging small bouncing ballerinas. All I could think about was Andrew, and how on earth I was going to make things right.

20

I Find Myself Falling, but Not in Love . . .

THINK IT'S WEIRD HOW YOU can't choose who you love. I mean, you can choose pretty much everything else in life. Chocolate or vanilla? Walk or take the bus? Sitcoms or the shopping network? But the really important stuff, like love—it's totally out of your control. Also, it's totally confusing.

When I got to school the next morning I found Andrew sitting alone on a bench, bent over an open notebook. I knew I had to talk to him and somehow let him know I didn't think of him like that. Not really. What happened in his basement last June had been nice, but my heart belonged to Gorgeous George—especially now that things were changing for me at school, and I might actually have a chance with him. I knew Andrew would understand in the long run. He's the most understanding person I know. . . .

"Finishing your homework?" I asked, sinking down a few feet away from him, planning to start off casual and find a way into the important stuff.

"I wish." He looked up, sticking his pencil behind his ear. "My mom asked me to write a letter to my grandma in Barbados. She says it will light up her life."

I leaned over to read what he had so far.

Dear Grandma. I am fine. How are you? How is lawn bowling? I hope it's fun. I grinned. "Well, I know that would light up my life."

Andrew gave an exaggerated sigh before sitting back. "What do *you* think I should write?"

"I don't know," I said. "Tell her something exciting."

"Like what?"

"I don't know," I said again, then I took the paper, grabbed the pencil from behind his ear, erased his last two sentences, and started to read aloud as I wrote. "How about: 'Dear Grandma. How are you? I am fine'?"

"I think I already had that," he pointed out.

"Shhh. Give me a sec, okay?" I cleared my throat. "'Yesterday, my class went on a field trip to the zoo.'"

"We didn't go on a field trip."

"Like she's going to know! Now, if you don't mind . . ." I brushed some eraser bits off the paper. *Or at least we tried to go to the zoo, but an alien spacecraft landed on the highway directly in front of the bus. Everyone was very frightened.* Andrew was leaning in now, watching me write. *But not me, because, thankfully, I spent the summer learning how to lawn bowl. I picked a giant boulder up off a nearby hill and rolled it right over the spacecraft, flattening it like a buckwheat pancake and saving the entire world. All the kids yelled "STRIKE," and it was awesome. Yours truly, Andrew.* He was laughing now. *P.S.,* I added, *I just made that all up. I hope you are fine.*

"You're kind of weird, Margot Button, you know that, right?" he said, smiling.

"Yeah. But at least I'm not boring."

"No. You're definitely not boring." He reached out to take his pencil back, but my hand was still on it. Our fingers overlapped, and we both looked down and froze. A second later I let go. But it was a second too late. Sarah, Maggie, and Joyce just so happened to be walking past, and Sarah stopped and stared.

"Sorry, Andrew," she called out. "Don't get your hopes up. You must have heard by now that she's a lesbian." When I ignored her, she narrowed her eyes, adding, "And no offense, Margot, but your eyebrows still look retarded."

It was a stupid, random Sarah-J.-style insult that would have normally had me fumbling for words, but—I don't know, maybe it was thanks to Andrew's letter—my creative juices were flowing. Or maybe it was Em's influence, and I'd picked up great comebacks by osmosis. Whatever the reason, like some kind of magical brain gift, the perfect insult came to me. I only hesitated a second—because this never happens to me.

"That lesbian rumor is really old," I said. "Don't you have anything better?" She looked at me in shock, but I went on, not giving her the chance to answer. "Also, I know my eyebrows don't look great. But they're growing back. At least my nose isn't crooked. That kind of deformity is permanent."

She paused. "Is she talking to me?" Sarah asked Joyce.

I turned to Andrew and said loudly, "I can't believe I never noticed it before"—I squinted at Sarah carefully—"but it curves to the left, doesn't it? Maybe it got knocked loose when Em hit her with that sandwich."

"What is she talking about?" Sarah turned to Maggie and Joyce, who shrugged before giving me dirty looks. "You don't know what you're talking about," she said lamely, then they walked off toward the concrete ledge. But as I watched them go, I swear to God, I saw Sarah put her hand up (just quickly) to touch her nose.

"Did you really just say that to her?" Andrew asked in awe, or shock, or maybe both.

"I really just did," I said, hardly believing it myself.

"Wow," he said. "Now, that's one side of you I've never seen before. You just lawn bowled Sarah J. flat." And I smiled, because I actually had.

As if to celebrate, Andrew bent down, scooped up a pile of bright leaves, and threw them up in the air. They floated down on us like confetti, and we never did end up having that important talk. But I figured it was okay. Why ruin the great feeling? We'd talk later.

After that, I spent the whole morning feeling pretty proud of myself for the hit I'd gotten in at Sarah J. (I'd even caught her checking her nose again in her locker mirror), but as good as it had felt, it still wasn't anywhere near enough to make her cry. Em was about to take care of that, and to win our bet.

It all started when Michelle showed up to English class wearing kitten-heel boots, which she was actually doing a pretty decent job of walking in. I admit I was impressed. I'd tried on a pair of Grandma Betty's chunky beige old-lady heels once and nearly tripped through a screen door.

"Aren't those a little formal for a school day?" Sarah said, taking Michelle in as she came down the aisle. "And no offense, but they almost make you look too tall. I don't think heels are meant for everyone. Just because Emily Warner from *New York* wears them doesn't make them stylish. . . ."

Obviously, Sarah was talking loudly enough to be overheard, like always, and Em wasn't about to take that one lying down.

"Right," she said from across the room. "Because Darling, Ontario, is a fashion mecca, so Sarah would know." Michelle kind of slid into her desk, crossing her legs underneath to hide the boots. "Don't listen to her, Michelle," Em said. "Most runway models are six feet tall, minimum. You look great in heels."

"Yeah, but Michelle's not a runway model." Sarah J. looked pointedly at Michelle's solid build.

"She's probably just jealous because you're an athlete, Michelle. And she's well . . . not."

"Excuse me?" Sarah J. stood up from her desk. "If you're trying to say that I'm fat, I'm not. I haven't gained a pound since the beginning of sixth grade."

"Oh, right. Sorry. I got confused. Maggie's the one who's fat. . . . Or at least that's what you've been telling people. No offense"—Em imitated Sarah's tone exactly—"but it's not very nice to talk about your friends like that."

Maggie looked down at her desk. Sarah J. glared at Em. Em smiled. Then Gorgeous George walked in with his earphones on, oblivious to it all.

Sarah J. waited until he'd almost reached his desk before walking over. "Hi, George," she said. He slid off his earphones. "I just thought I should let you know. There's no way Margot and Em have the new SubSonic single. Think about it. Everyone is waiting to hear 'Velocity.' K.wack'ed isn't going to hand it to some seventh grader with bad roots, even if she does know him, which I doubt." She fixed Em with a steady stare. "I'm sorry to disappoint you, but she's a liar and a big fake."

George looked from one girl to the other.

Sarah continued. "If you don't want to waste your time, why don't you just ask out my cousin's friend Shawna—that girl from the pool party? You guys can double with me and Matt at the movie on Saturday."

Em stood up.

"Dude," Ken called from across the room. "Duck! You're about to get caught in a catfight."

Em ignored him, walked forward, and smiled warmly at George. "Besides the single, K.wack'ed sent a whole box of autographed promotional posters. Obviously, you don't have to come, but I hope you will. I'm only going to play the song once." She turned and walked back to her seat, leaving Sarah J. to roll her eyes while George just stood there looking stunned.

At lunch, Ken came up to ask us if he could have any leftover autographed posters after the party to sell on eBay. Michelle got Em's phone number to give to her mom, and Zoe Daniels, an eighth grader, asked if she and her friend Kiki could sleep over. It didn't seem like Sarah J.'s little outburst had changed anybody's mind about showing up, which is why I don't know if I'll ever understand why Em did what she did next.

We were in the locker room, getting ready for gym class. I'd just finished tying my shoelaces when Em's phone buzzed. She took it out of her bag and read the text before handing it to me.

```
Message from Jason Wyatt
Still having a party this weekend?
```

"Ew," Em said. "He remembered."

"What are you going to tell him?" After all, we *had* kind of invited him that day at the 7-Eleven.

"I'm going to tell him it got canceled," Em said. "But wait. He goes to Sterling High, right? First I'm going to see if he knows Sarah's boyfriend."

"Why?" I asked.

"I don't know. Why not?" She keyed in a message with lightning-fast thumbs. Honestly, Em would have been awesome at War of the Druids if she'd ever given it a chance. The phone buzzed again and I leaned in to read the display.

```
Not really, but his girlfriend's my
lab partner. Why?
```

We exchanged a look. Three texts later, we knew this: Matt's *other* girlfriend's name was Tania Baker. The 7-Eleven guy wasn't positive they were going out, but they definitely made out sometimes. Also, she hated dissecting worms. That last part wasn't especially enlightening, but the rest was absolutely shocking.

"Do you think Sarah knows?" I whispered, feeling a little sorry for her, despite everything.

"Are you texting on school property?" I jumped when I heard Sarah J.'s voice behind me. She walked by with Maggie and Joyce, who were wearing nearly identical Lululemon Athletica outfits. "Don't make me report you."

Suddenly I didn't feel that sorry for her anymore. "Of course she doesn't know," Em whispered back as The Group girls pushed through the door and walked out into the hall, talking about how much they loved each other's groove pants.

"Should we tell her?" I asked.

Em looked at me like I was crazy. "Do you think she'd believe it, coming from us?" She had a point.

I shoved my stuff into my gym cubby. "Okay, then, we just act like we never found out Matt was cheating?"

"Well, we can't do that either," Em said.

"So?" I turned to her. We were the only two people left in the locker room now. "What *do* we do?"

She seemed to think about it for a second, then marched across the room. "We kill two birds with one cell phone." By the time I caught up with her, Em's arm was already deep inside Sarah J.'s backpack. "Found it," she said, lifting out a pink phone. She flipped it open and started pressing buttons.

"What are you doing?" I whispered. She passed me Sarah's phone. A sent text message was on the display.

```
Sorry, baby. Can't make it for our
date Saturday. My face is ugly right
now so I'm hiding in my house.
```

"What?" I shrieked, closing the phone and quickly wiping it on my shirt. The last thing we needed was for Sarah to find it covered in our fingerprints.

Em took it from me, flipped it open, and deleted the message history.

"She's going to find out we sent that to Matt, and then she's going to kill us!!" I said.

"Relax," Em said, passing me the phone. "It's going to be fine. Better than fine. Matt, the scumbag cheater, doesn't get his make-out date with Sarah J., and Sarah J. gets what she deserves. Justice has been done."

Sarah's phone started vibrating just then. It scared me so badly I almost dropped it on the floor.

```
Message from MattyPoo:
We'll go another time. I got stuff
I have to do anyway. What's up with
your face?
```

Em walked over, read it, deleted the message, then dropped the phone into Sarah's bag. She glanced at the clock. "You should go, or you'll be late for class. I'll be a minute. Can you tell Mrs. Rivera I just started my period or something? I'll be there in a sec."

"I don't mind being late," I said. I didn't want to walk into the gym alone. I was too scared Sarah would see the guilty look on my face, guess what we'd done, and strangle me with a jump rope from the equipment room. "I can wait."

"Really. Go," Em insisted. "I have to take care of one more thing."

I don't know what I thought. . . . Maybe she was going to text 7-Eleven guy back to say the party was canceled, or call her dad to arrange for the SubSonic autographs. So I went. It didn't seem like a big deal.

And it wasn't until we were changing back into our clothes after gym that I started to suspect something else might be up. Sarah J. was on the other side of the locker room, touching up her makeup when the freak-out started. "Oh my God," she said to Maggie and Joyce. "My face cream smells weird. Smell this."

She held it out, and both girls sniffed obediently.

"Ew. That's nasty."

"Do you think it went bad?"

"Check the expiration date."

"It doesn't have an expiration date."

"Yes it does."

"Oh my God. Guys. My face feels weird."

"It looks okay."

"No. It feels *really* weird." Sarah ran into the bathroom. I glanced over at Em, but she was calmly tying her shoes.

"Ready to go?" she asked, and we both picked up our bags. We stopped outside the locker room for a minute to give this girl Amber directions to Em's house, and were just starting up the stairs to French class when Sarah J. came shoving her way through the crowd behind us. "Move," she was ordering. "Get out of my way! Move!" she snapped at a group of eighth graders who were talking at the bottom of the stairs. It was over-the-top pushy, even for her. "You're dead, Margot," she said. "I can't believe you did this. Just because I made fun of your ugly eyebrows this morning." My heart started beating frantically. Obviously she knew what we'd done with her cell.

But Em didn't seem at all worried. "Ignore her," she said, pulling at my sleeve.

I glanced over my shoulder at Sarah J., feeling almost bad for her. Her face was splotchy and red. At first I thought she must have been crying about her canceled date, but then I noticed that something else about her looked different.

"Oh my God," I said. "What happened to your eyebrows?"

And that was about the last thing I remembered before I was suddenly falling backward. It was the same lurching, tidal-waves-in-your-stomach feeling you get on a roller coaster, but in slow motion. I remember looking for something to grab, but there were people between me and the banister. I remember the sharp edges of the stairs scraping against my thighs; noticing that somebody's shoelace was untied. And then, next thing I knew, I was lying on the floor at the bottom of the stairs, looking straight up and listening to somebody scream.

A minute later, Em was standing over me, plus Ken and Gorgeous George and a bunch of eighth graders. And then Andrew appeared out of nowhere, squatting down beside me. And the next thing I knew after that, I was in his arms, watching the fluorescent lights of the hallway pass over my head.

21

My Mother Behaves Like a Responsible Parent

I KNOW IT'S DUMB, BUT WHEN I was younger (okay, like six months ago), I used to have daydreams where I was in a forest. Oh, okay, what have I got to lose? It was an *enchanted* forest. Go ahead: laugh. Got it out of your system now? Good.

I'd be wearing this tattered dress—because I was a poor peasant, out gathering berries or looking for pixies. That part didn't really matter. And then this werewolf, or bear, or magical lion (that part also didn't matter) suddenly leaped out and attacked me. And I passed out. And the next thing I knew, my eyes were fluttering open and this handsome prince (who looked exactly like Gorgeous George), would be brushing my straight, tangle-free hair back from my face. He'd pick me up carefully in his very strong arms and lift me onto the back of his shiny, black horse.

After that, the fantasy would usually jump to this incredible canopy bed all covered in satin blankets, where I'd be waking up. And after that it would somehow work out that the prince would kiss me and we'd fall in love. But I didn't get that far very often. I was mostly obsessed with the horse part.

I know there's feminism now, and women are strong and can take care of themselves, and it's really great. But you've got to admit, there's something romantic about being rescued by a guy with strong arms.

In theory, anyway. In real life, it wasn't romantic because, first of all, it was the wrong guy. Not to be picky, but in the fantasy the prince never smelled like BO. And then there was the fact that Manning is no enchanted forest. Oh, and they don't have satin canopy beds in the emergency room at Darling General.

I do have to admit riding in an ambulance was cool. And after they called my mom and we waited eons to get an X-ray, I got a cast—which was another thing I'd always wanted, except it was made of fiberglass and you can't get people to sign it (which is the whole point of wanting a cast in the first place). This one was shiny and blue, and itched like crazy. Also, my shinbone was broken. The doctor said it wasn't a bad break, but it felt like somebody was zapping an electric shock from my heel to my knee. Constantly. Still, even though I was in agony, and pretty zoned out on painkillers, I didn't lose sight of what was important.

"Can I still sleep over at Em's house on Saturday night?" I asked my mom as she backed the van out of a parking space at the hospital.

Her response was so annoyingly momlike: "Absolutely not, Margot. You've only got one leg, and there will be other sleepover parties."

"Actually," I corrected her, "I've got two legs."

"Margot, don't be smart with me," she answered, signaling left. She was obviously shaken up about the whole broken leg thing. "I just don't understand. Why do you think Sarah would have pushed you down the stairs on purpose?"

"Because something happened to her eyebrows."

"What happened to them?" she asked.

"I don't know, they were blotchy. I only saw them for a second."

"And what did that have to do with you?"

"Nothing, really."

My mom gave me a concerned look. "I'm going to call Mrs. Vandanhoover as soon as we get home," she said, pulling up to a stoplight and turning toward me. "I don't like the sound of the way things are going for you at school this year."

It was almost too ironic for words. It was the first time in my entire educational history that things were actually going right for me, and *now* she was stepping in?

"Mom, please don't," I said, letting my head fall back against the seat. I closed my eyes for a second and sort of mini fell asleep, jerking back to consciousness a second later. Everything outside the window was moving faster than usual and seemed sort of wavy and far away. It was probably why the pharmacist had strictly forbidden me to operate heavy machinery. Smart pharmacist. I could have done some serious damage with a bulldozer right about then. "I can totally handle this," I said. "I lawn bowl girls like Sarah now." It made perfect sense in my mind, but my mom gave me a strange look. And then I just put my head against the window and fell asleep for real. It had been a long day.

And an even longer night followed, filled with weird drug-induced dreams about talking horses doing basketball drills on roller skates. Obviously, on Thursday morning, going to school wasn't even an option. Normally I would have been happy-dancing (at least with my arms), but for once in my life I actually wanted to be there . . . so I could keep planning the party with Em.

Needless to say, I was pretty excited when she showed up right after school to tell me what I'd missed.

"I'll be in the front room doing Mrs. Scott's reading if you need anything, Margot," Mom said, hovering in the living room door after showing Em in. Grandma Betty had taken the triplets out to the park so the house would be quiet.

"All right," I answered, wishing she'd go away. I didn't like the accusing way she was looking at Em. When she'd talked on the phone with Mrs. Vandanhoover the day before, my mom had learned that there was an ongoing fight between me, Em, and Sarah J., involving a sandwich and some posters. She'd asked me for details, and I'd told her none of it was our fault, but still, Mom had made a point of saying, "I'm not too keen about that new friend of yours."

As soon as she left, Em threw the October issue of *CosmoGirl* down on the table and bounced across the couch toward me. "Does it hurt?" she asked.

"A little," I said. It was the worst pain I'd ever experienced, but I didn't want Em to think I was a wimp.

"George was asking about you." Em grinned.

Enduring the pain suddenly got easier. "He was?"

"He wanted to know if your leg was broken or just sprained. I think he was really worried."

That settled it. I should have broken my leg ages ago. "And what's everyone else saying?"

"Well, Sarah's still totally denying that she pushed you. She told Vandanhoover you fell. Which is stupid. About eight people heard her say she wanted to kill you right before."

"What happened to her eyebrows, exactly, anyway?"

"I put Nair in her face cream," Em said, her jaw set. "Nobody calls me a liar and gets away with it. Seriously, you should see her. Her whole face is broken out in a rash, plus, most of one eyebrow is missing. She looks hilarious."

I didn't say anything because I didn't want Em thinking I was going to tattle on her, but it seemed like a crazy thing to do. What if it had gotten in Sarah's eyes? She could have been blinded for life. It also seemed unfair that I was the one Sarah had attacked when I'd actually had nothing to do with the eyebrow thing.

"And did she find out what we wrote to Matt?"

"Yeah. He told her, but it's not like she can prove we sent it. Plus, now it's all true. Sarah's face is really too ugly to go to the movies." She nudged one of my sisters' sticky sippy cups over on the coffee table to make room for her feet. "So, are you coming back to school tomorrow?"

"My mom says maybe Monday."

"Well, what about the Anti-Pork Party? You'd better be there."

"I don't think I can go," I said, bracing myself for Em's anger. I was just barely holding back tears of disappointment. "My mom said no, so she's not going to drive me. And I can't exactly walk there."

"Aren't there cabs in this city?" Em asked, like it was that simple.

"Yeah."

"Well, then. Call one."

"Is it expensive?" I asked.

"I don't know. Ten dollars, maybe," she answered. "Or fifteen. Just ask them when you call." She made it sound so easy. A cab. Why hadn't I thought of that? Now all I had to do was find some money.

Just after Em left, I heard my mom at the front door finishing up with Mrs. Scott. "I still can't get over the last reading," she was saying to my mom. "Remember how the judgment card came up and I said it didn't mean anything to me? Then, the next day, bam. A jury-duty notice in my mailbox."

"Well, the cards work in mysterious ways," Mom answered, laughing.

"You don't have to tell me twice. I'm heeding the warning of that four of pentacles. I'm going home right now to tell Carl we're donating that extra furniture to the homeless shelter. It's only by giving that we can receive."

But while Mom and her cards might have been in the mood for doling out that kind of touchy-feely advice, she definitely wasn't practicing what she preached.

"Mom," I said, as soon as she walked into the living room, "I need to talk to you. Erika's birthday is coming up in three weeks, and I really want to buy her a set of juggling pins. Can I have some money? Twenty dollars or something?"

"We'll see," she said, in a way that didn't sound promising. She sat down in the wingback chair. "First, I need to talk to *you*. I'm really concerned about this feud between you, Em, and Sarah Jamieson."

"Don't be. I can handle it."

"Can you?" She glanced at my cast. "Because I'm not sure

that any of you are working through it constructively."

I sighed. "You don't understand, Mom. There's no 'working through things constructively' with Sarah Jamieson. She's a horrible person. You know that. She's been making my life miserable since first grade. Remember the time she splashed green paint all over my backpack and I came home crying? That was just the beginning. Now that I'm friends with someone cool, like Em, she can't stand it. So she pushed me down the stairs."

"Margot, I think we need to be careful about making accusations here. Sarah is saying she didn't do it. Are you certain that she pushed you?"

"Of course I'm certain. She was mad because Em and I actually started standing up for ourselves, by throwing the sandwich and things, and she hates it."

"Margot, like I said before, I'm not sure how I feel about this new friend of yours. Em seems a little erratic."

"What's that supposed to mean?"

"I'm just saying, throwing a sandwich at someone is erratic." If my mom thought making a few Dijon stains was erratic, she'd definitely be furious about the cell phone and eyebrow stuff, so I was thankful Em hadn't admitted any of it to Vandanhoover.

"It's not erratic," I said. "It's hilarious." My mom looked shocked. "It's hilarious because Sarah deserved it. You don't know how much she deserved it."

Mom just looked sad now. "I don't think anyone deserves to be treated that way."

"Oh yeah? Well, tell that to Sarah. She's the one who humiliates me, and lots of other kids, almost every day. She put up those posters, Mom, saying that me and Em are lesbian lovers."

"You know there's nothing wrong with one woman loving another woman, right, Margot?"

I groaned. She was totally missing the point. *I* wasn't the one who was being homophobic.

"Of course I know that, Mom. But we're not actually lesbians. She just put up the posters to be mean, and to try to embarrass us. Plus, it's a lot of other things. She tells me almost every day that my eyebrows look retarded. Her friends make fun of me too, and she loves it. She whispers about fat kids behind their backs, and tall kids; any kids who are different. And she acts like she's so much better than everyone else."

My mom sighed, then brightened a little. "I know, what if I call up Sarah's mother? I could invite them over for some nice herbal tea and a snack. Maybe we could talk this out. Get to the bottom of things once and for all."

"Are you crazy?" I could just picture Sarah walking through our house, staring at the Goddess of Fertility painting, the cluttered kitchen and the messy shoe pile, storing up information to use against me at school. "Don't. Don't call her mom. I swear, if you call her, I'm never talking to you again."

"I'm sorry, Margot. I have to speak with her," Mom said. "It's what any responsible parent would do."

Anger bubbled up inside me, and I struggled to push myself upright on my crutches. It was too much. "Since when are you 'any responsible parent'?" My voice was shaking. "You think you're acting like a good mother by sticking your nose in, but you're not. Just let me deal with it, okay? You don't understand the first thing about what's going on at school. Since the

triplets were born, you've been totally clueless about my life."
She just sat quietly, looking at her lap as I glared at her, hard.
"If you invite Sarah and her mother over, you're just going
to make things so much worse for me. In case you haven't
noticed," I said, my voice getting harsher by the second, "I can
take care of myself. I always do. Also, I hate herbal tea. And
right now I kind of hate *you*." She didn't look up, and then I
went down the hall, slamming my bedroom door behind me
with my crutch.

22

I Hold the Blow-Dryer of Deceit

I
F MY MOM ENDED UP CALLING Sarah J.'s mother, I didn't give her a chance to tell me about it. I stayed in my room all night and most of the next day. She even tried to bring me lunch in bed, but as soon as she left, I pushed it out into the hallway with my crutch. The chunky, mud-colored VTV mushroom soup spilled all over the tray, but I didn't even care. I left it there and closed the door.

In fact, I barely came out again until Saturday afternoon, when I heard Grandma Betty's voice and the garage door opening as my mom and Bryan headed out to Costco to stock up on diapers. (This time they wisely left the triplets behind.) By then it was almost 4:00, and I'd promised Em I'd help her set up at 6:00. That meant I only had two hours left to figure out how I was going to get there, and I only had one option.

"Grandma?" I said, hopping into the living room on my crutches, which were really, really starting to hurt my armpits, by the way. "Can I ask you a question?"

"Of course, sweetheart," she said. She was managing to knit a perfect sweater while making sure the triplets didn't hit each other, stick their fingers in the electrical sockets, or cut

246

their own hair with their safety scissors.

I balanced myself on the arm of the sofa. "Can I borrow twenty dollars? Or maybe thirty?" She looked up, and I went on quickly. "I need it to buy flowers for Mom. You know we kind of had a fight on Thursday night, right?"

"She mentioned," Grandma said, setting her knitting down.

"I just thought I should apologize, with flowers. I'll pay you back as soon as I can save up enough allowance."

Her face softened and she reached for my hand, covering it with hers while her eyes glossed over with tears. "Of course, Margot. Your mother is lucky to have a daughter like you." She leaned over and kissed my cheek with her papery lips. "No need to pay me back. I'm happy to give you the money. I'll get my purse."

I waited until she was in the kitchen, then bit my lip and looked at the floor. I hated lying to my grandma, but it wasn't like I had a choice. Everything depended on the party. I had to be there.

I spent the rest of the afternoon in my room, watching the minutes go by and the raindrops trickle down the window, worrying obsessively about how frizzy my hair was going to be. My grandma snuck in at about 5:00 with a plate of contraband nonorganic macaroni and cheese.

She said my mom and Bryan were in the living room with the girls and asked if I needed anything else before she left. "I'm okay," I told her, lying on my bed with my comforter pulled up over my clothes. "I'm just going to stay here and rest." She nodded, taking her plastic rain bonnet out of her bag and tying it over her head.

"That's a good girl," she said.

I called the taxi at exactly 5:30. They said it would be fifteen minutes, so I sat on the edge of my bed for exactly seven and a half before getting up and peeking into the hallway. Luckily, my mom was still in the living room with the triplets, playing a noisy game of Hungry Hungry Hippos. That made it simple to sneak by and open the front door without being heard. I was almost disappointed by how easy it was.

The only part that didn't go so smoothly was waiting, in the pouring rain, for the seven and a half (or so) minutes it took for the taxi to get here. I completely forgot to bring an umbrella or a raincoat, and I couldn't risk going back in. Finally, a car with black-and-yellow diamonds painted on the sides pulled up. It looked so sleek and sophisticated, for a second I couldn't believe the driver was actually going to let me into it.

"It sure is coming down," the driver shouted as he got out of the car, pulling his jacket over his head. He ran around to the passenger side to open the door for me, then put my crutches in.

"Yeah. Really coming down," I answered, trying to seem older than I was.

The black wraparound Calvin Klein top Em had given me and my baggiest jeans (the only ones that would fit over the cast) were soaked. I was shivering, even though the driver had the heat on.

"How are you doing tonight?" he asked, once we'd started moving.

"Oh, fine," I said. "Just going out. You know, for the evening." And then, because that seemed good enough, we drove the rest of the way to Lakeshore in silence. I used the time to try to flatten down my hair, even though I could tell from my reflection in the window that it was hopeless.

"Enjoy your evening," the driver said as he helped me out of the taxi in front of the turret house.

"You too," I answered. "Even though it's a wet one." He laughed like I'd said something actually interesting.

Em's doorbell sang its entire little doorbell song before she answered.

"Thank God," she said. "I thought you were never coming." She noticed my soaked shirt and disastrous hair. "You look bad."

"Thanks," I said. She stepped aside and let me in. My crutches made a squeaking noise against the marble floor. "I had to wait outside for the taxi. Can I borrow some clothes?"

"Go upstairs. Take whatever. I'll be there in a sec. I'm just putting some breakable stuff away." She went down the basement stairs, leaving me on my own to get up to her room. It took a lot of work, but I eventually managed it by sitting on the bottom step of the curved staircase, then pushing myself up on my butt, one step at a time, pulling my crutches along.

Inside Em's room I found a sweater with a wide neck, a T-shirt to go underneath, and a pair of dark-wash jeans that looked like they'd fit even with the cast. I wriggled out of my wet clothes and put them on, then sat down on Em's desk chair and flipped my head upside down to start blow-drying. And that was when I noticed the photo on the side of the dresser, facing away from the door.

It was of a white guy in a suit. He was standing in front of some kind of theater, shaking hands with a big black man with dreads who was wearing a leather jacket, a long wool scarf, huge sunglasses, and a sun visor—even though it was nighttime. I recognized him from my Google search. It was K.wack'ed. Whoever took the photo was obviously standing in the crowd, because somebody's head was blocking one corner of the shot. It would have been a pretty unspectacular photo, actually, except for one big thing: it wasn't in a frame. And it wasn't taped up, or even thumbtacked. Instead, someone had taken a steak knife and stabbed it through the suit-wearing-man's chest, straight into the dresser.

I got chills, and not just because my hair was still partly wet. Was the white guy Em's dad? Who else would it be? I squinted at the star. It was definitely K.wack'ed. You could almost make out his pineapple ring. And the man in the suit looked exactly like Em had described her father: busy, powerful, and important.

I stared at the picture in confusion. Unlike my own radish-farming father who barely seemed to have the time to scribble a few lines on a card for me a couple of times a year, Em's dad actually called her—every day—even when he was busy because of SubSonic's new album. He'd sent her an unreleased single just so she could impress her friends. But all the same, if she'd stabbed him through the chest, he must have done something really bad. . . . Maybe even worse than calling your daughter's archenemy and inviting her and her mother over for herbal tea.

"You're wearing that?" Em said. I switched off the blow-dryer and quickly flipped my head up. I hadn't even heard her coming in.

"Well, you're wearing that, right?" She had on jeans and a plain black T-shirt that fit her just right. She looked great.

"No," she said, like I was nuts. "I'm not dressed yet." Em went to the closet and started pulling things out. A short strappy dress. A ribbed, off-the-shoulder sweater with see-through parts. A super-short flared white denim skirt. She scrunched up her face, thinking hard. "Oh, I know." She dug around in the back of the closet and pulled out something tight and black that ended up being a skirt with a matching top that had a small row of sequins across the front. "Except, you can't wear tights with that cast." Em frowned, then her face lit up and she opened a drawer. "Try these." She threw a pair of leg warmers at me. "They'll fit over your cast." She grabbed a small black bag with beading on it from a hook behind the door.

Then she found some clothes for herself and left to get dressed in her mom's bathroom. I seriously had my doubts about the coolness of the leg warmers, but when I'd finished struggling into the outfit and stood up to look in the mirror, I barely recognized myself. The clothes Em had given me a few days before had been a huge improvement on my regular wardrobe, but this was a whole different level. Instead of looking skinny, I looked willowy. Instead of seeming boobless, I seemed cute and spritelike. The magical outfit even made my hair look better. It wasn't frizzy, it was voluminous. And the little beaded bag, in which I stashed my pain meds and some lip gloss, added a touch of glamour. Em paused in the doorway on her way back in. "Much better," she said, before tossing a makeup bag on the bed. "Just one more thing." She sat me down on a chair and put eyeliner on for me.

Just as she finished smudging the lines, the doorbell rang. We both glanced at the clock: 6:44. At least we didn't have to sit around agonizing over whether or not anyone was actually going to show up. "Better get that," she said with an excited smile. "Oh, and bring those down when you come." She pointed to the desk where a stack of big, glossy SubSonic posters lay waiting.

"Sure," I said.

I hopped over. The picture was of the band standing in a desolate Arctic landscape. Sparkly snowflakes were blowing around them while gleaming, futuristic metal icebergs rose up from the ground. K.wack'ed, in the middle, was wearing a leather jacket and standing with his legs spread wide. The grumpy girl singer—in nothing but tight pants and a gold push-up bra, despite the bad weather—had one hand on her hip, while the other was raised in this tough pose, like she was personally commanding the snow. The last band member was dressed in baggy striped pants that were too short for him (for some reason, it was cool when *he* did it). I picked one up and examined the autograph on it. Even if K.wack'ed used way too much punctuation, at least his penmanship was good.

I straightened the pile, set it down, and was just about to reach for some blush on Em's bed when I noticed the black ink on my fingertips. At first I thought I must have accidentally rubbed my eye makeup off, but when I gently touched the *K*, a faint impression of it came off on my finger. I flipped through the rest. My breath caught in my throat. The ink was still wet on the top five posters.

The doorbell rang again.

"Hey, what's up?" I heard Ken's voice in the hallway downstairs.

"Bring on the 'Velocity,'" George cheered.

My heart started to beat faster. What about the SubSonic

song everyone was coming to hear? Was that a fake too?

The doorbell rang yet again. I didn't have time to wonder. Glancing back to make sure the door was closed, I opened the desk drawer and found a black marker. I fixed the smudged *K*, grabbed the blow-dryer, set the temperature to low, and pointed it at the "autograph," praying that the ink would dry quickly and that there was some kind of logical explanation for all of this. But the whole time, Sarah J.'s words were ringing in my head: "I'm sorry to disappoint you, but she's a liar and a big fake."

23

We Party

"HEY," I HEARD SOMEONE say as I came out of Em's bedroom. "Down here." It was Ken, standing at the bottom of the stairs.

"Hey," I said back unenthusiastically, hoping he'd go away. After all, I was going to have to slide down the stairs on my butt—wearing a miniskirt and leg warmers.

"How's it going with the leg thing?" he asked.

"Awesome," I said, but he didn't seem to get that I was being sarcastic. I waved good-bye so he'd maybe take the hint and join Em in the basement. He didn't.

"Do you need help or something?"

"No," I said. "I'm good." I approached the stairs carefully on my crutches while trying to hold the stack of posters under my arm. I didn't even make it down one step before I started wobbling and had to grab for the railing. The posters fell, sliding over one another down the stairs. My left crutch thudded after them. "Dammit," I muttered.

"Yeah," Ken said. "I can see that you're totally good." He came up the stairs, picking up posters and kicking my crutch out of his way. "Dude, you're crippled. You should let people help you."

"I'm not crippled!" I said.

"Fine. Disabled. Call it what you want." He took my other crutch from me and threw it down the stairs, then picked up my arm and put it around his shoulder. "Ready?" I hopped down a few steps, leaning on him for support. It was weird beyond belief. This was the same guy who'd oinked at me and stuffed ham sandwiches in my bag, and who—just a week ago—would tease me any chance he got. I kept expecting him to drop me, but he didn't. "So, have you heard the single yet?" he asked.

"No," I answered. "Em wants it to be like a big reveal." Now that I said it out loud, it sounded like a lame excuse. I was the cohost. Why *hadn't* Em played me the song?

He nodded like that made perfect sense. "This is gonna be awesome," he said as we reached the bottom of the stairs. "My brother heard them live in Seattle once. He said they blew his mind."

The doorbell rang just as Ken was handing me my crutches, and I walked over to let in Zoe Daniels—one of the eighth grade girls who'd tried on Em's shoes—along with her friend Kiki Yamanashi and three guys they'd brought. "Hey," Zoe said, closing a polka-dot umbrella. "I hope we're not late. Kiki had to tell her parents she was sleeping over at my place, so her dad dropped her off there first, then we took the bus. This is Steve, Anderson, and Kosta." She pointed to the guys, who were still standing outside the door, two of them with their jackets pulled up over their heads.

"Whoa, nice place," Zoe said, kicking off her shoes into

the pile by the door, which was starting to look like the shoe pile at my place—only wetter. Kiki and the boys followed her in.

"Everyone's downstairs," I said, pointing the way. Based on the shoe count, there must have been ten people already, and more were coming up the walkway.

Charlie Baker, from our class, and his girlfriend Amber were getting out of a red car that had pulled up to the curb. "Just pick us up on your way home," Charlie shouted to the driver—probably his older brother—over the thumping bass of some really loud techno song.

I was just about to close the door when I heard somebody call my name. Cynthia and Brayden from the girls' volleyball team were running up the street, pointlessly holding a flattened and soaked cardboard box over their heads. "Margot! Wait!" Brayden shouted. "Oh my God! Even my underwear is wet. And we only came from Cynthia's place." Drenched as they were, they still looked great. All three of them had dressed up in short skirts. I was extra glad that Em had made me change.

"Cute outfit," Brayden said to me as she stepped into the front hall. Water was dripping off the end of her ponytail like a leaky faucet. She turned to wave to Claire, another volleyball girl, who'd just gotten out of a black car and was clicking up the path in high-heeled boots, wobbling a little as she tried to avoid puddles. "Woo, work it, girl!" Brayden called.

"Hey guys. Basement's down the hall," I said, sounding casual even though inside I was a nervous wreck.

"Come on, Button," Ken said, closing the door and leading the way. "It's party time."

When we reached the rec room, George, Charlie Baker,

and Amber were already settled in on the big L-shaped couch. The guys were talking about hockey, while Amber sat silently. The eighth graders were on bar stools, set up next to the actual bar with a real working sink. When Em had brought me down there on the day of the invite list it had been fully stocked with different bottles of booze, but thankfully, she'd hidden them. The room also had a dartboard, a pool table the size of my entire bedroom, and the huge plasma TV. Definitely perfect for a party. While Em was busy offering dry clothes to some of the girls, I looked around for somewhere to sit.

"Oh my God," I heard someone say. "Margot, how *are* you?" The room was dark, so it took me a minute to figure out that it was Michelle. She was perched on an extra bar stool by the wall. Her friend Bethany was beside her.

"We heard your leg is broken. We were so worried," she added. "Here, sit." She hopped off her stool. It was such a change from the way they'd both smirked at me over the Ferris wheel picture the first day of school, but I wasn't about to complain.

"Margot," Em interrupted, "did you bring the autographed posters?"

I handed her the stack that Ken had carried down for me. "Hi girls," she said to Michelle and Bethany. "I watched *Reach for the Stars* last night, Bethany. So funny. And Michelle, you're so right. I loved Tanya Angel's outfits." Clearly they'd been hanging out while I was away from school. Michelle and Bethany grinned like Em had just crowned them both Miss America or something.

Em smiled back, then went to put the "autographed" posters down on the bar. People immediately started wandering up to get copies . . . everyone but Gorgeous George, who wasn't budging from the big couch where he'd staked out a spot close to one of the surround-sound speakers.

"Em," I said, sliding off my bar stool, "can I talk to you?" She nodded. "In the bathroom?" She gave me a confused look but led me down the hall, pushing open the door to a bathroom that had a huge Jacuzzi tub in it. "Look," I said, closing the door behind us. "I'm not going to tell anyone, but I know about the posters."

"What about the posters?"

"That the autographs aren't real."

"What do you mean?" she said, her face blank.

"I touched the ink upstairs, and it was still wet. So I know your dad didn't send them from New York. I know you signed them yourself."

"Are you calling me a liar?" She glared at me.

"No," I said, even though I maybe kind of was.

"Okay, look, Margot." She pulled open the medicine cabinet and took out a compact of powder, then started patting her face angrily with the puff. "I like you. But if you can't trust me, you can call a taxi and go home. I'm sick of people calling me a liar. I'd expect it from Sarah J., but not from you."

"But, Em, the ink was *wet*."

"Well, yeah," she said, like it was obvious. She snapped the compact shut. "Do you know anything about celebrities, Margot?" I knew that they had a lot of money. I knew they were better looking than regular people. "They're busy. Okay? Especially when he's about to release a new album and go on tour, K.wack'ed has tons to do. Do you think he actually has time to sign autographs?" She didn't wait for me to answer.

"He doesn't. So my dad sent me the posters, which, by the way, haven't even been released in stores yet, and I took care of the rest. So what? Most celebrity autographs are forged anyway. Get over it. Now, if you don't mind. I need to make sure nobody spills stuff on the sofa." She pushed past me and opened the door.

"Em. Wait," I said. She turned. "Sorry. I—I didn't know that. I don't think you're a liar."

"Whatever." She was already walking back to the rec room. I felt like an idiot. What had I been thinking? That the members of SubSonic were just sitting at home, dying to sign autographs for a bunch of seventh graders? It made sense that the signatures were fake. Still, it made me nervous. If the kids outside found out, they wouldn't be as understanding. And I couldn't shake a feeling of dread about the SubSonic song, even though I wanted so badly to believe in Em.

For the first part of the party she sat with the guys, barely looking in my direction. Meanwhile, I listened to the volleyball team gossip about the Cownie Hill Hyenas. How bad their serving technique was and how ugly their uniforms were. ("I don't even know what you'd call that color. Greige?")

I nodded and smiled and made agreeing noises in all the right places, but honestly, I was bored. I was still used to sleepover parties with Erika, where we watched a movie, played a board game, or put on face masks. This party was more like the standing-around-chatting potluck parties my mom used to drag me to—only without the adults or the hummus platter . . . and with way louder music. Now that Em had turned up the volume on the stereo, it was almost impossible to talk.

"Hey, Margot?" Michelle was shouting, but I could barely

hear her. "Do you want to go milk a cow?" Or at least I thought that was what she said.

"Huh?" I turned, and as I did, a bolt of pain shot through my leg, making me wince.

"Oh my God. Are you okay?" Michelle shouted, much louder this time. "Do you want me to get you something?" I looked at the clock. It *had* been four hours since I'd taken my last painkiller. And I was supposed to take them every two.

"Actually," I yelled back, "if you could get my bag." She returned about twenty seconds later with the little beaded purse Em had given me. I took out the prescription bottle, opened a can of ginger ale, and popped two pills into my mouth.

"I love your top," Zoe screamed into my ear, as she joined our group.

"Yeah, great skirt too, Margot," Kiki shouted in my other ear. I couldn't believe she actually knew my name. I was about to tell her that I liked her skirt too, but just then, Em turned the music down.

"Okay, guys. The moment has arrived." She held up the burned CD and a hush spread through the room. "As you know, this is an unreleased single off the new album *SubZero*. K.wack'ed is risking a lot by letting us have this, so don't tell anyone you heard it here, and don't ask me to burn you a copy because it's not happening. Enjoy." Em slid it into the player and turned the volume up as high as it would go. I kept my eyes on George, who was already leaning forward on the sofa to prepare himself for the optimum listening experience.

He was their biggest fan, after all. If the single was a fake, he was going to know it from the first note. The party, and any popularity we'd gained, would be over before we could blink. Em hit PLAY.

The song started with crackling noises, like someone was tuning an old-fashioned radio, then it moved into a warbly electric guitar solo. I held my breath, only letting it out when a man's voice started repeating in a robot-like refrain. "Vel-o-ci-ty. Vel-o-ci-ty. Ter-mi-nal vel-o-ci-ty. You will get a load of me when I reach my vel-o-ci-ty." The drums and bass kicked in, heavy and loud. George had his eyes closed. His head was bobbing to the deafening beat. Relief flooded through me.

Next, cranky bra-woman started singing/rapping, all ultra-tough: "They tried to bring me down. But just look at me now. I got the heat, I'm gaining speed, I'm a gonna rule this town."

The eighth grade girls got up to dance, doing these crazy rubber band body waves and lightning-fast hip shakes—and I closed my eyes, feeling the beat pulse through me and believing, just for a few seconds, that I was invincible too. When it ended, Em switched off the CD player and there was silence in the room before everyone broke into cheers.

"That's what I'm talking about!" George shouted, pumping his fist in the air.

"That was so good. Soooooo good," Zoe kept saying.

I found Em near the bar a few minutes later. She was perched on a stool while Charlie Baker, his girlfriend, and the eighth grade girls crowded around her, telling her how awesome the song was and asking questions about how many times she'd seen them live (she'd lost count), and if she was invited to the CD launch party (her dad was trying to get her on the guest list). When the crowd finally cleared and I could get her alone for a minute, I walked up.

"Hey, Em," I said, wobbling on my crutches. The pain-killers were definitely starting to kick in.

"Hey." Her tone was pretty cold.

"Listen, I'm *really* sorry I doubted you. The song was amazing."

"I know," she said, still not seeming to forgive me. In fact, she was barely even making eye contact with me. Instead, she was looking over my shoulder toward the stairs.

"So? Do you forgive me? Please?"

"Shut up, Margot," she said quietly, still not looking at me. My heart sank.

"Isn't there *anything* I can do?"

"You can stop talking," she said again, then motioned with her head. "We have a problem." I turned, and there, at the bottom of the stairs, was Sarah J.'s ninth grade boyfriend, Matt, dressed in a black leather coat that was glistening with rain. His hair looked even taller than before. And if I thought he seemed threatening, he was nothing compared to what stood behind him—one big East Asian guy in a wet red sweatshirt and an even bigger white guy with a shaved head.

"Hey. We heard there was a party," Matt said, all casual-like. Everyone was looking at them. Someone turned the music down.

Em stood up. "By invite only." She put her hands on her hips. "Who let you in?"

"The door was unlocked," Matt answered.

"You have a thing for trespassing, don't you? You should leave."

"Or else what? You're going to throw jelly beans at me?"

Matt smiled, taking a handful from one of the bowls we'd set out. The guys behind him laughed. The one with the shaved head flopped down on the sofa like he owned the place.

Em took a step forward. "Hey, hey," Matt said. "Chill. We're not staying long. We just want to hear that SubSonic single you claim to have." Matt walked over and joined his friend on the couch. "And also, I think you should tell me you're sorry about what you did to my girlfriend."

"I didn't do anything to your girlfriend. But your girlfriend broke my best friend's leg . . . so if anybody should be apologizing . . ." As terrified as I was, I still couldn't help doing a small happy-dance on the inside. *Best friend?!* "And sorry," Em went on, "but you already missed the premiere of the single." As she said this, Em grabbed a CD off the shelf behind her and held it up. "If you'd had an invitation, which you don't, you would have known you were supposed to be here at seven." She held the disk tightly against her stomach.

"Well, why don't you just play it again?" Matt suggested, putting his feet up on the coffee table to make it clear he wasn't going anywhere. The big East Asian guy stuck one hand out and leaned against the wall near the stairs, blocking the exit to make the same point. "Or better yet, give it to me. I'll listen to it at home," Matt added. Em stepped forward again so that she was directly in front of me. At first I thought it was sweet—like she was protecting me, her broken-legged best friend—but then she extended her arm, straight back . . . so quickly that nobody saw. I felt something cold and sharp touch my hand—the edge of a CD, *the real* CD. I took it, slipping my hand awkwardly behind my crutch and quickly shoving the disk down the back of my super-tight elasticized black skirt.

"Not happening," Em said, making a show of putting the fake CD behind her back.

Matt got up off the sofa and started walking toward her. "Listen, just give it to me, and then we'll leave. No problems." Ken, who'd been standing on the sidelines, stepped forward now, putting himself between Em and Matt.

"Just take off, man. Nobody wants you here."

"Like I said, I'll take off once she gives me the CD. What's the big deal anyway? She can burn herself another copy."

"This is an unreleased single," Em said, peering around Ken. "Nobody's going anywhere with it."

"Come on. Let's just make this easy, okay? Give me the CD." Matt lunged forward to get past Ken, but before he could reach Em, she'd darted around the other side and hurdled over the smaller sofa, knocking it down as she went. The big guy blocking the stairs made a grab for her, but she faked a left, then slipped around the right, dashing up the basement stairs. Matt chased after her, tripping on Ken's outstretched foot and crashing into the coffee table, spilling drinks everywhere. "Get her!" he shouted from the floor, and the two high school guys started after Em. Ken was right behind them . . . and Charlie Baker, Steve, Anderson, and most of the girls' volleyball team weren't far behind. I watched them go, knowing I couldn't follow on my crutches anyway. . . . Plus, I had bigger things to worry about. Em had trusted me with the most important job of all—keeping the SubSonic single safe. I couldn't let her down. And I could only think of one place where Matt and his goons wouldn't be able to get to it. I walked quickly down the hall—the CD pressing a cold circle against my back—and pushed open the door to the bathroom with my crutch. I flipped on the light.

"Hey!" I froze. There, washing his hands at the sink, was Gorgeous George.

"Sorry!" I squeaked, thankful at least that that was all I'd caught him doing. I came in and shut the door, locking it behind me. I didn't have time to explain. "You had the light off!"

He shrugged. "Couldn't find the switch." Then he made a move to get around me to the door. "Do you mind?"

"Yes," I said. "No. I mean, you can't go out there right now." I teetered on my crutches and nearly fell into the wall. George caught my arm and steadied me. I winced as my cast touched the floor. My leg was still killing me. "Sarah's boyfriend Matt is here with two of his friends. They're trying to get the SubSonic CD from Em, but she slipped it to me. I have to hide it in here. It's the only way!" I finished breathlessly, reaching around and pulling the CD basically out of my underpants. He stared at it, then at me. "So you have to stay in here," I explained. "To help me protect it. If this single falls into Matt's hands and gets leaked, do you know what it would do to K.wack'ed's career?" I didn't actually know if it would make any real difference, but it sounded urgent, and it worked.

"All right." George nodded. He walked around me and hopped into the Jacuzzi, where he stretched out his legs and reached his hands up behind his head. "If we're staying a while, I might as well get comfortable," he explained when I looked at him.

Suddenly, the hugeness of the situation hit me. I was alone, in a bathroom, with Gorgeous George. And not only that, he was in a Jacuzzi. With his clothes on, but still! For something to do, I opened the little purse Em had given me and took out my painkillers. I turned on the tap, cupped my hands underneath the water, and took two more. After all, my leg was really hurting, and I'd accidentally missed a dose earlier. I probably needed to catch up.

When I was done, I walked over, propped my crutches against the wall, and sat down on the edge of the Jacuzzi with my back to George. You could have cut the awkwardness with a knife. I was thankful that someone in the rec room had turned the music back up. The thumping beat gave me something to focus on.

"So. That song was awesome, eh?" I said finally.

"It rocked," he answered. "I wish I could hear it again."

"I know," I said, letting my head fall to one side against the tile wall. The cool ceramic felt nice on my cheek. "Me too."

We sat without talking for a minute—him, marveling at the incredibleness of the "Velocity" song; me, marveling at the incredibleness of sitting beside him. I closed my eyes. Overhead, we could hear crashing footsteps, then a thud, like more furniture tipping over.

"Did you see any of Shane Marlowe's tattoos when you met him?" George asked, out of nowhere.

"Huh? Tattoos?" I opened my eyes and blinked a few times to focus them.

"Like, the rabbit or the cobra?" I had no idea what he was talking about. And for some reason, when he said cobra, I heard korma, which is this Indian curry dish my mom used to make sometimes (in our pre-VTV days) when she was trying to honor my heritage. I don't really like it, though. Too spicy.

"He has a tattoo of korma? Who?" I asked.

"A cobra," George corrected. "Shane Marlowe . . . K.wack'ed."

"Oh!" I said, much too suddenly, remembering that, apparently, I was supposed to have met him once at an amazingly cool party. I started laughing. "Right. Duh. No. He was wearing long sleeves that day."

"The cobra tattoo is on his ankle."

"And pants. Obviously. It wasn't a naked party."

"Oh. Just, I thought you said he was wearing a bathing suit. So I thought maybe . . ."

"Right. Well. Yeah. But he was mostly in the water. And then he got dressed and came inside. It was raining. My hair looked *so* bad. But then it always looks bad." As soon as I said it, I started kicking myself internally. I hadn't even *been* at Em's modeling pool party. And since it was a huge lie anyway, I might as well have said that my hair looked amazing.

"I like your hair," he said. My heart almost stopped beating. I turned to look at him over my shoulder.

"Really?"

"Yeah. It's big." He closed his eyes and lay back against the headrest of the Jacuzzi, then took a deep breath like he was trying to inhale the moment. I watched him with a whole new level of adoration. All of a sudden I could see it so clearly. He liked me. I knew he did. I mean, there was nobody else there— just the two of us. He didn't *need* to tell me that he liked my big hair. There was no reason to lie to each other.

He opened his eyes, then flipped his hair, dispersing the ocean air smell of his shampoo. It was like breathing in a waft of pure dreaminess. I couldn't help myself. Before I knew what I was doing, I'd turned all the way around and reached into the hot tub to brush one of the stray strands back from his face. My fingers slid through so easily, I'd swear his hair was made of pure, spring-fed water.

"I like your hair too," I said. He turned to look at me. Our eyes locked, and suddenly we were connecting on a whole new level. I could just feel it. So I opened up my heart to him.

"Um—" he started to say, but I cut him off.

"I think you're gorgeous," I said, before the moment could slip away. "I think you're so cool."

"Umm. Okay." He narrowed his eyes at me, like I was mysterious, like he couldn't quite figure me out. "You're . . . pretty cool too. I guess."

"There was this time in third grade when we went on a field trip to the arena to skate. I kept falling down. And you came up to me and helped me up off the ice. You were wearing black mittens. Do you remember? With pictures of hockey sticks on them."

"Um. Not exactly," he said. "Third grade was a while ago."

"I know," I said. "But I've just always wanted you to know— that meant a lot to me."

There was a knock on the door and we both looked up.

"Somebody has to pee," I said seriously. "We should let them in. But I'm really glad we talked like this." I handed him the CD. "Stash it between those towels, okay?" He reached up to the shelf behind him and slid the disk in. Meanwhile, I silently congratulated myself for playing it so cool. After all, I didn't want to freak him out. Now that we'd established that we liked each other, there'd be plenty of time to tell him exactly how I felt about him. Plus, the CD would be safe in there.

When I stood up on my crutches, the world went black for just a second, but I only swayed slightly, taking a deep breath to steady myself, then I unlocked the door. "Oh, hi, Brayden." I smiled at the star setter of the girls' volleyball team. She looked over my shoulder at George, who was just climbing out of the Jacuzzi tub. "You can pee now if you want. We're done." Then I walked out to the L-shaped couch and lay my head against a cushion.

Before long, Em, Ken, the eighth grade guys, and the volleyball girls came back downstairs, telling the story of what had happened.

"Matt was so pissed," Em said, recounting how she'd eventually let him corner her in her mother's walk-in closet and wrestle a burned copy of a *Soothing Sounds of the Ocean* meditation CD from her hands.

"And we were all outside, just pounding on the closet door," Ken said.

"Seriously, I thought he might hurt you or something," Michelle added.

"But then, like a minute later he walks out and he's all like 'Uh, you guys. Let's bounce.'"

"What did you say to him?" Kiki asked, incredulous.

"I just let him know he didn't want to mess with me," Em answered, all mysterious, then she met my eyes from across the room and smiled, and I had a feeling I knew exactly what she'd said. I laughed and made a mental note to suggest we stop by the 7-Eleven soon and buy Jason-the-gerbil a swamp water Slurpee to thank him for the dirt on Matt's *other* girlfriend.

"Em Warner, you're the queen of cool," I said, letting my head fall back against the pillow. A few people laughed, then someone turned the music up even louder, and the party got back to normal. I remember a chocolate-bar-eating contest between the eighth grade guys . . . then Charlie Baker and James Stilton crawling into the space under the overturned sofa and declaring it a party fort . . . and someone starting a game of spin the bottle. After that, I must have fallen asleep or something because . . .

"Margot." The next thing I knew, I heard Em's voice.

"Yeah?" I answered, opening my eyes to see what she wanted. The music was still loud, but the room was emptier now. The entrance of the party fort had been covered with towels, and for some reason, a bunch of books had been pulled off the shelves and arranged like a cobblestone walkway leading up to it. Empty pop cans littered the carpet. George and Ken were on the L-shaped sofa with the bowl of jelly beans, tossing them up in the air and trying to catch them in their mouths.

"Your stepdad's here," Em said.

I sat up, rubbing my eyes. "Are you sure it's not somebody else's stepdad?"

"He says his name's Bryan."

I blinked a few times. It didn't make sense. As far as Bryan knew, I was in bed asleep. . . . But even if he *had* found out I'd gone to Em's house, he didn't know her address. I found my crutches on the floor beside the sofa and noticed the clock on the DVD player. It was 12:15. I'd meant to call a taxi at 11:00 at the latest.

By the time I managed to get to the bottom of the stairs, Bryan was already on his way down. I knew it was really him the second I saw his scuffed loafers. "What are you doing here?" I asked. He was wearing green plaid pajama bottoms underneath his yellow rain slicker. I could see him doing his best to take a yogic breath while he looked around the basement at the tipped furniture and general chaos.

"Margot, it's time to go home," he said firmly.

"How did you know I was here?" My voice squeaked.

He took another deep breath, then repeated: "Margot, I said time to go."

"I asked you a question," I said.

Before I realized what was happening, Bryan had picked me up. "Oh, no way," I shouted. "Don't touch me." He didn't even listen. For such a wimpy person, it was amazing that he actually managed to lift all one hundred pounds of me, even while I kicked at him with my good leg. "You have no right!" I shouted. He swung me around and carried me up the stairs without answering, then set me down at the top. Em followed behind with my crutches. "Go outside and get in the van," he said. Then he turned to Em. "Is there an adult in the house?"

"My mom's out right now." She dug her hands into her pockets and looked him straight in the eyes.

"Does she have a cell phone? I'd like to call her," Bryan said as Em led us out to the huge marble foyer.

"Awesome party, guys," Zoe yelled, as she and Kiki headed for the door.

"See you later, someone's dad," Kiki said, waving to Bryan, then she burst into a fit of giggles. Bryan didn't even react; he was still looking at Em, waiting for a phone number.

"Don't embarrass me in front of Em's mom," I pleaded. "Let's just leave, all right? I'm getting in the van. See?" I opened

271

the door. He didn't follow. "She said her mom isn't here. You can talk to her later, all right?"

Bryan finally gave in, but as we headed down the front path, he looked angrier than I'd ever seen him. Then again, he'd just embarrassed me on the best night of my life. I was pretty mad too.

24

I Teach Bryan the Basics
of Sign Language

THE THING ALL STEPPARENTS need to understand is that they should never try to act like real parents. Because they're not real parents. At all. They're more like random people your real parents decided to marry, usually against your wishes.

Think of it this way: It's not like I'd go pick up some kid I met on the street and bring him home and tell my mom, "Guess what! I found this kid. I think I'll make him my new brother. He's *your family* now, and you'd better be nice to him, and clean out a closet for him, and buy him Christmas presents."

But that's exactly how my mom expects me to be with Bryan. And this shouldn't be news to her (or to him) by now: it's not happening. The more "fatherly" things he tries to do, the more I want to murder him in his sleep.

I slammed the passenger-side door of the van shut and stared straight ahead, determined not to say a single word. Thankfully, Bryan didn't feel like talking either. The only sound in the van was the squeaking of the windshield wipers.

We would have probably made it the whole way home like

that, too, if it wasn't for the way my stomach turned against me. I tried to take deep breaths, then rolled down the window to get some air, but nothing helped. "Pull over," I groaned. "Pull over, pull over, pull over."

"Just a moment," Bryan said.

"No," I shouted. "Now. I'm going to be sick."

"Hold your horses, Margot." His voice was irritatingly calm. "I need to pull safely out of traffic." I gagged, but thankfully nothing came out.

After what felt like forever, he finally signaled and pulled off to the side of the road. I pushed the door open and leaned out as far as I could, which didn't turn out to be far enough. I threw up a little bit on the seat, a lot on the door, and even more on the floor of the van.

"Come on." I hadn't even noticed Bryan getting out, but he was suddenly in front of me. "Let's get you some fresh air." He helped me hop toward a bus shelter with a small metal bench in it. I sat down, leaning my head against the glass.

"Were you drinking?" Bryan asked.

"No," I said. "I swear I wasn't. I think it's the flu."

"What about your pain meds?"

"I took them," I said.

"Did you have anything to eat with them?"

"No."

"How many did you take?"

"Four," I answered.

"You know you're only supposed to take two every two hours," he said.

"I know," I answered. "But I missed a dose, so I took four. It's basic math."

"You can't take four at a time, Margot, even if you miss a dose. And you need to take those on a full stomach."

"Nobody told me that! All they said was don't operate bulldozers. Nobody tells me anything!" I leaned my head back again. All I wanted to do was get home and sleep. "How did you find me, anyway?" I asked.

Bryan jingled the van keys in his hand. "You left the Web site with the taxi information open on the computer screen," he said. "I called to find out where they'd driven you."

"You were spying in my room?" I said. "At my computer? Bryan, that's private."

"It's not private when we're worried about your safety," he answered in his fake-fatherly way. I rolled my eyes, but he was looking toward the van and didn't even notice. He was probably busy worrying about being illegally parked. "Are you feeling ready to go?" he asked, definitely eyeing the No Parking sign.

"So, what now?" I asked, after he'd gotten in and closed the door. "Are you and my mom going to punish me by making me babysit on weekends, too?"

Bryan did a shoulder check and pulled onto the street before answering. "As far as your mother knows, you're in bed."

I gave him a confused look.

"She asked me to check on you, but she was asleep by the time I got back to our bedroom. She's got so much on her plate these days, I couldn't face waking her up with bad news." He pulled up at a stoplight and turned to look at me. "And there's the fact that your mother and I had a conversation about my tendency to avoid conflict with you. She'd like to see me take on a more active parenting role."

I rolled my eyes again, not caring if he saw this time.

"I suppose," he said carefully, "we could keep this between us. As long as you promise to always tell your mother or myself where you're going in the future." The light changed and he stretched his neck out like a turtle, looking for cars, even though the streets were deserted. "It's important that we know you're safe."

The active-parenting stuff made me want to vomit all over again. But at the same time, I almost couldn't believe my luck.

"I'd still like to speak with Em's parents, though," he added.

"You can't," I said. "Her dad's dead." I don't even know why I said it. As far as I knew, he was alive and well, making multimillion-dollar music deals in New York, even if he *had* been symbolically stabbed through the chest with a steak knife.

"Well, that's unfortunate. I'm sorry for her loss. In that case, I'd like to speak with her mother."

"You can't. She's deaf."

He sighed. "Was she aware that an unsupervised party was going on in her home?"

"Oh, yeah. Em told her. Through sign language." I could tell he knew I was lying, but he didn't bother to say so.

Instead, he just took a deep cleansing breath. "Is there another adult in their home I could speak to?"

"They live alone." I bit my nails to keep from having to look him in the eyes. "You could still talk to her mom, though . . . if you learned sign language. I know some. This means 'micro-wave.'" I demonstrated the one sign I knew. Erika and I had learned it at a Brownie-pack sleepover once. "And this means 'I love you.'" Everyone knew that one.

"And how would that apply to a conversation about an

unsupervised party?" Now he sounded mad.

"I don't know," I admitted. We drove in silence for a while.

"When young teens get together, things can often get out of hand, Margot. Sometimes there's drinking, or fights break out, or worse. It's serious business."

"I know," I said, thinking about how scared I'd been when Matt had showed up.

"Prescription drugs can be dangerous too, if you don't follow the pharmacist's directions. I want you to promise me that you'll speak to your mother or me if you aren't sure how to take your medication."

I nodded. I wasn't planning to make that mistake again.

"All right," I said. "Fine. I promise." Then I closed my eyes the rest of the way home.

"I'll just clean up," Bryan said, after he'd opened the van door and handed me my crutches. "I'll be right in."

"Okay." I climbed out, being careful not to get puke on my shoe. I almost hated to admit it, but for once in his life, Bryan was actually acting kind of cool. When I got to the door, I even stopped, planning to say thank you, but he had his back turned. All I could see was the moon shining off his bald head while he uncoiled the garden hose at the side of the house.

25

I Am Both a Dog and a Two-Headed Doll

I N THE MORNING, I WOKE TO the sound of barking. I opened my eyes to look at the clock. It was 8:15. I flopped back down, trying to ignore the noise, but it only got louder.

Have I mentioned yet that we don't have a dog?

"Magoo," the triplets called. Six tiny paws hammered at my door.

When I didn't answer, they were quiet for a second, then they started barking again.

I put a pillow over my ear, then shouted as loudly as I could without hurting my own head: "Stop barking." My voice came out gravelly.

"No," Alice shouted back.

"We're doggies," said Aleene.

"A hundred and one damn nations," Alex added.

The barking started again.

"Go away!" They stayed put.

"I'll pay you a hundred dollars to stop barking." They didn't even consider it.

Then I had a stroke of brilliance. "The school bus is outside." I pulled the pillow off my head. "It's waiting for you. And it's full of dog bones." There was immediate silence in the hall, followed by the pitter-patter of tiny feet moving in the opposite direction. I took a deep breath, ready to drift back to sleep. But a minute later, my door opened.

"Margot?" Bryan was standing in the same pajama pants from the night before, with his hands on his hips. A patch of hair was poofing from his bathrobe. His face looked gray, like he'd barely slept, which, come to think of it, he probably hadn't. "Did you tell your sisters there was a school bus full of dog bones outside?"

I rolled over, pulling the blankets up all the way to my chin. "I was kidding."

I could hear screaming coming from the kitchen—the kind of anguished wailing only three two-year-olds deprived of a school bus full of dog bones are capable of. "I'd like it if you came and apologized. Then have some breakfast with us. I'm making scrambled tofu from scratch, with sun-dried tomatoes and feta."

The thought alone made me nauseous, but after what Bryan had done for me the night before, I owed him big-time— even if that meant eating tofu for breakfast, in the same room as my mother, who I was still furious with.

"Good morning, Margot," she said, once she'd finally gotten the triplets to stop whimpering and settled them down in their high chairs. "How's your leg feeling?"

"It hurts." I poked at my tofu with my fork and took a small bite. It wasn't as horrible as it sounded. At the very least, it wasn't VTV.

"I talked to Sarah's mother yesterday," she said.

I looked up.

"She declined my invitation for tea. In fact"—my mom stabbed a tofu chunk—"she barely gave me the time of day." I wasn't all that surprised to hear it. Meanness must run in the family. "According to her mother, Sarah says she didn't push you down the stairs or have anything to do with a poster campaign. And when I suggested that perhaps Sarah might have some long-standing issues with aggression, she actually hung up on me."

I couldn't believe my mom had actually said that to Sarah J.'s mother. . . . But before I even had the chance to tell her how embarrassing it was, Bryan stepped between us, setting down the triplets' bowls on their high-chair trays.

"Do you have something you want to say to your sisters, Margot?" he prodded. Mom glanced up, obviously impressed by his *active parenting*.

"Sorry I said there was a school bus full of dog bones when there wasn't," I mumbled. "That wasn't very nice of me. We can play dogs together after breakfast if you want, okay?"

And that's how I ended up spending my entire Saturday morning pretending to be a dog in a house made of sofa cushions.

It was after lunch before I got to the computer. There was an IM waiting from Em.

Em&Em: Hey Button, how are you feeling after your drug overdose?
Margot12: I didn't overdose! I had four pills!!
Em&Em: That's not what George told me. =) He said you were hilarious.

I felt my stomach flip. Hilarious? She obviously had no idea what had really happened between us.

Em&Em: He said you talked about a pair of mittens for five minutes straight.

I'd almost forgotten about the mittens. In the light of day, it *did* sound kind of dumb.

Em&Em: Anyway, don't worry. After you left, I told him you were flirting with him for a bet.

My stomach flipped again.

Margot12: You told him WHAT??
Em&Em: I didn't want him thinking you were easy or weird or anything.

I tried to remember everything I'd said to George the night before. I knew he'd told me he liked my hair. And he also said he thought I was pretty cool. Weren't those definite signs that he liked me? But then other memories started to surface, too. Like, did I actually say something to him about vegetable korma? Talking to George had felt so easy at the time, but now the events of the night seemed fuzzy around the edges, and I wasn't certain that I'd seemed nearly as charming and cool to him as I'd seemed to myself. What if I *had* acted like a weirdo? And now he thought I'd been using him for a bet . . . when, really, all these years I'd loved him.

I couldn't help it. Tears sprang to my eyes.

Margot12: Do you think he hates me
now?
Em&Em: Of course not, stupid! He
thought you were funny. He also said
you looked like a different person.

My heart leaped up again. I couldn't believe he'd actually
said that!

Em&Em: I was thinking we should invite
Maggie and Joyce to sneak out to the
sushi place for lunch on Monday and
NOT invite Sarah J. You in?

Maggie and Joyce? We were getting more popular, for sure,
and things were bound to be even better after word got out
about how good the party was. But Maggie and Joyce were
Sarah J.'s best friends. Would they actually sneak out with us?
Plus, wasn't sushi raw fish? Still, I knew better than to doubt
or contradict Em. If she'd suggested we eat dirt, I would have
probably done it.

Margot12: I'm in.

I quickly Googled "types of sushi," then picked one ran-
domly off the list so I'd sound convincing.

Margot12: I love unagi rolls.

Em&Em: Never had them. Anyway, see you Monday?

I desperately wanted to change the subject back to George before we stopped talking. Had he mentioned the moment when I touched his hair? Did she notice if he'd been looking at me when I was sleeping on the couch? What, exactly, did he say about me after I left? If it had been Erika, we would have analyzed the entire party, minute by minute, drawing diagrams of where everyone was sitting and what they were wearing, dedicating at least two hours to a serious discussion of the Gorgeous George thing and what it might mean . . . but this was Em. She'd already logged off.

After that I spent the rest of the day feeling exactly like this two-headed doll named Benita I'd had when I was little. She was made of cloth and had a skirt you could flip back and forth to hide whichever one of the heads you weren't using. One of the heads was frowning and had blue tears stitched to its face (sad Benita) and the other had rosy red circles on its cheeks and was grinning (glad Benita).

When I finished talking to Em, I lay on my bed for a long time with my sad-Benita head on. I was disgusting. There was no way he liked me. I cupped my hands over my mouth and exhaled into them, then tried to smell the air I'd breathed out. I had to do it a couple of times before I could tell for certain, but I definitely had bad breath. I also had a zit just starting to form beside my nose—the kind that hurts when you press on it. I was positive he'd noticed.

Eventually I dragged myself to the living room, where the triplets were building monsters out of giant Lego blocks.

I sat down beside Aleene on the couch and added two special googly-eyed blocks to the top of her monster, plus a red piece for a tongue sticking out. She looked up at me in amazement—like I was the number one top Lego builder on earth . . . and there was something in that look of surprise and delight that I recognized. I could have sworn that, as I'd reached out to touch his hair, I'd seen it cross George's face too. Then I remembered how sincere he'd sounded when he'd said he liked my hair.

But sad Benita showed up again when I was washing my face before bed and noticed that the zit had grown even bigger and that my eyebrows were still uneven. Then glad Benita pointed out that he *had* told Em I was hilarious and that I looked like a different person. Plus, what do guys know about eyebrows anyway?

Then sad Benita remembered the way he'd looked at me like I was an alien when I brought up the hockey stick mittens he'd worn in third grade. But glad Benita said if he really liked me, some weird conversation about mittens wasn't going to change it. Then sad Benita was like, "Oh please, mitten girl. Do you actually think he'd like *you?*"

And it basically went on like that until 12:30, when I couldn't sleep because the Benitas wouldn't shut up, and it occurred to me that this whole talking-to-myself thing might be kind of lame and pathetic, at which point sad Benita said, "Lame and pathetic? Kind of like telling him, out loud, that you think he's 'gorgeous and *so* cool'?" and even glad Benita was too depressed to think of a comeback.

26

I Taste the Gummi Frog of Acceptance

STILL, WEIRDLY ENOUGH, when my alarm went off the next morning, I felt ready to face anything. Bring it on, world! I thought. Of course, by the time Bryan dropped me off in front of the school, I felt like climbing up the maple tree and hiding all day so I wouldn't have to face George. . . . Which was partly why I was happy that the first person I saw was Andrew. He's always glad to see me. Or— he usually was. That morning there was something kind of sad or disappointed in his expression. Thankfully, only a few seconds passed before he helped me figure out why.

"Did you have an okay weekend," he asked, "even though we couldn't go to that party?" If I'd been able to do it while standing on one leg, I would have kicked myself for forgetting that I'd told Amir Em was going to invite them.

"Not bad," I said, barely hesitating before launching into yet another lie. I just couldn't face telling him that I'd gone without him. "I got to watch lots of TV." That part was true. "Anyway, sorry Em didn't get around to inviting you guys. I guess with all that happened . . ." I trailed off. "I'm sure we didn't miss much."

"Agreed," he said, holding the door open for me and seeming to brighten a little. "I saw a SubSonic video once. It was basically a really mad girl in a bra rapping about how cool she is." Now that he mentioned it, that described SubSonic almost exactly.

"How's the leg, anyway?" he asked.

"Not too bad," I answered. "But my armpits are killing me."

"Want an armpit massage?" he said, coming in prepared to tickle, but I fended him off with my crutch. "Damn. Now you're armed and dangerous. I don't stand a chance, do I?"

"You never did." I smiled. "Remember. I'm the dragon master." He laughed and followed me up the ramp to the door.

When we got inside, he pressed the elevator button for me before jogging up the stairs. "See you at lunch, Margot," he called over his shoulder.

"Sure," I called back. I breathed a sigh of relief, then smiled to myself as I got into the elevator. I'd barely made it through the door and already it was turning out to be a pretty good day. The Andrew situation was under control. The sun was shining. The air was crisp. Thanks to Em's magical frizz control serum, my hair looked good. I'd just found out I wasn't the only person on earth who secretly hated SubSonic. Then it got even better. Mr. Learner was still sitting behind Mrs. Collins's desk when I got to English class. Sarah J. was absent—and so were Maggie and Joyce. A whole bunch of people were saying hi and crowding around to talk to me.

"Welcome back, Margot!"

"Oh my God, how are you?"

"Can I see your cast?"

Em waved. Gorgeous George nodded when I smiled at him. My desk was covered in chocolates. Leprechauns were dancing underneath rainbows. Unicorns were prancing through fields of cotton candy. Okay, maybe those last two things didn't happen, but my desk *was* covered in chocolates. And cards. Well, one card, and one huge box of assorted chocolates. I picked up the envelope. The handwriting on the front looked messy and flat—like it had possibly been written by a guy. As I slid my finger under the flap, I tried not to make eye contact with George. I didn't want him to see me blushing in case it was from him.

The card had a cartoon chicken lying in bed eating soup. "Want some quackers with that?" I flipped it open. Inside was tons of tiny writing in different colors of pen. The whole class had signed. I forced myself to smile, despite my disappointment that it wasn't from George. "Thanks guys," I said to the whole room.

Mr. Learner put down his book and stood up. "Welcome back, Miss Button," he said, then he told us to get into our groups to keep working on our *Lord of the Flies* presentation.

"You're with me, Ken, and Tiffany," Em filled me in.

As people started pushing desks together, I opened the card from the class and scanned it, looking for George's signature. I found it in the bottom corner. *Broken legs suck. —From George.* Not exactly a love poem, but he'd probably signed it on Friday, before what happened at the party, so it didn't necessarily mean anything.

When the desks were all arranged, Ken took a pig-shaped drawing out of his binder.

"We're supposed to map out how we'd make our camp," Tiffany explained to me.

Ken, who had elected himself president of the island, was the one doing the drawing. So, needless to say, it looked horrible. He was busy drawing millions of little triangles.

"Stop putting tents all over the place," Em said. "We want the camp to be all together. For security."

"Who needs security?" Ken countered. "We're on an island. Plus, this way it looks like the pig's got spikes."

I tried to pay attention, but I could hardly concentrate. I was watching George out of the corner of my eye. He was sitting alone with Amir, who was bent over the drawing of their island. Obviously, some combination of Maggie, Joyce, or Sarah—who were all still missing—must have been their other group members.

"Button. Buuuuutton. Earth to Button." Ken was waving something green in front of my face. "You want one?"

"What? What is it?"

"A gummi frog. With a marshmallow center."

I gave Ken a strange look. Not because the marshmallow gummi frog sounded disgusting (it did), especially at 9:00 a.m., but because my first instinct was to wonder what was wrong with it. Had he dropped it on the floor? Or rubbed it in his armpit?

But Ken wasn't wearing his usual smirk. I took the frog candy and turned it over in my hand. It looked clean. I put it in my mouth and chewed. It was gross, but not in any abnormal way. "Want another one?" He held out the bag.

"Thanks," I said, reaching for it, amazed at how quickly and completely things could change.

At 9:30, Maggie and Joyce came to class. They sat down beside George and Amir, and I watched as they leaned in, telling George something. He listened intently, then glanced my way. I could hardly believe it. First the gummi frog and now this? I almost didn't want to let myself think it, but they must have been talking about the party, and about whether or not he liked me. What else could it be? By the time the bell finally rang, I couldn't stand the suspense a second longer. As everyone put their books and binders away, I reached out and tapped his shoulder.

"Hey." I tried to sound casual. "Did you have a good time at the party?"

"Yeah, not bad." He shrugged.

Not bad? I tried not to panic. "Not bad" could mean "could have been better," but you could also take it literally, in which case "not bad" was the opposite of bad, which was "good." I decided to go with that.

"I had a good time too." I paused, then added, with what I hoped was a meaningful look: "A great time."

He smiled nervously, and I felt a thrill go through me. He was nervous too!

"About what Em said—" I went on. I had to let him know I wasn't flirting with him because of some stupid bet. But he interrupted me.

"Can I ask you something?"

"What?" I looked deep into his eyes. The word "YES" was ready to burst out of my mouth. I pictured us holding hands in the yard, slow dancing under crepe paper decorations at the Valentine's dance, hanging out on the swings at the park during summer vacation.

"About Em. Is she going out with anyone?"

I leaned against the desk to steady myself. My stomach

lurched as my dreams crash-landed right in front of my eyes. "I don't know," I said. "I mean, I don't think so."

"Cool," he said, like it was no big deal. "See you." He walked out, leaving me alone, feeling like I might collapse and never be able to get back up.

And I didn't even get a minute to recover. Em was waiting for me outside the door. Maggie and Joyce were standing on either side of her. "Margot, I invited Maggie and Joyce to sneak out for sushi with us," she explained. "They said okay."

I just nodded and tried to smile. I was practically holding my breath to fight back the tears. It was the story of my life. The guy I'd been in love with since third grade just so happened to like my new best friend, who, by the way, had no right to show up from New York and steal him away. I took a deep breath and tried to be rational. It wasn't Em's fault. She couldn't help it that she knew famous people, and was so cool and pretty and smart.

"So?" Em asked. "What did loverboy say?"

I knew I should tell her and give her the chance to be with him. It was what a true friend would do. I tried to mentally replace the image of myself with an image of Em slow dancing with him under crepe paper cupids. It made my heart ache.

"He didn't say much," I answered. "We just talked about the party in general."

I couldn't do it. Not in front of Maggie and Joyce. I decided to tell Em later, when I could get her alone.

"George is hot," Maggie said. "Do you think he likes you?" I was sure she was being sarcastic, so I didn't answer.

"You'd be so lucky if he did. He's really sweet," Joyce added.

"I don't get it," Em said as we walked toward the doors. "I mean, maybe he's kind of cute, if you're into jocks, but he's not the brightest light on the Christmas tree. No offense, Margot. He's just not my type. He reminds me of a Ken doll."

Personally, I'd always thought Ken dolls were kind of hot, in a plastic underpants, hair-gelled-in-place sort of way.

"What's your type?" Joyce asked.

"I don't know. Rich, famous, incredibly smart, and unbelievably good-looking," Em answered. They both laughed.

Normally I would have jumped in to defend George's honor. He was so much more than a dumb jock. He was funny and stylish and thoughtful. But since Em obviously wasn't interested, there was no reason for her to know any of that, was there?

"Anyway," she said, "enough about the Ken doll. Margot, you aren't going to believe what happened. Maggie, tell her."

27

I Eat Sea Slugs and Put Socks in My Armpits

Three things I would rather do than ever eat sushi again:
  1. Go swimming in a pool filled with broken glass.
  2. Commit to a lifelong no-nacho diet.
  3. Be seen at the mall holding hands with my mother.

Not to be prejudiced, but I don't understand what the people of Japan have against fully cooked meat.

"Look, Margot," Em said when she opened the menu, "they have unagi."

"Huh?" I answered.

"Unagi. Remember how you said yesterday on IM that it's your favorite?"

I'd actually been eyeing the vegetarian rolls. "Oh right." I found the unagi and breathed a sigh of relief. "It's fifteen dollars, though. I only have ten."

"Whatever," Em said. "It's on me. We're celebrating. Sarah J. has finally been brought to justice for what she did to you."

The news Maggie had told me on the way had actually been almost enough to cheer me up. Sarah J. had been suspended.

And not only that—it had happened in the most unbelievable way. Her two best friends had turned her in.

"So? Tell us the details," Em said, spreading her napkin over her lap. "I mean, we thought you guys and Sarah were so tight."

"Right." Joyce held her empty teacup and spun it carefully on its bottom rim. "We thought that too." She glanced up at Maggie like she was waiting for her permission to go on. "But then we started hearing these rumors."

"Sarah thinks I'm fat. She would talk to Joyce about it behind my back, then she started passing notes about it in class."

Em picked up a set of wooden chopsticks joined at the top and split them apart angrily. "We know. Margot and I have both heard her say that before, but, Maggie, you're *not* fat."

"I know," she said, although she didn't say it with much conviction. "I mean, I went up a size since last year, but big deal. Anyway, that's not all. She was always talking to *me* about how Joyce has bad teeth."

"Let me see," Em said. Joyce opened her mouth and touched the two teeth on either side of her front ones. They overlapped slightly. "As if!" she exclaimed. "Drew Barrymore has the exact same teeth as you, Joyce. And they pay her millions of dollars to shoot lipstick commercials."

"I'm getting them fixed when I turn fourteen anyway," she said, then she picked up her set of chopsticks and tried to separate them too, but instead of snapping apart, hers kind of splintered.

Maggie and Joyce were both quiet for a while, feeling bad about their major flaws, I could only assume, which, honestly, were nonexistent. I'd never even looked at Joyce's teeth before.

Her perfect, pouty lips hid them. And as for Maggie, she looked great in whatever she wore. Like, for example, the olive green V-neck sweater she had on that matched her eyes exactly and was just tight enough to make it obvious she had a figure—unlike some of us.

"Anyway, when we both found out she'd been backstabbing us," Maggie said, "we just decided we'd had enough. Plus, we saw her push you down the stairs, Margot. I mean, making fun of people behind their backs is one thing, but actually breaking bones . . ." She snapped her chopsticks apart, and I winced involuntarily. "Plus, the whole lesbian poster thing," she added. "Totally not PC."

"Exactly," Joyce agreed. "I go to the gay pride parade every year. It's really fun. And anyway, even if you were a lesbian, which we know you're not, it's none of her business."

Even though I was pretty sure Maggie and Joyce must have helped her make, photocopy, and hang the posters in question, I still kind of appreciated the apology.

Just then, the waitress, dressed in a red kimono, came over to the table and bowed. Em grabbed my menu and passed it to her. "One order of unagi and the deluxe bento box," she said. Maggie and Joyce were still scanning the menu uncertainly.

"Do you have anything without fish?" Maggie asked, scrunching up her face.

"They'll have the California rolls," Em told the waitress. "Hold the crab." A minute later the waitress was back with a teapot.

"So, what happened this morning when you told Vandanhoover?" Em asked as she poured tea for everyone. "Tell us everything."

"Well," Maggie started, picking up her tea and smelling it suspiciously before taking a sip, "we were pretty sure we were going to do it, but not totally." She gave me a look that wasn't quite apologetic. "But then when I got to school this morning, Sarah was at the concrete ledge, and she goes, 'Hey, where's donkey teeth?'" Joyce looked down into her teacup as Maggie went on. "So then I said, 'Sarah, you know that's kind of a bitchy thing to say about someone who's supposed to be your friend, right?'"

"Did you actually use that word?" Joyce asked, looking up. Maggie nodded. "Oh my God. She must have freaked."

"She did. Anyway," Maggie said, after taking the tiniest possible sip from her cup, "that was when Joyce got there and we both confronted her."

"Right. And Sarah tried to deny it. She said she'd never called me donkey teeth."

"And I said, 'Right. Just like you never pushed Margot down the stairs?'"

"And that was when we went straight to Vandanhoover's office."

"My heart was beating so loud the whole time. I thought Sarah was going to burst into the office and try to stop us or something."

"Oh my God. Me too. When the secretary opened the door that time . . ."

"I totally thought it was her."

The waitress came up to the table with a tray of food, and Maggie and Joyce stopped talking for a minute while they watched the plates being set in front of them. They didn't look especially eager to dig in, and I couldn't blame them. The blackened hunks of meat sitting in a box of rice in front of me didn't look so appealing either. I rearranged my chopsticks in my hand, trying to get them into a position that would make them actually work.

Em eyed me. "I thought you said you had sushi all the time."

"I do," I lied. "I mean, I used to. It's been a while."

She held up her own chopsticks so I could see how she was holding them. Maggie and Joyce watched intently, too. "Like this."

"Oh, right." I practiced a few times before trying to pick up a piece of meat. It slipped and fell back into my bento box, but I tried again. I forced myself to swallow. According to the menu, unagi was grilled eel coated in a delicious sweet sauce. *Delicious* wasn't the word I would have chosen.

"Aren't eels the slugs of the sea?" Joyce asked as she scraped some rice off the side of her roll and ate it. I spit my second bite into my napkin and made an involuntary gagging noise. "Sorry!" she chirped.

"I'm not that hungry anyway," I said, and after that I just pushed the eel meat around on my plate with a chopstick.

While the rest of us stared down our meals, Em started expertly putting entire sushi rolls into her mouth through the next part of the story.

"Anyway, then Vandanhoover called her in," said Maggie.

"And she was pissed," added Joyce.

"So pissed. But with one eyebrow."

"And the peeling skin."

"Exactly. You have to remember to picture her like that every time we tell this story, because that makes it funnier," Maggie said.

296

Em stopped eating long enough to fill in the ending herself. It was the best part, after all. "And then she got suspended. For two days."

"I can't believe it." I raised my teacup. The liquid inside smelled like hay, but I drank it anyway.

"Yeah, well," Joyce said. "Nobody backstabs us and gets away with it."

"So, what are you going to do when she gets back?" Em asked.

Maggie shrugged.

Joyce just stared out the window. It was obvious they hadn't thought that far ahead. "If she tries to talk to us, we could just pretend she's invisible," she suggested.

"Or we could tell everyone she wears color contacts."

My mouth dropped open. I could have sworn Sarah J.'s eyes were too blue to be true.

"I don't know," Em said, glancing at her watch and waving to the waitress for the bill. "I'm not saying those are bad ideas, but they're exactly the kind of thing Sarah would do. Do you really want to sink to her level?"

Maggie swirled her tea, looking embarrassed. "Well, yeah," she said after a while. "I didn't mean we'd torture her forever. Just for a day or something. Until she learns her lesson."

"Obviously," Joyce put in.

"Okay, good," Em said. "I'm really glad you agree, because here's what I think we should do. . . ."

Besides the fact that there was no possible way my armpits could have hurt any worse, I didn't mind the short walk back to school after sushi. For one thing, I was glad to get away from the unagi. But also, we had phys ed, and for once in my life I was looking forward to it. I'd have my cast on for at least six weeks, which meant I'd be sitting out.

I left Em, Maggie, and Joyce at the doors of the locker room, planning to go straight to the gym to get started on my homework. But then I saw Andrew coming down the hall holding a basketball under his arm.

"Hey! Did you conquer the level-four dragon and find the doorway to the Maze of Mystery?" I asked.

"Yeah," he said, hardly turning to look at me.

"Excuse me?" I smiled and called to his back. "You're not even going to tell me how many heads the dragon had?"

He stopped. "If you wanted to see level four, you could have met us at lunch." I'd never seen him look so mad. "I saw you leave with Em and those Group girls."

"Sorry. You were with Mike and Amir anyway. I didn't think you'd care." And then I started to get mad that he was mad. Andrew had never cared when Erika and I used to eat lunch by ourselves. Or even when Em and I would go over to the maple tree. "Like, what? I'm not allowed to go eat lunch with other people all of a sudden?"

He exhaled loudly and turned to go.

"Just tell me why you're so mad."

Andrew stopped and looked at the floor. "I know you went to the party." He made a fist with one hand and drummed it against his thigh. "But you told me this morning you didn't go, then Amir heard you were there and you—" He paused. "You didn't have to lie to me. If you just didn't want to invite us, I would have understood."

I rocked back and forth on my crutches, feeling like an

idiot. Obviously, he would have heard that I'd been there. What had I been thinking when I'd lied to him that morning? "I'm sorry," I said, finally looking him in the eyes. And I meant it. "I didn't want to hurt your feelings."

"Yeah. Well." He looked off behind me at the clock on the wall. "I get it."

"Get what?"

"That I don't fit in with the new people you hang out with. I guess I just thought you wouldn't care. But obviously you do."

"It's not that—" I started. "Look, I'm sorry," I said again, lamely. What else was there to say?

"Sure," he said after a moment. "Anyway. I'd better get to class." He turned to go, then stopped. "Wait." He balanced the ball between his feet and opened his backpack. "I made these for you in family studies." He handed me two gym socks that had been filled with stuffed-animal fluff and sewn shut. "Armpit protectors," he explained.

"Thanks, they're . . ." My throat closed up. I couldn't think of a single thing to say.

"You're welcome." He shrugged and walked away.

Before going up to the gym, I took a detour to the girls' bathroom. I leaned my crutches up against the sink, then ran my fingers over the seams on the socks. He'd double stitched them in red thread—my favorite color. There was nobody else in the bathroom, so I tried them quickly, just to see. They were really comfortable. I felt awful, but as much as my armpits hurt, I couldn't walk around with Andrew's gym socks under my arms all day. I didn't have a choice, I thought as I pushed open the flap of the garbage can; I had to throw them away.

28

I Desperately Need a Bee-Proof Cave

WHEN MY GRANDPA Button was alive, and he and Grandma Betty lived in a big house on Chester Street, they used to do a lot of puzzles. They had a card table permanently set up in the den, and every time my mom and I would go for Sunday dinner there'd be something new: five hundred pieces of penguins, one-thousand pieces of the pyramids, or—I'm not even kidding—a five thousand piece puzzle of the sky.

"Come sit with me, Margot," Grandpa used to say while my mom and grandma were busy in the kitchen. "Tell me what's new in your world. We'll see if we can't get some edges in." He'd arrange the pieces in piles by color and put them together patiently while we talked until he had an entire cluster of clouds. Meanwhile, I'd be sighing in frustration over a small section of hot air balloon. "There you go," he'd say when I fit a single piece in. "You're getting it." But I wasn't really. I was just fumbling through, getting lucky enough, now and then, to find two pieces that went together.

My grandpa, on the other hand, had eons' worth of patience, and an unwavering faith that we'd get that puzzle done.

I miss him pretty much all the time, but on that afternoon, especially, I would have given anything to be able to sit and talk with him again while piecing together that impossible-seeming sky.

"Margot, lovely to see you back," Mrs. Rivera said unenthusiastically as I walked into the gym. She seriously had to be the most sedated person I'd ever met. All she ever seemed to do was sit in the gym office trying to tune out whatever was going on outside. I could picture her on Christmas morning as a little girl, sighing as she opened her presents. "A doll. How interesting," she'd say, before dropping it on the floor and turning to stare at the wall.

"I have a little job for you." She pointed to a pile of papers on her desk. "These equipment invoices need to be filed. Something to keep you busy these next few weeks."

Weeks? It was a big stack of paper, but not that big. "When you're done with those, you'll find more in the boxes." She waved her arms around to show me the boxes, which were, literally, everywhere . . . under her desk, on top of the filing cabinet, piled up behind the door. This had to be against some kind of child labor law.

The next hour of my life was spent sifting through one invoice at a time while I listened to the sounds of Mrs. Rivera crunching oatmeal cookies, humming along to soft rock radio, and flipping through the pages of a newspaper while the girls played basketball. Twice, one of them came to the door to report a foul, and Mrs. Rivera looked up just long enough to say, "Work it out."

It was easily the most boring period of my life. Not that I didn't learn anything. Like, for example, did you know that

Manning Middle School purchased thirty-two volleyballs in 1998? Me neither! Do you care? Me neither!

I was actually glad when the bell rang and I got to go to French class. That is, until I saw that Em was at George's desk in the back of the room. They were each sharing an earphone of his iPod, leaning in so close that their shoulders were almost touching. They must have gotten to an especially great part in the song, because he looked over at her, grinning and making a drumming motion in the air. I swallowed hard. Why hadn't I noticed it before? Just from the way his eyes lit up when he looked at her, it was so obvious he liked her. I opened my *cahier d'exercices* and started miserably practicing my *dictée* words. But a minute later, a bag landed in the middle of my page. I looked up, and there was Em.

"Okay," she whispered. "Besides SubSonic, your loverboy has awful taste in music. He just made me listen to this entire song about weasels. It was like, five minutes long."

I smiled, relieved.

"Anyway," she went on, "I forgot that I brought you your clothes. The wet stuff you left at my house. I put some other stuff in there, too. A few camisoles and things."

I smiled and was just about to open the bag to look at them when Mr. Patachou started to talk about the fascinating world of *passé composé* verbs and Em had to take her seat. She lay her head down on her desk, stuck her tongue out, and rolled her eyes at me. I let my head drop onto my desk too, doing a silent snore, except that it accidentally came out not-so-silent—like a big rhinoceros snort. Everyone turned to look at me.

"*Margot, ça ne t'amuse pas, le verbe finir?*" Mr. Patachou asked, and everyone laughed. I didn't really care, though. For once I got the feeling they were all laughing *with* me. Plus, I had new camisoles, Sarah J. was suspended, and Em and I had just gone out for lunch with two of the most popular girls in school. So my love life wasn't working out the way I'd planned? So Andrew was a little bit mad at me? So what? When I weighed the good things against the bad things, it had still been a decent day. Em gave me a mischievous look, and I smiled back, relaxing into my seat. She didn't like George. She'd said so herself.

Em met me at my locker after school, where I'd just finished pinning up my copy of the "autographed" SubSonic poster beside the pair of pears photo. Even though I knew it wasn't a real autograph, I liked the way it looked hanging there. A few other people who'd been at the party had put theirs in their lockers too.

"Your hair looks good today," Em said, coming up behind me.

"You think so?" I asked. "Thanks. That frizz control serum is amazing."

"I know." Em smiled, then looked at me more closely. "Your eyeliner's not bad either. But I'll bring you a new one tomorrow. Brown would be better on you for daytime." I'd done the best I could recreating my party eyes with my mom's crusty old black eyeliner pencil, but it hadn't been easy.

"Thanks," I said again. "That'd be cool."

A surge of hopefulness went through me as we walked out to the yard together. Maggie and Joyce were sitting on the concrete ledge and they waved us over. It felt weird to be approaching Sarah J.'s territory. Weirder, even, to be invited, but I propped up my crutches and hoisted myself onto the ledge. I had to admit, it was nice. The ledge was higher than most places in the yard, and it made me feel like royalty, looking out over my kingdom.

"God," Maggie lamented as she examined her pores in a compact, "my tan is totally gone. It's like the summer never even happened."

Joyce reached into her bag, unzipped a makeup case, and handed Maggie some bronzer.

"Thanks! You saved my life!" Maggie took it gratefully. "You're so lucky, Margot," she said to me as she started applying the gold powder to her cheekbones. "You never have to worry about being tanned."

I could have mentioned the many joys that come with permanently brown skin—like the fact that the pharmacy near our house barely carried any makeup that matched, or the loveliness of having a mustache I had to bleach—but instead I just smiled, taking the compliment, since it was the first real one she'd ever given me.

"Oh look," Em said as she hopped onto the ledge beside Joyce. "Here comes loverboy." George and Ken were coming straight for us.

"Stop calling him that!" I whispered, then I watched George's eyes carefully as he got closer, trying to see if he was focusing more on Em than on anyone else. It was hard to tell. If anything, he seemed to be looking at something off in the distance behind us.

"Is that your dad?" George asked, as soon as he reached the concrete ledge. I turned, and sure enough, Bryan was getting out of our rusty, hundred-year-old minivan, which he'd parked right in front of the school, where everyone would see it.

"Stepdad," I corrected. "Anyway. See you tomorrow." I grabbed my crutches and hopped off the ledge before the entire school yard had a chance to see how the driver's-side mirror was being held on with duct tape.

"You're not going to stay and hang out with us?" Ken looked almost genuinely disappointed. "You're breaking my heart, Button." I rolled my eyes at him.

Maggie and Joyce were still waving as Bryan shoulder checked five times and pulled into the street. Ken, who by then had already forgotten I existed, was sitting on the ledge, opening a bag of Doritos. But I couldn't see Em or George at all. I turned around farther in my seat, pretending to be waving back at Maggie and Joyce, and that was when I spotted them. They were standing together, talking. A bit apart from everyone else.

"Was that the same girl whose home you were at on Friday night?" Bryan asked, interrupting my minor panic attack. I pretended I hadn't heard him. "I'd still like to speak with her mother, but I'll need you to get me their number. It's unlisted."

"It's probably unlisted because they don't want people bugging them," I said, hoping he'd take the hint. "Her mom's an actor."

He nodded, not seeming all that impressed. "Your mother mentioned that. I also take it she isn't deaf."

I smiled sheepishly. "Would you believe that she magically regained her hearing?" Bryan didn't laugh, but he didn't look mad either.

"She used to be on *Destiny's World*," I told him. He still didn't seem awed, which kind of annoyed me. I mean, of all people, he should have known how hard it was to get good roles like that. "And *Chicago Dreams*. She's a big deal," I went on. "Also, Em's dad is a music agent for this amazing band, SubSonic, which is why they're so rich."

That seemed to get Bryan's attention, but not for the right reasons. "Are you sure about that?" he asked, as he shoulder checked again.

"Yeah. But don't tell anyone, okay? Em's trying to keep a low profile."

He seemed to be deep in thought for a second. "Margot, that strikes me as odd," he went on, signaling left. "You know, the acting community is smaller than you might think. I was talking with Jeff Fischer, from the Tylenol commercial." I knew the guy he meant. He was part of Bryan's old "dramatic arts collective," and he was the most famous actor in our town because he'd once pretended to have a backache for a national commercial spot. Then he'd moved to New York for a while to be on Broadway in some play about trains, which practically made Bryan die of envy.

"Jeff and Em's mother have a mutual friend," Bryan went on. "He mentioned she was a single mother who'd done very well for herself."

"What?" I looked straight at Bryan. "No. She's not a single mother. She's married. Em's dad lives in New York. She talks to him every day at lunch."

"Really? Because Jeff Fischer seemed quite sure about her situation. I just—"

"Bryan. She's practically my best friend. Who would know more about her life? Me, or the guy from the Tylenol commercial?"

"I don't know, Margot. I'm just giving you the facts as I've heard them. Is it possible your new friend isn't being entirely forthright with you?"

"Of course she's being *forthright*," I said, making a point of using his stupid word.

"I'm not trying to upset you, Margot. Sometimes people tell lies to cover up painful truths. It doesn't mean your friend isn't a good person at heart. But perhaps she's troubled."

So now Em was "erratic" *and* "troubled"?

"Perhaps she's grieving over something," he went on in this calm, wise, self-help-book voice. "People who are hurting inside often rebel against authority. It might explain why she felt the need to throw a party while her mother was out."

"Right." I stared out the window, but I couldn't deny it. No matter how I tried to rearrange the pieces of Em's story, and force them into place, they just didn't fit.

My mom's first tarot client still hadn't arrived when we got home. She was in the kitchen, still dressed in her 100% VEGAN T-shirt from that morning, picking at a VTV pasta entrée straight from the box while the triplets played with pots and Tupperware containers they'd scattered all over the floor. It looked like our kitchen cabinets had exploded, and the triplets were poor orphaned children playing in the wreckage.

Bryan went up behind my mom, massaged her shoulders, then kissed her on the lips.

"We just made a run to the pharmacy," Mom explained.

"Tough trip?" he asked.

"You wouldn't believe it," she answered. "All three of them threw tantrums because I bought store-brand diapers instead of the ones with Elmo. Then, while I was calming Aleene and

307

Alice down, I lost track of Alex. I found her in the feminine hygiene aisle. She'd opened a box of tampons, dumped them on the floor, and was using them to build a log cabin. She screamed the whole way home in the stroller," my mom finished weakly, shouting the last part of the story over Alice's wailing.

"My pot!!!!!" Alice was yelling, as Aleene wrestled it from her hands.

Mom stared at the ceiling like she was praying for the strength to survive another day of triple-toddler madness. Bryan stepped in to deal with the pot situation.

"Call me when your client gets here," I said as I picked my way through the Tupperware and pots on my crutches. "I have to start my homework." But instead I closed my door and flopped down on my bed. According to the clock on my bed-side table, it was 3:47. Em and George were probably sitting on the concrete ledge at this very second, exchanging childhood stories. I closed my eyes and tried to clear my head, but the second I opened them, my clock radio was staring me in the face again: 3:48. They'd probably moved from talking to tongue kissing. I groaned, then sat up and tried to calm down. After all, what had Em's exact words been? "No offense, but he's not my type." Then again, she'd lied about a lot of things. What's to say she wasn't lying about George, too?

There was a knock at my door. "Margot, dear." It was Grandma Betty. I hadn't even known she was at our house. "May I come in?" Unlike my mother, Grandma actually waited for an answer.

"Sure." I sat up.

"How was your day?" she asked, poking her head in. I was on the verge of saying "horrible" and launching into a big description of everything that had happened with George, and Andrew, and now Em . . . but I noticed the worried look on her face just in time. "All right," I lied.

"Good." She flashed me a quick smile, then went right back to her worried face. She stepped inside the room and closed my door partway. "Margot, I'm concerned about your mother. The girls are a handful. And then two jobs plus the housework. She's just plain exhausted."

I could see the Friend Request IM icon flashing on my computer screen and tried not to look at it too obviously while my grandma was talking.

"I was wondering if you'd had a chance to pick up those flowers yet. I think they'd give her a real boost." Grandma looked at me gently while my mind raced. Those flowers? What flowers?

Oh, right. The thirty dollars for the flowers. I glanced at my dresser, where I still had seventeen dollars of the money I'd borrowed.

"Oh no," I said with what I hoped sounded like real regret. "I forgot. I'll get them tomorrow. I promise."

"Good. I think your mom would like that." Grandma opened the door to let herself out. I *would* buy the flowers, of course, but mostly for her. "I'll let you get to your homework," she said, then left. I practically dove for my computer. The suspense was killing me.

Friend Request: SarahSXY (Sarah J.)

I stared in surprise. It was weird beyond belief to see the words *Sarah J.* and *Friend* in the same sentence. I hit *Accept.*

> **SarahSXY:** For the record, Margo, Maggie
> and Joyce are lying. I **didn't** push you
> down the stairs. It's stupid that I
> got suspended.

First of all, nice user name. She probably got more than her share of messages from random Internet perverts with that one. Second, she forgot the "t" in my name, and third, give me a break. Everyone knew she'd pushed me.

> **Margot12:** Technically, you **pulled** me
> down the stairs. But whatever. The
> point is that I broke my leg.
> **SarahSXY:** I think you should know it's
> true, what I said about Em. She's a
> liar. For example, she acts like she's
> your friend, but she's really not.
> **Margot12:** Right. And I should believe
> you because you always act like a good
> friend.

I knew I should log off and forget what I'd just read, but I couldn't help myself. I opened the next message.

> **SarahSXY:** The day after you broke your
> leg, when you weren't at school, she
> told George you had a huge crush on
> him, and they both laughed about it.
> They also shared a pop, using the same
> straw.

I felt sick to my stomach. Em wouldn't really do that to me, would she?

SarahSXY: Sorry to be the one to have to break it to you. :(

Except that she wasn't sorry. I wanted to reach right through the computer screen and strangle her, and her stupid frowny-face emoticon too.

Just then, Bryan knocked at my door. "Margot. Mrs. Carrington is here to consult the deck with your mother. And I have to leave for class. I've got study group until eight."

I sighed, logged off, and went into the living room, where the triplets were listening to Raffi. I usually loved that CD, but that night I couldn't get into it. Instead, I just stared at my reflection in the darkened window while they squealed and hopped around on the sofa cushions to the sandwich song.

After I put my sisters to bed I turned my IM back on, but the only person online was Erika, whose name disappeared instantly. I was just about to shut the computer down when there was a tiny knock at my door. "Magoo?" It was Alex. She was dragging her yellow blanket behind her. Tears were running down her face.

"What is it?" I said, bending down and hugging her.

Finally she managed between sobs, "I don't like da bees."

"The bees? Which bees?"

"Da bees in da story."

"Oh, those bees." One of the stories I'd read them before bed was *Mrs. Bunny's Bee Farm*. There's this one page where "the bees hear the banjo and they all go berserk." "Did you have a

311

dream about the bees?" I asked. She nodded, still sniffling. "Do you want me to build you a bee-proof cave?" She nodded again.

She slipped her tiny hand into mine and we walked back to her bedroom. Very quietly, so I wouldn't wake the other two, I took a queen-size bedsheet from the hall closet and hung it over the headboard and footboard of her toddler bed, then weighed it down to the floor with heavy books on either end. When I was done I peered inside. "No bees can get in now," I whispered. "I promise. Go to sleep, okay?"

"Okay," she whispered back.

My mom was working late. I heard her last tarot client leave at 7:45, and Bryan come in at 8:30, but I didn't leave my room again. Instead, I went to bed early and watched the headlights of passing cars streak across my cottage cheese ceiling and melt down my wall while thoughts went berserk like banjo bees in my head. What else was Em hiding from me, and why was she lying? Would I ever get used to how lonely my life felt without Erika? What about Andrew? Would he ever really forgive me for not inviting him to Em's party?

I missed my mom having time for me. I missed my grandpa being alive. I would have given anything right then just to have someone to talk to. Someone I could trust. Someone to build me a bee-proof cave where I could hide away until I figured it all out.

29

I Uncover Strange Clues, and a Quiet Person Speaks Loudly

WHEN I WOKE UP the next morning I knew I had to find out one way or the other. With a heavy feeling of dread, I turned my computer on and opened a browser window. I didn't know why I'd waited so long to do it, actually—maybe because I didn't *want* to know the truth. I searched the words *SubSonic* and *Agent*. A page on the band's site came up, telling how to book them for gigs. The contact listed didn't sound like Em's dad. His name was Collin Clarke, from L-Group Entertainment. But then again, lots of kids have their mother's last names, so it didn't necessarily mean Em was lying . . . even though it was looking more and more likely by the second.

"Margot! It's eight forty-five," my mom called. I ran out the door, still feeling confused by the things I'd learned about Em . . . but nevertheless appreciating her fashion sense. The night before, I'd opened up the bag she'd given me with my wet clothes in it. Inside were three really cute camisoles, one of which I had on. It was dark green, with tiny beaded flowers at the top, crossed straps, and three layers of gauzy fabric at the bottom.

In English class, I did my best to smile and act normal while Em admired it. "You see?" she said. "I know what looks good on you. You should always trust me." It was a weird thing to say under the circumstances. "Doesn't Margot's shirt look great, George?" she said.

"Yeah," he said, glancing back. "It's kind of fluffy at the bottom."

"See?" she said again, smiling at me.

"You're the best," I said, hoping it would come out sounding sincere. After all, I hadn't forgotten Em's reaction when I'd questioned her about the autographs. And I definitely hadn't forgotten what had happened to Sarah J.'s eyebrows after she'd called Em a liar. Plus, despite my own doubts and what Sarah had said on IM, I still wanted to believe there was a logical explanation for everything. I just had to figure out what it was.

That day we ate lunch with Maggie and Joyce on the ledge. I watched Em carefully, measuring everything she said against what I now suspected.

"So," Joyce asked Em, "how many times have you seen SubSonic live?"

Em counted off on her fingers. "Well, once in London, and pretty much every time they play New York."

"That's so cool," Joyce sighed.

"I heard their new tour is going to be huge," Maggie said.

"Yeah," I added, "I bet K.wack'ed's going to be really busy. Your family probably won't get to see him much."

"Probably not," she answered. "He'll be traveling nonstop all year. But then, we're living here, so it's not like we'd see him anyway."

"Yeah," I agreed. "He probably wouldn't ever come to

Darling. But your dad could still see him, right? Em's dad still lives in New York," I explained to Maggie and Joyce.

"Oh yeah? What does he do?" Maggie asked offhandedly.

"He's . . . a stockbroker," Em said, shooting me a warning look.

"Does he ever come visit you here?" I asked. "I mean, he must miss you and your mom."

I couldn't help noticing how she averted her eyes. "Work's been crazy, so he hasn't had time to yet. But at Christmas he might."

Maggie grabbed a lock of Joyce's blond hair and started braiding it, obviously bored by the stockbroker talk. "Hey, did you see how Des.ti.nee had her hair in the video for 'Bring It'? In, like, a thousand little braids? Joyce, your hair would look so good like that."

"Totally," I agreed. Then I looked to Em again. "Have you ever met her, Em?"

"Des.ti.nee? She actually gave me this shirt," Em answered. It was tight black lace with ruffled sleeves . . . a little see-through at the front, but she had a camisole underneath.

"Oh my God!" Maggie said, dropping Joyce's braid and grabbing the front of Em's shirt. "I thought this looked familiar. Didn't she wear this at the VMAs?" I was surprised. I'd never seen Des.ti.nee wear a shirt at all.

"Yeah," Em said.

They both screamed. "I can't believe she gave it to you. This must be worth like, millions. This is so amazing!" Maggie shrieked.

It *was* amazing. Kind of unbelievable, really.

* * *

315

And the clues, odd as they were, kept piling up. When I got to gym class that afternoon, Mrs. Rivera was sitting in her swivel chair, directing, while a few girls struggled to put up the volleyball nets. It was a good thing she was busy, too, because the second I walked into her office, I swore out loud, and I didn't say "fish sticks" either. The boxes of invoices had multiplied overnight. Not only were they on every surface, but now there was a huge pile stacked across the middle of the room. On the upside, though, the wall of boxes divided the office so it was almost like having my own mini-cubicle.

I opened a box marked 2000–2001, and a few minutes later I heard the sounds of the game starting up in the gym and Mrs. Rivera crunching her first cookie of the period.

Except for one paper cut and Mrs. Rivera forgetting I was there and turning up the radio to sing along to "Wind Beneath My Wings," most of the period passed uneventfully. But with ten minutes to go, I heard a knock on the office door.

"Oh, hello," Mrs. Rivera said. "What brings you to my gym?"

"Vanessa, hi." It was a voice I didn't recognize. "I was hoping to speak to Emily Warner for just a second. She's required to report to my office at lunch hour for counseling. It's twice now she hasn't shown. Yesterday, I gave her the benefit of the doubt, but today . . ."

"Right, Emily Warner." Mrs. Rivera said. "The dog girl. You know, I was expecting the worst, but she really hasn't given me any problems."

"Well, that much is good to hear. Do you mind?"

"Of course not. Take her for as long as you need."

As soon as the guidance counselor left the room, I cleared

my throat. Loudly. There was a second of silence while Mrs. Rivera remembered I'd been there the whole time. "Hello, Margot," she said, from the other side of the boxes, trying to sound casual. "How's the leg today?"

"Better, thanks," I said, picking up another stack of invoices. I heard her open the oatmeal-cookie drawer again.

The dog girl? I considered this weird bit of information while filing the last of the 2000–2001 invoices. I remembered what Em had told me that day in the hallway after I'd confessed about the glazed ham—that she ate dog food once to see how it tasted. Was that what the teachers were talking about? It was definitely odd, but then, when I was little I used to roll up those tubes of cherry ChapStick and bite the tops off (they smelled so good!), and nobody was making me go to counseling.

After French that day, Maggie, Joyce, Em, and I all walked out to the yard together like it was becoming a regular thing. The wind was strong, and the leaves were really starting to fall now. I shivered a little in Em's thin green jacket as we approached Ken and George, who were waiting for us by the ledge, trying to throw Swedish Berries into each other's mouths and mostly missing.

"Button," Ken called. "Catch!" He threw a berry at me, and it bounced off my shoulder. I was just about to tell him to grow up when I heard someone saying my name. "Oh, man," Ken said. "It's my competition."

I turned to see Amir standing about ten feet away, over toward the basketball courts. Mike was behind him, but Andrew was nowhere in sight. "Margot," he called again.

"What does he want?" Em said.

"Just gimme a sec," I said to The Group. I walked slowly toward Amir, who was standing with his feet firmly planted, both hands deep in the pockets of his khaki pants.

"Don't leave me, Margot!" Ken called out behind me, but I just ignored him.

"Hey, what's up?" I said as I came to a stop and balanced on my crutches. I nodded to Mike.

"What's *up*?" Amir repeated angrily. "You mess with our man Andrew, you mess with us."

"Excuse me?" I answered.

"You destroyed him. You know that? He couldn't sink a single shot at practice today."

I knew Andrew was upset that I'd lied to him about the party, but saying I'd *destroyed* him seemed to be taking things a little far.

"You and George Wainscott. In the bathroom, at Emily Warner's party. Okay?" Amir added, reading my confusion. "We know. Andrew knows, and we know."

"What?"

"We know that you were"—Amir looked uncomfortable and also disgusted—"with him. Whatever. All the girls on the volleyball team were talking about it in the gym yesterday morning."

Yesterday morning? So when Andrew confronted me in the hallway about not being invited to the party, he was really upset about this? My entire face flushed.

"It wasn't like that," I tried to explain. "Brayden walked in on us, and she must have totally misunderstood. George was just in the hot tub and we talked about mittens." It sounded so stupid.

"Please, Margot. Don't insult our intelligence, okay? You go to this party, you don't invite us, and suddenly you're hanging out with them—with him"—he motioned toward George—"every day." He bit his lip in frustration. "You knew Andrew liked you. And then you went in a bathroom with *George Wainscott*. Do you think he even knew your last name a few weeks ago? Do you think he would have spent an entire morning taking down posters for you or sewing you armpit cushions?"

"Wait a second—"

"If you didn't like Andrew back, you could have just told him that instead of giving him hope. He would have still wanted to be your friend. He thinks the sun rises and sets on you, but honestly, Margot, sometimes I don't get why."

Amir turned and started across the yard. Mike went to follow, but stopped, blowing his long bangs up off his forehead. For a second I thought he was just going to stare at me disapprovingly, or shake his head, but then he actually spoke.

"You screwed up. Big-time," he said, summing it up like no other words could. Then he walked away too.

30

I Learn About Bad Egg Salad

MOST MISUNDERSTANDINGS are easy to fix. Like in first grade, when Grandpa Button left his white pipe near my toys and I poured bubble stuff into it, and then he inhaled a mouthful of dish soap. (I just explained that I couldn't find my bubble pipe so I borrowed his. And he admitted that he shouldn't have left his real pipe near my toy box. And then he bought me a new bubble pipe.) Or last week, when Bryan asked me to take out the garbage, and I said "yeah-yeah," because I was watching TV. And then I didn't do it. (I just explained that I can't focus on what he's saying when *Decorating by Design* is on. And he said next time he'd ask me when I wasn't watching TV.)

But other misunderstandings are not so easy to resolve . . . especially when the person who misunderstood you is refusing to even talk to you, like Erika-with-a-K, and now Andrew, Mike, and Amir. When I passed them in the yard the next morning, they barely even looked my way. And Amir spent the whole day avoiding me, even taking the long way around in math to get to the pencil sharpener. Still, even though I felt awful, I didn't have all that much time to obsess about it. Because, aside from being an occasion when *all* of my old friends were officially furious with me, the day also marked Ṣarah J.'s return to school after her suspension—and it wasn't pretty.

We were all trying to act like we didn't care, but secretly I was a disaster. Maggie and Joyce seemed anxious too. I could tell from the way they were talking even faster than usual, and constantly glancing at the door. Em didn't seem worried, though—even when Sarah walked back into English class wearing a new suede jacket and Lucky jeans. Through some miracle of makeup, you couldn't even see the gap in her eyebrow, and her skin had stopped peeling. In fact, it looked annoyingly peachy and perfect.

She sank down into her usual seat, tossing her hair in her usual way. Bethany and Charlie were whispering about her at the back of the room, but she silenced them with a glare. Still, nobody went over to talk to her. And even Mr. Learner seemed to know that it was best to leave her alone, skipping over her entirely when he was calling out people to read sections of *Lord of the Flies*.

Maggie and Joyce hung out with us at lunch hour, and we all thought that would be when Sarah would snap, but instead she just waved to us carelessly as she left the yard. "I'm going to meet Matt behind the mini-mart," she said, as if we'd asked.

Then after gym, Em told me that Sarah had even changed in a different corner of the locker room, not looking once in their direction.

But she couldn't avoid us forever. When we got to French class, Mr. Patachou had the TV set up. *"Aujourd'hui, nous commençons notre unité au sujet des annonces publicitaires."* A bunch of us looked confused. "Television commercials," he explained. Oh. We understood now. Then he explained that we were going to stop the TV after each commercial and talk about the technique the advertiser was using to sell products.

The first commercial was for deodorant. It showed two girls, both flirting with a guy at a party. They were wearing low-cut black dresses, and when a waiter came by with a tray of food, they both reached for it. The camera zoomed in on one girl's armpits, and a red circle appeared around the white stain on her dress so we'd be sure not to miss it. Then, in the next scene, you saw the guy leaving the party with the girl who didn't have marks on her dress. Mr. Patachou stopped the tape.

Nobody raised their hand, so I figured I'd try. *"Ils utilizent la technique de . . . ummm . . ."* I stalled. "You know," I said, giving up on French, "they want girls to be scared they'll never get a date if they use the wrong deodorant."

"C'est ça," Mr. Patachou said, before telling me to say it in French next time.

Next we watched a car commercial that was apparently trying to use the technique of humor to sell hatchbacks, only none of us got the jokes. Then another one for diapers that showed all kinds of pictures of newborn babies, which made a lot of the girls go "Awww." Clearly they'd never had to deal with newborn triplets. If they had, they'd be too busy thinking about what would be *in* those diapers to find it adorable.

After we'd watched a few more, Mr. Patachou told us to get into groups of five. We were supposed to invent a product and make our own French TV commercial to sell it. Each group was going to take one of the school's video cameras home to film it.

322

Em, Maggie, Joyce, and I all looked at each other. I almost felt bad for Sarah. She was staring down at her notebook so she wouldn't have to make eye contact with anyone. I knew the feeling. She'd end up having to tell Mr. Patachou she didn't have a group. And he'd add her to a group of friends who didn't really want her there.

"Sarah," Em shouted. "We need a fifth." Maggie, Joyce, and I all gave her confused looks, but she just mouthed, "Don't worry."

Sarah took her time shutting her notebook and gathering her stuff, like it was no big deal, but she must have been relieved. The only other group that didn't have five yet was Amir, Erik Frallen, Cameron Ruling, and Stuart Smythe. And they'd probably end up inventing some kind of space travel helmet that would have totally ruined Sarah's hair.

"So, New York." Sarah sat down. "Why don't you just do this project for us, since you know so many celebrities and you're from New York and you probably know everything about directing movies."

"Okay," Em said pointedly. "As director, my first decision is that Sarah takes the notes. Everyone else good with that?" We all nodded. Sarah glared at us, but she knew she was outnumbered. She picked up her pen.

"We could do some kind of cosmetic," Maggie suggested.

"Yeah!" Sarah agreed. "Like, what about a face cream that burns off your eyebrows? Oh wait"—she smirked at me—"somebody already invented that. Oh, I've got one," she went on. "What about a shampoo with bleach so you don't have ugly roots all the time?" She looked at Em. "Or mustache bleach? Margot, no offense, but you could use some of that."

"Screw you, Sarah," I said. I'd just bleached a few days before. Was it honestly that bad already? Still, I wasn't about to let her know that she was getting to me by going to the bathroom to check, so I pulled myself together. "Okay, seriously," I went on. "I like the idea of using the technique of social fear, like that deodorant ad. What about a product for people with really big, crooked noses?"

"*Ici on parle français,*" Mr. Patachou announced to the room in general.

"I mean, *les personnes avec les nez très grands et crooked.*"

"What about concealer that makes your nose look smaller?"

"Or a nose-job center?"

"Or . . . a cone that you wear on your nose so people won't notice how big it is!"

"That's the stupidest thing I've ever heard," Sarah finally spoke up. "Who would wear a cone on their nose?"

"Nobody," Em said. "That's why it's so funny."

Sarah rolled her eyes.

"We could call it Les Clothes de Nose," I suggested.

"Perfect!" Em said. It wasn't exactly French, but it sounded good. And anyway, practically half of French is English anyway, like *le weekend* and *les hot dogs.*

As we worked, I kept looking behind me, pretending to read the giant calendar on the bulletin board, but really trying to see what George was doing and if he was watching Em. He was in a group with Ken, who was busy making his trademark farting noises with his armpits. You could tell they were going to end up with a really mature commercial.

"Can you type that up in good copy for tomorrow?" Em asked Sarah, when the bell rang. Sarah rolled her eyes again.

"Didn't your grandma ever tell you your face could get stuck like that?"

"Didn't your grandma ever tell you not to tell huge lies about everything?" Sarah mumbled at Em, almost too quietly for anyone to hear.

Em slapped her binder shut, making everyone jump. "I was asking you nicely. Type it up in good copy." Her voice had a definite "don't mess with me" tone. She picked up her bag and started for the door. Maggie, Joyce, and I followed.

"Okay, so you hook the hose up to your butt, right, and then it connects to the gas tank, but how do you power yourself? I mean, where does all that gas come from?" Ken was talking to George as they walked up to our lockers after class.

"Burritos," George answered.

"Of course." Ken slapped himself on the forehead. "Why didn't I think of that? Dude, you're a genius." George flipped his flippy hair, looking proud of himself.

"So we put burrito holders here and here." Ken had opened his binder and was pointing to a drawing with his pencil. "And here."

"Do we even want to know?" Em turned to us. We all shook our heads.

"It's a fuel-efficient, fart-powered family sedan," Ken explained. "L'Auto Fart-O. Revolutionizing the automotive world and saving the environment, one fart at a time."

"You're so immature," I said to Ken.

"And you're so beautiful," he said back, obviously just to bug me and shock me into silence. Maggie and Joyce said "Awww," at the same time, then started laughing. I turned to get something out of my locker so Ken wouldn't see that I was blushing.

"You guys want to hang out for a while?" Em asked.

"Sure, why not?" Sarah J. stuck her giant crooked nose into the conversation.

"I don't think anyone invited you," Maggie said softly.

Sarah just looked straight at Em, though, like she knew who was really in charge.

"We're just going to sit on the ledge," Em said. "It's a free country." Sarah gave Maggie a smug look. "Just don't go assuming it means we've forgiven you or anything," Em added, which left Sarah looking less self-satisfied. Still, she followed us as we walked to the door, which just goes to show how desperate she must have been to have a group of people to be seen with.

Bryan was already waiting outside, so I waved good-bye to everyone quickly.

"See you tomorrow, Margot," Em called, as The Group settled themselves on the ledge.

Ken blew me a kiss, which I pretended to ignore.

"Did you have an enjoyable day?" Bryan asked as he put my crutches in the backseat. He was already dressed for his real estate class in a denim button-up shirt and black pants, along with his usual scuffed loafers.

"I don't know." I flipped the sun visor down and opened the flap on the tiny mirror to check how bad my mustache really was.

"You don't know?"

"That's what I said." I leaned in closer. There were two especially dark hairs, almost right under my nose. Disgusting. It was definitely time to bleach again. I leaned back, closed my eyes, and opened them again quickly, trying to pretend like I was seeing my own face for the first time, like a stranger would. Minor mustache problem aside, I wasn't ugly. I could admit that much. But I definitely wasn't *so beautiful.*

"You don't know if your day was enjoyable?"

"Right," I said, probably a little more impatiently than I needed to. I flipped the mirror shut.

Bryan nodded quietly without taking his eyes off the road. Of course, then I felt bad because I'd obviously hurt his feelings. Again. "Okay," I admitted, "it wasn't the greatest. A few people are mad at me because of something I did, that's all."

"Well, if it's anything you want to talk about, Margot, you know I—"

But that last thing I'd said had reminded me of something.

"Oh, can we stop?" I asked suddenly, as we got near the corner store at Larson and Springlade. "I just remembered. I have to get something." Bryan glanced at the clock on the dashboard. His real estate class started at 4:30, sharp. It was only 3:27 . . . but he always had to be at least a half hour early for everything.

"It's something I *really* need," I added urgently, in a way that suggested it might be maxi pads. He pulled into the first available parking spot.

"Do you need money?" he asked.

"I've got some." I felt my pocket just to be certain. The three five-dollar bills and the toonie left over from my taxi/flower money were all there.

I went inside and was standing at a pathetic little card rack trying to decide between a card with a sailboat on it and another with a bird, when the shop bells above the door jingled and two girls walked in.

"I think we should get the kind with almonds today," one of them was saying. "Almonds are high in vitamin E and healthy fats."

"Sure, I guess," the other answered. My heart leaped up at the sound of her voice. I turned my back and pretended to be studying the card in my hand intently so Erika wouldn't see me there, or—if she did—she'd think I hadn't seen her. Erika and the other girl walked up to the cash register and put something on the counter.

"Trail mix again?" The cashier laughed. "You girls are going to deplete my stock." I glanced over. The girl standing beside Erika was in a Sacred Heart uniform too. Her red hair was in a single thick braid down her back. I didn't see her face, but everything else about her—right down to her choice of snack foods—screamed Goody Two-shoes.

"I hope this one will be fresher," the girl said in a matter-of-fact tone. "In the pack we had yesterday, the sunflower seeds were chewy." No kidding, I thought. Because nobody buys trail mix at a convenience store. It was probably nineteen years old.

"Well, if you have any problems with that one, bring it right back, you hear?" the woman said, smiling. They both turned to go, and as they did, Erika's eyes caught mine for the briefest second. They went wide and questioning when she saw the cast on my leg, then we both looked away. I waited until the door closed behind them before quickly grabbing a spider plant (the only flowerlike thing they had) and the bird card.

So *that* explained it, I thought miserably as I paid the cashier. Erika had a new friend. There was no reason for her to return my phone call, or the e-mail I'd sent her. She'd replaced me with trail-mix girl as easily as she'd replace a pair of too-tight pants, a pen that had run out of ink, or that ruffly thing on the bottom of her bed when her mom got her a new coordinating sheet set. Well fine, I thought as I pushed the shop door open angrily with one shoulder, accidentally bashing the bag with the spider plant into the glass and nearly dropping one crutch as I stumbled sideways. Fine. I didn't need her anymore anyway.

When we got home, my mom was coming into the kitchen, pulling her hair back in a ponytail. I set the bag with the plant down in the corner, where she wouldn't notice it right away. "Mom," I said. "Can I talk to you?" She started gathering dishes and piling them in the sink.

"Sorry, Margot," she said. "Connie McMaster will be here in five minutes, and you know how she always comes in through the kitchen. I need to get these dishes done." Mrs. McMaster, the mayor's wife, was one of my mom's most high-profile clients. She always snuck in the kitchen door so no voters would spot her and think the new location of the landfill site was being partly decided by the Wheel of Fortune card.

"I just—"

"Is that jacket warm enough?" Mom interrupted, glancing at me critically as she started to run the water.

"Yes," I lied. Obviously it was way too thin now that it was nearly October, but I wasn't going to switch to my puffy winter jacket until I had to.

She shook some water off her hands and pinched the fabric on my arm, leaving wet fingerprints behind. "Where's your Gore-Tex jacket?"

"I lost it." I bit my lip, waiting.

"You lost it?"

"Well, not exactly. But I can't find it." It was technically true. The last time I'd seen it was when Em threw it in the trash can. For all I knew, a homeless person might be wearing it.

"Well look for it." She put her hands on her hips. "Honestly, Margot."

"I know," I said, not looking her in the eye. Everything I said or did just seemed to make her mad, but I had to tell her one last thing. "By the way," I said, bracing myself, "I have to do a group project for French tomorrow after school at a friend's house. So I can't babysit."

"Tomorrow, Margot? You couldn't have given me a little more notice?" She was totally annoyed now.

"I only found out today!" I said.

"That's all right," Grandma Betty called soothingly, overhearing our argument from the living room, where she was busy measuring the triplets for Halloween costumes. Through the door I could see my grandma wrapping the measuring tape around Aleene, just underneath her armpits, then trying to hold it steady while Aleene giggled and wiggled uncontrollably. "Let me babysit tomorrow. Grandma loves her girls." She tickled Aleene on purpose now. "That way Margot can focus on her schoolwork."

My mom sighed but didn't argue. "Leave the phone number where you'll be on the table," she said. "And how are you going to get home?"

"I'll wait at my friend's house until Bryan's done with class," I said.

Mom glanced at her watch. It looked like I'd lucked out again. She was definitely on the verge of a lecture, but Connie McMaster would be there any second to ask the cards whether she and the mayor should buy a new car or plan a ski vacation.

"Well, work it out with him, then."

"I will." I picked up the bag with the spider plant and went to hide it in my room. By the time I got back, my mom had gone into the front room and closed the door. Grandma was folding up her measuring tape.

"How's your leg, dear? Are you in much pain?" She pointed to the sofa. "Sit. I'll fix you some dinner."

"My leg is okay. I can make dinner, Grandma."

She waved the suggestion away like she was shooing a fly. "I've half a mind to speak to your mother." She bent down stiffly, tidying up some books and toys on the floor. "Baby-sitting every day is too much for you right now. You need to focus on your recovery and your schoolwork." She dumped an armload of toys into the bin and looked up. "Now, if you'll work that VCR, I'll go see about dinner."

I didn't bother pointing out that it was actually a DVD player, and I also didn't protest about her making dinner. She was right. I wasn't even thirteen yet. Nobody else my age had to come home every single day after school to babysit for free.

Before Cruella De Vil's thugs had kidnapped their first puppy, Grandma Betty was back, balancing a tray with bowls on it. "Careful, girls, it's a little warm." She handed them each a spoon.

"Thanks, Grandma. This is really good," I said as I took my first bite. I recognized it as VTV Three-Bean Casserole, but I didn't complain.

She just gave me a quick smile. "Now, tell me. Why haven't I seen Erika these past few weeks?" she asked.

"I guess she's busy."

Grandma lowered her spoon. "Why don't you tell me what's really happening?"

I blew on a navy bean to cool it down. "She sort of hates me now."

"Why would she hate you?" Grandma Betty turned, giving me her full attention.

"I told her I'd meet her somewhere and then I forgot to go." It didn't sound so bad when I said it like that. "But then my new friend, Em, she kind of slammed the door in Erika's face. By accident."

"Well, that's just a misunderstanding," Grandma Betty said reasonably. "Why don't you call her up and explain that it slipped your mind and that Em didn't mean to slam the door?"

"I tried. She doesn't want to talk to me," I answered. "I even saw her at the store today. She pretended I was invisible."

My grandma looked deep in thought for a second. "I'm going to tell you a little story," she said. "Do you remember your great-aunt Clara?" I nodded, even though I wasn't exactly certain. Was she was the one who lived in the Maritimes and sewed tea cozies shaped like boats? "Well, she was my sister." Grandma explained. "We were close." She put a hand on my knee. "Then just after Grandpa Button and I moved to Darling, our father died of lung cancer. A terrible disease. Clara was devastated. We both were. It happened so fast. But I was the oldest, so I had to be the strong one." I understood completely. I always had to be the strong, responsible one with my sisters too.

"I went home and ordered the flowers, wrote the obituary, planned the service, made the finger sandwiches for the reception. And meanwhile, Clara just cried. At first I didn't mind.

She'd always been sensitive. But after a while I got impatient with her. I'd just lost my father too, but I was still putting one foot in front of the other." I nodded, remembering again how she'd been so busy looking after me and my mom that she'd barely even cried when Grandpa Button died.

"And then the day of the burial . . . that was the last straw. The funeral home arranged two cars for the family. Clara and her husband rode in one, and Grandpa Button, your mother, and I were in the other. Well, when we got to the cemetery, Clara didn't get out of the car. Can you imagine? She was so caught up in her own drama that she didn't even bother. She had the driver let her husband out at the grave site and then drive her away. After all the arrangements I'd made, she didn't even have the decency to pay her last respects to the man who'd raised us."

She slapped me lightly on the arm to make her point. I waited for the rest of the story, but she didn't go on. We watched the Dalmatians in silence for a few minutes. Finally, I had to ask.

"But you forgave her, right?"

"I'm glad you asked." She paused to smile before she went on. "The next day when she called, she didn't apologize. Didn't even mention it."

"So how did you finally make up?"

"We didn't. Not for a long time. I refused to take her calls. Before long, she gave up. They moved out east on account of Great-uncle Todd's business, and things being as they were, we lost touch for nearly twenty years."

She paused as if to emphasize just how long twenty years was. "It wasn't until your aunty Corinne's wedding that I finally saw Clara again and told her what I thought of her insulting our father's memory. I asked her straight out, 'What would make a person behave that way?' And do you know what she said?"

"What?" I asked.

"Bad egg salad."

"Bad egg salad?"

"On the way to the cemetery, she'd developed a case of the runs. *Diarrhea*," Grandma Betty whispered, in case I hadn't understood. "Well, you know how it is. She had to use the washroom right away. That was why she drove off. And when it was all said and done, she was too embarrassed to mention it. Then when I didn't return her phone calls, she assumed I was angry with her over something else. She couldn't even exactly remember what anymore."

I laughed out loud, and Grandma did too.

"And it's funny. But it's also sad, isn't it? I lost out on twenty years of friendship with my sister for no good reason." Grandma shook her head. "It's my biggest regret."

She finished her casserole and slid her bowl onto the coffee table. "Margot, learn from an old lady's mistakes. Don't let a little bad egg salad come between you and Erika. Give her a call. Tell her what's in your heart."

I nodded, but I knew I wasn't going to. It just wasn't that simple. Even if Erika—or Andrew, for that matter—would agree to talk to me, things could never be the same. Like Mike said, I'd screwed up. Big-time.

It wasn't until Grandma finally left for her apartment and I'd put the triplets to bed that I remembered the spider plant, still in its bag on my bedside table.

Maybe I couldn't fix my friendships with Erika and Andrew, but I could at least try to fix things with my mom. It was true that she expected a lot from me—probably too much. And I wished she hadn't called Sarah J.'s mother like that, but on the other hand, maybe she couldn't help herself. She might not be your typical lamp-shade-dusting, pot-roast-cooking, or business-suit-wearing mother, but deep down she was *still* a mother in the ways that counted. And maybe—I hated to admit this—sometimes she did the annoying things that she did because she loved me. I took a deep breath, peeled the cellophane off the bird card, and wrote the first words that came into my heart.

31

A Bichon Frise and a Ham Have More in Common Than You Think

The Top Three Worst Things I've Ever Done
(until I did what I did yesterday, which tops them all):
1. Stole a glazed ham
2. Ditched my former best friend Erika in a cemetery, and lied to my other friend, Andrew
3. Told my mother I hated her

Before I go any further, though—and before you judge me—I just want to say that I didn't wake up yesterday morning planning to do something terrible. It just happened. Like dominoes. One thing led to another, and before I knew it, the whole situation had come crashing down, out of control.

At lunch hour, probably because of the little talk she'd had during gym with Mrs. Martine, Em suddenly had "something to take care of" again. She disappeared when the bell rang, leaving me alone on the concrete ledge with Maggie and Joyce, who were discussing extremely important stuff.

"Whatever."

"Oh, please. Whatever."

"Okay. Margot will settle it for us. What do you like

better? Watermelon or honey vanilla?"

"Honey vanilla, I guess," I answered.

"Totally. Me too," Maggie said, like it was amazing we had so much in common. "See?" She turned to Joyce.

"You guys are so clueless." Joyce shook her head. "Watermelon lip gloss rocks."

"Sucks," Maggie said.

"Rocks," Joyce corrected.

"Sucks," Maggie said again. They probably would have been able to keep that fascinating argument going for ages, if Ken hadn't showed up and interrupted.

"Girls, girls, girls," he said, putting a hand on each of their shoulders. "Let me settle this for you." He looked deep in thought for a second. "It rocks."

Maggie cocked her head to one side. "You don't even know what we're talking about."

Ken shrugged. "You guys seen George?" he asked.

We all shook our heads.

"How about Em?" When we shook our heads again, he nodded. "Oh," he said, giving Maggie and Joyce a meaningful look. "Right."

"What's that supposed to mean?" I said, my heart skipping a beat. "Em's probably—" I was about to say "in the Student Support Office," but caught myself just in time. "She's probably talking to her dad. She usually calls him at lunch." I glanced at my watch. It was 12:45. Em was always back by then. I stood up. "I'm going to go look for her. Be right back."

"Margot, I don't think you should," Maggie said.

"Yeah, why don't you just wait here?" said Joyce.

There was something in their tones that made me know

what was going on even before I stood up, ignoring their suggestions to just stay and hang out; even before I walked across the yard; even before I turned the corner and reached the little nook in the wall beside the stairs (where kids sometimes went for privacy); even before I saw it with my own eyes.

George was sitting with his back to the wall, his legs bent in front of him. Em was kneeling beside him, her fingers laced through his, leaning across his body to reach his lips. She was kissing him gently, tilting her head to one side. I felt my stomach drop. I don't know how long I stood there watching, frozen in place, but I do know I felt hot and dizzy and sick. And then I just turned on my crutches and started walking away as fast as I could. That was when she must have seen me.

"Margot!" Em called, but I didn't stop. I kept going until I reached the far end of the concrete ledge, where nobody was sitting, and nobody would see the tears streaming down my face. "Wait, Margot." Em came across the yard breathlessly and sat down beside me. I focused my eyes straight ahead on a four-square line drawn on the ground. I honestly had nothing to say to her.

"Okay, so you're pissed at me," she started. "I get it." It wasn't much of an apology. Not that it mattered. What I'd just seen was unforgivable. "I was going to tell you. It's not like I wanted you to find out like this." I wiped at my cheeks with the back of my hand. The worst part was that I'd known it. I'd known all along I couldn't trust her, and I'd let it happen anyway.

"Margot, look." She exhaled heavily. "I know you have a thing for him. *Everybody* knows. But he doesn't like you. Not like that. Look, I even asked him outright, that day you weren't here. He said he didn't think of you that way. You have to move on." Did she actually think she was helping me to "move on"? Did she *honestly* believe she'd done me some kind of a favor by telling him I liked him and completely embarrassing me?

"It's over," I said finally, in a low voice.

"What's over?"

"Our friendship. Don't talk to me. Don't pass me notes. Don't IM me. Don't even look at me."

"Margot." She grabbed my wrist tightly, but I shook my arm to get loose.

"You told me you didn't like him," I said. "You said he wasn't your type, but you lied. You lied about everything." There, I'd said it. I didn't even care if she burned my eyebrows off. I couldn't stand holding it in anymore. "I know you don't have a music agent for a dad. You're just making him up. You go to the Student Support Office at lunch because you got in trouble and you need counseling, and it wasn't just for skipping school." She took all of this in calmly until I added my last accusation. "And I know you're the dog girl."

"What?" she said. "Who told you about that?"

I didn't answer.

"Margot, who told you that?" she said sharply, but it wasn't working. She could get as mad at me as she wanted. I didn't care. I was *more* mad at her, and I had every right to be. "Okay, look. You can hate me for what you just saw," she went on. "That's fine, but I'm begging you, please don't tell anyone about the dognapping. It's the whole reason my mom and I left New York. She'll kill me if anyone here finds out." There was a pleading tone in her voice that I'd never heard before. I looked over, amazed to see actual tears in her eyes.

"I just did it because he's really my father. I *know* he is, but he won't admit to it. He can deny it all he wants, but I have proof. I found papers at home that said he was my mom's agent before I was born, and now he's saying he never even met her? So I had to make him confess. And I took really good care of his stupid dog after I kidnapped it. I even fed it this expensive dog food that was supposed to taste like lobster, even though I tried it, and it didn't."

"Who's really your father?" I asked, totally confused. "You kidnapped a dog?"

She looked up, brushing away her tears. An expression of horror crossed her face. "You mean you *don't* know?"

"I just heard a teacher call you the dog girl, that's all," I said.

"Oh great," Em said, letting her head fall into her hands. "Well, I guess you pretty much know now anyway." She opened her backpack and pulled out her binder, then slid a piece of newspaper out from a hidden pocket in one of her dividers and handed it to me.

Preteen Pleads Guilty to Dognapping of NY Agent's Bichon Frise

There was a photo of a man in a business suit, holding a fluffy white dog with bows in its hair. I read on:

Mr. Honey, the pampered pooch of NY music agent Collin Clarke and wife, Annabeth McDowell, has been reunited with the couple after a terrifying week spent in canine captivity. The dog was taken last Monday from outside a SoHo

Starbucks, where the couple's dog walker had tied it to a post. "I just wanted a tall nonfat no-foam soy latte," says Angela Todd, of Tails 'n' Tiaras Dog Walking Service. "I never meant for any of this to happen!"

The dognapper, turned in by a neighbor who recognized Mr. Honey from the couple's repeated televised pleas, is the twelve-year-old daughter of a daytime drama actress whose name has been withheld to protect her daughter's identity. Sources say the preteen believed Clarke to be her biological father and was demanding an undisclosed amount of cash in unmarked bills in exchange for Mr. Honey's safe return.

"She came into my office posing as a potential client several weeks ago," Clarke reports, "but before that, I'd never met this girl or her mother in my life."

The girl will face charges of mischief and theft. And as for Mr. Honey, he's reported to be dog tired, but in good health, enjoying the comforts of home once again.

"Debbie swears my dad was this minor actor who played Dead Guy Number Two in an episode of *Destiny's World*, but I know she's lying and that this guy's blackmailing her, or something. Just look." Em pointed to the picture at the top of the article. "We're identical."

They *did* look alike. It was their noses and the shape of their mouths. I wasn't sure why I was supposed to care, though. If anything, it just made me angrier because it proved what I'd been suspecting for a while now: that she'd lied to me—and to everyone else—about everything.

"You're lucky," Em went on. "At least you know who your dad is, even if you don't live with him. At least he cares about you. All my dad cares about are his rock star clients, his dumb blond wife, and his stupid dog."

She was wrong, of course. All my real dad cared about was . . . well, I didn't even know. Radishes, maybe? Or falcons? He definitely didn't care about me. But that didn't mean I thought I had the right to go out and kidnap somebody's dog, lie about who I was, give out fake autographs, and steal my friend's crush.

Em took the article from me, folded it up carefully, and hid it away in her binder. "So, can I trust you?" she asked.

I stared straight at her without blinking. "Why should I do you any favors?"

More tears sprung to her eyes. "Because you're my best friend," she said. Her shoulders started to shake. "I always meant to tell you the truth about this. I swear. From that very first time in the bathroom, when you told me about stealing the glazed ham . . . but I felt like too much of an idiot to say it out loud. I was going to tell you about George, too. I was going to do it today, even. I never wanted you to find out like this."

I still couldn't look at her.

"Best friends don't let guys come between them, right?" she went on. Obviously untrue. "Right? Look, I told you, he's not even my type." She could have fooled me, the way she'd been trying to inhale his lips. "I'll go break up with him. I'll do it right now if you want me to."

Break up? So they were actually going out? I dug my fingernails into my palms.

"It's just . . ." She let her hands fall heavily into her lap. "Margot, I don't have a lot of experience with this kind of thing, okay? I don't have a lot of friends. Not a lot of *real* friends. At my last school, my best friend ditched me, and everyone else started spreading rumors and whispering behind my back. I mean, I kidnapped a bichon frise." She swirled her index finger near her right ear, which, don't quote me on this, I'm pretty sure is the official sign language word for *I'm totally nuts*.

"When that story came out in the tabloids and people in the industry were talking about it, Debbie was so embarrassed that she made us move here so she could lie low until it blew over. Now I have to have a social worker and a counselor who watch my every move. Plus, they made me go to that stupid self-esteem workshop. I thought I was losing everything. But then I met you, and you actually liked me and looked up to me. . . . What I'm trying to say is, don't throw our friendship away. Please?" Her voice had gotten so soft I could barely hear her.

"I know what I did with George was wrong," she started again. "It just happened. . . ." She studied the ground, then took a deep breath and looked up. "But I'm going to make it right. I'm going to go over there and break up with him right now." She stood up, tucking a piece of hair behind her ear.

"Em, wait," I said.

I was still mad at her for kissing George, and furious that she'd been lying to me all this time. But I also couldn't help thinking how strange it was that we'd somehow found each other: the Hamburglar and the dognapper. In a way, it made perfect sense. Em wanted to pretend to be somebody she wasn't. So did I. Also, I couldn't help it—part of me felt sorry for her. She'd made a very dumb, idiotic mistake, and now she was paying for it, big-time. If anyone knew what that felt like, wouldn't it be me?

"Don't break up with him," I said. "You're right. He doesn't like me anyway." The words caught in my throat, but I knew they were true. "If he makes you happy . . ." Now it was my turn to trail off. I felt my eyes glaze over with tears. "You should be with him."

She looked at me like she didn't believe what I was saying. Honestly, after devoting three years of my life to obsessing over him, I didn't believe I was saying it either. "I knew he liked you. He pretty much told me." I paused, waiting to see if she'd be mad. "You said he wasn't your type, but I should have told you anyway. Maybe I haven't been the world's greatest friend either."

She sat down on the ledge beside me, and we looked off in different directions. Something was bugging me, and I had to ask.

"If your dad isn't really an agent, how did you get the SubSonic single?"

"He *is* my dad," Em said sternly, but then her tone softened. "I went to Collin Clarke's office pretending to be a new client. And I stole it when he went to the bathroom. I took an unreleased Punky Fish album too," she said. "And the posters, and a whole pile of breath mints. I figured it was the least he owed me. He never even bought me a birthday present, or paid my mom child support." We were both silent again for a minute, until we saw Ken coming toward us.

"You guys seen George?" he shouted.

"Over here." George waved and stood up, being careful to avoid making eye contact with either one of us.

"George-man," Ken said. "I got another idea for the Auto Fart-O. It came to me in a dream. Instead of honking, the car horn should fart."

Em looked at me and pinched her lips into a tight smile. I rolled my eyes. It wasn't exactly a big warm hug or even a handshake, but we both got the meaning. Despite what had happened—as impossible as it seemed—we were going to stay friends.

Or, that was what I believed all through gym class as I sat in the office filing invoices and watching the girls play volleyball through the window. Sarah J. was wearing this really tight T-shirt and what must have been a padded bra (unless her boobs had magically grown two sizes overnight), and Em kept trying to make me laugh by sticking her chest way out and imitating the girly way Sarah was running. I also believed it all through French as Em passed me notes with drawings of Ken's fart car on them. It got a little harder to believe, though, when George started holding Em's hand at the lockers after school.

"You guys," Maggie whispered urgently, stepping in front of them so I wouldn't see.

"It's all right," Em said. "She knows. She saw us at lunch." I stood there feeling like the world's biggest loser.

"She found out?" Sarah J., who had obviously been eavesdropping again, came up behind us. Even Sarah J. knew?

"You told everyone except me?" I turned on Em. "Even her?"

"Not on purpose. Trust me," she said. "She was following us around after school, and she found out." That, at least, made me feel a fraction of a bit better. "I told her I'd kill her if she told you." She shot Sarah a look that suggested she might still kill her. Any second now. "I wanted to tell you myself."

"Well, I didn't," Sarah J. said to Em, sounding exasperated. "Tell her, I mean. So relax. Do you want some water so you can take a chill pill?" It was the kind of thing that used to make Maggie and Joyce nearly die laughing, but now they didn't even smile.

"Nobody wants you here." I was having a bad enough day without having to deal with her stupid comments. Or I *thought* I was having a bad enough day. What I didn't know was that it was about five seconds away from getting much worse.

A bunch of eighth grade guys were standing across the hall from us, jostling each other around, and it wasn't until they started for the doors that I noticed Andrew was on the other side of the hall too, near the water fountain. He was crouched down tying his shoelace. Sarah J. just so happened to notice him too.

"I mean, look on the bright side, Margot," she said. "George doesn't want you, but at least now you can be with your true love, Andrew. You two losers were made for each other."

Andrew looked up at the sound of his name. "I'm *not* a loser," I said, staring Sarah J. down. Andrew's mouth dropped open a little, and so did mine as I realized what I'd accidentally just said and, more important, *not* said. Then he stood up, looked straight at me, shook his head sadly, and walked away. He hadn't even taken the time to finish with his shoes. And as I watched him disappear around the corner with the ends of his laces dragging along the ground, I suddenly couldn't stand it anymore. I started crying—full-out, face-turning-red, snot-everywhere, on-the-verge-of-hyperventilating crying.

"Margot?" Em said.

"Oh my God, Margot, are you okay?" Joyce asked.

"What's wrong?" Maggie echoed. As if it wasn't obvious: everything was wrong.

32

Revenge Tastes Like Lemons

EVERYONE SPENT THE REST of the day tiptoeing around me like I was some kind of scary, emotional time bomb waiting to go off.

"I think Margot should play the part of Pretty Girl," Em said, as we studied our Nose Clothes scripts in her living room.

"Definitely," Joyce agreed. "Margot, you've got the nicest nose of us all."

It was a lie. My nose was second worst, right after Sarah's. Still, I appreciated the thought. "I should probably be the announcer," I said, "because of my leg."

"Oh, right," Em said. "Maggie can be Pretty Girl, then. Sarah, you're Ugly Girl." She ignored the look Sarah gave her. "Joyce, you're Sleazy Fireman. And I'm the camera person. Did you guys make the Nose Clothes last night?"

Joyce dumped a ziplock bag full of colored triangles onto the sofa. There was a striped one, one with flowers, one with a leopard print that had rhinestones glued to it, and another that was kind of plaid. "They don't stay on that well," Maggie explained. "We'll have to use tape."

Em picked up one with orange polka dots and held it over her nose. "How do I look, Margot?" she asked.

"Good," I said.

"Just good? How about this one?" She put on the leopard-print one.

"You look like a moron," Sarah offered.

"Didn't ask you," Em said, without blinking. "Margot?" She batted her eyelashes.

I couldn't just say "good" again. She was wearing a nose cone for me. She was trying so hard to make me laugh, or smile, or at least talk. "Way better." I tried to sound enthusiastic, but it came out forced. "That one's really hot."

"I know." Em smiled. "*C'est super sexy, non?*" Everyone laughed. Well, everyone except for me (because I wasn't in a laughing mood) and Sarah J. So, really, what I mean by *everyone* is Maggie and Joyce.

Em got up and rifled through a drawer. "I can't find any tape," she said after a while. "Just use this." She threw a pack of grape bubble gum into Sarah's lap.

Sarah looked at the package like it was crawling with maggots. "I'm *not* putting gum on my nose."

"Yes you are." Em opened the camera case and started unwrapping cables.

"You guys," Sarah whined. No one reacted. "Well, do you at least have sugar-free? I'm on a diet."

"You want me to chew it for you?" I offered. Everybody (and this time I mean everybody except Sarah) laughed.

"Hold still," Maggie scolded, turning Sarah's head back toward her. She had appointed herself head makeup artist, and she was busy "enhancing" Sarah's nose.

I let myself sink back into the cushy white couch as I looked around Em's lavish living room. Everything, as usual, was polished and in its place. Nearly too perfect to be true.

"Your house is amazing," Maggie said suddenly. "Is your dad's place in New York like this?" Maggie and Joyce had been pretty awestruck ever since the car with the black-tinted windows had pulled up in front of the school to get us. They couldn't get over the plush seats and the driver wearing a suit with a pin that said DARLING CAR SERVICE. I had to admit, even *I* thought it was pretty cool.

Em just shrugged at Maggie's question. She fiddled with the lens cover, probably so she wouldn't have to look me in the eye while she stretched the truth again. "His penthouse is a little smaller than this. But then, everyone lives in apartments in New York." Em held the camera up. "Are we ready?"

Maggie leaned back to get a better look at Sarah's enhanced nose. "Perfect," she proclaimed. I almost snorted. Maggie had used a ton of my deep olive foundation, plus half a thing of brown eye shadow. Sarah's entire nose looked like it had a huge bruise. The funniest part was that Sarah had no idea how bad it was.

"Places, please. Scene one. Take one." Em directed as if she'd done this a hundred times. But then, she did everything with confidence, right down to the way she kidnapped dogs and seduced her best friend's crush.

Maggie and Sarah sat on the comfy sofa and pretended to be reading magazines.

"ACTION," Em said.

Maggie flipped a page of her magazine then uncrossed and recrossed her legs. She sniffed the air. "Oh no. Do you smell that?" She said in a sweet, surprised voice, only, obviously, in incredibly bad French.

"I think it's a fire," Sarah said, sounding like she could have fallen asleep from boredom.

"CUT." Em stopped the camera. "Your house is on fire. Say it like you're actually worried." She started the camera again.

"I think it's a fire," Sarah said, with a bit more effort.

Maggie ran to the door, pretending to try the handle. "It's locked!" she shouted. "We're trapped!"

"What will we do?" Sarah said, again with the bored voice. Em shot her a look of death from behind the camera.

Suddenly, Joyce burst through the door. She was wearing a plastic fire helmet and carrying a garden hose. "I'll save you!" she shouted. She looked Maggie up and down, made kissy lips at her, and winked at the camera. "She's foxy." Then she pointed at Sarah's nose and made a gagging noise. "She's ugly."

Joyce grabbed Pretty-Girl-Maggie's hand, pulled her through the door to safety and shut it behind her, leaving Ugly-Girl-Sarah behind in the burning room. Sarah pounded on the door. "Okay, cut," Em yelled. "Cue the announcer."

I cleared my throat and started in a deep announcer tone, my voice cracking partway through, "Don't let this happen to you! If your nose is huge and ugly, get Nose Clothes right away."

Em stopped the camera. "Okay, put on the first one." Sarah made a face as she pulled the purple gum out of her mouth and stuck it on her nose.

"ACTION," Em said again. She zoomed in on Sarah's nose in profile.

"Nose Clothes come in eight attractive designs to match any outfit choice," I read. "For a fraction of the cost of a nose job, you can cover up that ugly nose and be fashionable at the same time." Sarah switched nose cones as I read on. "Nose Clothes are made of one hundred percent recycled materials and smell like popcorn. Now, let's see that scene again."

Maggie and Sarah took their places on the sofa, this time with Sarah wearing Nose Clothes. Maggie crossed and uncrossed her legs exactly as she'd done before, then sniffed the air. "Oh no, do you smell that?"

When Joyce the fireman came through the door this time, she looked at Maggie, made the kissy lips, winked at the camera and said, "She's foxy," then she looked Sarah up and down, too. "Va-va-va-voom!" she said in a deep voice, tapping her own nose to show it was the nose cone that made Sarah look hot. She grabbed them both by the hand and pulled them out the door.

"Portez les Nose Clothes," I said, then held up a sign in front of the camera. It was in English (even though we knew we'd lose points). "Because who 'nose' what might happen today!"

Em panned over to the door, which opened to show Sarah and Maggie pushing Joyce the Sleazy Fireman back into the burning room.

"And, CUT," Em said. "That's a wrap." We all sank down onto the supersoft sofas while Em started fiddling with the cord to plug the camera into the TV.

"Hello, girls." Em's mom came into the living room. She was wearing a hot pink dress, these crazy high-heeled shoes, and tons of makeup. Her hair was swept back, too, making her look exactly like a soap-opera star. I was half expecting her to faint suddenly, hit her head on the coffee table, develop a case of amnesia, and accidentally get pregnant with her ex-husband's baby. She snapped open her sparkly evening bag and looked through it while she talked to Em. "Emily, I'm leaving for the benefit now. Are you almost done with whatever you're doing?"

"We just finished." It was the first time I'd seen Em's mom since we got there.

"I left my gold card in the kitchen. Order some pizza for your friends."

"Sure," Em mumbled.

"And don't stay up too late," her mom added. "It's a school day tomorrow." She gave us all a quick smile, then glanced at herself in the mirror over the fireplace.

"Your mom lets you use her Visa card?" Maggie said once she'd left. "That's so cool."

"I'm starving. Can we get a large?" Joyce asked.

"We can get five larges. She won't care." Em put the camera down on the mantel. We all followed her into the kitchen. "Write down what you want." She threw a pad of paper onto the table.

"No anchovies," Maggie started.

"Seriously," Joyce added. "Who eats anchovies?"

"Double cheese," Maggie went on.

"Pepperoni," Joyce said.

"Double pepperoni," Maggie corrected.

"Okay. Sick." Sarah J. came back from the bathroom, where she'd gone to wash the makeup and gum residue off her nose. "Do you know how much fat is in pepperoni?" She looked at Maggie. "And oil." She looked at me.

I glared at her. I had exactly one zit, and I'd totally smothered it in concealer that morning. It was barely noticeable. Or at least I'd thought it was.

"Triple pepperoni," I said, staring her straight in the eyes, daring her to say another word about my zit.

"Quadruple," Maggie put in, backing me up.

"Margot's skin is gorgeous. She always has a tan, and you can hardly even see her blemish. And, Sarah? Maggie's *not* fat. Just order an entire box of pepperoni with no pizza crust attached," Joyce said.

"Okay," Em said. "But ask for melted cheese on the box. I love cheese." We all laughed, except Sarah, who was looking horrified at the thought of how many calories would be in a cheese-covered cardboard box of pepperoni.

"Okay, seriously," I said, "how about just triple?"

We ended up ordering five of the weirdest pizzas ever invented, including one with double cheese, triple pepperoni, quadruple pineapple, and one-eighth olives. We made Sarah call and place the order because nobody else could do it without laughing.

"They said forty-five minutes." Sarah hung up the phone. She'd made sure to order herself a Diet Coke and a Caesar salad, which she made a big deal of saying was the only thing she'd be eating.

"Why do you have a stick up your butt, Sarah?" Em asked. Obviously, Sarah didn't answer.

"I'm hungry," Joyce whined. "Forty-five minutes is forever. Do you have any chips?"

"Sorry," Em answered. "My mom only eats seaweed and rice."

And then I had an idea. It seemed brilliant at the time, but now I'd give anything to go back and change the words that came out of my mouth. "Let's play mystery on a spoon!"

"Oh my God," Em trilled. "I'll get the blindfold."

While she was gone, I explained the rules to the others, emphasizing that the blindfolded person has to swallow what's on the spoon, no matter how bad it tastes.

"I'm not playing," Sarah J. said.

"Yes you are," I answered.

"Either play or we'll have to punish you," Em added, coming into the room behind me.

"We'll give you some time to think about your decision. I'll go first," I offered. It was a strategic move. I'd only had to play mystery on a spoon once to figure out that the stuff got more disgusting each turn.

Em put the blindfold over my eyes. I heard the fridge opening and closing, a cupboard slamming, then a shaking noise like popcorn kernels in a jar, but softer.

"Open wide," Em said. At first, the taste was salty and sort of peppery, then it got sweet. The texture was creamy and crunchy at the same time. I ripped off the blindfold and reached for the glass of water. "Easy," I said. "Soy sauce, mustard, and crushed Smarties."

"Oh my God." Em clapped her hands. "You're amazing."

Maggie was next. She turned out to be hopeless. "Tomato juice, crackers, and jam?" she guessed. It was actually pineapple juice, crushed Cheerios, and salt.

Joyce was even worse. "Yogurt, lemon juice, and pepper?" To be fair, though, Em had tricked her by only putting one thing on the spoon: Dijon mustard.

Sarah sat watching, rolling her eyes. "You guys make me want to puke." Nobody paid her any attention. We were all waiting to see what Maggie would feed Em. It didn't end up being worth the wait.

"A little effort, please," Em said as she took off her blindfold. "Ketchup."

"And?" Maggie prompted, trying to trip her up.

"And just ketchup," Em said with complete certainty. Maggie tipped her head back and sighed in defeat while Em held the blindfold out to Sarah J. "Your turn."

Sarah shook her head. "Not a chance."

"Stop acting like a bitch, Sarah," Joyce said, shocking us all.

"Put it on," I added. "Or else."

"Or else what?" She turned to me. "Or else you'll cry some more?"

"You don't want to push me any more today," I warned. It didn't escape me that I sounded exactly like my mom when she was dealing with a carload of screaming triplets.

"You know," Sarah went on, "you don't really have a right to be all pissed off with me. Did you really think you had a chance with George? I mean, look at yourself."

Maggie and Joyce stared her down. "That's so mean," Joyce said.

"Not to mention rude," Maggie put in. "And untrue."

I stood up from my chair and was about to tackle her to the ground, broken leg or not, when Em stepped between us. "Okay, enough. Guys, violence isn't the answer."

"Yeah, tell her that," I spat. "She's the one who pushed me down the stairs."

"I wouldn't have done it if you guys hadn't been trying to ruin my life and burn my face off. Just so you know, you deserved it."

"Sit," Em said to Sarah, holding up the blindfold.

Sarah stood up. "I'm going home," she said, but Maggie

grabbed her arm before she could get very far. "Let go," Sarah said, trying to shake Maggie off, but then Joyce grabbed hold too.

"Wait a sec. Keep holding her," Em said, and ran from the room. She was back a second later with an armload of her mom's scarves. "Tie her to the chair," she instructed, throwing a few to Maggie and a bunch to Joyce.

"What? You're going to hold me prisoner? This is retarded," Sarah said, but she let herself be pushed into a chair. When we were done, she looked like she'd been taken hostage by a gang of ladies with very expensive taste. I know because Erika's mom gets Burberry catalogues in the mail. The scarves that were holding Sarah down were probably worth two thousand dollars.

"You just have to play the spoon game, like we asked you to nicely a hundred times, and then you can go," Em explained. She tied the blindfold over Sarah's eyes, then handed me the spoon with a smile.

When it was my turn, I'd tried to peek, so I knew you really couldn't see through the blindfold. Still, Sarah seemed to sense what was going on. "I'm not eating anything if Margot is putting it on the spoon," she said.

"Maggie's doing it," Em said. "Right, Maggie?"

"Un-huh," Maggie lied.

I opened the fridge and took my time considering my options. This was my moment of long-awaited revenge. Somehow, nothing seemed disgusting enough.

There was a cut lime in a plastic container. There were about ten thousand different kinds of salad dressing. A huge jug of dark green juice. There was an open bottle of white wine. Some leftover coleslaw. A few eggs. I grabbed one and cracked it into a bowl. Then I moved on to the pantry. A bottle of red wine vinegar caught my eye, so I added a bit. And then—it wasn't that I wasn't aware of rule number one (only three things on the spoon), but if Sarah wanted to declare all-out war, which she obviously did, playing by the rules hardly mattered anymore. I added peanut butter.

"Are you going to make me sit here forever?" Sarah asked, making a pathetic effort to pull her hand free from one of the scarves.

"Almost done," Maggie said, opening and shutting a cupboard door for added effect. "Hang on."

I opened another cabinet, and that's where I found my final ingredient. It violated rule number two, sort of, but like I said, the rules had pretty much gone out the window. The bottle said it was all-natural, environmentally friendly, and contained "Real Lemon Essence," so even if I wouldn't have picked it for a snack, it was practically edible.

I whisked my mixture together, smiled, then scooped up a big, runny, brown spoonful and handed it to Maggie. I could see her biting her lip to keep from laughing as she walked toward Sarah, trying not to spill.

"Open wide," Maggie said.

Sarah shook her head. "It smells disgusting," she answered through clenched teeth. "I'm *not* eating it."

Em pulled up a chair. "I'm giving you one last chance before I pinch your big crooked nose shut." Sarah just clamped her lips more tightly together.

Em motioned for me to take the spoon from Maggie. "When she opens her mouth, shove it in." She grabbed Sarah's nose and pinched hard. Sarah managed to hold her breath for a ridiculously long time. She probably could have held it longer, too, because when she finally opened her mouth, it wasn't to breathe.

"I hate you guys so—" she started, but she didn't get to the "much" part before I'd shoved the mystery spoon into her mouth. She scrunched up her face and tried to spit, but I covered her mouth with my hand. I wanted to see her suffer—just a little.

"Swallow," Em instructed. "Just swallow and it will be over."

Sarah swallowed, then Em let go of her nose. She took a deep breath before complaining. "That was the most—" but again, she didn't get to the "disgusting" part before Em pinched her nose and I shoved the spoon into her mouth one more time. "Swallow," I said. When she'd finished, she gagged, but Em immediately pinched her nose again.

"Em . . ." I said tentatively.

"One more bite." Em waved my concern away.

"Maybe we shouldn't," Maggie agreed.

"Oh, give me that." Em grabbed the spoon with her free hand and got one more in that way.

Sarah was really starting to gag. "I think she ate a lot already," I said. "Let's stop."

After Em set the bowl down on the counter, I pulled off Sarah's blindfold, expecting to find her glaring at us with murderous tigerlike rage in her eyes. But instead, a flood of tears spilled down her cheeks. The blindfold, already soaked, felt wet and warm against my palm. A big trail of drool was dribbling out of her mouth, and her breath was coming in little gasps. I think she was sweating, too, because her whole face was wet.

I picked up a glass of water that Maggie had just poured.

"Here," I said, holding it up to Sarah's lips. The word came out harsher than I had intended it to. "Drink," I added more nicely, and she took a sip. "You won the game."

"Yeah, you totally won," Maggie said cheerfully, putting a hand on Sarah's shoulder. "Nobody else could have eaten so much of that."

Sarah didn't answer, though. She closed her eyes. The sound of her breathing filled the quiet kitchen.

Suddenly she lunged forward in the chair. I jumped back, thinking she was trying to break through the scarves to attack me, and just managed to get myself out of the path of a gush of vomit that came shooting out of her mouth. It landed in a watery brown puddle on the cream-colored kitchen tiles.

"Oh my God," Joyce shrieked, stepping back until she was pressed against the cabinets. Maggie was already clear across the kitchen.

"I'm not cleaning that up," Em said.

Sarah started retching again. "I have to leave the room," Joyce said weakly, "or I'll throw up too." Maggie escaped with her.

They left just in time: Sarah threw up again, but this time, instead of hitting the floor, it got all over her clothes and the expensive scarves.

"We have to untie her," I said, pulling at the scarves. The smell was disgusting, but living with two-year-olds, I was pretty used to disgusting things.

"That's just nasty," Em said, stepping around the puddle of barf.

"Go get some towels," I instructed. Em nodded. She left the kitchen, seeming relieved to have an excuse to go.

"I don't feel good," Sarah said in a small voice.

"I know." I worked at a knot in the scarf tied around her waist.

"I really don't feel good," she repeated.

"Just a second, okay?" I pulled the scarf off her waist, then loosened the last one, which had been holding down her right arm.

"Do you want more water?" She took a single sip, then barfed again. I took the glass from her, trying not to look at the throw up that was floating in it, mixing with the water. "Do you want to lie down?" She nodded and stood up, but she'd barely taken two steps before she sank to her knees.

"No, Sarah, not here," I said. Her face was a scary shade of white, and I didn't want her to see how terrified I was. I tried to pull her back up while balancing on one crutch, but it was useless. "Let's go into the living room, okay?" I said in the calmest voice I could manage. Then I thought of the over-stuffed, expensive-looking white couches, and revised that plan. "Or maybe Em's room? Can you get upstairs?"

She didn't answer. She was pressing her face against the cool floor tiles, breathing in and out heavily. I put a hand against her forehead. Her skin felt clammy. That was when I walked across the kitchen to the cabinet and took out the Tru-Glo Lemon Scent Furniture Polish. I frantically skimmed the small print on the label. KEEP OUT OF REACH OF CHILDREN, it said in bold type. POISONOUS IF INGESTED. I broke out in a sweat, as the full reality of the situation hit. This wasn't edible. *Of course* it wasn't edible. It was furniture polish. And it was poisonous. I had poisoned Sarah J. "Sarah?" I asked. "Are you okay? Can you talk to me?" She just groaned softly.

Em came back in with a single towel draped over her arm. She glanced at the huge mess, then threw it on the table. "Oh my God," she said, clearly panicking. "Margot, sometimes my mom comes home from fund-raisers early if they don't have an open bar. She can't see this. You have to clean it up now. I'm serious. Right now. And we have to get her out of here."

Did she honestly think Sarah was in any condition to be walking home?

"Em," I whispered, "I put furniture polish in that bowl, and you made her eat a lot. We poisoned her. This is *really* serious."

"I know. I saw you. But you didn't put in that much, right?" she whispered back.

"I don't know. A few spoonfuls."

Em waved her hand. "She puked it all out. She's being a drama queen."

Sarah was still lying on the floor, moaning softly.

"I think maybe we should call an ambulance," I said.

"No!" Em answered with complete certainty. "We shouldn't. She's going to be fine. Trust me. I've seen this a million times with mystery on a spoon." I obviously didn't look convinced. "Margot, think about it," Em said softly. "If we call an ambulance, they're going to find out she got poisoned. The police might even get involved. Then we'll both be screwed for something you did." She glared at me like she was daring me to contradict her, but I could see the fear in her eyes. "And we don't even know," she said. "What if they *actually* arrest us?" The possibility hadn't crossed my mind, but she was right. "The first time you get in trouble with the law, they go easy on you. But the second time? Considering our pasts, you and I can't

361

risk that. Plus, trust me, it's out of her system by now."

As if to prove her wrong, Sarah heaved again and threw up a little on the sleeve of her shirt.

I looked from Em to Sarah and back again. I knew what I had to do. I knew what the consequences would be, and how badly it would suck. "Okay," I said to Em. "You're right." Her entire face relaxed. "She's probably going to be fine. But we need more towels. If you go get some, I'll start cleaning up."

"Good," she said. "Be right back." Then she turned and left. As soon as I heard her footsteps on the stairs I pushed myself up and hopped across the floor, taking care not to slip in any puke. I grabbed the cordless phone.

"Sarah?" I said again. When she still didn't answer, I punched in the number.

"Police, fire, or ambulance?" a woman asked.

"Ambulance." My voice quivered. My heart started pounding loudly.

"Address, please."

"Um. Lakeshore," I said. "I don't know the house number. My friend is throwing up a lot. I just—"

"Is there anyone there who knows the house number?"

What choice did I have? I couldn't leave Sarah, so I covered the receiver with my hand and yelled as quietly as possible into the living room. "Maggie, Joyce! Can you go check the house number and tell me what it is?"

"What do you want?" Maggie yelled back.

"She said the house number, I think," I heard Joyce explain to Maggie. "Why do you want the house number?" she yelled. "We don't know it."

"No, go check it. It's on the front of the house," I said in my loudest whisper, but by then Em must have heard us.

She came running down the stairs and into the kitchen, holding practically an entire closetful of fluffy white towels. "Who are you talking to?"

I probably should have lied, but I couldn't think straight enough to come up with something. "9-1-1," I said.

"Give me that." She grabbed the phone from my hand, pushed the hang-up button, and slammed it back on the charger. "Why are you such an idiot, Margot? Do you know how close you just came to getting us all in major trouble? I told you! She's going to be fine."

I turned away from Em, lowered myself onto the floor, and lifted a strand of Sarah's hair off her face, tucking it behind her ear. Her forehead was really sweating now. She reached out for my hand, and I held on to hers tightly. "Well, shouldn't we at least call an adult?" I asked. "I could call my stepdad. He won't tell anyone. I know he won't." I knew that wasn't true, but it was a risk I was willing to take.

"No," Em repeated.

"Okay, fine. Well, can you at least get me a wet washcloth?" I asked. "And a clean shirt for her?"

Em sighed heavily. "I'll be right back. Don't you *dare* try anything else like that," she said, then walked out, taking the phone with her.

My mind started racing. Maybe there was a phone in the next room I could get to. Or maybe I could convince Maggie or Joyce to find one. But just after Em left, Sarah sat up. She wiped her cheek with the back of her hand. "Are you okay?" I rubbed her back a little. "Do you want some more water?"

She shook her head. "I think I'm dying," she said, putting

her hand to her forehead. "What did I eat?"

I told her.

"Oh my God." She covered her mouth. At first I thought she was just reacting to the grossness of what was on the spoon, but then she actually heaved and vomited again. Em came into the kitchen just in time to see it. She took a step back, making a face before tossing me a washcloth and a white T-shirt.

I folded the cloth into thirds and pressed it against Sarah's forehead like my mom used to do when I was sick. "Aren't you at least going to help me?" I said.

"No. This is your problem. You're the one who decided what went on the spoon." Em turned to go, but before she could leave the room, the doorbell rang. Her eyes went wide. "Did you call somebody else?" she accused.

"No," I said. "You took the phone, remember? It's probably just the pizza guy."

She breathed a sigh of relief. "Can you get that?" she called to Maggie and Joyce. "Tell him I'll come with the credit card in a sec." Then she turned back to me, but I never found out what she was going to say next. The pizza guy was obviously in a hurry. He was banging on the door now. Hard. And then we heard a deep voice in the front hallway.

"A 9-1-1 call was traced to this residence. What's going on here, girls?"

Em poked her head through the doorway. When she turned back, she was glaring at me. Her jaw was clenched. "Fantastic," she spat, her eyes narrowing. "Awesome job, Button. The cops are here."

33

We "Talk It Out"

D O YOU KNOW WHAT I hate most about hospitals? More than the disinfectant smell of the floors? More than the sick people in blue gowns that gape at the back? Even more than the constant PA announcements about people code-redding, code-blueing, and code-yellowing? It's the waiting.

I hate waiting at the best of times, but hospital waiting is the worst because you're almost always waiting for life-altering news. Like, it's a boy . . . or it's a girl (or it's three girls) . . . or the surgery was a success . . . or, I'm so sorry, we did everything we could.

I'd been checking my watch obsessively ever since I'd sat down on the orange plastic waiting-room chair. It had only been twenty-five minutes since Bryan and I had arrived at the hospital to check on Sarah, but they'd been the longest twenty-five minutes of my life. I couldn't stop thinking about what had happened.

Back at Em's house, there'd been two police officers: a man and a woman. Em had tried to keep them outside, but they'd pushed past her. The male officer had hardly taken two steps into the kitchen before he reached for his belt. I thought he was going to pull his gun on us, but he was only reaching for his radio to call an ambulance.

The female officer bent down beside Sarah to ask her name and how she was feeling, then she asked if I was the one who'd made the call. I was certain she was going to start yelling at me for hanging up before giving the full address, but instead she patted my knee. "Good girl," she said.

Minutes later, the ambulance showed up. The female officer stayed in the kitchen with Sarah and the paramedics while the policeman took us into the living room to ask questions, writing everything down on a notepad. Then they made us call our parents.

Bryan was the first to arrive, coming through the door breathlessly like he'd run all the way there from real estate class. I was expecting him to freak out, but instead he caught me up in a bony-armed Bryan hug, smushing me against his chest so I could hardly breathe. Em looked on with an expression of absolute hatred. While Bryan was giving the officer our address, she took one finger and drew it across her throat while clearly mouthing the words "You're dead, Button." I just looked away.

A few minutes after that, Maggie's and Joyce's moms showed up and made a big commotion before taking them home. That's when Em completely zoned out. Her mom was missing in action. Apparently her phone was off, and Em claimed she couldn't remember where the benefit was. So the officers had to take her with them.

I wonder if I'll ever see her again.

* * *

"You must be Margot." I looked up from a brochure about multiple sclerosis, which I'd been unsuccessfully trying to read to distract myself. Standing in front of me was a blond woman. She was old, but younger than middle-aged—maybe thirty. I'd never seen her before. "The nurse told me you were waiting outside." She held out her hand. "I'm Angela." I must have looked at her blankly. "Sarah's sister."

Bryan stood up. "Margot's stepfather, Bryan."

Angela shook his hand, then sat down in the seat beside me. I'd never known Sarah had a sister, let alone a much older one. "I was just in with her," she explained. "They're getting her settled into a room for the night."

"Is she going to be okay?" I hadn't said a word since we got there. My voice came out squeaky and strange.

"She'll be fine," Angela said. "They thought they might have to pump her stomach, but they won't. She's thrown up so many times."

I felt a huge wave of relief wash through me. "That's good," I said softly, trying to hold back the tears, which were threatening to start again. I unfolded and refolded the brochure in my hands.

"Can I ask you something?" Angela said, setting her purse down at her feet. I looked up. "Why did you do it?"

It was a simple question, but the answer was so complicated. Because Sarah was mean. Because she'd always hated me. Because, even though I'd hated her, I wanted to be like her and have what she had. And then by trying to be like her, I'd become somebody I barely recognized. I wished now, of course, that I'd never made that stupid bet with Em, and that I'd never let things get so out of hand.

"I don't know," I said. "I guess I was really mad at her. She's not always very nice." I didn't mean to, but I glanced down at my cast as I said it.

"I figured," Angela said. "I actually came out here to thank you."

"Thank me?"

"For calling 9-1-1," she explained. She obviously saw the look of disbelief on my face. "No. Really. There are a lot of people who would have panicked instead of telling the truth. I'm sorry about your leg," she said. "Sarah . . . she's the baby of the family. It's like my parents think she can do no wrong. Anyway." She stood up. "She can have visitors now, Margot, if you want to come in with me. My mom's busy with paperwork, so it would be a good time to get her alone."

I *so* didn't want to get her alone. Really. If somebody had asked me which I would have rather done—sing the national anthem naked in front of everyone in the room or go talk to Sarah, I would have been stripping off my clothes and humming the first few bars of "O Canada." Unfortunately, though, nobody was giving me that choice.

"I've talked with my mom," Angela said. "We're going to ask the police to drop any charges." A second wave of relief washed through me. "On one condition. Whatever's going on between you, it stops today."

Bryan leaned forward in his seat, giving me a meaningful look.

"Agreed," he said, as if anyone had asked him.

"I'll come in with you," Angela said, "to make sure you and Sarah talk it out." She passed me my crutches, and I stood up reluctantly. "Don't worry," she said. "She's had some time to cool off. I'm sure she'll want to thank you for what you did today."

I swallowed hard, imagining all the ways I was sure Sarah would want to thank me. Clubbing me over the head with an IV pole was the first thing that came to mind.

When we got to the elevator, Angela pushed the button. "You okay?"

I nodded, but I was picturing Sarah pacing the floor of her room, sharpening a scalpel, and planning to plunge it into my heart. The elevator door dinged open and we got inside.

"You can do this," Angela said, once the doors shut. "Trust me, she's not as scary as she seems."

Of course, that got way harder to believe when I stepped into the room. Sarah was sitting up in bed surrounded by pillows, flipping through a fashion magazine. She turned her head, took one look at me, and freaked right out.

"Oh no," she said. "Angela. Get her out of here. I told you, I'm not talking to her. She tried to kill me." Sarah glared at me.

"I didn't—" I started.

"You did," Sarah said. "You poisoned me." She paused, then added dramatically, "In cold blood."

"It was an accident," I said. "I didn't mean—"

"In cold blood," Sarah repeated, glaring at her sister now.

I looked helplessly at Angela. Obviously this whole talking-it-out thing wasn't going to work.

"Kind of like the way you pushed Margot down the stairs?" Angela asked calmly.

"That was so different." She paused. "I only meant to grab her backpack and make her stumble a little, and then she went flying. It wasn't the same."

"I was just going to give you one spoonful," I explained. "And then, I don't know. Things got out of control."

"Sounds kind of the same to me," Angela said.

"Yeah. Out of control, Margot? I almost *died.*"

"Nobody almost died," Angela said reasonably. "Nobody was trying to kill anybody else. Can we at least agree on that?"

"We can agree on that when Margot stops trying to kill me," Sarah shot back. "And when she stops stealing all my friends."

"I didn't steal your friends." I was starting to get really mad. "Like it's my fault you were talking behind both their backs."

"Whatever," Sarah answered. "What about Erika Davies?" I looked at her blankly. "Oh, come on. Like you don't remember?" As far as I knew, Sarah J. had always thought Erika-with-a-K and I were unworthy of being in her presence. "In first grade?" she prompted. I still had no idea. "My birthday party?" She looked irritated that she was going to have to explain. "Me and Erika were best friends, okay? I invited her, and she said she'd come. But next thing I knew, she changed her mind because you invited her to some stupid singing hayride thing."

And then I remembered: the apple-picking hayride at Organic Orchards. They always had two big horses pulling a wagonful of hay, and they'd hand out these song sheets that had normal songs converted into lame lyrics about apples. Stuff like, "Hi-ho, the derry-o, the farmer picks an *apple.*"

My mom used to take me every year, and come to think of it, there was a photo somewhere of me and Erika with a basket of apples. I didn't remember anything about Sarah's birthday party, though, and I definitely didn't remember anything about the two of them being best friends.

"And I know you told her not to come," Sarah accused, "because you were jealous I didn't invite you."

"I don't even remember that," I said honestly.

Angela looked amazed. "And that's why you pushed Margot down the stairs, Sarah?"

"Well, duh. Of course not," Sarah answered, letting her head fall back against the pillows. "It wasn't just that. She's *always* hated me."

"You've always hated *me*!" I shot back.

"Well, you've always hated me *more*," she said.

"And you've always hated Erika!" I added. "You call her Nerdette."

"So?" Sarah said. "I liked Erika." She paused and looked out the window. "She used to give me the Fruit Roll-Ups from her lunch." She paused. "And then you and your new friend started throwing sandwiches at me, and trying to break up me and my boyfriend, and burning my eyebrows off. And you purposely didn't invite me to your party, just to get back at me for the time I didn't invite you to mine."

In first grade? Did she seriously think anyone would hold a grudge that long?

"We didn't invite you because you called us lesbians."

"Well, I only called you lesbians because you acted like lesbians."

"Okay, stop," Angela said, and held up her hands. The room got quiet. "I don't care who didn't invite who to whose party. I don't care who called who what. This ends. Today." She took another breath. "Are you listening to yourselves? You're not in first grade anymore. You're big girls now."

She reminded me of myself for a second; the way I often

told the triplets how big girls were supposed to behave: "Big girls don't throw things and hurt other people. . . . Big girls don't whine. . . . Big girls say please and thank you. . . . Big girls use the potty." It was true. Sarah and I were almost thirteen. But (with the exception of that last point about the potty) we'd forgotten some pretty basic things.

There was no excuse for the way I'd treated her. I was a better person than that. Or at least I wanted to be. "I'm sorry," I said, and I meant it, "about feeding you furniture polish." The words caught in my throat. "And also about all the mean things Em and I have said and done to you since school started. That's what I came in here to say. I'm not going to fight with you anymore."

Angela smiled. "Sarah?" she prodded. "Is there something you'd like to say to Margot?"

Sarah pretended to be looking out the window. I was just beginning to think she wasn't going to say anything at all when she finally turned her head. "If you tell anyone I held your hand in the kitchen, you're dead," she spat.

Angela sighed heavily. "Sarah! For God's sake!"

"Oh fine." Sarah gave in. "And I'm sorry. About pushing you down the stairs, and also about a lot of other things." I didn't know if she meant it, but it didn't really matter. I wasn't scared of her anymore, and I definitely wasn't jealous.

Angela took a deep breath. "So we're good here?" Neither of us answered.

"See you at school, Margot," Sarah said, opening her magazine.

"Yeah," I answered. "See you at school." Then I walked out to meet Bryan.

34

I Smell the Old Spice

I DON'T REMEMBER THIS, BUT apparently, when I was little, I asked my grandpa Button what it was like to live before color was invented. He was confused until I went to the shelf, pulled down some old photo albums, and showed him how all the pictures of him and Grandma Betty as newlyweds were in black-and-white.

"Margot has always had an interesting mind," he used to finish the story.

Still, even after he explained the wonders of full-color versus black-and-white film, I was always bored to death when he or my grandma would take out those pictures and start meandering down memory lane.

It's weird, isn't it, how other people's photos are boring . . . but you can look at a photo from your own life for ages. You see yourself, six years old, standing in your princess pajamas, grinning at the camera in the kitchen of the house where you used to live. Suddenly you can remember what it was like to run your tongue over the gap where you'd just lost a tooth; the sound of the radio—which was always on—playing some boring talk radio show; the way the air smelled like lilacs when the back window was open in the spring.

When we got home I went straight to the garage, moving aside the sports equipment, to get to the box of old photos we'd never unpacked. I found what I was looking for halfway through the first album. It was a sunny fall day in the photo. We were dressed in Windbreakers. Erika had bangs, two thick braids, and huge, crooked front teeth. She was crouched beside a barrel of red apples, but she wasn't looking at the camera. She was looking at me, and I was looking back, grinning. Except for the fact that I was smaller and my hair was frizzier, I looked pretty much the same.

I took the picture out of its plastic sleeve and brought it back to my room, where I flipped it over. There was my mom's slanted handwriting: "Margot and Erika at Orchard Fest. First grade. Best of friends!"

First grade. That was two years before my grandpa died. Three years before my mom and Bryan met. Four whole years before the triplets had been born. I flipped the photo again. We looked like we'd just thought up the world's funniest joke. We probably had.

Just then, there was a knock at the door. I was expecting my mom and the lecture of a lifetime, but my grandma's face appeared. She came and sat on the bed beside me. "Bryan told me what happened."

I stared at the outline of a quilted butterfly on my overturned blanket so I wouldn't have to look her in the eyes.

"I'm not here to be hard on you, Margot. I know you. You'll be hard enough on yourself. I just wanted to let you know that I love you." She kissed my cheek. Somehow, I would have rather she'd given me a stern look, or even a speech about the dangers of household cleaners. I didn't deserve her understanding and her love. It made my cheeks burn with shame.

The rest of the night, I tossed and turned in bed, waiting for my mom to come talk to me, but nobody else knocked on my door.

All of which brings me to this morning, when I woke up and found my mom waiting for me in the kitchen. She took one look at my face. "Do you want some coffee?" she asked.

"I hate coffee," I said.

"I know," she answered. "But do you want some?"

I nodded. She handed me a mug and sat down across from me.

"Do you want to tell me what happened?"

I took a sip and resisted the urge to spit it back into the cup. It didn't even have sugar in it. I looked at my mom, but didn't know where to begin. "Is it all right if I say no?" I asked.

Mom took a sip before answering. "No."

"Well, is it all right if I say not right now?"

She thought about it again. "Okay," she answered. We sat in silence. Well, sort of in silence. The triplets were having a screaming fit over who had more milk in their cereal bowl and why it wasn't fair, which my mom was ignoring.

"I have to get ready for school now," I said finally. Mom nodded vaguely, like she was a million miles away.

"I'm going to cancel my clients tonight," she said. "I'll be here when you get home. Maybe we can talk then?" I nodded and went to get dressed, and that's when I noticed the bag on my dresser with the spider plant in it (a little worse for wear, because I hadn't watered it or given it any sunlight since I got it). Before leaving for school I put the plant and the note on the coffee table in the living room, where my mom would find them.

I was in no rush to get to school. I asked Bryan to take the scenic route, but I still ended up getting there five minutes before the bell. Bryan opened the van door for me and handed me my crutches.

"I'll be here to get you the minute school lets out," he promised.

As I made my way through the yard, I could feel people turning to look at me. Michelle whispered something to Bethany, who shrugged. Maggie and Joyce, already perched on the concrete ledge, didn't say a word, but stared hard at my back. Andrew, Mike, and Amir all stopped the game of basketball they were playing. For a second it looked like Andrew was going to walk toward me, but Amir put a hand on his arm to stop him.

The one thing I was thankful for was that Em didn't seem to be around.

Still, everywhere I looked, there were reminders of what I'd done. "Why do you think the boys killed Simon?" Mr. Learner asked, balancing an open copy of Lord of the Flies on his thigh as he perched awkwardly on the corner of Mrs. Collins's desk. "Anyone? Ken?" I waited for the inevitable smart-assed pig pun.

Ken sucked at his teeth. "It's like they forgot how to be decent," he said. Mr. Learner nodded for Ken to go on. "They were stuck-up choirboys, but then they got stranded on this island and just went nuts."

We'd just finished reading a scene from the book out loud, and it had sent chills down my spine. There was this one quiet kid on the island, called Simon. He was a bit of a loner.

Probably the most mature of them all, though. And when he'd only been trying to reason with everyone, they'd all taken out their spears and stabbed him to death. They were chanting: "Kill the beast. Kill the beast."

"Good," Mr. Learner said. You could tell from his tone that he was surprised. "That was a thoughtful response, Ken.

"Anyone else? Margot?" I looked up from my book. The fact that I'd barely slept the night before was starting to catch up with me. All I wanted to do was lay my head down on my desk.

"They forgot who they were," I answered. "Kind of like Ken said." Ken gave himself a thumbs-up. "And they didn't even realize Simon was a person anymore. All they could see him as was, like, the enemy."

Mr. Learner nodded, satisfied with my answer. He moved on. I wished I could have moved on as easily, but every time I looked over at Sarah J.'s empty desk, a fresh wave of guilt washed over me. And every time I glanced to my left, the sight of Em's empty desk filled me with dread.

I lay my cheek against my hand, trying to focus, but it was useless. So instead I looked out the window and counted shoes for a while. I got to ten sets before the bell rang.

"Ladies and gentlemen," Mr. Learner said, holding up his hand, "this is good-bye. I'd like to thank you for your attendance, your attention, and your insights. Mrs. Collins will be returning tomorrow." A collective groan went up, and Mr. Learner smiled for the first time. "Your misery warms my heart," he said. "Before you go—" He held up a stack of marked essays and started calling names. "Tiffany Abraham, Amir Ahmed, Bethany Bluffs . . ."

"Sir?" Amir raised his hand when he got his paper. Mr. Learner waved him up to the front to see what the problem was. While they talked quietly over the essay, George turned around in his seat.

"So they're moving back to New York." I looked up in surprise. He was the first person who'd said a word to me all morning. "You know you ruined everything for her, right?"

Amir and Mr. Learner had finished talking by now. "Margot Button," he called, passing my test paper down the aisle. When it got to George, he turned, placing it facedown on my desk. "Oh, and one more thing . . . she told me you never met K.wack'ed." If I hadn't been so totally depressed, I might even have laughed. Of all the things that had happened, and all the lies Em had told, *this* was what George was upset about?

He flipped his hair, and suddenly I could see it. Em hadn't been that far off when she'd said he was like a Ken doll. Gorgeous George was always cool, always well dressed, and he was incredibly hot. But he was also kind of empty, and a little bit plastic. Like another accessory in Barbie's closet.

I turned my paper over and stared at it hard until George faced the front. I got an A+. Mr. Learner had scrawled a comment in red ink using totally unreadable handwriting. As the class started to empty out, I gathered my stuff and walked to the desk where the teacher was sitting. "Excuse me, sir?" I interrupted him. "What does this say?"

"What do you think it says?" Mr. Learner asked, without looking up from his paperback.

I squinted at his handwriting. "'A zaythful onlys. You're a right squirl, Margot'?"

"Hmmm. I don't recall writing that." Even *he* had to

squint. "Right," he said, and read in a monotone voice: "A thoughtful analysis. You're a bright girl, Margot."

"Really?" I couldn't help smiling just a little.

"Really," he answered, turning his attention back to his book.

I desperately wanted to ask Mr. Learner which part of the essay he'd liked best, but I could tell I was only bugging him, so I turned to go. I was almost at the door when I heard his voice. "Don't let the bastards bring you down," he said. "You're too smart for that." I looked back to see who he was talking to. "Yes, you," he said, glancing up as he turned the page. "They can call you names and fart at you with their armpits and behave like animals, but don't let them break you." He waved his book at me. "Now get lost."

I like trees, I thought, as I sat alone under the red maple at lunch. They're so leafy, so barky, so rooted to the ground. They never lie to you about who they are; never glare at you, whisper behind your back, or try to trip you in the hall—like Ken had done after math class. "Way to get my man George's girlfriend kicked out of the country," he said. (So much for thinking I was *so beautiful*.)

Friends are for losers. Trees are for winners, I told myself as I sat miserably in a pile of leaves.

"I heard they had to pump her stomach and that she was like, clinging to life by a thread," an eighth grade girl said as she walked past with her friend.

"What did the other girl feed her anyway?"

"I think it was gasoline and lighter fluid. She could have easily died."

"Then that blond girl. The one who threw the party with the SubSonic song? She got sent to juvenile detention or something."

"God. Seventh graders are so dumb."

I lay my head back against the trunk and closed my eyes, trying to block it all out. After all, Em was gone and nobody was going to believe anything I said about what had really happened, so what was the point of even caring about my reputation anymore?

I was about one breath away from falling asleep when I heard a bang and felt the whole trunk shake. I jumped, expecting to find Ken standing beside me, kicking my tree for revenge, but when I looked around, nobody was there. Then a basketball rolled by and came to a stop beside my cast. I looked in the direction it had come from and saw Andrew walking across the yard, his hands in his pockets.

"Sorry," he muttered when he reached me. He picked up his ball and turned to go back to the court, where Amir and Mike were waiting.

"Andrew," I called. "Wait." But he kept walking. "Andrew." I tried again; my voice came out small and shaky. I noticed a crushed 7Up can sitting on the ground. It was within reach, so I grabbed it and threw it. I hadn't played War of the Druids in at least a week, but the improved hand-eye coordination was obviously long-lasting, because it hit Andrew's heel. He stopped and turned to see where the ball had come from.

"I was calling you," I explained, trying to hold back tears. "But you didn't hear me, so I had to resort to throwing stuff at you." He took a small step toward me, looking doubtful. "I know I've been acting like a total idiot lately," I started, talking fast, trying to get it all out before he could turn and walk away again. "I should never have ditched you for Em. Or lied to you about the party. You didn't deserve that. And about what I said yesterday in the hall with Sarah J.—"

"Classic Margot." He cut me off flatly, shaking his head as he switched the ball from one arm to the other.

"What?"

"Classic Margot. You know, always saying something you shouldn't."

"Yeah," I answered, biting my lower lip.

"I hear you're poisoning people now," he went on. "So that makes you, what? A ham-stealer-slash-attempted-murderer?"

"I guess . . ."

He nodded. "I don't know if I can be friends with a person like you. Bad influence, you know." I looked at the ground. I understood. After all, I wouldn't want to be friends with me either if I were him. "Are you crying?" I wiped a tear from my cheek with the back of my hand. "Margot, I was kidding!" He walked back and crouched down in front of me, but I could hardly look at him. "Do you seriously think I'd believe you tried to murder someone?" I didn't answer. "And as for the other stuff, no big deal. I forgive you, okay? When have I ever *not* forgiven you?" He paused. "Okay, maybe there was that one time in fourth grade when you said my cursive letter Q's looked like little flowers. I still can't write the word *quiet* without feeling kind of girly. Or *quail* or *quicksand* . . ."

Was he actually making a joke? "But how can you forgive me?" I said. "I lied to you. And then you found out I was in the bathroom with George Wainscott . . . even though, seriously, nothing happened. But that's not the point. I should have been honest with you, and told you I didn't like you . . . I mean, *like that*. Not that there's any reason why I shouldn't. You're such a great guy, it's just that—"

"It's okay," he said, looking off toward the fence before meeting my gaze. "You can't change how you feel, right? I can take the rejection." He shrugged and smiled. "Anyway, there are, like, hundreds of girls waiting to get my number." He glanced behind him as if he was looking for the imaginary lineup. "Sorry to disappoint you, but you'll just have to settle for being my friend. Here," he said suddenly. "Catch."

He threw the ball at me. I tried to react, but it was too late. It had already hit me in the face. My nose started bleeding immediately, but I was almost relieved. At least now we could both pretend the tears running down my cheeks had to do with the pain.

"Oh God," Andrew said. "Sorry." Before I realized what he was doing, he had taken his sweaty shirt off and was pressing it against my face. "Pinch here," he instructed, demonstrating on his own nose. "Lean forward." I did, letting the tears flow, too. I held my breath for as long as possible to avoid having to smell the shirt, but when I finally did take a breath, I was amazed. It smelled clean, like soap, and also fresh, like ocean air. It was a smell I recognized. I closed my eyes and breathed in again. It came to me instantly: Gorgeous George.

"What's this smell like?" I asked, still pinching the bridge of my nose.

"My mom got me deodorant," he said. "Old Spice. She says I stank." He shrugged. "Did I?" I nodded. I was never going to lie to him again. "Well, I would have thought *you* of all people would have said something." He rolled his eyes at me. "I'd tell you if you stunk, which, by the way, you do."

I elbowed him in the arm as hard as I could without letting go of my nose or the shirt. "Wait here," he said, pulling himself up suddenly. "I'm going to get another shirt from my locker."

He started jogging across the yard. "You can keep that one," he yelled behind him, and flashed me a smile that lit up his entire face. As I watched him go, all I could think was this: one day, Andrew was going to make some girl so happy, and one day, I wouldn't be all that surprised to find myself regretting that it wouldn't be me.

35

I Am the Fool

IF YOU'D ASKED ME A MONTH AGO, I would have told you I was mature for my age. I drink coffee, after all (even though I hate it). And I sometimes watch the local news (mostly because I'm waiting for something else to come on, but it counts). Still, as I rode home with Bryan, mentally preparing myself to tell my mother everything I'd done, I felt like a little kid again. I could already picture the disappointed look on her face. "What were you thinking?" she'd ask. And I'd have to admit, yet again, that I didn't know.

So I was incredibly relieved when I got in and found the door to the front room shut. Grandma Betty was in the kitchen helping the triplets make necklaces out of Organic Oaty-O's, so, obviously—even though my mom said she was going to cancel her readings—she was with a client. Probably some emergency. Maybe Sheila Wheeler met another guy on Lavalife, or Kathy Malloy needed help choosing the best fertilizers for her feng shui shrubs.

"Your mother's waiting for you in the front room, Margot." Grandma Betty poured more Oaty-O's onto the table.

"But the door's closed," I said.

"I know, dear. But she said for you to go right in."

I stood up uncertainly. Opening the door to the reading room went against everything I'd ever learned in life. "Are you sure she said that?" I asked. Grandma nodded, but I still had my doubts.

I went down the hall and pushed the door open a fraction of an inch. A strong waft of sandalwood incense drifted out. My mom was definitely doing a reading. I tried to look through the tiny crack with one eye, but all I could make out was a sliver of the sofa.

"Margot?" I heard my mother's voice call sharply. I jumped twelve feet and slammed the door shut. I was already heading for my room when the door opened wide.

"I was wondering where you were." I turned to face my mom. She was wearing a brown peasant skirt with a purple button-up blouse. Her hair was pulled back into a loose ponytail. For the first time in a long time she looked relaxed. She'd even put on earrings. They were big and dangly and gold. They made her look like herself. In the room behind her, the tarot deck was on the table, wrapped in its silk scarf. "Come in," she said.

"I'll come back when you're done with your client," I said. The last thing I wanted was to tell her the awful things I'd done, and ruin her good mood.

"You *are* my client." She stepped aside, leaving the doorway open.

"I am?" It literally didn't make sense to my brain.

"I know," she said, possibly psychically reading my mind. "You're not eighteen yet. Come in anyway." I followed her into the room, not about to argue.

"Please, have a seat." She pointed to a chair on one side of the card table. "Can I offer you anything to drink? Water? Herbal tea?" It was beyond weird to hear her talking to me like I was an actual client.

"I hate herbal tea," I said, then caught myself: "I mean, no thank you."

"Well then, let's get started." Mom smoothed the back of her skirt and sat down. "Is this your first reading?" she asked, even though she obviously knew it was. She went into a big description of the history of the cards and the powers they held—all of which I pretty much knew. Then she told me to put my fingertips on the deck and close my eyes. She did the same, and we sat in silence for a minute. When we were done, she placed the deck against my palm. I shifted the cards a little in my hand, watching how the soft light in the room reflected off the gold edges. "While you shuffle, I'd like you to focus on a problem you've been having, or a question you'd like to ask the cards." I tried as hard as I could to concentrate on Erika; on how much I missed her; on how lonely I was. *Can't things just go back to how they were before?* I mentally asked the deck.

I handed it back to my mom, who laid the cards out in a cross pattern.

She got very quiet for a minute. "This card speaks to us of the recent past." She pointed to a card with a picture of a man on it. He was carrying one of those sticks with a bundle of stuff tied to it.

"It's called The Fool," she said. "You've done something you're not proud of. Right now you feel like you're back at zero. Starting all over again." I gulped as I thought of this afternoon, sitting alone with the red maple tree in the school yard. "It seems like a negative card," my mom explained, "but it's hopeful, too. The card represents a foolish act, but it also represents a fresh start. See this pack he's carrying?" I nodded. "The fool is on a journey. He doesn't know how he'll find his way from here, but not knowing is part of his adventure.

"This card represents a situation." She pointed to a person carrying an armload of swords. "The Seven of Swords. Someone is stealing something from you. Your ideas? Or your time?" Nothing was coming to mind, unless it was Mr. Tannen and the solid hour of math homework he'd given us for the weekend. "Or they might be stealing your honor by spreading gossip about you. You might want to be confrontational, but this card is telling you to stay calm and be strong." My eyes must have been wide with amazement, because Mom looked up and smiled. There was no way she could have known how Maggie and Joyce had told people their version of the mystery-on-a-spoon story (in which they were blameless and Em and I were monsters); how all the kids were mixing up the facts and making it even worse . . . except that, somehow, she did.

"This one tells us about the near future." It was a king in a red gown. "The Hierophant. It's good news. You know how to solve your problem. It's not a quick fix, but it's doable. The solution is there in front of you, Margot.

"And this card," she said, "is in the 'self' position." It looked like a naked lady inside a Christmas wreath. "It's called The World. It's about wisdom. Here you are, The Fool, taking the final step in your journey only to discover that you're right back at the start . . . at the edge of the same cliff you've stepped off before." All I'd wanted was to be somebody

387

different, somebody better, and here I was anyway: just Margot with the crazy hair. Margot who always said the wrong thing at the wrong time. Just Margot . . . unpopular, sarcastic, not at all photogenic. Only now I was missing my best friend.

"But this time around you see things differently. That's the key." She sat back in her chair. "Now," she said, suddenly sounding like my mother again, "do you want to tell me what all of that means to you?"

I took a deep breath and started at the beginning. My mom's face went from calm (when I told her how Em and I first met at the self-esteem workshop) to worried (when I got to our bet to make Sarah cry) to sad (when I told her that Erika and I hadn't talked for weeks) to furious (when she heard about the party Bryan and I had kept secret from her), but when I was finished, the look she was left with was something else. Something I barely recognized.

She sat for a while, going over all of it in her mind. "I'm sorry, Margot," she said finally. "I let you down." Her expression was apologetic, which was confusing, to say the least. "If you ever needed a parent, it was this past month. And I've been so overworked and overtired." She looked down at her hands. I was afraid she was going to start crying, but she just shook her head a little. Her earrings made a soft, tinkling sound, like wind chimes attached to her head. "Do you know why I wanted to do this reading for you today?" She motioned toward the side table. The spider plant was sitting there, still looking a bit wilted. "You've always told me you were mature for your age," she said. "And you're right."

Okay, now I was seriously confused. Maybe it would have made sense if I'd brought home a report card with straight A's, or started a waste-free bagged-lunch program at my school. But not only had I done neither of those things, I'd behaved in some of the most immature ways I could think of.

She took the card off the table and handed it to me. I flipped it open.

Dear Mom,

    Sorry I said I hate you. I was just mad because you said Em was "erratic." For the record, I think you were right, which goes to show you are a responsible parent. But sometimes I miss when you weren't always being responsible. Like when we used to go to the store and buy Twinkies. Or you'd let me stay up late when there was a good movie on TV. I love the triplets, and Bryan isn't a <u>total</u> loser. But I miss when it was just you and me.

    I haven't always been nice to you lately, but I'm going to be better. I don't want you to be so tired and unhappy. Bryan, the triplets, and I need you. You're the ringleader in our circus . . . the peaches in our pie . . . the cherry on the ice-cream sundae of our family. You get the idea.

    Love,
    Margot

p.s. Sorry I killed this plant.
p.p.s. Can I also say that I miss your cooking? VTV dinners suck!!
p.p.p.s. Bryan thinks so too, but he's too nice to tell you.

She walked around the table and hugged me from behind. I read the note twice, trying to pick out the part that made my mom think I was mature, but I couldn't find it.

Thankfully, Mom helped me out. "You were honest with me," she said. "For months I've been trying to figure out how to reach you, and you finally told me. I know this has been a big adjustment for you." She paused like she was working up the nerve to say something. "I love our new life," she went on, "but sometimes I miss the days when it was just you and me, too." That made my eyes well up with tears.

She hugged me again, then said with a huge, goofy smile: "You also called Bryan your family." I read it again and realized with a shudder that she was pretty much right. "I know you're still getting used to him, but Margot, I hope you can see how good he is for us. He's reliable, for one thing, and he's also thoughtful and generous and devoted to you. When your grandpa died, I didn't think you'd ever have a male role model like that again . . . Bear with me while I get mystical on you"— she smiled—"but sometimes I wonder if Grandpa Button didn't have something to do with Bryan coming into our lives when he did."

My mom wiped a tear off her cheek, and another off mine. "You've been through a lot these past few weeks, sweetie. And maturity doesn't happen overnight. It comes from making mistakes and learning from them." She leaned over and picked The World card off the table. "This is a good card," she said, studying the picture. "The Fool approaches the same cliff. He takes the same step. But this time, instead of falling, he soars."

36

I Realize What's Been Right in Front of Me

THIS AFTERNOON IN MY room, I kept going over the reading in my mind. It was spooky how right on it was.

Of all the cards I'd drawn, the one I kept thinking about was The Hierophant. "The solution is there in front of you, Margot," my mom had said. I kept looking at things that were right in front of me, but none of them seemed likely to make Erika forgive me.

A list of things right in front of me:
1. My nose. I could flatter Erika into forgiving me by telling her she smells good?
2. My bedroom door. I could walk right out it and tell Erika I am sorry. . . . Except she isn't outside my bedroom door, so I'd only end up apologizing to the hallway, and what good would that do?
3. A magazine on the nightstand. I could buy her a gift subscription as an apology present . . . but it just so happens to be <u>Home Style Today</u>. Her mom already subscribes.

4. Dirty Snoopy underwear on the floor. Not even a little bit useful.
5. A nearly empty box of Kleenex. At least I could use it to dry my tears when I come home from school for the rest of the year and have nobody to talk to.

I gave up and got up to turn on the computer, but half-way there, one of my crutches slipped sideways over a hardcover book. (My room still looked way better since I'd redecorated, but the de-cluttering part hadn't exactly worked out for me.) I fell hard on my butt. Two feet of laundry cushioned my fall, so it didn't really hurt, but tears sprang to my eyes anyway, mostly from exhaustion and frustration.

I pulled one crutch up from under me and leaned it against the bed, but when I went to pull up the second one, it wouldn't come free. It took a bit of digging, but I finally discovered what it was caught on: Erika's stupid Parasuco jeans, which I hadn't returned. I tried to pull them off the crutch, but my room is so small, and the crutch is so long, it was like trying to twirl a baton in a closet. I came an inch from smashing the lamp on top of my bookshelf, and I knocked everything off my bedside table, including the nearly empty box of Kleenex, the magazine, and the apple festival photo of me and Erika.

That was when I gave up and yelled as loudly as I could, "Mom? Can you come help me?"

"Just a second," she called back from the kitchen. "I'm knee-deep in couscous, chickpeas, and anise seed." It sounded gross, but weirdly enough, it made me happy. My mom was actually cooking . . . without a microwave!

About ten minutes later, she finally appeared at the door, wiping her wet hands on her skirt. "Margot." She rushed over as soon as she saw me on the floor. "Why didn't you tell me you'd fallen?"

"I'm fine," I said. "I just slid on some clutter." She picked up the crutch and started pulling the jeans off of it. It's a funny thing, but when you're stuck sitting on the floor for ten minutes, waiting for your mom to finish with her couscous, the wheels in your brain start turning.

"After dinner, can you drive me to Erika's house?" I asked. It was the kind of request that, lately, would have made my mom sigh heavily.

This time, though, she gave me her hand and pulled me up. "As long as your grandma doesn't mind putting the girls to bed."

An hour and a half later, my mom, the jeans, and I pulled up in front of Erika's house on Park Street. "Do you want me to wait?" she asked, turning off the ignition. I nodded. There was no telling how this was going to go.

As I walked down the landscaped pathway, I ran over what I was planning to say in my mind. *Erika, I need to talk to you.* With each step I took, I felt a little more certain. I was going to be confident. I was going to be mature. We were going to resolve this like adults. I checked my reflection in the leaded glass of the door, then grabbed hold of the familiar brass knocker and banged it three times.

A few seconds later, the door swung open and there was Erika, dressed in a pair of sweatpants and a matching Sacred Heart sweatshirt. She'd cut her hair to shoulder length. It looked really grown-up. And it instantly made me really sad. I should have been with her to help her decide whether or not she should do layers and how short her bangs should be.

"Erika" I said, "I need to talk to—" but before I could finish, she took a single step back and slammed the door so hard that the windows on either side of it shook. A gush of warm air from inside the house came at me. It smelled like the little pots of dried flowers Erika's mom keeps in the hallway.

I desperately wanted to go back to the van. I'd been rejected enough for one day. But I knew I'd never forgive myself if I didn't do what I'd come to do. I reached for the knocker again.

"What?" Erika said when she opened the door. "I don't want any Girl Scout cookies, okay?" She spat the words at me. I knew I deserved them.

"Erika," I started again. "I need to talk to you. . . ."

And that's kind of where my plan fell apart. In the script in my head, at that point she was supposed to also start acting like a mature adult. I mean, of the two of us, she was the one who always said thank you to the bus driver and who knew which fork to use for dessert. She was raised to be ultrapolite. She was supposed to say something like: "I'm glad you're here. Let's discuss this." Except she didn't. She just stood there glaring at me.

"Anyway," I improvised, skipping ahead in the script, "I brought back your jeans." I took them out from under my armpit and handed them to her.

She held them by the waistband, shaking them out and inspecting them as if she was looking for stains. Then she folded them in half, lengthwise, and draped them over her arm. "It's about time." Then, with her hand on the door, she added, "Is that all?"

I exhaled in frustration. She was supposed to thank me

for returning them. If she didn't want to behave like a rational person, how was I supposed to make her forgive me?

"No. Wait." I slid my hand into my pocket. "Do you remember this?" I held out the photo from the apple festival. She squinted at it under the porch light.

"I guess," she said. "The hayride thing."

"Yeah," I said, a bit too brightly. "We're seven years old in this photo." This was the part where she was supposed to remember all the good times we'd had growing up. I'd even envisioned a tear trickling down her cheek as she hugged me and said, "I can't believe how close we came to throwing it all away!"

"Well." I hesitated. "Do you want to go this year? With me? It's this weekend."

She looked out at the street behind me. There was an uncomfortable silence. I heard two cars pass and some cats fighting a few yards over. "We're not really friends anymore." She passed the photo back to me. "Plus, it's kind of for kids."

"Yeah." I looked down at my feet, then shook my head like I should have realized. "You're totally right. It's for kids. Anyway . . ." The beams from someone's headlights washed across her thighs and over the stone path before disappearing into the dark. A car door slammed somewhere. "My mom's waiting." I motioned toward the street. "So . . ." I trailed off and turned around to go. Mom must have seen me, because the van started with its usual coughing, wheezing, about-to-keel-over-and-die noise.

And then, of all the things in the world I could have said, these words came out of my mouth: "I like your new haircut." I knew Erika was still standing there because I hadn't heard the click of the front door closing yet. "It makes you look older."

The cats had stopped fighting. Everything was silent, except, of course, for the wheezing of the van. I turned back toward Erika as my mom switched off the ignition again.

"Thanks," she said, but she didn't sound very thankful. There was another pause. "Your new bangs are . . ."

"Horrible." I helped her out. "I know." After what had happened with Em and the mystery spoon, I'd felt wrong wearing any of the head scarves she'd given me. I even felt iffy about the frizz-control serum—but I'd decided to keep using it anyway. Just for the next couple of days. Just until I could save up enough to buy my own bottle.

"When you told me on the phone that you'd cut them, I didn't expect them to look so . . ."

"Ugly?" I supplied.

"Different," she said coldly. As if sensing that things had taken another turn for the worse, Mom turned the key in the ignition again. The van wheezed to life.

"Yeah," I agreed. "Anyway." I motioned to the street. The engine revved noisily, then went quiet. Mom was obviously getting sick of not knowing if I was leaving or staying. Just then, I heard the van door open and slam shut.

"Goddamn it," my mom said, coming up the path. The wind whipped her cotton skirt around her ankles. "It's dead," she said, throwing up her hands. "We should all just admit it. It's finished."

She was right. I'd tried everything I could think of and it hadn't changed anything. Erika hated me. Our friendship was really and truly and finally over. "I know," I agreed, feeling numb.

"It leaks coolant. The shocks are gone. The windshield

wipers get stuck every time you go over a bump. The mirrors are cracked. The paint is rusting. The cup holders are too small." My mom listed off on her fingers. "And now," she finished, "the engine won't start." She glanced back at the van and sighed. "Hi, Erika," she said. "It's good to see you. Could I use your phone?"

Erika smiled warmly. "Of course, Ms. Button." She stepped aside to let my mom in.

"Yoo-hoo," Mom called. She kicked off her shoes in the front hall as though nothing had changed. "Anybody home?" Erika's mom appeared at the top of the stairs, a little too quickly for my liking. I'd bet anything she'd been eavesdropping the entire time. "I just drove Margot over to have a talk with Erika, and the van's finally kicked the bucket," Mom explained. "Just when we've barely got two cents left to rub together."

"Oh, you poor thing," Erika's mom cooed, as if she knew anything about rubbing cents together. "Come into the kitchen. I'll make you a cup of decaf while you use the phone."

Erika and I were left standing alone in the hallway, both wishing we were anyplace else on earth. "I guess you're going to be here awhile. Would you like to sit down?" Erika asked in a very formal, unwelcoming way. I actually would have rather stood freezing my butt off outside, except that she was right—there was no telling how long we'd be there. Erika led me into the good living room—the one with big flower-print couches, where there were always vacuum marks on the carpet.

"Would you like something to drink?" she asked in the same cold voice.

"No thank you," I said. We sat stiffly for a long time, like two strangers at a tea party. Finally, though, Erika's curiosity got the better of her.

"What happened to your leg?" she asked.

"Sarah J. pushed me down the stairs," I answered. I could tell that she was surprised, and I could also tell that she wanted the details (how could she not?), but she didn't ask.

"That's unfortunate," she said. There was another long silence.

"How's Sacred Heart?" I asked.

"Very nice, thank you," she responded. "And Manning?"

"Lovely," I shot back. Two could play at this game. "Splendid."

"Mmmmm." Erika pinched her lips into a tight smile, like she was so pleased to hear it. "And your blond friend? What was her name again?" It was a trick question, obviously. Erika had never met Em . . . not unless you counted the two seconds before she'd slammed the door in her face.

"Liesalot McDognapper," I answered in the same polite tone. I don't even know why I said it.

"What an unusual name." Erika didn't even crack a smile.

"It's her pseudonym," I said, "for modeling." She nodded as if that made sense and was a very interesting fact.

"Have you made any friends at Sacred Heart?" I tried to sound uninterested, like I was asking about the weather.

"Yes," she smiled smugly. "Several. My best friend is Gabriella Whipplechuck." *Her best friend? Traitor!* It had taken us years to be as close as we were—or as close as we used to be. Plus, what kind of a stupid name was Gabriella Whipplechuck?

"How nice," I said, practically spitting venom.

"It *is*," Erika said. "She was here after school today, actually. We watched the Discovery Channel and ate nachos." She paused for maximum effect. "She makes good nachos."

I'd been practically biting a hole in my tongue to keep from saying something rude, but now she was taking things too far. "That's nice," I said again, but I couldn't help it. The words felt like hot lava trapped inside my throat. I was a natural disaster waiting to happen. "Really nice, Erika," I snapped. "Really frigging nice. Just throw our friendship away like the past six years were made of rancid potatoes. Just go and replace me with a new best friend as easily as you'd replace a"—I paused, trying to think of the right words, and then gave up, saying whatever came into my head—"maxi pad."

"Rancid potatoes?" She stood up. "A maxi pad? Do I need to remind you that you're the one who ditched me? That you're the one who had a new friend within days of starting school? And do I need to remind you that it took you weeks to come over and apologize? Or, actually, not even apologize, because you haven't even apologized yet. Like, what, Margot? Did you expect me to put my life on hold forever?"

I hung my head. I felt two inches tall. She had a point. She had lots of points, actually. Everything I'd said and done since coming over was meant to show her I was sorry, but it had all come out wrong, as usual. "I sent an e-mail," I said. "You never answered. *And* I called."

"Well, yeah," she said, like that much was obvious. "One e-mail. One phone call."

And then I got it . . . the answer . . . the thing that had been right in front of my face. I'd slammed the door on Erika, and now she was going to slam it on me. Right in my face. She had every right to. This was a big screwup. The kind that might need hundreds of apologies. And Erika was the kind of friend who was worth knocking on the door for. And then knocking on the door for again. And then knocking on the door for again, no matter how many times she had to slam it in my face before she felt better.

"I'm an idiot," I said. "I don't deserve your forgiveness." She didn't disagree. "And that girl, Liesalot McDognapper? She's an idiot too. We're not friends anymore."

Erika sat back down on the sofa across from me. She folded her hands in her lap. Neither of us said anything for a very long time.

"I'm sorry," I said finally. "I'll do whatever it takes if you'll just think about forgiving me."

She let out a long exasperated breath while she picked at the fabric on the sofa.

"I'll grovel," I said. "I'll eat cement. I'll tattoo your name on my forehead. I'll go to school naked. Oh, I'll wear bell-bottoms. For a month. Without washing them." She didn't smile. "I'll shave my head?" I looked up at the ceiling. "I'll give up ice cream. Oh! I'll do the chicken dance in my underpants. I'll crank call your most hated teacher. I'll do your homework for six months . . . only not math . . . and, come to think of it, you probably don't want me to do your French either. But I'll do English. I just got an A-plus on an essay."

I couldn't tell for sure, but the corners of her mouth seemed to lift into a tiny smile, just for a second. "Shut up, Margot," she sighed.

We sat quietly again, listening to the muffled voices of our moms in the kitchen. Finally Erika broke the silence. "My mom probably wants to make pies for Thanksgiving," she said, sounding annoyed. I looked at her, confused. What did pies have to do with anything? "And we could make fun of the songs, I guess." I still didn't get it. "The apple thing," she said impatiently. "I should probably go buy my mom some apples. For her stupid pies."

"Oh," I said, resisting the urge to grin. "Okay." I could already picture us on the hayride, singing all the words to the stupid songs just a little bit too loudly, stuffing hay down the backs of each others' shirts, being on the lookout for cute guys even though there wouldn't be any.

"I already have plans with Gabriella this weekend, though, so she'll have to come too," Erika said. I felt my heart sink again. Suddenly there was a new person in the picture, sitting between us. I pictured her rolling her eyes at the songs; refusing to get her face painted, even as a joke. She was probably the girl from the corner store. The trail-mix-eating, ultra-Goody Two-shoes, red-haired, Catholic schoolgirl. I hated her already. But Erika was looking at me expectantly. I knew what I had to do, so I took a deep breath.

"Great," I said, smiling. And for once, I said the exact right thing at the exact right time. "I can't wait to meet her."

Acknowledgments

There are lots of thank-you's to say, but it's easy to know where to start: with my former teachers and classmates from Canterbury High School's Literary Arts program. You taught me everything I know about writing, revising, and revising again.

Huge thank-you's to my husband, Brent, for his unwavering support; to my daughter, Gracie, and my son, Elliot, for giving me the best reason on earth to go after my dream (then taking really long naps so I could do it); to those who read drafts, offered feedback, and helped with research (Jamila-Khanom Allidina, Farrah Khan, Jane Moore, Taylor Guitard, and Keith Malcolm); and to my immediate and extended family for their encouragement—my mom especially, who, by example, taught me that the things you want are worth working really hard for.

Thank you to my former agent, Nikki Van De Car (of Sterling Lord Literistic), who came like magic into my life and made it all happen; and to my new agent, Rebecca Friedman (of Hill Nadell Literary Agency), for being so enthusiastic about what I might do next. To Emily Schultz, my editor at Disney•Hyperion, a million scoops of thanks with a cherry on top. You made Margot a better person, and you made me a better writer. Thanks, too, to Catherine Onder, for stepping in and seeing the book through production.

Heaps of gratitude to the City of Toronto through Toronto Arts Council and the Canada Council for the Arts for providing financial support. And last but definitely not least, thank you to everyone who ever truly believed there'd be books in the world with my name on them (that's mostly you, Dad).